VOYAGEUR CLASSICS

BOOKS THAT EXPLORE CANADA

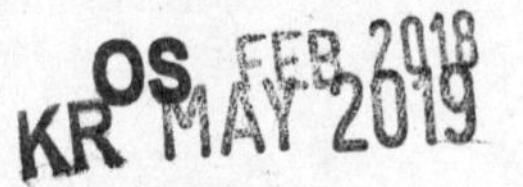

Michael Gnarowski — Series Editor

The Dundurn presents the Voyageur Classics series, building on the tradition of exploration and rediscovery and bringing forward time-tested writing about the Canadian experience in all its varieties.

This series of original or translated works in the fields of literature, history, politics, and biography has been gathered to enrich and illuminate our understanding of a multi-faceted Canada. Through straightforward, knowledgeable, and reader-friendly introductions the Voyageur Classics series provides context and accessibility while breathing new life into these timeless Canadian masterpieces.

The Voyageur Classics series was designed with the widest possible readership in mind and sees a place for itself with the interested reader as well as in the classroom. Physically attractive and reset in a contemporary format, these books aim at an enlivened and updated sense of Canada's written heritage.

Michael Gnarowski co-edited *The Making of Modern Poetry in Canada*, compiled *The Concise Bibliography of English Canadian Literature*, and edited the Critical Views of Canadian Writers series for McGraw-Hill Ryerson. He has written for *Encyclopedia Americana*, *The Canadian Encyclopedia*, *The McGraw-Hill Encyclopedia of World Biography*, and *The Oxford Companion to Twentieth-Century Poetry*. Gnarowski is professor emeritus at Carleton University in Ottawa.

OTHER VOYAGEUR CLASSICS TITLES

The Blue Castle by Lucy Maud Montgomery, introduced by Dr. Collett Tracey 978-1-55002-666-5

Canadian Exploration Literature: An Anthology, edited and introduced by Germaine Warkentin 978-1-55002-661-0

Combat Journal for Place d'Armes: A Personal Narrative by Scott Symons, introduced by Christopher Elson 978-1-55488-457-5

The Donnellys by James Reaney, introduced by Alan Filewod 978-1-55002-832-4

Empire and Communications by Harold A. Innis, introduced by Alexander John Watson 978-1-55002-662-7

The Firebrand: William Lyon Mackenzie and the Rebellion in Upper Canada by William Kilbourn, introduced by Ronald Stagg 978-1-55002-800-3

In This Poem I Am: Selected Poetry of Robin Skelton, edited and introduced by Harold Rhenisch 978-1-55002-769-3

The Letters and Journals of Simon Fraser 1806–1808, edited and introduced by W. Kaye Lamb, foreword by Michael Gnarowski 978-1-55002-713-6

Maria Chapdelaine: A Tale of French Canada by Louis Hémon, translated by W.H. Blake, introduction and notes by Michael Gnarowski 978-1-55002-712-9

The Men of the Last Frontier by Grey Owl, introduced by James Polk 978-1-55488-804-7

Mrs. Simcoe's Diary by Elizabeth Posthuma Simcoe, edited and introduced by Mary Quayle Innis, foreword by Michael Gnarowski 978-1-55002-768-6

Pilgrims of the Wild, edited and introduced by Michael Gnarowski 978-1-55488-734-7

The Refugee: Narratives of Fugitive Slaves in Canada by Benjamin Drew, introduced by George Elliott Clarke 978-1-55002-801-0

The Scalpel, the Sword: The Story of Doctor Norman Bethune by Ted Allan and Sydney Ostrovsky, introduced by Julie Allan, Dr. Norman Allan, and Susan Ostrovsky 978-1-55488-402-5

Selected Writings by A.J.M. Smith, edited and introduced by Michael Gnarowski 978-1-55002-665-8

Self Condemned by Wyndham Lewis, introduced by Allan Pero 978-1-55488-735-4

The Silence on the Shore by Hugh Garner, introduced by George Fetherling 978-1-55488-782-8

Storm Below by Hugh Garner, introduced by Paul Stuewe 978-1-55488-456-8

A Tangled Web by Lucy Maud Montgomery, introduced by Benjamin Lefebvre 978-1-55488-403-2

The Yellow Briar: A Story of the Irish on the Canadian Countryside by Patrick Slater, introduced by Michael Gnarowski 978-1-55002-848-5

FORTHCOMING

Duncan Campbell Scott: Selected Writings, edited, selected, and introduced by Michael Gnarowski 978-1-45970-144-1

The Kindred of the Wild: A Book of Animal Life by Charles G.D. Roberts, introduced by James Polk 978-1-45970-147-2

The Town Below by Roger Lemelin, introduced by Michael Gnarowski 978-1-55488-803-0

VOYAGEUR CLASSICS

BOOKS THAT EXPLORE CANADA

ROBERT W. SERVICE

SELECTED POETRY AND PROSE

EDITED, SELECTED, AND INTRODUCED BY
MICHAEL GNAROWSKI

DUNDURN
TORONTO

Project Editor: Michael Carroll
Copy Editors: Cheryl Hawley and Britanie Wilson
Design: Jennifer Scott
Printer: Webcom

Library and Archives Canada Cataloguing in Publication

Service, Robert W., 1874-1958
Robert W. Service : selected poetry and prose / by Robert W. Service ; edited by Michael Gnarowski.

(Voyageur classics)
Includes bibliographical references.
Issued also in electronic formats.
ISBN 978-1-55488-938-9

I. Gnarowski, Michael, 1934- II. Title. III. Series: Voyageur classics

PS8537.E78A6 2011 C811'.52 C2011-901137-9

1 2 3 4 5 16 15 14 13 12

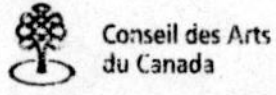

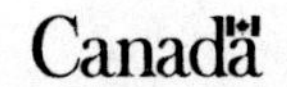

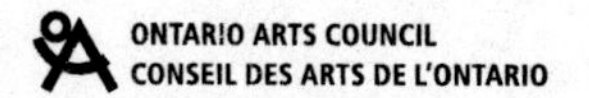

We acknowledge the support of the **Canada Council for the Arts** and the **Ontario Arts Council** for our publishing program. We also acknowledge the financial support of the **Government of Canada** through the **Canada Book Fund** and **Livres Canada Books**, and the **Government of Ontario** through the **Ontario Book Publishing Tax Credit** and the **Ontario Media Development Corporation**.

Care has been taken to trace the ownership of copyright material used in this book. The author and the publisher welcome any information enabling them to rectify any references or credits in subsequent editions.

J. Kirk Howard, President

Printed and bound in Canada.
www.dundurn.com

Dundurn
3 Church Street, Suite 500
Toronto, Ontario, Canada
M5E 1M2

Gazelle Book Services Limited
White Cross Mills
High Town, Lancaster, England
LA1 4XS

Dundurn
2250 Military Road
Tonawanda, NY
U.S.A. 14150

CONTENTS

INTRODUCTION

BY MICHAEL GNAROWSKI

Most readers know Robert William Service as the author of two signature poems: "The Shooting of Dan McGrew" and "The Cremation of Sam McGee," two ballad-like verse narratives that, it may now be said, anchor Service's first published collection of verse, which he called *Songs of a Sourdough.*[1] The popularity of the two ballads was quickly established, and they were frequently quoted, recited from the stage and on the radio and, in one case, made into a short film. More knowledgeable readers may be able to identify Service as the premier poet of the Canadian North or, as he became known, as the Bard[2] of the Yukon, a role that Service took on readily, making the spell of the North an almost hypnotic reference in his early collections of verse.

His contemporaries were only too happy to grant Service "poet in residence in the North" status and accept him as one with the hardy types who braved unimaginable hardships to join the gold rush and, in Service's immortal phrase, "to moil for gold." This series of mining discoveries that drew thousands into the brutal environments of Alaska and the near-Arctic of the Canadian North also inscribed the word *Klondike* on the map of the imagination and acted as a powerful stimulus to the creative urges of Service.

We know that he was born in 1874 of British stock, although there was a strong element of the Scottish in his roots, and the iconic presence of Robert Burns and the border ballads of Sir Walter Scott remained strongly established in his mind. Throughout his life and his writing career, Service maintained a careful reticence about the biographical facts of his life,[3] so much so that even some reference works are at a loss as to dates and events of his circumstances. His biographer, Carl Klinck, saw fit to refer to him as "this otherwise unknown man." What is particularly curious is that even his publishers were either bullied or persuaded to join in this act of authorial privacy and were content to reveal precious little by way of biographical notes or introductory remarks about their markedly prolific author who had managed to draw to his writing if not to himself a large and loyal readership.

Robert William Service (the "William" eventually disappeared from the covers and the title pages of his many books) was a Lancashire lad whose family, due to an improved financial situation, moved to Glasgow where Service was educated at Hillhead public school. Thus, dipped into a Scottish environment, Service saw himself as a Scotsman, linked in spirit to the great

The jacket of Bar-Room Ballads *(1940).*

Scottish bard Robert Burns, and thus inclined to work Scots vernacular into his verse, endowing his best piece of prose writing, the romance *The Trail of Ninety-Eight* (1910)[4] with a Scottish flavour. The question of Service's national identity would dog him and his biography during his entire career. Most contemporary reference works recognize that Service was British by birth, sometimes being more specific and calling him a British-born Canadian poet. This suggestion of ambiguity would continue to haunt his placement in literature and may explain, if only in part, how poorly he has fared in literary history.

School was not always a happy experience for Service who proved to be independent-minded and a not particularly attentive pupil much given to daydreaming and fantasy and the reading of adventure stories. At the age of fifteen he was expelled from school and forced to enter the world of employment. He first secured an apprentice clerkship in a ship chandler's office, but soon after found a very junior position with the Commercial Bank of Scotland. Unbeknownst to him, this early experience in banking would serve him especially well and usher him into employment with a Canadian bank and a posting to Canada's North, but not before, as a newly arrived immigrant, Service would taste hard work as a labourer on a farm near Duncan, British Columbia.

He arrived in Canada on an "emigrant" ship in 1896 and travelled by train westward across great expanses of country, nursing romantic notions about carefree travel and adventure in North America. It was not to be quite the life he had fantasized about as far back as his adolescent days in Scotland. Here Service's story became a mixture of all the awkwardness, social maladjustment, and difficulty of an immigrant fitting into a seemingly classless new world environment in which Service found himself trying to adapt and to feel at home. He undertook all kinds of work, most of it manual, and seemed to thrive on the sheer physical demands of haying, harvesting, and looking after animals. Some of this appealed to him because it demanded personal fitness, something that became a bit of an obsession with him in later years.

But Service did not settle down or put out roots in the new land. The "drifter" urge that became a powerful undertow in his life pulled him into a kind of benign vagabondism that sent him southward into the United States. What little we know of this fairly extensive period of Service's life survives as echoes and recollections that went into the making of his later writing. We must bear in mind that Service left Scotland for Canada at the age of twenty-two, and that after arriving in Canada he spent at least half a dozen years as an itinerant labourer and hobo doing odd jobs before he found his way back to Canada, specifically Victoria, British Columbia. There, seriously at loose ends and almost penniless, he was prompted by a stranger to try his luck by applying for a job at the bank across the street from the park bench where he found himself. He applied, and very likely on the strength of his past banking experience in Scotland, he was hired by the Canadian Bank of Commerce, transforming himself, late in 1903, from a guitar-strumming hobo and jack of all trades into a bank clerk with a regular wage. A year later the bank sent him to Whitehorse in Yukon Territory, and his fate and his fiction were, so to speak sealed. Service was locked into a future that would make him widely known as the Bard of the Yukon, even though he had missed the gold rush by some five years. He was thirty years old.

Earlier on, in the course of the years of his so-called vagabondage, Service had heard from time to time of the excitement of the Klondike Gold Rush. The discovery of placer gold in the Klondike River occurred in 1896 and occasioned the gold rush of 1897–98. When Service arrived in Whitehorse in 1904, the tumult and the shouting had pretty much died down, but yarn-spinning old-timers were still about and their stories quickly captivated the young bank clerk. He was struck by the powerful scenery, the sense of brutal adventure, and the rich vein of local

RHYMES *of a*
RED CROSS MAN
by
ROBERT W SERVICE
Author of 'The Spell of the Yukon'
'Ballads of a Cheechako' Etc.
ILLUSTRATED BY
CHARLES L. WRENN
NEW YORK
BARSE & HOPKINS
PUBLISHERS

The title page of Rhymes of a Red Cross Man *(1916).*

lore that fired his imagination. Although most of the prospectors who had made the gold rush such a colourful event in Canadian history had moved on, stories of lucky miners striking it suddenly rich, of gambling on a grand scale, of ruffians, con artists, and harlots, lingered on and were happily told and retold by grizzled northerners given to embroidering their long memories.

Somehow, sometime, someone had mentioned in Service's hearing that the Klondike needed its own Bret Harte (1836–1902), the American writer who had successfully used the California gold rush of the mid-1800s as material for his stories such as those collected in *The Luck of Roaring Camp* (1870), with titles like "The Outcasts of Poker Flats," the tone of which echoed eerily for Service. And, of course, the success of Jack London (1876–1916) with *The Call of the Wild* (1903) and *White Fang* (1906), to name only two gripping adventure stories fuelled by London's experiences in the North when he was one of the thousands who swarmed into the Yukon gold fields, very likely prompted Service to try his hand at his own brand of tales of the Northland (as he liked to call it) — only his would be recounted in strongly rhythmed verse.

Service had discovered a talent for rhyming and versifying at an early age. He had also scribbled and published occasionally what he described self-deprecatingly as newspaper verse during his vagabond travels. Now, established in a steady job, and with not a great deal available as entertainment or diversion, he settled into a cabin and into writing in his free time. Harte and London were near contemporaries, and although Service had not had the benefit of an extensive education, he was a reader and had his literary models in the likes of Rudyard Kipling, Robert Burns, Walter Scott, and Robert Louis Stevenson to draw upon.

After his stint in Whitehorse, Service was transferred to Dawson City, but all in all, he did not have a particularly long stay in the North. A few years in the teller's cage at the bank, some travel and solitary writing in his Dawson City cabin, resulted in a sheaf of poems about which Service felt good enough to be prepared to pay out of his own carefully husbanded savings for its publication. Although biographically Service is not all that forthcoming, he does tell us something of what his life in the Northland had been like, which gives us an insight into how certain poems came to be written, and the style of life that had occasioned them.

At this point in his life Service was in his thirties, and except for much rambling travel mostly along the Pacific coast and in Mexico, the occasional piece of fugitive verse published somewhere in a newspaper, and work at the bank, Service had neither a profession nor a career to call his own. The saving step would be authorship of some kind duly enshrined in book form. The first stepping stone of what would become a wildly successful career as a writer was a clutch of thirty-three pieces of verse, mostly cast in Service's idea of what a ballad might be, a form that one attempt at definition described as "the name given to a type of verse of unknown authorship dealing with episodes or simple motifs rather than sustained themes written in stanzaic form more or less found suitable for oral transmission."What also must have appealed to Service with his notions of itinerant minstrelsy was that the ballad lent itself to recitation or song.

Appropriately his first book was called *Songs of a Sourdough*, and his second *Ballads of a Cheechako*. In one fell swoop Service had pushed two obscure terms into the limelight of the English language, with *sourdough* meaning a grouchy or peevish individual, and *cheechako* meaning a greenhorn or novice. Both terms appear to have been current among the hard-bitten mining folk of the gold fields of Alaska and the Yukon. *Northland*, another special word, carried with it the ethos of that near-Arctic roof of the American continent, and it was an ethos that Service took happily and readily as his own.

For Service verse-making became a kind of minstrelsy that blended easily with the uncomplicated music that so attracted him. In addition, the North of the gold rush had its own saloon culture echoing richly with song, dance, and sentiment. A recent archaeological find has brought up a music-playing machine, perhaps an early version of the gramophone, which was recovered from the sunken wreck of a riverboat in the Klondike River. Disks on this machine have survived with two pieces of popular music from that time. Hitherto unknown, the pieces were "My Onliest One" and "Rendezvous Waltz." Clearly stuff of Service's time, and for Service, verses were ballads, and ballads meant music.

Once launched on this stream of composition, a regular outflow of collections of verse followed for the rest of Service's creative life, with the evocative use of words such as *rhymes*, *carols*, *songs*, *ballads*, and *lyrics* artfully used in the titles of new collections of verse. Critically speaking, though, one discerns a definite falling off in quality and inventiveness in his writing after the appearance of *Rhymes of a Rolling Stone* (1912) and *Rhymes of a Red Cross Man* (1916).

Earlier, on the heels of the success of his first collection of verse, Service had decided to try his hand at fiction. He crafted a romance adventure that was published in 1911 as *The Trail of '98* with the subtitle *A Northland Romance*, which ranks as one of his better achievements in prose writing, dependent as it is on the flavour of the gold fields. It also hinted at his penchant for what became known as the "romance" genre in which Service worked with notable success for fifteen years. Not only did his fiction find a readership, most likely helped by his reputation as a highly readable and entertaining versifier, but it also gave him entry into the burgeoning domain of the world of movies where his romances lent themselves readily to being made into films.

Service had honed his storytelling skills with his ballad stories, which he had salted with intriguing and colourful characters with names like One-Eyed Mike, Muckluck Meg, the Dago Kid, and Blasphemous Pete. It was an easy step into the riff-raff and *apache*[5] lives of the Paris underworld. Shady adventure romances were the kind of material sought after by Hollywood's movie mills, which in their turn were a rewarding source of a goodly portion of Service's growing wealth. Reticent as he tended to be about his private life, he had no compunction about referring to himself as "rich." And that he clearly was. From a house in a seaside village in Brittany to a luxurious two-storey apartment in a chic district of Paris to an equally self-pampering flat in Monte Carlo and life in Nice and on the French Riviera, all suggest considerable wealth.

When Service arrived in Paris in 1913, one has a sense that he hoped to become part of the avant-garde literary and artistic community that was beginning to establish itself in that unique city of the arts. The bohemianism of Paris life attracted him greatly, but the wanderlust that had taken him widely in the world still tugged at him, and we find that Service, who had developed some skills in journalism reporting on the Balkan wars, was also successfully sending in reports on travels by bicycle and walking in rural France to a Toronto newspaper. But what Service really craved was acceptance by the literati of the time. It seems that this

Robert and Germaine Service in Paris, October 1913.

was not to be and Service had to suffer unjust rejection, in one instance being told by an envious contemporary that his writing was not bad for newspaper verse, and in another case showing the handsomely designed *Rhymes of a Rolling Stone* to an eminent British man of letters who, without bothering to open the book, told Service that he admired the binding. Unable to win serious acceptance among the bohemians of the Latin Quarter, Service cultivated a coterie of journalists who were resident in Paris and with whom he had a sense of affinity.

In 1913, Service met a young Frenchwoman, Germaine Bourgoin, younger daughter of the owner of a distillery. They were married in June of that year, and Service entered upon a very happy but very different style of life. One supposes that he had also noticed the ticking of life's clock when he decided, as he tells it, to get "hitched." He was almost forty and confessed to a friend that he thought the time had come "for the greatest of all adventures — Marriage." We can get an idea of what they settled into from his second novel *The Pretender: A Story of the Latin Quarter* (1914). That year the Great War was upon Europe and the

Service in uniform in 1916.

world, and Service dutifully sought to do his share. Too old for the trenches, he did journalistic work writing for the *Toronto Star* and then found himself in the medical service, driving an ambulance and caring for the wounded. The result was a collection of verse, both patriotically stirring but with overtones of regret for the suffering and the death, and with a pacifist sentiment.

After the end of the First World War, Service's writing career entered a new and radically different phase. The verse-making continued at a steady pace, but the major effort was directed to the writing of fiction. Between 1922 and 1927 he produced four novels which, as mentioned earlier, won favour in Hollywood. In 1928, having developed problems with his heart, Service published a celebration of physical fitness with *Why Not Grow Young? or Living for Longevity*. Although he was only in his early fifties, what is evident is that Service had entered the last phase of his life. The verses kept coming, sadly not particularly original, mainly personal and domestic in their inspiration, and predictable in their tone and sentiment. That the summing-up was coming was signalled by the publication of *The Complete Poems* in 1933. This was followed by two autobiographical volumes, *Ploughman of the Moon: An Adventure into Memory* in 1945 and *Harper of Heaven: A Record of Radiant Living* (1948). *Later Collected Verse* (1960) appeared after his death.

Service displaying his muscles in a photograph that appeared on the jacket of Why Not Grow Young? *(1928).*

Service spent his declining years happily as a long-time resident expatriate in France and died of a heart attack at his cottage in Brittany on September 11, 1958. He left a legacy of a sensible outlook on life that permeated a large body of work in which there is a tolerant interplay between what is not always entirely good or wholly bad, and in which gentle irony was his instrument of fine persuasion. There is a modest credo in these lines:

Aye, though a godless way I go,
And sceptic is my friend,
A faith in something I don't know
Might save me in the end.

NOTES

1. First published in 1907 by William Briggs of Toronto and T. Fisher Unwin in London, and also in the same year in its American edition under the title of *The Spell of the Yukon*

by Barse and Hopkins in New York and F. Stern & Co. in Philadelphia. All in all, quite remarkable for a first book, but then its enormous appeal may be gauged by the fact that the Canadian edition had been reprinted thirty-one times by 1911.

2. The idea of a "bardic" identity would have appealed to Service whose penchant for the ballad, which he associated with minstrelsy and the notion of the poet as a kind of itinerant entertainer who accompanied his narratives with music — the guitar or accordion in Service's case — would have blended nicely with his sense of Celtic tradition.
3. Although Service wrote and published two ample volumes of autobiography, these tend to focus on incidents and travel adventures that formed an important component of his life, but the connected narrativity that one normally expects to find in life writing is tightly controlled and not inviting or revelatory of Service's human side.
4. While the title of the book printed on the cover reads *The Trail of Ninety-Eight* [:] *A Northland Romance*, the bibliographically correct title since it appears on the title page reads *The Trail of '98* {;} *A Northland Romance*. What is noteworthy is that this first and best major work of prose fiction by Service was illustrated by Maynard Dixon (1875–1946), an American painter and illustrator largely of western themes whose origins in California and much painting of the American West and Southwest celebrated territory through which Service had drifted in his hobo days and for which he had an affinity. An appropriate if unusual choice. Dixon, not unlike Service, was also a self-taught artist.
5. The term *apache* was current in the 1920s and 1930s and was used to describe pimps and hustlers and the general — usually male — low-life of the Paris underworld.

The front jacket of Harper of Heaven *(1948).*

SELECT BIBLIOGRAPHY

Principal Works of Robert William Service

Poetry

Songs of a Sourdough (1907)
Ballads of a Cheechako (1909)
Rhymes of a Rolling Stone (1912)
Rhymes of a Red Cross Man (1916)
Ballads of a Bohemian (1921)
The Complete Poems of Robert Service (1933)
Bar-Room Ballads: A Book of Verse (1940)
Rhymes of a Roughneck: A Book of Verse (1950)
More Collected Verse (1955)
Later Collected Verse (1960)

Prose

The Trail of '98: A Northland Romance (1910)

The Pretender: A Story of the Latin Quarter (1914)
The Poisoned Paradise: A Romance of Monte Carlo (1922)
The Roughneck: A Tale of Tahiti (1923)
The Master of the Microbe: A Fantastic Romance (1926)
The House of Fear: A Novel (1927)
Why Not Grow Young? or Living for Longevity (1928)
Ploughman of the Moon: An Adventure into Memory (1945)
Harper of Heaven: A Record of Radiant Living (1948)

About Robert Service

There is considerable fugitive journalism about Service, but Carl F. Klinck's *Robert Service: A Biography* (New York: Dodd, Mead, 1976) remains the best study to date of a remarkable life.

Frontispiece photograph of a mature, healthy Service that appeared in Ploughman of the Moon: An Adventure into Memory *(1945).*

FROM

The Spell of the Yukon and Other Verses

Robert Service's log cabin in Dawson City, Yukon.

The Law of the Yukon

This is the law of the Yukon, and ever she makes it plain:
"Send not your foolish and feeble; send me your strong and
your sane —
Strong for the red rage of battle; sane, for I harry them sore;
Send me men girt for the combat, men who are grit to the core;
Swift as the panther in triumph, fierce as the bear in defeat,
Sired of a bulldog parent, steeled in the furnace heat.
Send me the best of your breeding, lend me your chosen ones;
Them will I take to my bosom, them will I call my sons;
Them will I gild with my treasure, them will I glut with my meat;
But the others — the misfits, the failures — I trample under my
feet.
Dissolute, damned and despairful, crippled and palsied and slain,
Ye would send me the spawn of your gutters — Go! take back
your spawn again.

"Wild and wide are my borders, stern as death is my sway;
From my ruthless throne I have ruled alone for a million years
and a day;
Hugging my mighty treasure, waiting for man to come,
Till he swept like a turbid torrent, and after him swept — the
scum.
The pallid pimp of the deadline, the enervate of the pen,
One by one I weeded them out, for all that I sought was — Men.
One by one I dismayed them, frighting them sore with my
glooms;
One by one I betrayed them unto my manifold dooms.
Drowned them like rats in my rivers, starved them like curs on
my plains,
Rotted the flesh that was left them, poisoned the blood in their
veins;

Burst with my winter upon them, searing forever their sight,
Lashed them with fungus-white faces, whimpering wild in the
night;

"Staggering blind through the storm-whirl, stumbling mad
through the snow,
Frozen stiff in the ice pack, brittle and bent like a bow;
Featureless, formless, forsaken, scented by wolves in their flight,
Left for the wind to make music through ribs that are glittering
white;
Gnawing the back crust of failure, searching the pit of despair,
Crooking the toe in the trigger, trying to patter a prayer;
Going outside with an escort, raving with lips all afoam,
Writing a cheque for a million, driveling feebly of home;
Lost like a louse in the burning ... or else in the tented town
Seeking a drunkard's solace, sinking and sinking down;
Steeped in the slime at the bottom, dead to a decent world.
Lost 'mid the human flotsam, far on the frontier hurled;
In the camp at the bend of the river, with its dozen saloons aglare,
Its gambling dens ariot, its gramophones all ablare;
Crimped with the crimes of a city, sin-ridden and bridled with
lies,
In the hush of my mountained vastness, in the flush of my
midnight skies.
Plague-spots, yet tools of my purpose, so natheless I suffer them
thrive,
Crushing my Weak in their clutches, that only my Strong may
survive.

"But the others, the men of my mettle, the men who would
'stablish my fame
Unto its ultimate issue, winning me honour, not shame;
Searching my uttermost valleys, fighting each step as they go,

Shooting the wrath of my rapids, scaling my ramparts of snow;
Ripping the guts of my mountains, looting the beds of my creeks,
Them will I take to my bosom, and speak as a mother speaks.
I am the land that listens, I am the land that broods;
Steeped in eternal beauty, crystalline waters and woods,
Long have I waited lonely, shunned as a thing accurst,
Monstrous, moody, pathetic, the last of the lands and the first;
Visioning campfires at twilight, sad with a longing forlorn,
Feeling my womb o'er-pregnant with the seed of cities unborn.
Wild and wide are my borders, stern as death is my sway,
And I wait for the men who will win me — and I will not be
won in a day;
And I will not be won by weaklings, subtle, suave and mild,
But by men with the hearts of vikings, and the simple faith of a
child;
Desperate, strong and resistless, unthrottled by fear or defeat,
Them will I gild with my treasure, them will I glut with my meat.

"Lofty I stand from each sister land, patient and wearily wise,
With the weight of a world of sadness in my quiet, passionless eyes;
Dreaming alone of a people, dreaming alone of a day,
When men shall not rape my riches, and curse me and go away;
Making a bawd of my bounty, fouling the hand that gave —
Till I rise in my wrath and I sweep on their path and I stamp
them into a grave.
Dreaming of men who will bless me, of women esteeming me
good,
Of children born in my borders of radiant motherhood,
Of cities leaping to stature, of fame like a flag unfurled,
As I pour the tide of my riches in the eager lap of the world."

This is the Law of the Yukon, that only the Strong shall thrive;
That surely the Weak shall perish, and only the Fit survive.

Dissolute, damned and despairful, crippled and palsied and slain,
This is the Will of the Yukon, — Lo, how she makes it plain!

The Spell of the Yukon

I wanted the gold, and I sought it;
    I scrabbled and mucked like a slave.
Was it famine or scurvy — I fought it;
    I hurled my youth into a grave.
I wanted the gold, and I got it —
    Came out with a fortune last fall, —
Yet somehow life's not what I thought it,
    And somehow the gold isn't all.

No! There's the land. (Have you seen it?)
    It's the cussedest land that I know,
From the big, dizzy mountains that screen it
    To the deep, deathlike valleys below.
Some say God was tired when He made it;
    Some say it's a fine land to shun;
Maybe; but there's some as would trade it
    For no land on earth — and I'm one.

You come to get rich (damned good reason);
    You feel like an exile at first;
You hate it like hell for a season,
    And then you are worse than the worst.
It grips you like some kinds of sinning;
    It twists you from foe to a friend;
It seems it's been since the beginning;
    It seems it will be to the end.

I've stood in some mighty-mouthed hollow
That's plumb-full of hush to the brim;
I've watched the big, husky sun wallow
In crimson and gold, and grow dim,
Till the moon set the pearly peaks gleaming,
And the stars tumbled out, neck and crop;
And I've thought that I surely was dreaming,
With the peace o' the world piled on top.

The summer — no sweeter was ever;
The sunshiny woods all athrill;
The grayling aleap in the river,
The bighorn asleep on the hill.
The strong life that never knows harness;
The wilds where the caribou call;
The freshness, the freedom, the farness —
O God! how I'm stuck on it all.

The winter! the brightness that blinds you,
The white land locked tight as a drum,
The cold fear that follows and finds you,
The silence that bludgeons you dumb.
The snows that are older than history,
The woods where the weird shadows slant;
The stillness, the moonlight, the mystery,
I've bade 'em goodbye — but I can't.

There's a land where the mountains are nameless,
And the rivers all run God knows where;
There are lives that are erring and aimless,
And deaths that just hang by a hair;
There are hardships that nobody reckons;
There are valleys unpeopled and still;

There's a land — oh, it beckons and beckons,
    And I want to go back — and I will.

They're making my money diminish;
    I'm sick of the taste of champagne.
Thank God! when I'm skinned to a finish
    I'll pike to the Yukon again.
I'll fight — and you bet it's no sham-fight;
    It's hell! — but I've been there before;
And it's better than this by a damsite —
    So me for the Yukon once more.

There's gold, and it's haunting and haunting;
    It's luring me on as of old;
Yet it isn't the gold that I'm wanting
    So much as just finding the gold.
It's the great, big, broad land 'way up yonder,
    It's the forests where silence has lease;
It's the beauty that thrills me with wonder,
    It's the stillness that fills me with peace.

The Call of the Wild

Have you gazed on the naked grandeur where there's nothing
    else to gaze on,
  Set pieces and drop-curtain scenes galore,
Big mountains heaved to heaven, which the blinding sunsets
    blazon,
  Black canyons where the rapids rip and roar?
Have you swept the visioned valley with the green stream
    streaking through it,
  Searched the Vastness for a something you have lost?

Have you strung your soul to silence? Then for God's sake go
and do it;
Hear the challenge, learn the lesson, pay the cost.

Have you wandered in the wilderness, the sagebrush desolation,
The bunch-grass levels where the cattle graze?
Have you whistled bits of ragtime at the end of all creation,
And learned to know the desert's little ways?
Have you camped upon the foothills, have you galloped o'er the
ranges,
Have you roamed the arid sun-lands through and through?
Have you chummed up with the mesa? Do you know its
moods and changes?
Then listen to the Wild — it's calling you.

Have you known the Great White Silence, not a snow-gemmed
twig aquiver?
(Eternal truths that shame our soothing lies.)
Have you broken trail on snowshoes? mushed your huskies up
the river,
Dared the unknown, led the way, and clutched the prize?
Have you marked the map's void spaces, mingled with the mon-
grel races,
Felt the savage strength of brute in every thew?
And though grim as hell the worst is, can you round it off with
curses?
Then hearken to the Wild — it's wanting you.

Have you suffered, starved and triumphed, groveled down, yet
grasped at glory,
Grown bigger in the bigness of the whole?
"Done things" just for the doing, letting babblers tell the story,
Seeing through the nice veneer the naked soul?

Have you seen God in His splendors, heard the text that nature
renders?
(You'll never hear it in the family pew.)
The simple things, the true things, the silent men who do
things —
Then listen to the Wild — it's calling you.

They have cradled you in custom, they have primed you with
their preaching,
They have soaked you in convention through and through;
They have put you in a showcase; you're a credit to their
teaching —
But can't you hear the Wild? — it's calling you.
Let us probe the silent places, let us seek what luck betide us;
Let us journey to a lonely land I know.
There's a whisper on the night-wind, there's a star agleam to
guide us,
And the Wild is calling, calling … let us go.

The Heart of the Sourdough

There where the mighty mountains bare their fangs unto the
moon,
There where the sullen sun-dogs glare in the snow-bright,
bitter noon,
And the glacier-glutted streams sweep down at the clarion call of
June.

There where the livid tundras keep their tryst with the tranquil
snows;
There where the silences are spawned, and the light of hellfire
flows

Into the bowl of the midnight sky, violet, amber and rose.

There where the rapids churn and roar, and the ice floes bel-
lowing run;
Where the tortured, twisted rivers of blood rush to the setting
sun —
I've packed my kit and I'm going, boys, ere another day is done.

I knew it would call, or soon or late, as it calls the whirring
wings;
It's the olden lure, it's the golden lure, it's the lure of the timeless
things,
And tonight, oh, God of the trails untrod, how it whines in my
heartstrings!

I'm sick to death of your well-groomed gods, your make-
believe and your show;
I long for a whiff of bacon and beans, a snug shakedown in the
snow;
A trail to break, and a life at stake, and another bout with the
foe.

With the raw-ribbed Wild that abhors all life, the Wild that
would crush and rend,
I have clinched and closed with the naked North, I have learned
to defy and defend;
Shoulder to shoulder we have fought it out — yet the Wild
must win in the end.

I have flouted the Wild. I have followed its lure, fearless, familiar,
alone;

By all that the battle means and makes I claim that land for mine
own;
Yet the Wild must win, and a day will come when I shall be
overthrown.

Then when as wolf-dogs fight we've fought, the lean wolf-land
and I;
Fought and bled till the snows are red under the reeling sky;
Even as lean wolf-dog goes down will I go down and die.

The Pines

We sleep in the sleep of ages, the bleak, barbarian pines;
The grey moss drapes us like sages, and closer we lock our lines,
And deeper we clutch through the gelid gloom where never a
sunbeam shines.

On the flanks of the storm-gored ridges are our black battalions
massed;
We surge in a host to the sullen coast, and we sing in the ocean
blast;
From empire of sea to empire of snow we grip our empire fast.

To the niggard lands were we driven, 'twixt desert and floes are
we penned;
To us was the Northland given, ours to stronghold and defend;
Ours till the world be riven in the crash of the utter end;

Ours from the bleak beginning, through the aeons of death-like
sleep;
Ours from the shock when the naked rock was hurled from the
hissing deep;

Ours through the twilight ages of weary glacier creep.

Wind of the East, Wind of the West, wandering to and fro,
Chant your songs in our topmost boughs, that the sons of men
may know
The peerless pine was the first to come, and the pine will be the
last to go!

We pillar the halls of perfumed gloom; we plume where the
eagles soar;
The North-wind swoops from the brooding Pole, and our
ancients crash and roar;
But where one falls from the crumbling walls shoots up a hardy
score.

We spring from the gloom of the canyon's womb; in the valley's
lap we lie;
From the white foam-fringe, where the breakers cringe, to the
peaks that tusk the sky,
We climb, and we peer in the crag-locked mere that gleams like
a golden eye.

Gain to the verge of the hog-back ridge where the vision
ranges free:
Pines and pines and the shadow of pines as far as the eye can
see;
A steadfast legion of stalwart knights in dominant empery.

Sun, moon and stars give answer; shall we not staunchly stand,
Even as now, forever, wards of the wilder strand,
Sentinels of the stillness, lords of the last, lone land?

The Song of the Wage-Slave

When the long, long day is over, and the Big Boss gives me
my pay,
I hope that it won't be hellfire, as some of the parsons say.
And I hope that it won't be heaven, with some of the parsons
I've met —
All I want is just quiet, just to rest and forget.
Look at my face, toil-furrowed; look at my calloused hands;
Master, I've done Thy bidding, wrought in Thy many lands —
Wrought for the little masters, big-bellied they be, and rich;
I've done their desire for a daily hire, and I die like a dog in a
ditch.
I have used the strength Thou hast given, Thou knowest I did
not shirk;
Threescore years of labour — Thine be the long day's work.
And now, Big Master, I'm broken and bent and twisted and
scarred,
But I've held my job, and Thou knowest, and Thou will not
judge me hard.
Thou knowest my sins are many, and often I've played the fool —
Whiskey and cards and women, they made me the devil's tool.
I was just like a child with money; I flung it away with a curse,
Feasting a fawning parasite, or glutting a harlot's purse;
Then back to the woods repentant, back to the mill or the
mine,
I, the worker of workers, everything in my line.
Everything hard but headwork (I'd no more brains than a kid),
A brute with brute strength to labour, doing as I was bid;
Living in camps with menfolk, a lonely and loveless life;
Never knew kiss of sweetheart, never caress of wife.
A brute with brute strength to labour, and they were so far
above —

Yet I'd gladly have gone to the gallows for one little look of
Love.
I, with the strength of two men, savage and shy and wild —
Yet how I'd ha' treasured a woman, and the sweet, warm kiss of
a child!
Well, 'tis Thy world, and Thou knowest. I blaspheme and my
ways be rude;
But I've lived my life as I found it, and I've done my best to be
good;
I, the primitive toiler, half naked and grimed to the eyes,
Sweating it deep in their ditches, swining it stark in their sties;
Hurling down forests before me, spanning tumultuous streams;
Down in the ditch building o'er me palaces fairer than dreams;
Boring the rock to the ore-bed, driving the road through the fen,
Resolute, dumb, uncomplaining, a man in the world of men.
Master, I've filled my contract, wrought in Thy many lands;
Not by my sins wilt Thou judge me, but by the work of my
hands.
Master, I've done Thy bidding, and the light is low in the west,
And the long, long shift is over … Master, I've earned it — Rest.

The Shooting of Dan McGrew

A bunch of the boys were whooping it up in the Malamute
saloon;
The kid that handles the music box was hitting a jag-time tune;
Back of the bar, in a solo game, sat Dangerous Dan McGrew,
And watching his luck was his light-o'-love, the lady that's
known as Lou.

When out of the night, which was fifty below, and into the din
and the glare,

There stumbled a miner fresh from the creeks, dog-dirty, and
loaded for bear.
He looked like a man with a foot in the grave and scarcely the
strength of a louse,
Yet he tilted a poke of dust on the bar, and he called for drinks
for the house.
There was none could place the stranger's face, though we
searched ourselves for a clue;
But we drank his health, and the last to drink was Dangerous
Dan McGrew.

There's men that somehow just grip your eyes, and hold them
hard like a spell;
And such was he, and he looked to me like a man who had
lived in hell;
With a face most hair, and the dreary stare of a dog whose day
is done,
As he watered the green stuff in his glass, and the drops fell one
by one.
Then I got to figgering who he was, and wondering what he'd
do,
And I turned my head — and there watching him was the lady
that's known as Lou.

His eyes went rubbering round the room, and he seemed in a
kind of daze,
Till at last that old piano fell in the way of his wandering gaze.
The ragtime kid was having a drink; there was no one else on
the stool,
So the stranger stumbles across the room, and flops down there
like a fool.
In a buckskin shirt that was glazed with dirt he sat, and I saw
him sway;

Then he clutched the keys with his talon hands — my God!
but that man could play.

Were you ever out in the Great Alone, when the moon was
awful clear,
And the icy mountains hemmed you in with a silence you most
could *hear*;
With only the howl of a timber wolf, and you camped there in
the cold,
A half-dead thing in a stark, dead world, clean mad for the
muck called gold;
While high overhead, green, yellow and red, the North Lights
swept in bars? —
Then you've a hunch what the music meant … hunger and
night and the stars.

And hunger not of the belly kind, that's banished with bacon
and beans,
But the gnawing hunger of lonely men for a home and all that
it means;
For a fireside far from the cares that are, four walls and a roof
above;
But oh! so cramful of cosy joy, and crowned with a woman's
love —
A woman dearer than all the world, and true as Heaven is
true —
(God! how ghastly she looks through her rouge, — the lady
that's known as Lou.)

Then on a sudden the music changed, so soft that you scarce
could hear;
But you felt that your life had been looted clean of all that it
once held dear;

That someone had stolen the woman you loved; that her love was a devil's lie;
That your guts were gone, and the best for you was to crawl away and die.
'Twas the crowning cry of a heart's despair, and it thrilled you through and through —
"I guess I'll make it a spread misere," said Dangerous Dan McGrew.

The music almost died away ... then it burst like a pent-up flood;
And it seemed to say, "Repay, repay," and my eyes were blind with blood.
The thought came back of an ancient wrong, and it stung like a frozen lash,
And the lust awoke to kill, to kill ... then the music stopped with a crash,
And the stranger turned, and his eyes they burned in a most peculiar way;

In a buckskin shirt that was glazed with dirt he sat, and I saw him sway;
Then his lips went in in a kind of grin, and he spoke, and his voice was calm,
And "Boys," says he, "you don't know me, and none of you care a damn;
But I want to state, and my words are straight, and I'll bet my poke they're true,
That one of you is a hound of hell ... and that one is Dan McGrew."

Then I ducked my head, and the lights went out, and two guns blazed in the dark,

And a woman screamed, and the lights went up, and two men
lay stiff and stark.
Pitched on his head, and pumped full of lead, was Dangerous
Dan McGrew,
While the man from creeks lay clutched to the breast of the
lady that's known as Lou.

These are the simple facts of the case, and I guess I ought to know.
They say that the stranger was crazed with "hooch," and I'm
not denying it's so.
I'm not so wise as the lawyer guys, but strictly between us two —
The woman that kissed him and — pinched his poke — was
the lady that's known as Lou.

The Cremation of Sam McGee

There are strange things done in the midnight sun
By the men who moil for gold;
The Arctic trails have their secret tales
That would make your blood run cold;
The Northern Lights have seen queer sights,
But the queerest they ever did see
Was that night on the marge of Lake Lebarge
I cremated Sam McGee.

Now Sam McGee was from Tennessee, where the cotton
blooms and blows.
Why he left his home in the South to roam 'round the Pole,
God only knows.
He was always cold, but the land of gold seemed to hold him
like a spell;

Though he'd often say in his homely way that "he'd sooner live
in hell."

On a Christmas Day we were mushing our way over the
Dawson trail.
Talk of your cold! through the parka's fold it stabbed like a
driven nail.
If our eyes we'd close, then the lashes froze till sometimes we
couldn't see;
It wasn't much fun, but the only one to whimper was Sam
McGee.

And that very night, as we lay packed tight in our robes beneath
the snow,
And the dogs were fed, and the stars o'erhead were dancing heel
and toe,
He turned to me, and "Cap," says he, "I'll cash in this trip, I
guess;
And if I do, I'm asking you that you won't refuse my last
request."

Well, he seemed so low that I couldn't say no; then he says with
a sort of moan:
"It's the cursèd cold, and it's got right hold till I'm chilled clean
through to the bone.
Yet 'tain't being dead — it's my awful dread of the icy grave that
pains;
So I want you to swear that, foul or fair, you'll cremate my last
remains."

A pal's last need is a thing to heed, so I swore I would not fail;
And we started on at the streak of dawn; but God! he looked
ghastly pale.

He crouched on the sleigh, and he raved all day of his home in
Tennessee;
And before nightfall a corpse was all that was left of Sam McGee.

There wasn't a breath in that land of death, and I hurried,
horror-driven,
With a corpse half hid that I couldn't get rid, because of a
promise given;
It was lashed to the sleigh, and it seemed to say: "You may tax
your brawn and brains,
But you promised true, and it's up to you to cremate those last
remains."

Now a promise made is a debt unpaid, and the trail has its own
stern code.
In the days to come, though my lips were dumb, in my heart
how I cursed that load.
In the long, long night, by the lone firelight, while the huskies
round in a ring,
Howled out their woes to the homeless snows — O God! how
I loathed that thing.

And every day that quiet clay seemed to heavy and heavier
grow;
And on I went, though the dogs were spent and the grub was
getting low;
The trail was bad, and I felt half mad, but I swore I would not
give in;
And I'd often sing to the hateful thing, and it hearkened with a
grin.

Till I came to the marge of Lake Lebarge, and a derelict there
lay;

It was jammed in the ice, but I saw in a trice it was called the
"Alice May."
And I looked at it, and I thought a bit, and I looked at my frozen
chum;
Then "Here," said I, with a sudden cry, "is my cre-ma-tor-eum."

Some planks I tore from the cabin floor, and I lit the boiler fire;
Some coal I found that was lying around, and I heaped the fuel
higher;
The flames just soared, and the furnace roared — such a blaze
you seldom see;
And I burrowed a hole in the glowing coal, and I stuffed in Sam
McGee.

Then I made a hike, for I didn't like to hear him sizzle so;
And the heavens scowled, and the huskies howled, and the wind
began to blow.
It was icy cold, but the hot sweat rolled down my cheeks, and I
don't know why;
And the greasy smoke in an inky cloak went streaking down
the sky.

I do not know how long in the snow I wrestled with grisly fear;
But the stars came out and they danced about ere again I ven-
tured near;
I was sick with dread, but I bravely said: "I'll just take a peep inside.
I guess he's cooked, and it's time I looked"; ... then the door I
opened wide.

And there sat Sam, looking cool and calm, in the heart of the
furnace roar;
And he wore a smile you could see a mile, and he said: "Please
close that door.

It's fine in here, but I greatly fear you'll let in the cold and storm —
Since I left Plumtree, down in Tennessee, it's the first time I've
been warm."

There are strange things done in the midnight sun
By the men who moil for gold;
The Arctic trails have their secret tales
That would make your blood run cold;
The Northern Lights have seen queer sights,
But the queerest they ever did see
Was that night on the marge of Lake Lebarge
I cremated Sam McGee.

The Men That Don't Fit In

There's a race of men that don't fit in,
A race that can't stay still;
So they break the hearts of kith and kin,
And they roam the world at will.
They range the field and they rove the flood,
And they climb the mountain's crest;
Theirs is the curse of the gypsy blood,
And they don't know how to rest.

If they just went straight they might go far;
They are strong and brave and true;
But they're always tired of the things that are,
And they want the strange and new.
They say: "Could I find my proper groove,
What a deep mark I would make!"
So they chop and change, and each fresh move
Is only a fresh mistake.

And each forgets, as he strips and runs
With a brilliant, fitful pace,
It's steady, quiet, plodding ones
Who win in the lifelong race.
And each forgets that his youth has fled,
Forgets that his prime is past,
Till he stands one day, with a hope that's dead,
In the glare of the truth at least.

He has failed, he has failed; he has missed his chance;
He has just done things by half.
Life's been a jolly good joke on him,
And now is the time to laugh.
Ha, ha! He is one of the Legion Lost;
He was never meant to win;
He's a rolling stone, and it's bred in the bone;
He's a man who won't fit in.

The Rhyme of the Remittance Man

There's a four-pronged buck a-swinging in the shadow of my cabin,
And it roamed the velvet valley till today;
But I tracked it by the river, and I trailed it in the cover,
And I killed it on the mountain miles away.
Now I've had my lazy supper, and the level sun is gleaming
On the water where the silver salmon play;
And I light my little corncob, and I linger, softly dreaming,
In the twilight, of a land that's far away.

Far away, so faint and far, is flaming London, fevered Paris,
That I fancy I have gained another star;

Far away the din and hurry, far away the sin and worry,
  Far away — God knows they cannot be too far.
Gilded galley-slaves of Mammon — how my purse-proud
    brothers taunt me!
  I might have been as well-to-do as they
Had I clutched like them my chances, learned their wisdom,
    crushed my fancies,
  Starved my soul and gone to business every day.

Well, the cherry bends with blossom and the vivid grass is
    springing,
  And the star-like lily nestles in the green;
And the frogs their joys are singing, and my heart in tune is
    ringing,
  And it doesn't matter what I might have been.
While above the scented pine-gloom, piling heights of golden
    glory,
  The sun-god paints his canvas in the west,
I can couch me deep in clover, I can listen to the story
  Of the lazy, lapping water — it is best.

While the trout leaps in the river, and the blue grouse thrills the
    cover,
  And the frozen snow betrays the panther's track,
And the robin greets the dayspring with the rapture of a lover,
  I am happy, and I'll nevermore go back.
For I know I'd just be longing for the little old log cabin,
  With the morning glory clinging to the door,
Till I loathed the city places, cursed the care on all the faces,
  Turned my back on lazar London evermore.

So send me far from Lombard Street, and write me down a
    failure;

Put a little in my purse and leave me free.
Say: "He turned from Fortune's offering to follow up a pale lure,
He is one of us no longer — let him be."
I am one of you no longer; by the trails my feet have broken,
The dizzy peaks I've scaled, the campfire's glow;
By the lonely seas I've sailed in — yea, the final word is spoken,
I am signed and sealed to nature. Be it so.

The Low-Down White

This is the payday up at the mines, when the bearded brutes
come down;
There's money to burn in the streets tonight, so I've sent my
klooch to town,
With a haggard face and ribband of red entwined in her hair of
brown.

And I know at the dawn she'll come reeling home with the
bottles, one, two, three —
One for herself, to drown her shame, and two big bottles for me,
To make me forget the thing I am and the man I used to be.

To make me forget the brand of the dog, as I crouch in this
hideous place;
To make me forget once I kindled the light of love in a lady's
face,
Where even the squalid Siwash now holds me a black disgrace.

Oh, I have guarded my secret well! And who would dream as I
speak
In a tribal tongue like a rogue unhung, 'mid the ranch-house
filth and reek,

I could roll to bed with a Latin phrase and rise with a verse of
Greek?

Yet I was a senior prizeman once, and the pride of a college
eight;
Called to the bar — my friends were true! but they could not
keep me straight;
Then came the divorce, and I went abroad and "died" on the
River Plate.

But I'm not dead yet; though with half a lung there isn't time to
spare,
And I hope that the year will see me out, and, thank God, no
one will care —
Save maybe the little slim Siwash girl with the rose of shame in
her hair.

She will come with the dawn, and the dawn is near; I can see its
evil glow,
Like a corpse-light seen through a frosty pane in a night of
want and woe;
And yonder she comes by the bleak bull-pines, swift staggering
through the snow.

The Tramps

Can you recall, dear comrade, when we tramped God's land
together,
And we sang the old, old Earth-song, for our youth was
very sweet;
When we drank and fought and lusted, as we mocked at tie and
tether,

And the road to Anywhere, the wide world at our feet —

Along the road to Anywhere, when each day had its story;
When the time was yet our vassal, and life's jest was still unstale;
When peace unfathomed filled our hearts as, bathed in amber glory,
Along the road to Anywhere we watched the sunsets pale?

Alas! the road to Anywhere is pitfalled with disaster;
There's hunger, want, and weariness, yet O we loved it so!
As on we tramped exultantly, and no man was our master,
And no man guessed what dreams were ours, as, swinging heel and toe,
We tramped the road to Anywhere, the magic road to Anywhere,
The tragic road to Anywhere, such dear, dim years ago.

L'Envoi

You who have lived in the land,
You who have trusted the trail,
You who are strong to withstand,
You who are swift to assail:
Songs have I sung to beguile,
Vintage of desperate years
Hard as a harlot's smile,
Bitter as unshed tears.

Little of joy or mirth,
Little of ease I sing;
Sagas of men of earth
Humanly suffering,

Such as you all have done;
Savagely faring forth,
Sons of the midnight sun,
Argonauts of the North.

Far in the land God forgot
Glimmers the lure of your trail;
Still in your lust are you taught
Even to win is to fail.
Still you must follow and fight
Under the vampire wing;
There is the long, long night
Hoping and vanquishing.

Husbandman of the Wild,
Reaping a barren gain;
Scourged by desire, reconciled
Unto disaster and pain;
These, my songs, are for you,
You who are seared with the brand.
God knows I have tried to be true;
Please God you will understand.

The March of the Dead

The cruel war was over — oh, the triumph was so sweet!
We watched the troops returning, through our tears;
There was triumph, triumph, triumph down the scarlet glittering street,
And you scarce could hear the music for the cheers.
And you scarce could see the house-tops for the flags that flew between;

The bells were pealing madly to the sky;
And everyone was shouting for the Soldiers of the Queen,
And the glory of an age was passing by.

And then there came a shadow, swift and sudden, dark and drear;
The bells were silent, not an echo stirred.
The flags were drooping sullenly, the men forgot to cheer;
We waited, and we never spoke a word.
The sky grew darker, darker, till from out the gloomy rack
There came a voice that checked the heart with dread:
"Tear down, tear down your bunting now, and hang up sable black;
They are coming — it's the Army of the Dead."

They were coming, they were coming, gaunt and ghastly, sad and slow;
They were coming, all the crimson wrecks of pride;
With faces seared, and cheeks red smeared, and haunting eyes of woe,
And clotted holes the khaki couldn't hide.
Oh, the clammy brow of anguish! the livid, foam-flecked lips!
The reeling ranks of ruin swept along!
The limb that trailed, the hand that failed, the bloody fingertips!
And oh, the dreary rhythm of their song!

"They left us on the veldt-side, but we felt we couldn't stop
On this, our England's crowning festal day;
We're the men of Magersfontein, we're the men of Spion Kop,
Colenso — we're the men who had to pay.
We're the men who paid the blood-price. Shall the grave be all our gain?
You owe us. Long and heavy is the score.
Then cheer us for our glory now, and cheer us for our pain,

And cheer us as ye never cheered before."

The folks were white and stricken, and each tongue seemed weighted with lead;
Each heart was clutched in hollow hand of ice;
And every eye was staring at the horror of the dead,
The pity of the men who paid the price.
They were come, were come to mock us, in the first flush of our peace;
Through writhing lips their teeth were all agleam;
They were coming in their thousands — oh, would they never cease!
I closed my eyes, and then — it was a dream.

There was triumph, triumph, triumph down the scarlet gleaming street;
The town was mad; a man was like a boy.
A thousand flags were flaming where the sky and city meet;
A thousand bells were thundering the joy.
There was music, mirth and sunshine; but some eyes shone with regret;
And while we stun with cheers our homing braves,
O God, in Thy great mercy, let us nevermore forget
The graves they left behind, the bitter graves.

FROM
Ballads of a Cheechako

To the Man of the High North

My rhymes are rough, and often in my rhyming
I've drifted, silver sailed, on seas of dream,
Hearing afar the bells of Elfland chiming,
Seeing the groves of Arcadie agleam.

I was the thrall of Beauty that rejoices
From the peak snow-diademed to regal star;
Yet to mine aerie ever pierced the voices,
The pregnant voices of the Things That Are.

The Here, the Now, the vast Forlorn around us;
The gold-delirium, the ferine strife;
The lusts that lure us on, the hates that hound us;
Our red rags in the patchwork quilt of Life.

The nameless men who nameless rivers travel,
And in strange valleys greet strange deaths alone;
The grim, intrepid ones who would unravel
The mysteries that shroud the Polar Zone.

These will I sing, and if one of you linger
Over my pages in the Long, Long Night,
And on some lone line lay a calloused finger,
Saying: "It's human-true — it hits me right";
Then will I count this loving toil well spent;
Then will I dream awhile — content, content.

The Ballad of the Black Fox Skin

I

There was Claw-fingered Kitty and Windy Ike living the life of shame,
When unto them in the Long, Long Night came the man-who-had-no-name;
Bearing his prize of a black fox pelt, out of the Wild he came.

His cheeks were blanched as the flume-head foam when the brown spring freshets flow;
Deep in their dark, sin-calcined pits were his sombre eyes aglow;
They knew him far for the fitful man who spat forth blood on the snow.

"Did ever you see such a skin?" quoth he; "there's nought in the world so fine —
Such fullness of fur as black as the night, such lustre, such size, such shine;
It's life to a one-lunged man like me; it's London, it's women, it's wine.

"The Moose-hides called it the devil-fox, and swore that no man could kill;
That he who hunted it, soon or late, must surely suffer some ill;
But I laughed at them and their old squaw-tales. Ha! Ha! I'm laughing still.

"For look ye, the skin — it's as smooth as sin, and black as the core of the Pit.
By gun or by trap, whatever the hap, I swore I would capture it;

By star and by star afield and afar, I hunted and would not quit.

"For the devil-fox, it was swift and sly, and it seemed to fleer at
me;
I would wake in fright by the campfire light hearing its evil glee;
Into my dream its eyes would gleam, and its shadow would I see.

"It sniffed and ran from the ptarmigan I had poisoned to excess;
Unharmed it sped from my wrathful lead ('twas as if I shot by
guess);
Yet it came by night in the stark moonlight to mock at my
weariness.

"I tracked it up where the mountains hunch like the vertebrae
of the world;
I tracked it down to the death-still pits where the avalanche is
hurled;
From the glooms to the sacerdotal snows, where the carded
clouds are curled.

"From the vastitudes where the world protrudes through clouds
like seas up-shoaled,
I held its track till it led me back to the land I had left of old —
The land I had looted many moons. I was weary and sick and
cold.

"I was sick, soul-sick, of the futile chase, and there and then I
swore
The foul fiend fox might scathless go, for I would hunt no more;
Then I rubbed mine eyes in a vast surprise — it stood by my
cabin door.

"A rifle raised in the wraith-like gloom, and a vengeful shot
that sped;
A howl that would thrill a cream-faced corpse — and the
demon fox lay dead....
Yet there was never a sign of wound, and never a drop he bled.

"So that was the end of the great black fox, and here is the prize
I've won;
And now for a drink to cheer me up — I've mushed since the
early sun;
We'll drink a toast to the sorry ghost of the fox whose race is
run."

II

Now Claw-fingered Kitty and Windy Ike, bad as the worst were
they;
In their roadhouse down by the river trail they waited and
watched for prey;
With wine and song they joyed night long, and they slept like
swine by day.

For things were done in the Midnight Sun that no tongue will
ever tell;
And men there be who walk earth-free, but whose names are
writ in hell —
Are writ in flames with the guilty names of Fournier and Labelle.

Put not your trust in a poke of dust would ye sleep the sleep of
sin;
For there be those who would rob your clothes ere yet the
dawn comes in;
And a prize likewise in a woman's eyes is a peerless black fox skin.

Put your faith in the mountain cat if you lie within his lair,
Trust the fangs of the mother wolf, and the claws of the lead-
ripped bear;
But oh, of the wiles and the gold-tooth smiles of a dance-hall
wench beware!

Wherefore it was beyond all laws that lusts of man restrain,
A man drank deep and sank to sleep never to wake again;
And the Yukon swallowed through a hole in the cold corpse of
the slain.

III

The black fox skin a shadow cast from the roof nigh to the
floor;
And sleek it seemed and soft it gleamed, and the woman stroked
it o'er;
And the man stood by with a brooding eye, and gnashed his
teeth and swore.

When thieves and thugs fall out and fight there's fell arrears to
pay;
And soon or late sin meets its fate, and so it fell one day
That Claw-fingered Kitty and Windy Ike fanged up like dogs at
bay.

"The skin is mine, all mine," she cried; "I did the deed alone."
"It's share and share with a guilt-yoke pair," he hissed in a preg-
nant tone;
And so they snarled like malamutes over a mildewed bone.

And so they fought, by fear untaught, till haply it befell

One dawn of day she slipped away to Dawson town to sell
The fruit of sin, this black fox skin that had made their lives a
hell.

She slipped away as still he lay, she clutched the wondrous fur;
Her pulses beat, her foot was fleet, her fear was as a spur;
She laughed with glee, she did not see him rise and follow her.

The bluffs uprear and grimly peer far over Dawson town;
They see its lights a blaze o' nights and harshly they look down;
They mock the plan and plot of man with grim, ironic frown.

The trail was steep; 'twas at the time when swiftly sinks the
snow;
All honeycombed, the river ice was rotting down below;
The river chafed beneath its rind with many a mighty throe.

And up the swift and oozy drift a woman climbed in fear,
Clutching to her black fox fur as if she held it dear;
And hard she pressed it to her breast — then Windy Ike drew
near.

She made no moan — her heart was stone — she read his smil-
ing face,
And like a dream flashed all her life's dark horror and disgrace;
A moment only — with a snarl he hurled her into space.

She rolled for nigh an hundred feet; she bounded like a ball;
From crag to crag she caromed down through snow and timber
fall; . . .
A hole gaped in the river ice; the spray flashed — that was all.

A bird sang for the joy of spring, so piercing sweet and frail;
And blinding bright the land was dight in gay and glittering
  mail;
And with a wondrous black fox skin a man slid down the trail.

IV

A wedge-faced man there was who ran along the river bank,
Who stumbled through each drift and slough, and ever slipped
  and sank,
And ever cursed his Maker's name, and ever "hooch" he drank.

He travelled like a hunted thing, hard harried, sore distrest;
The old grandmother moon crept out from her cloud-quilted
  nest;
The aged mountains mocked at him in their primeval rest.

Grim shadows diapered the snow; the air was strangely mild;
The valley's girth was dumb with mirth, the laughter of the
  wild;
The still sardonic laughter of an ogre o'er a child.

The river writhed beneath the ice; it groaned like one in pain,
The yawning chasms opened wide, and closed and yawned
  again;
And sheets of silver heaved on high until they split in twain.

From out the road-house by the trail they saw a man afar
Make for the narrow river-reach where the swift cross-currents
  are;
Where, frail and worn, the ice is torn and angry waters jar.

But they did not see him crash and sink into the icy flow;
They did not see him clinging there, gripped by the undertow,
Clawing with bleeding fingernails at the jagged ice and snow.

They found a note beside the hole where he had stumbled in:
"Here met his fate by evil luck a man who lived in sin,
And to the one who loves me least I leave this black fox skin."

And strange it is; for, though they searched the river all around,
No trace or sign of black fox skin was ever after found;
Though one man said he saw the tread of *hoofs* deep in the
ground.

The Ballad of One-Eyed Mike

This is the tale that was told to me by the man with the crystal eye,
As I smoked my pipe in the campfire light, and the Glories swept the sky;
As the Northlights gleamed and curved and streamed, and the bottle of
"hooch" was dry.

A man once aimed that my life be shamed, and wrought me a
deathly wrong;
I vowed one day I would well repay, but the heft of his hate was
strong.
He thonged me East and he thonged me West; he harried me
back and forth,
Till I fled in fright from his peerless spite to the bleak, bald-
headed North.

And there I lay, and for many a day I hatched plan after plan,
For a golden haul of the wherewithal to crush and to kill my
man;

And there I strove, and there I clove through the drift of icy
streams;
And there I fought, and there I sought for the pay-streak of my
dreams.

So twenty years, with their hopes and fears and smiles and tears
and such,
Went by and left me long bereft of hope of the Midas touch;
About as fat as a chancel rat, and lo! despite my will,
In the weary fight I had clean lost sight of the man I sought to
kill.

'Twas so far away, that evil day when I prayed the Prince of
Gloom
For the savage strength and the sullen length of life to work his
doom.
Nor sign nor word had I seen or heard, and it happed so long
ago;
My youth was gone and my memory wan, and I willed it even
so.

It fell one night in the waning light by the Yukon's oily flow,
I smoked and sat as I marvelled at the sky's port-winey glow;
Till it paled away to an absinthe grey, and the river seemed to
shrink,
All wobbly flakes and wriggling snakes and goblin eyes a-wink.

'Twas weird to see and it 'wildered me in a queer, hypnotic dream,
Till I saw a spot like an inky blot come floating down the stream;
It bobbed and swung; it sheered and hung; it romped round in
a ring;
It seemed to play in a tricksome way; it sure was a merry thing.

In freakish flights strange oily lights came fluttering round its
head,
Like butterflies of a monster size — then I knew it for the
Dead.
Its face was rubbed and slicked and scrubbed as smooth as a
shaven pate;
In the silver snakes that the water makes it gleamed like a dinner
plate.

It gurgled near, and clear and clear and large and large it grew;
It stood upright in a ring of light and it looked me through and
through.
It weltered round with a woozy sound, and ere I could retreat,
With the witless roll of a sodden soul it wantoned to my feet.

And here I swear by this Cross I wear, I heard that "floater" say:
"I am the man from whom you ran, the man you sought to slay.
That you may note and gaze and gloat, and say 'Revenge is
sweet,'
In the grit and grime of the river's slime I am rotting at your
feet.

"The ill we rue must e'en undo, though it rive us bone from
bone;
So it came about that I sought you out, for I prayed I might
atone.
I did you wrong and for long and long I sought where you
might live;
And now you're found, though I'm dead and drowned, I beg
you to forgive."

So sad it seemed, and its cheekbones gleamed, and its fingers
flicked the shore;

And it lapped and lay in a weary way, and its hands met to
implore;
That I gently said: "Poor, restless dead, I would never work you
woe;
Though the wrong you rue you can ne'er undo, I forgave you
long ago."

Then, wonder-wise, I rubbed my eyes and I woke from a horrid
dream.
The moon rode high in the naked sky, and something bobbed
in the stream.
It held my sight in a patch of light, and then it sheered from the
shore;
It dipped and sank by a hollow bank, and I never saw it more.

This was the tale he told to me, that man so warped and grey,
Ere he slept and dreamed, and the campfire gleamed in his eye in a
wolfish way —
That crystal eye that raked the sky in the weird Auroral ray.

The Man from Eldorado

I

He's the man from Eldorado, and he's just arrived in town,
In the moccasins and oily buckskin shirt.
He's gaunt as any Indian, and pretty nigh as brown;
He's greasy, and he smells of sweat and dirt.
He sports a crop of whiskers that would shame a healthy hog;
Hard work has racked his joints and stooped his back;
He slops along the sidewalk followed by his yellow dog,
But he's got a bunch of gold-dust in his sack.

He seems a little wistful as he blinks at all the lights,
And maybe he is thinking of his claim
And the dark and dwarfish cabin where he lay and dreamed at nights,
(Thank God, he'll never see the place again!)
Where he lived on tinned tomatoes, beef embalmed and sourdough bread,
On rusty beans and bacon furred with mould;
His stomach's out of kilter and his system full of lead,
But it's over, and his poke is full of gold.

He has panted at the windlass, he has loaded in the drift,
He has pounded at the face of oozy clay;
He has taxed himself to sickness, dark and damp and double shift,
He has laboured like a demon night and day.
And now, praise God, it's over, and he seems to breathe again
Of new-mown hay, the warm, wet, friendly loam;
He sees a snowy orchard in a green and dimpling plain,
And a little vine-clad cottage, and it's — Home.

II

He's the man from Eldorado, and he's had a bite and sup,
And he's met in with a drouthy friend or two;
He's cached away his gold-dust, but he's sort of bucking up,
So he's kept enough tonight to see him through.
His eye is bright and genial, his tongue no longer lags;
His heart is brimming o'er with joy and mirth;
He may be far from savoury, he may be clad in rags,
But tonight he feels as if he owns the earth.

Says he: "Boys, here is where the shaggy North and I will shake;
I thought I'd never manage to get free.

I kept on making misses; but at least I've got my stake;
There's no more thawing frozen muck for me.
I am going to God's Country, where I'll live the simple life;
I'll buy a bit of land and make a start;
I'll carve a little homestead, and I'll win a little wife,
And raise ten little kids to cheer my heart."

They signified their sympathy by crowding to the bar;
They bellied up three deep and drank his health.
He shed a radiant smile around and smoked a rank cigar;
They wished him honour, happiness and wealth.
They drank unto his wife to be — that unsuspecting maid;
They drank unto his children half a score;
And when they got through drinking very tenderly they laid
The man from Eldorado on the floor.

III

He's the man from Eldorado, and he's only starting in
To cultivate a thousand-dollar jag.
His poke is full of gold-dust and his heart is full of sin,
And he's dancing with a girl called Muckluck Mag.
She's as light as any fairy; she's as pretty as a peach;
She's mistress of the witchcraft to beguile;
There's sunshine in her manner, there is music in her speech,
And there's concentrated honey in her smile.

Oh, the fever of the dance-hall and the glitter and the shine,
The beauty, and the jewels, and the whirl,
The madness of the music, the rapture of the wine,
The languorous allurement of a girl!
She is like a lost madonna; he is gaunt, unkempt and grim;
But she fondles him and gazes in his eyes;

Her kisses seek his heavy lips, and soon it seems to him
He has staked a little claim in Paradise.

"Who's for a juicy two-step?" cries the master of the floor;
The music throbs with soft, seductive beat.
There's glitter, gilt and gladness; there are pretty girls galore;
There's a woolly man with moccasins on feet.
They know they've got him going; he is buying wine for all,
They crowd around as buzzards at a feast,
Then when his poke is empty they boost him from the hall,
And spurn him in the gutter like a beast.

He's the man from Eldorado, and he's painting red the town;
Behind he leaves a trail of yellow dust;
In a whirl of senseless riot he is ramping up and down;
There's nothing checks his madness and his lust.
And soon the word is passed around — it travels like a flame;
They fight to clutch his hand and call him friend,
The chevaliers of lost repute, the dames of sorry fame;
Then comes the grim awakening — the end.

IV

He's the man from Eldorado, and he gives a grand affair;
There's feasting, dancing, wine without restraint.
The smooth Beau Brummels of the bar, the faro men, are there;
The tinhorns and purveyors of red paint;
The sleek and painted women, their predacious eyes aglow —
Sure Klondike City never saw the like;
Then Muckluck Mag proposed the toast, "The giver of the show,
The livest sport that ever hit the pike."

The "live one" rises to his feet; he stammers to reply —
    And then there comes before his muddled brain
A vision of green vastitudes beneath an April sky,
    And clover pastures drenched with silver rain.
He knows that it can never be, that he is down and out;
    Life leers at him with foul and fetid breath;
And then amid the revelry, the song and cheer and shout,
    He suddenly grows grim and cold as death.

He grips the table tensely, and he says: "Dear friends of mine,
    I've let you dip your fingers in my purse;
I've crammed you at my table, and I've drowned you in my wine,
    And I've little left to give you but — my curse.
I've failed supremely in my plans; it's rather late to whine;
    My poke is mighty wizened up and small.
I thank you each for coming here; the happiness is mine —
    And now, you thieves and harlots, take it all."

He twists the thong from off his poke; he swings it o'er his head;
    The nuggets fall around their feet like grain.
They rattle over roof and wall; they scatter, roll and spread;
    The dust is like a shower of golden rain.
The guests a moment stand aghast, then grovel on the floor;
    They fight, and snarl, and claw, like beasts of prey;
And then, as everybody grabbed and everybody swore,
    The man from Eldorado slipped away.

V

He's the man from Eldorado, and they found him stiff and dead,
    Half covered by the freezing ooze and dirt.
A clotted Colt was in his hand, a hole was in his head,
    And he wore an old and oily buckskin shirt.

His eyes were fixed and horrible, as one who hails the end;
The frost had set him rigid as a log;
And there, half lying on his breast, his last and only friend,
There crouched and whined a mangy yellow dog.

The Wood-Cutter

The sky is like an envelope,
One of those blue official things;
And, sealing it, to mock our hope,
The moon, a silver wafer, clings.
What shall we find when death gives leave
To read — our sentence or reprieve?

I'm holding it down on God's scrap-pile, up on the fag-end of earth;
O'er me a menace of mountains, a river that grits at my feet;
Face to face with my soul-self, weighing my life at its worth;
Wondering what I was made for, here in my last retreat.

Last! Ah, yes, it's the finish. Have ever you heard a man cry?
(Sobs that rake him and rend him, right from the base of the chest.)
That's how I've cried, oh, so often; and now that my tears are dry,
I sit in the desolate quiet and wait for the infinite Rest.

Rest! Well, it's restful around me; it's quiet clean to the core
The mountains pose in their ermine, in golden the hills are clad;
The big, blue, silt-freighted Yukon seethes by my cabin door,
And I think it's only the river that keeps me from going mad.

By day it's a ruthless monster, a callous, insatiate thing,
With oily bubble and eddy, with sudden swirling of breast;
By night it's a writhing Titan, sullenly murmuring,
Ever and ever goaded, and ever crying for rest.

It cries for its human tribute, but me it will never drown.
I've learned the lore of my river; my river obeys me well.
I hew and launch my cordwood, and raft it to Dawson town,
Where wood means wine and women, and, incidentally, hell.

Hell and the anguish thereafter. Here as I sit alone
I'd give the life I have left me to lighten some load of care:
(The bitterest part of the bitter is being denied to atone;
Lips that have mocked at Heaven lend themselves ill to
prayer.)

Impotent as a beetle-pierced on the needle of Fate;
A wretch in a cosmic death-cell, peaks for my prison bars;
'Whelmed by a world stupendous, lonely and listless I wait,
Drowned in a sea of silence, strewn with confetti of stars.

See! from far up the valley a rapier pierces the night,
The white search-ray of a steamer. Swiftly, serenely it nears;
A proud, white, alien presence, a glittering galley of light,
Confident-poised, triumphant, freighted with hopes and
fears.

I look as one looks on a vision; I see it pulsating by;
I glimpse joy-radiant faces; I hear the thresh of the wheel.
Hoof-like my heart beats a moment; then silence swoops from
the sky.
Darkness is piled upon darkness. God only knows how I
feel.

Maybe you've seen me sometimes; maybe you've pitied me
then —
The lonely waif of the wood-camp, here by my cabin door.
Some day you'll look and see not; futile and outcast of men,
I shall be far from your pity, resting forevermore.

My life was a problem in ciphers, a wear and profitless sum.
Slipshod and stupid I worked it, dazed by negation and doubt.
Ciphers the total confronts me. Oh, Death, with thy moistened thumb,
Stoop like a petulant schoolboy, wipe me forever out!

FROM
Rhymes of a Rolling Stone

From Rhymes of a Rolling Stone

A Rolling Stone

There's sunshine in the heart of me,
My blood sings in the breeze;
The mountains are a part of me,
I'm fellow to the trees.
My golden youth I'm squandering,
Sun-libertine am I;
A-wandering, a-wandering,
Until the day I die.

I was once, I declare, a Stone-Age man,
And I roomed in the cool of a cave;
I have known, I will swear, in a new lifespan
The fret and the sweat of a slave:
For far over all that folks hold worth,
There lives and there leaps in me
A love of the lowly things of earth,
And a passion to be free.

To pitch my tent with no prosy plan,
To range and to change at will;
To mock at the mastership of man,
To seek Adventure's thrill.
Carefree to be, as a bird that sings;
To go my own sweet way;
To reck not all what may befall,
But to live and to love each day.

To make my body a temple pure
Wherein I dwell serene;
To care for the things that shall endure,
The simple, sweet and clean.

To oust out envy and hate and rage,
    To breathe with no alarm;
For Nature shall be my anchorage,
    And none shall do me harm.

To shun all lures that debauch the soul,
    The orgied rites of the rich;
To eat my crust as a rover must
    With the rough-neck down in the ditch.
To trudge by his die whate'er betide;
    To share his fire at night;
To call him friend to the long trail-end,
    And to read his heart aright.

To scorn all strife, and to view all life
    With the curious eyes of a child;
From the plangent sea to the prairie,
    From the slum to the heart of the Wild.
From the red-rimmed star to the speck of sand,
    From the vast to the greatly small;
For I know that the whole for good is planned,
    And I want to see it all.

To see it all, the wide world-way,
    From the fig-leaf belt to the Pole;
With never a one to say me nay,
    And none to cramp my soul.
In belly-pinch I will pay the price,
    But God! let me be free;
For once I know in the long ago,
    They made a slave of me.

In a flannel shirt from earth's clean dirt,
Here, pal, is my calloused hand!
Oh, I love each day as a rover may,
Nor seek to understand.
To *enjoy* is good enough for me;
The gypsy of God am I;
Then here's a hail to each flaring dawn!
And here's a cheer to the night that's gone!
And may I go a-roaming on
Until the day I die!

Then every star shall sing to me
Its song of liberty;
And every morn shall bring to me
Its mandate to be free.
In every throbbing vein of me
I'll feel the vast Earth-call;
O body, heart and brain of me
Praise Him who made it all!

The Land of Beyond

Have ever you heard of the Land of Beyond,
That dreams at the gates of the day?
Alluring it lies at the skirts of the skies,
And ever so far away;
Alluring it calls: O ye the yoke galls,
And ye of the trail overfond,
With saddle and pack, by paddle and track,
Let's go to the Land of Beyond!

Have ever you stood where the silence brood,
And vast the horizons begin,
At the dawn of the day to behold far away
The goal you would strive for and win?
Yet ah! in the night when you gain to the height,
With the vast pool of heaven star-spawned,
Afar and agleam, like a valley of dream,
Still mocks you a Land of Beyond.

Thank God! there is always a Land of Beyond
For us who are true to the trail;
A vision to seek, a beckoning peak,
A fairness that never will fail;
A pride in our soul that mocks at a goal,
A manhood that irks at a bond,
And try how we will, unattainable still,
Behold it, our Land of Beyond!

The Idealist

Oh you who have daring deeds to tell!
And you who have felt Ambition's spell!
Have you heard of the louse who longed to dwell
In the golden hair of a queen?
He sighed all day and he sighed all night,
And no one could understand it quite,
For the head of a slut is a louse's delight
But he pined for the head of a queen.

So he left his kinsfolk in merry play,
And off by his lonesome he stole away,
From the home of his youth so bright and gay,

And gloriously unclean.
And at last he came to the palace gate,
And he made his way in a manner straight
(For a louse may go where a man must wait)
To the tiring-room of the queen.

The queen she spake to her tiring-maid:
"There's something the matter, I'm afraid.
Tonight ere for sleep my hair ye braid,
Just see what may be seen."
And lo, when they combed that shining hair
They found him alone in his glory there,
And he cried: "I die, but I do not care,
For I've lived in the head of a queen!"

Barbwire Bill

At dawn of day the white land lay all gruesome-like and grim,
When Bill Mc'Gee he says to me: "We've *got* to do it, Jim
"We've got to make Fort Liard quick. I know the river's bad,
"But, oh! the little woman's sick … why! don't you savvy, lad?"
And me! Well, yes, I must confess it wasn't hard to see
Their little family group of two would soon be one of three.
And so I answered, careless-like: "Why Bill! you don't suppose
"I'm scared of that there 'babbling brook'? Whatever you say — goes."

A real live man was Barbwire Bill, with insides copperlined,
For "barbwire" was the brand of "hooch" to which he most inclined.
They knew him far; his igloos are on Kittiegazuit strand

They knew him well, the tribes who dwell within the Barren
Land.
From Koyokuk to Kuskoquim his fame was everywhere;
And he did love, all life above, that little Julie Claire,
The lithe, white slave-girl he had bought for seven hundred skins,
And taken to his wickiup to make his moccasins.

We crawled down to the river bank and feeble folk were we,
That Julie Claire from God-knows-where, and Barbwire Bill
and me.
From shore to shore we heard the roar the heaving ice floes make,
And loud we laughed, and launched our raft, and followed in
their wake.
The river swept and seethed and leapt, and caught us in its stride;
And on we hurled amid a world that crashed on every side.
With sullen din the banks caved in; the shore-ice lanced the
stream;
The naked floes like spooks arose, all jiggling and agleam.
Black anchor-ice of strange device shot upward from its bed,
As night and day we cleft our way, and arrow-like we sped.

But "Faster still!" cried Barbwire Bill, and looked the live-long
day
In dull despair at Julie Claire, as white like death she lay.
And sometimes he would seem to pray and sometimes seem to
curse.
And bent above, with eyes of love, yet ever she grew worse.
And as we plunged and leapt and lunged, her face was plucked
with pain,
And I could feel his nerves of steel a-quiver at the strain.
And in the night he gripped me tight as I lay fast asleep:
"The river's kicking like a steer … run out the forward sweep!
"That's Hell-gate Canyon right ahead; I know of old its roar,

"And … I'll be damned! *the ice is jammed!* We've *got* to make the shore."

With one wild leap I gripped the sweep. The night was black as sin.
The float-ice crashed and ripped and smashed, and stunned us with its din.
And near and near, and clear and clear I heard the canyon boom;
And swift and strong we swept along to meet our awful doom.
And as with dread I glimpsed ahead the death that waited there,
My only thought was of the girl, the little Julie Claire;
And so, like demon mad with fear, I panted at the oar,
And foot by foot, and inch by inch, we worked the raft ashore.

The bank was staked with grinding ice, and as we scraped and crashed,
I only knew one thing to do, and through my mind it flashed:
Yet while I groped to find the rope, I heard Bill's savage cry:
"That's my job, lad! It's me that jumps. I'll snub this raft or die!"
I saw him leap, I saw him creep, I saw him gain the land;
I saw him crawl, I saw him fall, then run with rope in hand.
And then the darkness gulped him up, and down we dashed once more,
And nearer, nearer drew the jam, and thunder-like its roar.

Oh God! all's lost … from Julie Claire there came a wail of pain,
And then — the rope grew sudden taut, and quivered at the strain;
It slacked and slipped, it whined and gripped, and oh, I held my breath!
And there we hung and there we swung right in the jaws of death.

A little strand of hemp rope, and how I watched it there,
With all around a hell of sound, and darkness and despair;

A little strand of hempen rope, I watched it all alone,
And somewhere in the dark behind I heard a woman moan;
And somewhere in the dark ahead I heard a man cry out,
Then silence, silence, silence, fell, and mocked my hollow shout.
And yet once more from out the shore I heard that cry of pain,
A moan of mortal agony, then all was still again.

That night was hell with all the frills, and when the dawn broke
dim,
I saw a lean and level hand, but never sign of him.
I saw a flat and frozen shore of hideous device,
I saw a long-drawn strand of rope that vanished through the ice.
And on that treeless, rockless shore I found my partner — dead.
No place was there to snub the raft, so — *he had served instead*;
And with the rope lashed round his waist, in last defiant fight,
He'd thrown himself beneath the ice, that closed and gripped
him tight;
And there he'd held us back from death, as fast in death he lay....
Say, boys! I'm not the pious brand, but — I just tried to pray.
And then I looked to Julie Claire, and sore abashed was I,
For from the robes that covered her, *I — heard — a — baby —
cry....*

Thus was Love conqueror of death, and life for life was given;
And though no saint on earth, d'ye think — Bill's squared his-
self with Heaven?

The Headliner and the Breadliner

Moko, the Educated Ape is here,
The pet of vaudeville, so the posters say,
And every night the gaping people pay

To see him in his panoply appear;
To see him pad his paunch with dainty cheer,
    Puff his perfecto, swill champagne, and sway
    Just like a gentleman, yet all in play,
Then bow himself off stage with brutish leer.

And as tonight, with noble knowledge crammed,
    I 'mid this human compost take my place,
I, once a poet, now so dead and damned,
    The woeful tears half freezing on my face:
"O God!" I cry, "let me but take his shape,
    Moko's, the Blest, the Educated Ape."

The Squaw Man

The cow-moose comes to water, and the beaver's overbold,
The net is in the eddy of the stream;
The teepee stars the vivid sward with russet, red and gold,
And in the velvet gloom the fire's a-gleam.
The night is ripe with quiet, rich with incense of the pine;
From sanctuary lake I hear the loon;
The peaks are bright against the blue, and drenched with sunset
    wine,
And like a silver bubble is the moon.

Cloud-high I climbed but yesterday; a hundred miles around
I looked to see a rival fire a-gleam,
As in a crystal lens it lay, a land without a bound,
All lure, and virgin vastitude, and dream.
The great sky soared exultantly, the great earth bared its breast,
All river-veined and patterned with the pine;
The heedless hordes of caribou were streaming to the West,

A land of lustrous mystery — and mine.

Yea, mine to frame my Odyssey: Oh, little do they know
My conquest and the kingdom that I keep!
The meadows of the musk-ox, where the laughing grasses grow,
The rivers where the careless conies leap.
Beyond the silent Circle, where white men are fierce and few,
I lord it, and I mock at man-made law;
Like a flame upon the water is my little light canoe,
And yonder in the fireglow is my squaw.

A squaw man! yes, that's what I am; sneer at me if you will.
I've gone the grilling pace that cannot last;
With bawdry, bridge and brandy — Oh, I've drunk enough to
kill
A dozen such as you, but that is past.
I've swung round to my senses, found the place where I belong;
The City made a madman out of me;
But here beyond the Circle, where there's neither right or wrong,
I leap from life's straitjacket, and I'm free.

Yet ever in the far forlorn, by trails of lone desire;
Yet ever in the dawn's white leer of hate;
Yet ever by the dripping kill, beside the drowsy fire,
There comes the fierce heart-hunger for a mate.
There comes the mad blood-clamour for a woman's clinging
hand,
Love-humid eyes, the velvet of a breast;
And so I sought the Bonnet-plumes, and chose from out the band
The girl I thought the sweetest and the best.

O wistful women I have loved before my dark disgrace!
O women fair and rare in my home land!

Dear ladies, if I saw you now I'd turn away my face,
Then crawl to kiss your footprints in the sand!
And yet — that day the rifle jammed — a wounded moose at
    bay —
A roar, a charge ... I faced it with my knife:
A shot from out the willow-scrub, and there the monster lay....
Yes, little Laughing Eyes, you saved my life.

The man must have the woman, and we're all brutes more or less,
Since first the male ape shinned the family tree;
And yet I think I love her with a husband's tenderness,
And yet I know that she would die for me.
Oh, if I left you, Laughing Eyes, and nevermore came back,
God help you, girl! I know what you would do....
I see the lake wan in the moon, and from the shadow black,
There drifts a little, *empty* birch canoe.

We're here beyond the Circle, where there's never wrong nor
    right;
We aren't spliced according to the law;
But by the gods I hail you on this hushed and holy night
As the mother of my children, and my squaw.
I see your little slender face set in the firelight glow;
I pray that I may never make it sad;
I hear you croon a baby song, all slumber-soft and low —
God bless you, little Laughing Eyes! I'm glad.

The Man Who Knew

The Dreamer visioned Life as it may be,
And from his dream forthright a picture grew,
A painting all the people thronged to see,

And joyed therein — till came the Man Who Knew,
Saying: "'Tis bad! Why do ye gape, ye fools!
He painteth not according to the schools."

The Dreamer probed Life's mystery of woe,
And in a book he sought to give the clue;
The people read, and saw that it was so,
And read again — then came the Man Who Knew,
Saying: "Ye witless ones! this book is vile:
It hath not got the rudiments of style."

Love smote the Dreamer's lips, and silver clear
He sang a song so sweet, so tender true,
That all the marketplace was thrilled to hear,
And listened rapt — till came the Man Who Knew,
Saying: "His technique's wrong; he singeth ill.
Waste not your time." The singer's voice was still.

And then the people roused as if from sleep,
Crying: "What care we if it be not Art!
Hath he not charmed us, made us laugh and weep?
Come, let us crown him where he sits apart."
Then, with his picture spurned, his book unread,
His song unsung, they found their Dreamer — *dead.*

FROM
Rhymes of a Red Cross Man

The Volunteer

Sez I: My Country calls? Well let it call.
I grins perlitely and declines wiv thanks.
Go, let 'em plaster every blighted wall,
'Ere's *one* they don't stampede into the ranks.
Them politicians with their greasy ways;
Them empire-grabbers — fight for 'em? No fear!
I've seen this mess a-comin' from the days
Of Algyserious and Aggydear:
    I've felt me passion rise and swell .
    But … wot the 'ell, Bill? Wot the 'ell?

Sez I: My Country? Mine? I likes their cheek.
Me mud-bespattered by the cars they drive,
Wot makes my measly thirty bob a week,
And sweats red blood to keep meself alive!
Fight for the right to slave that they may spend,
Them in their mansions, me 'ere in my slum?
No, let 'em fight wot's something to defend:
But me, I've nothin' — let the Kaiser come.
    And so I cusses 'ard and well,
    But … wot the 'ell, Bill? Wot the 'ell?

Sez I: If they would do the decent thing,
And shield the missis and the little 'uns,
Why, even *I* might shout "God save the King,"
And face the chances of them 'ungry guns.
But we've got three, another on the way;
It's that wot makes me snarl and set me jor:
The wife and nippers, wot of 'em, I say,
If I gets knocked out in this blasted war?
    Gets proper busted by a shell,

But … wot the 'ell, Bill? Wot the 'ell?

Ay, wot the 'ell's the use of all this talk?
Today some boys in blue was passin' me,
And some of 'em they 'ad no legs to walk,
And some of 'em they 'ad no eyes to see.
And — well, I couldn't look 'em in the face,
And so I'm goin', goin' to declare
I'm under forty-one and take me place
To face the music with the bunch out there.
A fool, you say! Maybe you're right.
I'll 'ave no peace unless I fight.
I've ceased to think; I only know
I've gotta go, Bill, gotta go.

The Man from Athabaska

Oh the wife she tried to tell me that 'twas nothing but the
thrumming
Of a woodpecker a-rapping on the hollow of a tree;
And she thought that I was fooling when I said it was the
drumming
Of the mustering of legions, and 'twas calling unto me;
'Twas calling me to pull my freight and hop across the sea.

And a-mending of my fish nets sure I started up in wonder,
For I heard a savage roaring and 'twas coming from afar;
Oh the wife she tried to tell me that 'twas only summer
thunder,
And she laughed a bit sarcastic when I told her it was War;
'Twas the chariots of battle where the mighty armies are.

Then down the lake came Half-breed Tom with russet sail
a-flying,
And the word he said was "War" again, so what was I to do?
Oh the dogs they took to howling, and the missis took to crying,
As I flung my silver foxes in the little birch canoe:
Yes, the old girl stood a-blubbing till an island hid the view.

Says the factor: "Mike, you're crazy! They have soldier men
a-plenty.
You're as grizzled as a badger, and you're sixty year or so."
"But I haven't missed a scrap," says I, "since I was one and twenty.
And shall I miss the biggest? You can bet your whiskers — no!"
So I sold my furs and started ... and that's eighteen months ago.

For I joined the Foreign Legion, and they put me for a starter
In the trenches of the Argonne with the Boche a step away;
And the partner on my right hand was an *apache* from
Montmartre;
On my left there was a millionaire from Pittsburgh, U.S.A.
(Poor fellow! They collected him in bits the other day.)

But I'm sprier than a chipmunk, save a touch of the lumbago,
And they calls me Old Methoosalah, and *blagues* me all the day.
I'm their exhibition sniper, and they work me like a Dago,
And laugh to see me plug a Boche a half a mile away.
Oh I hold the highest record in the regiment, they say.

And at night they gather round me, and I tell them of my roaming
In the Country of the Crepuscule beside the Frozen Sea,
Where the musk-ox runs unchallenged, and the cariboo goes
homing;
And they sit like little children, just as quiet as can be:
Men of every crime and colour, how they harken unto me!

And I tell them of the Furland, of the tumpline and the paddle,
Of secret rivers loitering, that no one will explore;
And I tell them of the ranges, of the pack-strap and the saddle,
And they fill their pipes in silence, and their eyes beseech for more;
While above the star-shells fizzle and the high explosives roar.

And I tell of lakes fish-haunted, where the big bull moose are
calling,
And forests still as sepulchres with never trail or track;
And valleys packed with purple gloom, and mountain peaks
appalling,
And I tell of my cabin on the shore at Fond du Lac;
And I find myself a-thinking: Sure I wish that I was back.

So I brag of bear and beaver while the batteries are roaring,
And the fellows on the firing steps are blazing at the foe;
And I yarn of fur and feather when the *marmites* are a-soaring,
And they listen to my stories, seven *poilus* in a row,
Seven lean and lousy *poilus* with their cigarettes aglow.

And I tell them when it's over how I'll hike for Athabaska;
And those seven greasy *poilus* they are crazy to go too.
And I'll give the wife the "pickle-tub" I promised, and I'll ask her
The price of mink and marten, and the run of cariboo,
And I'll get my traps in order, and I'll start to work anew.

For I've had my fill of fighting, and I've seen a nation scattered,
And an army swung to slaughter, and a river red with gore,
And a city all a-smoulder, and ... as if it really mattered,
For the lake is yonder dreaming, and my cabin's on the shore;
And the dogs are leaping madly, and the wife is singing gladly,
And I'll rest in Athabaska, and I'll leave it nevermore.

Pilgrims

For, oh, when the war will be over
We'll go and we'll look for our dead;
We'll go when the bee's on the clover,
And the plume of the poppy is red:
We'll go when the year's at its gayest,
When meadows are laughing with flow'rs;
And there where the crosses are greyest,
We'll seek for the cross that is ours.

For they cry to us: *Friends, we are lonely,*
A-weary the night and the day;
But come in the blossom-time only,
Come when our graves will be gay:
When daffodils all are a-blowing,
And larks are a-thrilling the skies,
Oh, come with the hearts of you glowing,
And the joy of the Spring in your eyes.

But never, oh, never come sighing,
For ours was the Splendid Release;
And oh, but 'twas joy in the dying
To know we were winning you Peace!
So come when the valleys are sheening,
And fledged with the promise of grain;
And here where our graves will be greening,
Just smile and be happy again.

And so, when the war will be over,
We'll seek for the Wonderful One;
And maiden will look for her lover,
And mother will look for her son;

And there will be end to our grieving,
And gladness will gleam over loss,
As — glory beyond all believing!
We point … to a name on a cross.

The Stretcher-Bearer

My stretcher is one scarlet stain,
And as I tries to scrape it clean,
I tell you wot — I'm sick with pain
For all I've 'eard, for all I've seen;
Around me is the 'ellish night,
And as the war's red rim I trace,
I wonder if in 'Eaven's height,
Our God don't turn away 'Is face.

I don't care 'oose the Crime may be;
I 'olds no brief for kin or clan;
I 'ymns no 'ate: I only see
As man destroys his brother man;
I waves no flag: I only know,
As 'ere beside the dead I wait,
A million 'earts is weighed with woe,
A million 'omes is desolate.

In drippin' darkness, far and near,
All night I've sought them woeful ones.
Dawn shudders up and still I 'ear
The crimson chorus of the guns.
Look! like a ball of blood the sun
'Angs o'er the scene of wrath and wrong. …
"Quick! Stretcher-bearers on the run!"
O Prince of Peace! 'Ow long, 'ow long?

The Song of the Pacifist

What do they matter, our headlong hates, when we take the toll
of our Dead?
Think ye our glory and gain will pay for the torrent of blood
we have shed?
By the cheers of our Victory will the heart of the mother be
comforted?

If by the Victory all we mean is a broken and brooding foe;
Is the pomp and power of a glitt'ring hour, and a truce for an
age or so:
By the clay cold hand on the broken blade we have smitten a
bootless blow!

If by the Triumph we only prove that the sword we sheathe is
bright;
That justice and truth and love endure; that freedom's throned
on the height;
That the feebler folks shall be unafraid; that Might shall never
be Right;

If this be all: by blood-drenched plains, by the havoc of fire and
fear,
By the rending roar of the War of Wars, by the Dead so doubly
dear....
Then our Victory is a vast defeat, and it mocks us as we cheer.

Victory! there can be but one, hallowed in every land:
When by the graves of our common dead we who were foe-
men stand;
And in the hush of our common grief hand is tendered to hand.

Triumph! Yes, when out of the dust in the splendour of their
release
The spirits of those who fell go forth and they hallow our
hearts to peace,
And, brothers in pain, with worldwide voice, we clamour that
War shall cease.

Glory! Ay, when from blackest loss shall be born most radiant
gain;
When over the gory fields shall rise a star that never shall wane:
Then, and then only, our Dead shall know that they have not
fall'n in vain.

When our children's children shall talk of War as a madness that
may not be;
When we thank our God for our grief today, and blazon from
sea to sea
In the name of the Dead the banner of Peace … *that will be
Victory.*

FROM

Ballads of a Bohemian

From Ballads of a Bohemian

Prelude

Alas! upon some starry height,
The Gods of Excellence to please,
This hand of mine will never smite
The Harp of High Serenities.
Mere minstrel of the street am I,
To whom a careless coin you fling;
But who, beneath the bitter sky,
Blue-lipped, yet insolent of eye,
Can shrill a song of Spring;
A song of merry mansard days,
The cheery chimney-tops among;
Of rolics and of roundelays
When we were young … when we were young;
A song of love and lilac nights,
Of wit, of wisdom and of wine;
Of Folly whirling on the Heights,
Of hunger and of hope divine;
Of Blanche, Suzette and Celestine,
And all that gay and tender band
Who shared with us the fat, the lean,
The hazard of Illusion-land;
When scores of Philistines we slew
As mightily with brush and pen
We sought to make the world anew,
And scorned the gods of other men;
When we were fools divinely wise,
Who held it rapturous to strive;
When Art was sacred in our eyes,
And it was Heav'n to be alive….

O days of glamour, glory, truth,
To you tonight I raise my glass;

O freehold of immortal youth,
Bohemia, the lost, alas!
O laughing lads who led the romp,
Respectable you've grown, I'm told;
Your heads you bow to power and pomp,
You've learned to know the worth of gold.
O merry maids who shared our cheer,
Your eyes are dim, your locks are grey;
And as you scrub I sadly fear
Your daughters speed the dance today.
O windmill land and crescent moon!
O Columbine and Pierrette!
To you my old guitar I tune
Ere I forget, ere I forget....

So come, good men who toil and tire,
Who smoke and sip the kindly cup,
Ring round about the tavern fire
Ere yet you drink your liquor up,
And hear my simple songs of earth,
Of youth and truth and living things;
Of poverty and proper mirth,
Of rags and rich imaginings;
Of cock-a-hoop, blue-heavened days,
Of hearts elate and eager breath,
Of wonder, worship, pity, praise,
Of sorrow, sacrifice and death;
Of lusting, laughter, passion, pain,
Of lights that lure and dreams that thrall ...
And if a golden word I gain,
Oh, kindly folks, God save you all!
And if you shake your heads in blame ...
Good friends, God love you all the same.

FROM "BOOK ONE: SPRING"

I

MONTPARNASSE,
April 1914.

All day the sun has shone into my little attic, a bitter sunshine that brightened yet did not warm. And so as I toiled and toiled doggedly enough, many were the looks I cast at the three faggots I had saved to cook my evening meal. Now, however, my supper is over, my pipe alight, and as I stretch my legs before the embers I have at last a glow of comfort, a glimpse of peace.

My Garret

Here is my Garret up five flights of stairs;
Here's where I deal in dreams and ply in fancies,
Here is the wonder-shop of all my wares,
My sounding sonnets and my red romances.
Here's where I challenge Fate and ring my rhymes,
And grope at glory — aye, and starve at times.

Here is my Stronghold: stout of heart am I,
Greeting each dawn as songful as a linnet;
And when at night on yon poor bed I lie
(Blessing the world and every soul that's in it),
Here's where I thank the Lord no shadow bars
My skylight's vision of the valiant stars.

Here is my Palace tapestried with dreams.
Ah! though tonight ten *sous* are all my treasure,
While in my gaze immortal beauty gleams,

Am I not dowered with wealth beyond all measure?
Though in my ragged coat my songs I sing,
King of my soul, I envy not the king.

Here is my Haven: it's so quiet here;
Only the scratch of the pen, the candle's flutter;
Shabby and bare and small, but O how dear!
Mark you — my table with my work a-clutter,
My shelf of tattered books along the wall,
My bed, my broken chair — that's nearly all.

Only four faded walls, yet mine, all mine.
Oh, you fine folks, a pauper scorns your pity.
Look, where above me stars of rapture shine;
See, where below me gleams the siren city …
Am I not rich? — a millionaire no less,
If wealth be told in terms of Happiness.

FROM "BOOK TWO: EARLY SUMMER"

The Philistine and the Bohemian

Last night MacBean introduced me to Saxon Dane the Poet. Truly, he is more like a blacksmith than a Bard — a big bearded man whose black eyes brood somberly or flash with sudden fire. We talked of Walt Whitman, and then of others.

"The trouble with poetry," he said, "is that it is too exalted. It has a phraseology of its own; it selects themes that are quite outside of ordinary experience. As a medium of expression it fails to reach the great mass of the people."

Then he added: "To hell with the great mass of the people! What have they got to do with it? Write to please yourself, as if not a single reader existed. The moment a man begins to be conscious of an audience he is artistically damned. You're not a Poet, I hope?"

I meekly assured him I was a mere maker of verse.

"Well," said he, "better good verse than middling poetry. And maybe even the humblest of rhymes has its uses. Happiness is happiness, whether it be inspired by a Rossetti sonnet or a ballad by G.R. Sims. Let each one who has something to say, say it in the best way he can, and abide the result.... After all," he went on, "what does it matter? We are living in a pygmy day. With Tennyson and Browning the line of great poets passed away, perhaps forever. The world today is full of little minstrels, who echo one another and who pipe away tunefully enough. But with one exception they do not matter."

I dared to ask who was his one exception. He answered, "Myself, of course."

Here's a bit of light verse which it amused me to write today, as I sat in the sun on the terrace of the Closerie de Lilas:

She was a Philistine spick and span,
He was a bold Bohemian.
She had the *mode*, and the last at that;
He had a cape and a brigand hat.
She was so *riante* and *chic* and trim;
He was so shaggy, unkempt and grim.
On the rue de la Paix she was wont to shine;
The rue de la Gaîté was more his line.
She doted on Barclay and Dell and Caine;
He quoted Mallarmé and Paul Verlaine.
She was a triumph at Tango and teas;
At Vorticist's suppers he sought to please.
She thought that Franz Lehar was utterly great;
Of Strauss and Stravinski he'd piously prate.
She loved elegance, he loved art;

They were as wide as the poles apart:
Yet — Cupid and Caprice are hand and glove —
They met at a dinner, they fell in love.

Home he went to his garret bare,
Thrilling with rapture, hope, despair.
Swift he gazed in his looking-glass,
Made a grimace and murmured: "Ass!"
Seized his scissors and fiercely sheared,
Severed his buccaneering beard;
Grabbed his hair, and clip! clip! clip!
Off came a bunch with every snip.
Ran to a tailor's in startled state,
Suits a dozen commanded straight;
Coats and overcoats, pants in pairs,
Everything that a dandy wears;
Socks and collars, and shoes and ties,
Everything that a dandy buys.
Chums looked at him with wondering stare,
Fancied they'd seen him before somewhere;
A Brummel, a D'Orsay, a *beau* so fine,
A shining, immaculate Philistine.

Home she went in a raptured daze,
Looked in the mirror with startled gaze,
Didn't seem to be pleased at all;
Savagely muttered: "Insipid Doll!"
Clutched her hair and a pair of shears,
Cropped and bobbed it behind the ears;
Aimed at a wan and willowy-necked
Sort of a Holman Hunt effect;
Robed in subtile and sage-green tones,
Like the dames of Rossetti and E. Burne-Jones;

Girdled her garments billowing wide,
Moved with an undulating glide;
All her frivolous friends forsook,
Cultivated a soulful look;
Gushed in a voice with a creamy throb
Over some weirdly Futurist daub —
Did all, in short, that a woman can
To be a consummate Bohemian.

A year went past with its hopes and fears,
A year that seemed like a dozen years.
They met once more.... Oh at last! At last!
They rushed together, they stopped aghast.
They looked at each other with blank dismay,
They simply hadn't a word to say.
He thought with a shiver: "Can this be she?"
She thought with a shudder: "This can't be he?"
This simpering dandy, so sleek and spruce;
This languorous lily in garments loose;
They sought to brace from the awful shock:
Taking a seat, they tried to talk.
She spoke of Bergson and Pater's prose,
He prattled of dances and ragtime shows;
She purred of pictures, Matisse, Cezanne,
His tastes to the girls of Kirchner ran;
She raved of Tschaikowsky and Caesar Franck,
He owned that he was a jazz band crank!
They made no headway. Alas! alas!
He thought her a bore, she thought him an ass.
And so they arose and hurriedly fled;
Perish Illusion, Romance, you're dead.
He loved elegance, she loved art,
Better at once to part, to part.

And what is the moral of this rot?
Don't try to be what you know you're not.
And if you're made on a muttonish plan,
Don't seek to seem a Bohemian;
And if to the goats your feet incline,
Don't try to pass for a Philistine.

II

A SMALL CAFÉ IN A SIDE STREET,
June 1914.

The Bohemian Dreams

Because my overcoat's in pawn,
I choose to take my glass
Within a little *bistro* on
The rue du Montparnasse;
The dusty bins with bottles shine,
The counter's lined with zinc,
And there I sit and drink my wine,
And think and think and think.

I think of hoary old Stamboul,
Of Moslem and of Greek,
Of Persian in a coat of wool,
Of Kurd and Arab sheikh;
Of all the types of weal and woe,
And as I raise my glass,
Across Galata bridge I know
They pass and pass and pass.

I think of citron trees aglow,
Of fan-palms shading down,
Of sailors dancing heel and toe
With wenches black and brown;
And though it's all an ocean far
From Yucatan to France,
I'll bet beside the old bazaar
They dance and dance and dance.

I think of Monte Carlo, where
The pallid croupiers call,
And in the gorgeous, guilty air
The gamblers watch the ball;
And as I flick away the foam
With which my beer is crowned,
The wheels beneath the gilded dome
Go round and round and round.

I think of vast Niagara,
Those gulfs of foam a-shine,
Whose mighty roar would stagger a
More prosy bean than mine;
And as the hours I idly spend
Against a greasy wall,
I know that green the waters bend
And fall and fall and fall.

I think of Nijni Novgorod
And Jews who never rest;
And womenfolk with spade and hod
Who slave in Buda-Pest;
Of squat and sturdy Japanese
Who pound the paddy soil,

And as I loaf and smoke at ease
they toil and toil and toil.

I think of shrines in Hindustan,
Of cloistral glooms in Spain,
Of minarets in Ispahan,
Of St. Sophia's fane,
Of convent towers in Palestine,
Of temples in Cathay,
And as I stretch and sip my wine
They pray and pray and pray.

And so my dreams I dwell within,
And visions come and go,
And life is passing like a Cin-
Ematographic Show;
Till just as surely as my pipe
Is underneath my nose,
Amid my visions rich and ripe
I doze and doze and doze.

FROM "BOOK FOUR: WINTER"

IV

A Lapse of Time and a Word of Explanation

THE AMERICAN HOSPITAL, NEUILLY,
January 1919.

Four years have passed and it is winter again. Much has happened. When I last wrote, on the Somme in 1915, I was sickening with typhoid fever. All that spring I was in hospital.

Nevertheless, I was sufficiently recovered to take part in the Champagne battle in the fall of that year, and to "carry on" during the following winter. It was at Verdun I got my first wound.

In the spring of 1917 I again served with my Corps; but on the entry of the United States into the War I joined the army of my country. In the Argonne I had my left arm shot away.

As far as time and health permitted, I kept a record of these years, and also wrote much verse. All this, however, has disappeared under circumstances into which there is no need to enter here. The loss was a cruel one, almost more so than that of my arm; for I have neither the heart nor the power to rewrite this material.

And now, in default of something better, I have bundled together this manuscript, and have added to it a few more verses, written in hospitals. Let it represent me. If I can find a publisher for it, *tant mieux*. If not, I will print it at my own cost, and anyone who cares for a copy can write to me —

STEPHEN POORE,
12 *bis*, RUE DES PETITS MOINEAUX,
PARIS.

Michael

"There's something in your face, Michael, I've seen it all the day;
There's something quare that wasn't there when first ye wint
away...."

"It's just the Army life, mother, the drill, the left and right,
That puts the stiffinin' in yer spine and locks yer jaw up tight...."

"There's something in your eyes, Michael, an' how they stare
and stare —
You're lookin' at me now me boy, as if I wasn't there...."

"It's just the things I've seen, mother, the sights that come and
come,
A bit o' broken, bloody pulp that used to be a chum...."

"There's something on your heart, Michael, that makes ye wake
at night,
And often when I hear ye moan, I trimble in me fright...."

"It's just a man I killed, mother, a mother's son like me;
It seems he's always hauntin' me, he'll never let me be...."

"But maybe he was bad, Michael, maybe it was right
To kill the inimy you hate in fair and honest fight...."

"I did not hate at all, mother; he never did me harm;
I think he was a lad like me, who worked upon a farm...."

"And what's it all about, Michael; why did you have to go,
A quiet, peaceful lad like you, and we were happy so? ..."

"It's thim that's up above, mother, tit's thim that sits an' rules;
We've got to fight the wars they make, it's us as are the fools...."

"And what will be the end, Michael, and what's the use, I say,
Of fightin' if whoever wins it's us that's got to pay? ..."

"Oh, it will be the end, mother, when lads like him and me,
That sweat to feed the ones above, decide that we'll be free...."

"And when will that day come, Michael, and when will fightin'
cease,
And simple folks may till their soil and live and love in peace? ..."

"It's coming soon and soon, mother, it's nearer every day,
When only men who work and sweat will have a word to say;
When all who earn their honest bread in every land and soil
Will claim the Brotherhood of Man, the Comradeship of Toil;
When we, the Workers, all demand: 'What are we fighting for?' …
Then, then we'll end that stupid crime, that devil's madness —
War."

FROM

Bar-Room Ballads

The Ballad of Salvation Bill

'Twas in the bleary middle of the hard-boiled Arctic night,
I was lonesome as a loon, so if you can,
Imagine my emotions of amazement and delight
When I bumped into that Missionary Man.
He was lying lost and dying in the moon's unholy leer,
And frozen from his toes to fingertips;
The famished wolf pack ringed him; but he didn't seem to fear,
As he pressed his ice-bound Bible to his lips.

'Twas the limit of my trapline, with the cabin miles away,
And every step was like a stab of pain;
But I packed him like a baby, and I nursed him night and day,
Till I got him back to health and strength again.
So there we were, benighted in the shadow of the Pole,
And he might have proved a priceless little pard,
If he hadn't got to worrying about my blessed soul,
And a-quotin' me his Bible by the yard.

Now there was I, a husky guy, whose god was Nicotine.
With a "coffin nail" a fixture in my mug;
I rolled them in the pages of a pulpwood magazine,
And hacked them with my jackknife from the plug.
For, oh to know the bliss and glow that good tobacco means,
Just live among the everlasting ice....
So judge my horror when I found my stock of magazines
Was chewed into a chowder by the mice.

A woeful week went by and not a single pill I had,
Me that would smoke my forty in a day;
I sighed, I swore, I strode the floor; I felt I would go mad:
The gospel-plugger watched me in dismay.

The brow was wet, my teeth were set, my nerves were rasping
raw;
And yet that preacher couldn't understand:
So with despair I wrestled there — when suddenly I saw
The volume he was holding in his hand.

Then something snapped inside my brain, and with an evil start
The wolf-man in me woke to rabid rage.
"I saved your lousy life," says I; "so show you have a heart,
And tear me out a solitary page."
He shrank and shrivelled at my words; his face went pewter white;
'Twas just as if I'd handed him a blow;
And then … and then he seemed to swell, and grow to
Heaven's height,
And in a voice that rang he answered: "No!"

I grabbed my loaded rifle and I jabbed it to his chest:
"Come on, you shrimp, give up that Book," says I.
Well sir, he was a parson, but he stacked up with the best,
And for grit I got to hand it to the guy.
"If I should let you desecrate this Holy Word," he said,
"My soul would be eternally accurst;
So go on, Bill, I'm ready. You can pump me full of lead
And take it, but — you've got to kill me first."

Now I'm no foul assassin, though I'm full of sinful ways,
And I knew right there the fellow had me beat;
For I felt a yellow mongrel in the glory of his gaze,
And I flung my foolish firearm at his feet.
Then wearily I turned away, and dropped upon my bunk,
And there I lay and blubbered like a kid.
"Forgive me, pard," says I at last, "for acting like a skunk,
But hide the blasted rifle…." Which he did.

And he also hid his Bible, which was maybe just as well,
For the sight of all that paper gave me pain;
And there were crimson moments when I felt I'd go to hell
To have a single cigarette again.
And so I lay day after day, and brooded dark and deep,
Until one night I thought I'd end it all;
Then rough I roused the preacher, where he stretched pretending
sleep,
With his map of horror turned towards the wall.

"See here, my pious pal," says I, "I've stood it long enough....
Behold! I've mixed some strychnine in a cup;
Enough to kill a dozen men — believe me it's no bluff;
Now watch me, for I'm gonna drink it up.
You've seen me bludgeoned by despair through bitter days and
nights,
And now you'll see me squirming as I die.
You're not to blame, you've played the game according to your
lights....
But how would Christ have played it? — Well, goodbye...."

With that I raised the deadly drink and laid it to my lips,
But he was on me with a tiger-bound;
And as we locked and reeled and rocked with wild and wicked
grips,
The poison cup went crashing to the ground.
"Don't do it, Bill," he madly shrieked. "Maybe I acted wrong.
See, here's my Bible — use it as you will;
But promise me — you'll read a little as you go along....
You do! Then take it, Brother; smoke your fill."

And so I did. I smoked and smoked from Genesis to Job,
And as I smoked I read each blessed word;

While in the shadow of his bunk I heard him sigh and sob,
And then … a most peculiar thing occurred.
I got to reading more and more, and smoking less and less,
Till just about the day his heart was broke,
Says I: "Here, take it back, me lad. I've had enough, I guess.
Your paper makes a mighty rotten smoke."

So then and there with plea and prayer he wrestled for my soul,
And I was racked and ravaged by regrets.
But God was good, for lo! next day there came the police patrol,
With paper for a thousand cigarettes….
So now I'm called Salvation Bill; I teach the Living Law,
And Bally-hoo the Bible with the best;
And if a guy won't listen — why, I sock him on the jaw,
And preach the Gospel sitting on his chest.

The Ballad of Lenin's Tomb

This is the yarn he told to me
As we sat in Casey's Bar,
That Rooshun mug who scrammed from the jug
In the land of the Crimson Star;
That Soveet guy with the single eye,
And the face like a flaming scar.

Where Lenin lies the red flag flies, and rat-grey workers wait
To tread the gloom of Lenin's tomb, where the Comrade lies in state.
With lagging pace they scan his face, so weary yet so firm;
For years a score they've laboured sore to save him from the worm.
The Kremlin walls are grimly grey, but Lenin's Tomb is red,

And pilgrims from the Sour Lands say: "He sleeps and is not
dead."
Before their eyes in peace he lies, a symbol and a sign,
And as they pass that dome of glass they see — a God Divine.
So Doctor's plug him full of dope, for if he drops to dust,
So will collapse their faith and hope, the whole combine will
bust.
But stay, Tovarich; hark to me ... a secret I'll disclose,
For I did see what none did see; I know what no one knows.

I was Cheka terrorist — Oh I served the Soviet's well,
Till they put me down on the bone-yard list, for the fear that I
might tell;
That I might tell the things I saw, and that only I did see,
They held me in quod with a firing squad to make a corpse of
me.
But I got away, and here today I'm telling my tale to you;
Though it may sound weird, by Lenin's beard, so help me God
it's true.
I slouched across the great Red Square, and watched the
waiting line.
The mongrel sons of Marx were there, convened to Lenin's
shrine;
Ten thousand men of Muscovy, Mongol and Turkoman,
Black bonnets of the Aral Sea and Tatars of Kazan.
Kalmuck and Bashkir, Lett and Finn, Georgian, Jew and Lapp,
Kirghiz and Kazakh, crowding in to gaze at Lenin's map.
Aye, though a score of years had run I saw them pause and pray,
As mourners at the Tomb of one who died but yesterday.
I watched them in a bleary daze of bitterness and pain,
For oh, I missed the cheery blaze of vodka in my brain.
I stared, my eyes were hypnotized by the saturnine host,
When with a start that shook my heart I saw — I saw a ghost.

As in foggèd glass I saw him pass, and peer at me and grin —
A man I knew, a man I *slew*, Prince Boris Mazarin.

Now do not think because I drink I love the flowing bowl;
But liquor kills remorse and stills the anguish of the soul.
And there's so much I would forget, stark horrors I have seen,
Faces and forms that haunt me yet, like shadows on a screen.
And of these sights that mar my nights the ghastliest by far
Is the death of Boris Mazarin, that soldier of the Czar.

A mighty nobleman was he; we took him by surprise;
His mother, son and daughters three we slew before his eyes.
We tortured him, with jibes and threats; then mad for glut of
gore,
Upon our reeking bayonets we nailed him to the door.
But he defied us to the last, crying: "O carrion crew!
I'd die with joy could I destroy a hundred dogs like you."
I thrust my sword into this throat; the blade was gay with blood;
We flung him to his castle moat, and stamped him in its mud.
That mighty Cossack of the Don was dead with all his race....
And now I saw him coming on, dire vengeance in his face.
(Or was it some fantastic dream of my besotted brain?)
He looked at me with eyes a-gleam, the man whom I had slain.
He looked and bade me follow him; I could not help but go;
I joined the throng that passed along, so sorrowful and slow.
I followed with a sense of doom that shadow gaunt and grim;
Into the bowels of the Tomb I followed, followed him.

The light within was weird and dim, and icy cold the air;
My brow was wet with bitter sweat, I stumbled on the stair.
I tried to cry; my throat was dry; I sought to grip his arm;
For well I knew this man I slew was there to do us harm.
Lo! he was walking by my side, his fingers clutched my own,

This man I knew so well had died, his hand was naked bone
His face was like a skull, his eyes were caverns of decay …
And so we came to the crystal frame where lonely Lenin lay.

Without a sound we shuffled round. I sought to make a sign,
But like a vice his hand of ice was biting into mine.
With leaden pace around the place where Lenin lies at rest,
We slouched, I saw his bony claw go fumbling to his breast.
With ghastly grin he groped within, and tore his robe apart,
And from the hollow of his ribs he drew his blackened heart….
Ah no! Oh God! A *bomb*, a BOMB! And as I shrieked with dread,
With fiendish cry he raised it high, and … swung at Lenin's head.
Oh I was blinded by the flash and deafened by the roar,
And in a mess of bloody mash I wallowed on the floor.
Then Alps of darkness on me fell, and when I saw again
The leprous light 'twas in a cell, and I was racked with pain;
The ringèd round by shapes of gloom, who hoped that I would
die;
For of the crowd that crammed the Tomb the sole to live was I.
They told me I had dreamed a dream that must not be revealed,
But by their eyes of evil gleam I knew my doom was sealed.

I need not tell how from my cell in Lubianka gaol,
I broke away, but listen, here's the point of all my tale …
Outside the "Gay Pay Oo" none knew of that grim scene of
gore;
They closed the Tomb, and then they threw it open as before.
And there was Lenin, stiff and still, a symbol and a sign,
And rancid races come to thrill and wonder at his Shrine;
And hold the thought: if Lenin rot the Soviet's will decay;
So there he sleeps and calm he keeps his watch and ward for aye.
Yet if you pass that frame of glass, peer closely at his phiz,
So stern and firm it mocks the worm, it looks like wax … *and is.*

They tell you he's a mummy — don't you make the bright
mistake:
They tell you — he's a dummy; aye, a fiction and a fake.
This *eye* beheld the bloody bomb that bashed him on the bean.
I heard the crash, I saw the flash, yet ... there he lies serene.
And by the roar that rocked the Tomb I ask: how could that be?
But if you doubt that deed of doom, just go yourself and see.
You think I'm mad, or drunk, or both.... Well, I don't care a
damn:
I tell you this: their Lenin is a waxen, showcase SHAM.

Such was the yarn he handed me,
Down there in Casey's Bar,
That Rooshun bug with the scrambled mug
From the Land of the Commissar.
It may be true, I leave it you
To figger out how far.

The Ballad of Casey's Billy-Goat

You've heard of "Casey at The Bat,"
And "Casey's Tabble Dote";
But now it's time
To write the rhyme
Of "Casey's Billy-goat."

Pat Casey had a billy-goat he gave the name of Shamus,
Because it was (the neighbours said) a national disgrace.
And sure enough that animal was eminently famous
For masticating every rag of laundry round the place.
From shirts to skirts prodigiously it proved its powers of chewing;
The question of digestion seemed to matter not at all;

But you'll agree, I think with me, its limit of misdoing
Was reached the day it swallowed Missis Rooney's ould red shawl.

Now Missis Annie Rooney was a winsome widow woman,
And many a bouncing boy had sought to make her change her
name;
And living just across the way 'twas surely only human
A lonesome man like Casey should be wishfully the same.
So every Sunday, shaved and shined, he'd make the fine occasion
To call upon the lady, and she'd take his hat and coat;
And supping tea it seemed that she might yield to his persuasion,
But alas! he hadn't counted on that devastating goat.

For Shamus loved his master with a deep and dumb devotion,
And everywhere that Casey went that goat would want to go;
And though I cannot analyse a quadruped's emotion,
They said the baste was jealous, and I reckon it was so.
For every time that Casey went to call on Missis Rooney,
Beside the gate the goat would wait with woefulness intense;
Until one day it chanced that they were fast becoming spooney,
When Shamus spied that ould red shawl a-flutter on the fence.

Now Missis Rooney loved that shawl beyond all rhyme or
reason,
And maybe 'twas an heirloom or a cherished souvenir;
For judging by the way she wore it season after season,
It might have been as precious as a product of Cashmere.
So Shamus strolled towards it, and no doubt the colour pleased
him,
For he biffed it and he sniffed it, as most any goat may do;
Then his melancholy vanished as a sense of hunger seized him,
And he wagged his tail with rapture as he started in to chew.

"Begorrah! you're a daisy," said the doting Mister Casey
To the blushing Widow Rooney as they parted at the door.
"Wid yer tenderness an' tazin' sure ye've set me heart a blazin',
And I dread the day I'll nivver see me Annie anny more."
"Go on now wid yer blarney," said the widow softly sighing;
And she went to pull his whiskers, when dismay her bosom smote....
Her ould red shawl! 'Twas missin' where she'd left it bravely drying —
Then she saw it disappearing — down the neck of Casey's goat.

Fiercely flamed her Irish temper. "Look!" says she, "the thavin' divvle!
Sure he's made me shawl his supper. Well, I hope it's to his taste;
But excuse me, Mister Casey, if I seem to be oncivil,
For I'll nivver wed a man wid such a misbegotten baste."
So she slammed the door and left him in a state of consternation,
And he couldn't understand it, till he saw that grinning goat;
Then with eloquence he cussed it, and his final fulmination
Was a poem of profanity impossible to quote.

So blasting goats and petticoats, and feeling downright sinful,
Despairfully he wandered in to Shinnigan's shebeen;
And straightway he proceeded to absorb a mighty skinful
Of the deadliest variety of Shinnigan's potheen.
And when he started homeward it was in the early morning,
But Shamus followed faithfully, a yard behind his back;
Then Casey slipped and stumbled, and without the slightest warning
Like a lump of lead he tumbled — right across the railway track.

And there he lay, serenely, and defied the powers to budge him,
Reposing like a baby, with his head upon a rail;

But Shamus seemed unhappy, and from time to time would
    nudge him,
Though his prods of protestation were without the least avail.
Then to that goatish mind, maybe, a sense of fell disaster
Came stealing like a spectre in the dim and dreary dawn;
For his bleat of warning blended with the snoring of his master
In a chorus of calamity — but Casey slumbered on.

Yet oh, that goat was troubled, for his efforts were redoubled;
Now he tugged at Casey's whisker, now he nibbled at his ear;
Now he shook him by the shoulder, and with fear becoming
    bolder,
He bellowed like a foghorn, but the sleeper did not hear.
Then up and down the railway line he scampered for assistance;
But anxiously he hurried back and sought with tug and strain
To pull his master off the track … when sudden! in the distance
He heard the roar and rumble of the fast approaching train.

Did Shamus faint and falter? No, he stood there stark and splendid.
True, his tummy was distended, but he gave his horns a toss.
By them his goathood's honour would be gallantly defended,
And if their valour failed him — he would perish with his boss.
So dauntlessly he lowered his head, and ever clearer, clearer,
He heard the throb and thunder of the Continental Mail.
He would face that mighty monster. It was coming nearer, nearer;
He would fight it, he would smite it, but he'd never show his tail.

Can you see that hirsute hero, standing there in tragic glory?
Can you hear the Pullman porters shrieking horror to the sky?
No, you can't; because my story has no end so grim and gory,
For Shamus did not perish and his master did not die.
At this very present moment Casey swaggers hale and hearty,
And Shamus strolls beside him with a bright bell at his throat;

While the recent Missis Rooney is the gayest of the party,
For now she's Missis Casey and she's crazy for that goat.

You're wondering what happened? Well, you know that truth is
stranger
Than the wildest brand of fiction, so I'll tell you without shame....
There was Shamus and his master in the face of awful danger,
And the giant locomotive dashing down in smoke and flame....
What power on earth could save them? Yet a golden inspiration
To gods and goats alike may come, so in that brutish brain
A thought was born — *the ould red shawl*.... Then rearing with
elation,
Like lightning Shamus *threw it up* — AND FLAGGED AND
STOPPED THE TRAIN.

FROM

Later Collected Verse

My Rocking Chair

When I am old and worse for wear
I want to buy a rocking chair,
And set it on a porch where shine
The stars of morning glory vine;
With just beyond, a gleam of grass,
A shady street where people pass;
And some who come with time to spare,
To yarn beside my rocking chair.

Then I will light my corncob pipe
And dose and dream and rarely gripe.
My morning paper on my knee
I won't allow to worry me.
For if I know the latest news
Is bad,— to read it I'll refuse,
Since I have always tried to see
The side of life that clicks with glee.

And looking back with days nigh done,
I feel I've had a heap of fun.
Of course I guess that more or less
It's you yourself make happiness
And if your needs are small and few,
Like me you may be happy too:
And end up with a hope, a prayer,
A chuckle in a rocking chair.

The Ghosts

Said Lenin's ghost to Stalin's ghost:
    "Mate with me in the Tomb;
Then day by day the rancid host
    May gaze upon our doom.
A crystal casket we will share;
    Come, crusty Comrade come,
And we will bear the public stare,
        Ad nauseum."

Said Stalin's spook to Lenin's spook:
    "Long have you held your place.
The masses must be bored to look
    Upon your chemic face.
A change might be a good idear,
    And though I pity you,
There is within the Tomb, I fear,
        No room for two."

Said Lenin's wraith to Stalin's wraith:
    "You're welcome to my job;
Let millions of our mighty faith
    Gaze on your noble nob.
So when to goodly earth I've gone,
    (And I'll be glad to go),
Your carrion can carry on
        Our waxwork show."

The Visionary

If fortune had not granted me
  To suck the Muse's teats,
I think I would have liked to be
  A sweeper of the streets;
And city gutters glad to groom,
  Have heft a bonny broom.

There — as amid the crass and crush
  The limousines swished by,
I would have leaned upon my brush
  With visionary eye:
Deeming despite their loud allure
  That I was rich, they poor.

Aye, though in grab terrestrial,
  To Heaven I would pray,
And dream with broom celestial
  I swept the Milky Way;
And golden chariots would ring,
  And harps of Heaven sing.

And all the strumpets passing me,
  And heelers of the Ward
Would glorified Madonnas be,
  And angels of the Lord;
And all the brats in gutters grim
    Be rosy cherubim.

My Inner Life

'Tis true my garments threadbare are,
  And sorry poor I seem;
But inly I am richer far
  Than any poet's dream.
For I've a hidden life no one
  Can ever hope to see;
A sacred sanctuary none
  May share with me.

Aloof I stand from out the strife,
  Within my heart a song;
By virtue of my inner life
  I to myself belong.
Against man-ruling I rebel,
  Yet do not fear defeat,
For to my secret citadel
  I may retreat.

Oh you who have an inner life
  Beyond this dismal day
With wars and evil rumours rife,
  Go blessedly your way.
Your refuge hold inviolate;
  Unto yourself be true
And shield serene from sordid fate
    The Real You.

Surtax

When I was young and Scottish I
Allergic was to spending;
I put a heap of bawbees by,
But now my life is ending,
Although I would my hoarded pelf
Impetuously scatter,
Each day I live I find myself
Financially fatter.

Though all the market I might buy,
There's nothing to my needing;
I only have one bed to lie,
One mouth for feeding.
So what's the good of all that dough
Accumulating daily?
I should have spent it long ago
In living gaily.

So take my tip, my prudent friend,
Without misgiving;
Don't guard your fortune to the end,
But blow it living.
Better on bubbly be it spent,
And chorus cuties,
Then pay it to the Government
For damned Death Duties.

Plebeian Plutocrat

I own a gorgeous Cadillac,
    A chauffeur garbed in blue;
And as I sit behind his back
    His beefy neck I view.
You let me whisper, though you may
    Think me a queer old cuss,
From Claude I often sneak away
    To board a bus.

A democrat, I love the crowd,
    The bustle and the din;
The market wives who gab aloud
    As they go out and in.
I chuckle as I pay my dime,
    With mien meticulous:
You can't believe how happy I'm;
    Aboard a bus.

The driver of my Cadillac
    Has such a haughty sneer;
I'm sure he would give me the sack
    If he beheld me here.
His horror all my friends would share
    Could they but see me thus:
A gleeful multi-millionaire
        Aboard a bus.

The Goat and I

Each sunny day upon my way
    A goat I pass;
He has a beard of silver grey,
    A bell of brass.
And all the while I am in sight
    He seems to muse,
And stares at me with all his might
    And chews and chews.

Upon the hill so thymy sweet
    With joy of Spring.
He hails me with a tiny bleat
    Of welcoming.
Though half the globe is drenched with blood
    And cities flare,
Contentedly he chews the cud
    And does not care.

Oh gentle friend, I know not what
    Your age may be,
But of my years I'd give the lot
    Yet left to me,
To chew a thistle and not choke,
    But bright of eye
Gaze at the old world-weary bloke
    Who hobbles by.

Alas! though bards make verse sublime,
    And lines to quote,
It takes a fool like me to rhyme
    About a goat.

Husbands

Some husbands are a sorry lot
　　(Of course *you* are not one)
Who stop at bars and act the sot
　　And come home with a bun;
Some play the ponies, pledge their pay,
　　And stint their weary wives;
While some chase after blondes and may
　　　Lead double lives.

Though some men avaricious are,
　　While some choleric be,
I deem the worst default by far
　　Is *mental* cruelty.
A criticism harshly tuned,
　　Let careless husbands know,
A gentle woman's heart can wound
　　　More than a blow.

The sadic mate who sulks apart,
　　And fails to praise and bless,
Goes far to break a woman's heart
　　In life's togetherness.
Than loud and brutish language worse,
　　Or evil jealousy,
In wedded life the greatest curse
　　　Is Mental Cruelty.

Our Bosses

The power behind the race called human
I dare to deem is mostly Woman.
'Tis she who pulls the puppet strings,
Of pimps and parsons, clowns and kings.
By woman's wiles we men are swayed,
Bewitched, befuddled and betrayed.

Just scan the page of History,
And in its texture you will see
Key parts in the dramatic scene
Are played by courtesan and queen;
The while men brawl with brutal arms
The women win with wanton charms.

So may we males of modest mien
Who lumber the domestic scene,
Let wives with eloquence of jaw,
And lily hands lay down the law.
Behold I greet with heart of grace
Woman, the glory of the race
An all-wise God made man to vex
From Adam's rib — the Super Sex.

FROM

Ploughman of the Moon

FROM "BOOK ONE: CHILDHOOD"

Chapter One

The Long Grey Town

"Please, Aunt Jeannie, can I go out and look at the hens?"

Over her spectacles my aunt gazed at me suspiciously. "Whit fur, Rubbert Wullie, do you want to look at the hens?"

"I don't know whit fur, I jist want to look at them."

"Ye'd be faur better lookin' at yer bonnie Bible. Don't ye like yer wee Bible?"

"Ay, but I like the hens better."

My aunt was inclined to be shocked; however I was paying her a pretty compliment, for her Plymouth Rocks were her heart's pride. Still she hesitated; when Grandfather, peering from under his spectacls, broke in.

"Whit fur will ye no' let we Wullie look at the hens? He'll no dae them ony herm."

My aunt seemed doubtful. To her my capacity for doing harm was only limited by my awakeness. Grudgingly she consented, and no released prisoner ever sighed with more profound relief. It was the afternoon of the Sabbath and I was richly miserable. My new boots pinched me, my white collar choked me. My hair was smugly flat, my Sunday suit skin-tight. My winter woollens were prickly, while my thick stockings made my legs itch. For a boy of five could worse torture be conceived?

How well I remember that little parlour! The furniture, padded with horsehair, was glossy black. Antimacassars draped armchairs and sofa, while on the wall was Moses in the Bulrushes, done in coloured wool by Aunt Jeannie. The bookcase was grim with volumes of sermons, and the pendulum of the grandfather's clock swung with relentless austerity. Under a glass bell was a collection of wax fruits — apples, pears, peaches, grapes. I had never tasted the last two, but as I gazed at them my mouth watered. Could they be as delicious as they looked?

My three aunts sat round the glowing fire. Aunt Jeannie was reading *Good Words*, Aunt Bella the *Quiver*, and Aunt Jennie *Sunday at Home*. The only reading I was allowed was Fox's *Book of Martyrs*, whose pictures of burning saints gave me a gruesome delight. My aunts wore black silk skirts, and in front of the fire they drew them up over their knees. I was supposed to be too young to notice, but the fatness of their legs disgusted me. Grandfather would doze on the sofa till his snores awoke him. He had a crinkly white beard, and for long my idea of God was a grandiose edition of Grandfather.

I lived with him and my three aunts in the little Ayrshire town. Grandfather was postmaster; Aunt Bella sold stamps, while Aunt Jennie jiggled a handle that in some inconceivable way sent off telegrams. Aunt Jeannie ran the house and looked after the garden and the hens. All three were virgins. They might have married, but they were jealous of each other, and when a man came "spierin'" one of them the others crabbed his style, so that the poor laddie gave up.

Gazing through the grating of the hen-yard, I regained my serenity. The hens calmed me. I liked them, all but the cock, a truculent bully, strutting amid his meek wives. I was angry when he would pounce on one of his consorts, jump on her back, and with pecks and flapping wings flatten her to the ground. With stones I would go to the rescue, but one day Aunt Jeannie witnessed my intervention and stopped me.

"Leave him alone, he's no' hurtin' them," she said pensively. I recall to this day the look in her eyes. It seemed to say: "Oh, for a human rooster!"

For six days of the week I was happy, but the Sabbath was misery. We rose late. The house was hushed, the Post Office dark. Newspapers had been put away and whistling was forbidden. I asked Aunt Jeannie if I might whistle hymns, but she vetoed the idea. "Ye don't know the tunes well enough to stick to them," she objected. After breakfast of "parrich and finnan haddie" came preparation for church. All of us went, except one of my aunts who stayed to prepare lunch. Happy was I when I was sick enough to keep her company. Together we would stand behind the Nottingham lace curtains and watch the churchgoers.

Our town consisted of a single street of whin-grey houses and was about two miles long. The population were churchgoers to the last child. There were three churches, the Established, the Free and the U.P., and the rivalry between them was so bitter members of one denomination would scarcely speak to the others. We belonged to the Auld Kirk and looked down on the U.P. and the Free with disdain. We would not patronize a shopkeeper who did not belong to our sect, and Aunt Jeannie ceased to sell her eggs to a grocer when he became a "Wee Free."

About ten the bells began to ring, and from the far ends of the long town the worshippers formed into procession. It was a solemn march, every one dressed in Sunday best, with face grave. Black was the dominant colour, and to show a bit of brightness was to shock convention. As they walked, their slow steps never faltered, while conversation consisted of side whispers; for all knew that behind the lace curtains of every house eyes were on them and tongues were wagging.

"Look! Mrs. McWhinnie's got a new bunnet, an' her man no' ten months pit awa'."

Or "Puir auld Jimmie Purdie. His step's gettin' gey feeble. I'm thinkin' whuskey's no' sae good a cure for the rheumatics after a'."

Again: "Hoo changed yon Gillespie lass looks sin' she went to work in Glesca. I wonner if she's better than she ought to be. An' her mither deid o' the gallopin' consumption."

Always the same barbed remarks as the procession went by to the sound of the bells. And how I loved to watch it when I got the chance! That wasn't often, though. Generally I was told to wash behind my ears, plaster down my hair, don my Sunday suit and get ready to join the throng. My aunts were busy putting the finishing touches to their black silk dresses and their bonnets with the crape and sequins. We were always in mourning, although the last death had occurred years before. When we were ready Aunt Jeannie's last act was to straighten my Glengarry bonnet, to which I had given a jaunty tilt. It was my new one. My school bonnet had neither ribands nor a "toorie," as one of my first acts on going to school was to tear off those sissy appendages. If questioned about the mutilation I would blame it on the older boys. Incidentally, my Sunday Glengarry had a red "toorie"; but Aunt Jeannie thought it wasn't proper for church, so she inked it black.

Grandfather preceded us to church by half an hour, because he stood by one of the plates where people piled their pennies. He donned a frock coat, faded to green, and ruffled top hat that transformed him into a dignified elder. Last of all, he would slip into an inside pocket a "wee gill." From this the vestrymen would nip during the service, and on the rare occasions when Grandfather joined us in the pew he would be chewing a clove.

Before leaving, Aunt Jeannie would gaze at herself in the glass and pull faces till she finally achieved her Sabbath simper. As I trotted to church by her side, she would say: "Dinna kick the stanes, wee Wullie. An' tak' longer steps. Mind, ye've got on yer new boots." But my mind was on something else — the ordeal I dreaded, putting my penny in the plate. Really, it was a ha'penny, for only grown-ups gave pennies. Once I asked Aunt Jeannie why she gave me a ha'penny and she answered tartly: "Because I havena' got a farthin'."

The reason I dreaded putting my copper in the plate was Mister McCurdie. He was a crony of Grandfather's, and a great joker; but to me he always presented a grim aspect. There were two doors leading into church and he stood at the right while Grandfather had the left. Grandfather on these occasions did not deign to recognize me, but Mister McCurdie's specs had a minatory glitter. It was through his door I had to pass, and there he stood behind his plate piled high with coppers. Occasionally a sixpence glimmered among them. Once, indeed, I saw a shilling; but that must have got in by mistake, and was regarded as exultant vigilance by both elders.

As I approached shrinkingly with my small coin, my Cerberus, towering down on me, would fix me with an accusing eye. Then one day he bent forward and whispered: "Look oot. I'm watchin' ye. Ye're yin o' they lads that pits in a penny an' tak's oot tippence." At this dreadful accusation I blushed and shrank away like a sneak-thief. After that, I held out my small coin at arm's length and dropped it from about a foot above the plate. Once it missed the edge and rolled to the floor, where I had to retrieve it. Cringing under his look of reprobation, I sneaked into church feeling as if all eyes were upon me, a suspected thief. I began to wonder if I really wasn't one. I felt fearfully in my pockets to see if no twopence were lurking there. I almost expected the minister to arise and denounce me from the pulpit.

Our pew was at the back of the church. It was varnished pine and so constructed as to ensure a maximum of discomfort. The seats were narrow, the backs at an awkward angle to discourage drowsiness. In all the church there was not a cushion. When the congregation was seated, the bells ceased and the Minister entered, preceded by the Beadle, carrying the big Bible. Once, going up to the pulpit, the Minister tripped over his gown and said: "Tut! Tut!" His neck got very red; and always after that I watched eagerly, hoping he would trip again and say: "Tut! Tut!"

My aunts went to church early, so that they could see the others arrive. It was their great moment. Their eyes missed nothing, as they stored spicy comment for lunchtime conversation. Then we settled down to two hours of worship. At the prayers I was told to keep my head bent and close my eyes. But I dared to open them, for there was a brown knot in the wood in front of me that fascinated me. I tried to gouge it out under cover of the prayers, but even with my new pocket knife I never succeeded.

The Minister, the Reverend Mister Lamb, had a bald head of lustrous polish and mutton-chop whiskers. Usually his discourse was prosy, but in inspired moments his voice rose to a yowl. This would occur at least once in every sermon, and I awaited the moment with an expectant thrill. Yet somehow, when it came I was secretly ashamed. Even at that age public displays of emotion embarrassed me. I felt sorry for him because he felt so badly about sin and all that; but when he relapsed into dreariness again, I thought it would be a relief to hear him yowl.

By us he was looked upon as an Intellectual. Had he not preached a sermon entitled man and the Monkeys, putting in his place a whippersnapper of a scientist called Darwin, who had dared to voice a ridiculous theory utterly at odds with Holy teaching. Indeed, the congregation thought so much of it they had it printed as a pamphlet. But, whatever his other gifts, the Reverend Lamb was surely long-winded. Usually he began his sermon with *Firstly* and worked up to *Seventhly*. Then to my relief he would begin *Lastly*. But to my irritation he would go on to *Finally.* And when he would drone, *"In Conclusion,"* I was too exhausted for further mental protest. Then, as I slumped on the bench, Aunt Jeannie would pass me a peppermint and a stern look that made me sit upright again. This peppermint was an extra, because at the beginning of the sermon we would each receive one. The custom was general. All round church you could see peppermints being passed, as if the congregation was bracing itself for an ordeal.

Returning home was so different from going to church. It was as if everyone had been relieved of a burden. Duty grimly done, we walked joyously, heads high, eyes smiling. We formed groups, greeting, gossiping, even joking. At lunch Grandfather was pawky and aromatic, while my aunts discussed the sermon with critical comments on the garments of the other women. They knew what bonnets were re-trimmed, what dresses dyed. Over the cold meat, rice and prunes, they tore their neighbours apart. Released from the strain of "unco guidness," everyone became human again.... But the respite was short. Soon it was time for Sunday school. Aunt Jeannie had taught there for thirty years and was now Lady Superintendant. It was unthinkable I should ever miss, but really I did not dislike it. We had to memorize tiny texts printed on gilt tickets, and this I did with exultant ease. Besides, I enjoyed the hymns, which often had likeable tunes. Indeed, in later years I slightly altered some of the melodies and turned them into comic songs.

After Sunday school Aunt Jeannie usually suggested a walk to the cemetery. It was her idea of divertissement. There, hanging over tombs, she would sniffle and sigh. When at a certain point her handkerchief was produced, I hotly resented the dear departed; however, to her it was an orgy of sentiment she enjoyed to the last fat tear.

These childish memories may seem trivial, but they reveal traits that were to distinguish my whole life. To this day I shun graveyards with their melancholy evocations; and I refuse to attend funerals, for in a few years I will have to be available at my own.

But above all do I hold my horror of the Scotch Sabbath. Indeed it has left me with a distaste for churchgoing of any kind. Yet I approve of piety … for others. Oh, yes, I send my cheque to the vicar and applaud those who hold down the family pew, but I would rather worship in my own kale-yard. If I am not a pillar of the church, I am, at least, one of the pagan columns that support it from the outside.

Chapter Two

Barefoot Boy

After the dour Sabbath came six days of joy. My grandfather and aunts must have been very kind to me, for I never remember being afraid of them. Aunt Jeannie was cross sometimes and shook me, but only once did she want me whipped. I cannot recall what I had done, though no doubt I deserved punishment. However, she had not the heart to do it herself, so she begged Grandfather to take action. He complied with bad grace. Calling me into his room and shutting the door he swung a heavy strap.

"Bend over," he told me sternly. I was trembling but I would not beg for mercy. I presented my little buttocks expecting to feel the tang of the strap. I was determined not to cry. To my amazement he began to belabour the cushion of his chair.

"Greet ye wee devil," he hissed in my ear. "Pretend ye're greetin'."

So I bawled for all I was worth, while he whacked the cushion till the dust flew. Outside the door Aunt Jeannie was begging him to stop.

"The laddie's had enough," she shrieked.

"Dinna tell," said Grandfather; "but don't do it again. Next time I'll give ye a proper leatherin'."

I promised, and Aunt Jeannie greeted me with a look of commiseration. "Ye needna hae been sae brutal aboot it," she said to Grandfather, caressing my small posterior affectionately. But though they were gentle, my aunts were never demonstrative. Kissing was rarely practised. Sweethearts kissed and mothers kissed; but outside of that, osculation was taboo. I never saw any kissing in my family. If I had, I think I would have been shamed, for any show of emotion embarrassed me. We Scotch are a gritty race, with a habit of reserve.

I had another aunt who died when I was very young. She was little more than a girl, and I only remember her vaguely. I was always told not to go too near her. "Puir Aggie, she's got the consumption," they would whisper, but I couldn't understand. To me she was the loveliest of the family. She had such a waxen complexion and such pink cheeks. She never did any work and often sat apart, brooding sadly. In these moods she would repulse me when I tried to caress her; but I think it was more from a fear of infecting me than from any irritation she felt. Sometimes, however, as if yielding to an uncontrollable tenderness, she would hug me to her, and once she brought out some delicately written poems and read them to me. She said they were her own and I thought them beautiful.

To the others it must have been agony to see her fading away. Perhaps a southern climate would have helped her, but in our harsh Scotland she had not a chance. However, I doubt if we had the means to send her to Italy or Switzerland; and in any case such a thing was simply not done in our humble circles. She was regarded as doomed; we just waited for her to die. It was decided that she had better live in the little summer house, and there a bed was installed for her. I remember I thought it was a jolly idea and I envied her but she wept bitterly. From then on I would see little of her, though sometimes, through the blackcurrant bushes, I would glimpse her watching me haggardly. I tried to get in to her but the door was barred.

Soon after that she died. They took her into the house towards the end and put her in the best bedroom. It had one of those stuffy enclosed beds; and there she sat, smoking some herbal cigarettes that were supposed to help her breathing. I laughed delightedly to see her smoking, but the others did not share my mirth. I recall the unearthly brightness of her eyes and the burning glow in her cheeks. She smoked her cigarettes like a real lady. Then, after a little, she asked if she might kiss me, and hugged me ever so tightly to her nightdress. And that night she died....

As she lay in the best parlour we waited for the undertaker to screw her down. But before they closed the coffin I saw Grandfather rise and put his hand on her waxen brow, saying:

"Puir lassie ... My wee Aggie ... She's cauld, sae cauld."

Yet she lay there, indifferent to us all, victim of a sad destiny. She had not asked for life, and what a fate had been forced on her! What a burden she had borne so patiently! Oh, that one could make up to her for what she suffered! And there are so many like her. I did not understand then, but now I realize how stoically she awaited death who had never really known life.

When I was five I was sent to the parish school, because there was no other. Even the Minister's son went there. And this brings me to the matter of social standing in the Long Grey Town. First, there was the Earl in his castle; but he and his family were spoken of with bated breath. They were seen only on the rarest of occasions and spent most of their time in London or Cannes. To them, our town was almost non-existent. Then there was the Quality — landed gentry who rode to hounds and treated us with disdain. Next came the professional class, our doctors, bankers, lawyers, who held themselves aloof from the common tradesmen. The latter, with the office men, the shopkeepers and employers of labour, formed a large middle class to which we belonged. Below them were the skilled workers, and last of all, the unskilled labourers.

Each of these sections looked down upon the one immediately below, while they accepted the patronage of the class above. It was quite in the order of things. We were told: "Keep in your place and don't try to imitate your betters." But, besides this social demarcation, the town was notable for three types of citizens … First came the weavers, working in their low cottages, their handlooms visible through the small windows. They were pale and inclined to be intellectual. They were of Huguenot origin, responsible for the town's foundation, and its most worthy citizens. By contrast there were the farmers, ruddy and intelligent, but hardly well-read. They too were a fine type.… Lastly, about two miles out of town, were the coal pits and iron works, but the colliers and furnacemen were regarded as beyond the pale. When they came into town on Saturday night, to drink their pay, they seemed a race apart. The pitman, especially, were pallid, stunted creatures, and to me in my childish days a source of fear and repulsion.

In school there were all classes, from Willie Lamb, the Minister's son, to Nellie Purdie, whose mother was in the almshouse. In summer all of us went barefoot except Willie, whom we twitted on having to wear boots. He was a poor spindling, but he looked enviously at our bare feet. However, on the sharp gravel of the playground, he had the best of us. In winter, too, many of the pupils went barefoot, because their parents were too poor to buy them shoes. I have seen them coming to school when the ground was hard with frost, their feet cracked and purple with cold. But they were spartan about it and scorned our pity. Nay, they rather claimed our admiration. On winter days we would huddle outside the school door, crying:

> "Teacher, teacher, let me in;
> My hands are cold, my shoes thin."

I can testify to the hands, for often I returned home with fingers frozen; and, oh, how bitterly I wept as they thawed out!

One incident of my school I recall vividly. Seated at the desk near me was the girl Nellie, whose mother was on the parish. She was a frail lass, with bare feet and ragged gown, but she had a mass of pale gold hair that I admired in spite of its untidiness. Then one day the teacher stooped over her and said in a tone of disgust:

"Nellie, you're a dirty girl. You have beasties in your hair."

Nellie hung her head and began to cry. I felt sorry for her, so I rose, holding up my hand.

"Please, Teacher, Auntie Jeannie caught ten in my head last night."

The teacher said: "No doubt you got them from Nellie."

"Oh, no," I said chivalrously, "I'm sure she got them from me."

Our teacher told me to hush and retired behind her desk to laugh chokingly. When I got home that night I told the family of the incident. Aunt Jeannie went as red as a beet, but the others laughed a lot. Then she got out the small-tooth comb and gave me a thorough going-over. I enjoyed seeing the little beasties drop on the paper and hearing the crack under my thumbnail.

I do not remember much more about this school except that one day the Head Master stopped me on the playground. He was a bearded man, as all Heads were in those days.

"What are you going to be when you grow up?" he asked.

"A philosopher," I said gravely.

He laughed heartily and told the story to the family, confirming their belief in my originality. Years after, Aunt Jeannie wrote to me: "You did not become a philosopher, but you became a poet, which is much better." I rather doubted it, but I was pleased that she was pleased.

Once I heard my grandfather remark: "Yon's a queer wee callant. He's sooner play by himsel' than wi' the other lads." This was true. Rather than join the boys in the street I would amuse myself alone in the garden, inventing imagination games. I would be a hunter in the jungle of the raspberry canes; I would be an explorer in the dark forest of the shrubbery; I would squat by my lonely campfire on the prairie, a little grass plot where the family washing was spread. I was absorbed in my games, speaking to myself or addressing imaginary companions. No wonder the others thought me a queer one. I looked forward to bedtime; for then, about half an hour before dropping off to sleep, I had the most enchanting visions. Shining processions of knights and fair ladies passed before my eyes: warriors, slaves and pages emerged and faded. I did not seem to imagine them. They just presented themselves, a radiant pageantry. They gave me a rare delight, and I was loath to fall asleep. But all at once this gift of visioning left me, and, alas! it has never returned.

I used to sleep with Aunt Jeannie, who cuddled me a lot. Every Saturday night she would change her chemise and tell me not to look while she was doing it. But one night I dared to peep. What I saw made me duck my head under the blankets. "If women undressed are as ugly as that," I pondered, "I never want to get married."

Aunt Jeannie was housekeeper; Aunt Bella liked to scrub and work in the open air; but Aunt Jennie was accounted the literary one of the family, because she read books. The others only read papers. She encouraged me to learn poetry from the school primers. These selections were mostly from Campbell and Longfellow.

So standing on a chair I would spout: "The boy stood on the burning deck," or "It was the schooner Hesperus." The more I ranted and gestured, the more they applauded. In those days I was not troubled by an inferiority complex, and to outsiders must have been an egregious little pest. I was undoubtedly precocious, but if they spoiled me it was not my fault. There was, in fact, quite a literary tradition in our family. My great-grandfather had been a crony of Robert Burns and claimed him as a second cousin. One of our parlour chairs had often been warmed by the rump of the Bard; for, besides being a rhymester, my ancestor had been a toper; so I expect if that chair could have talked it could have told of wild nights with John Barleycorn. To my folks anything that rhymed was poetry, and Robbie Burns was their idol.

Perhaps something of this atmosphere affected me; but poetry attracted me from the first — largely, I suppose, because of the rhyming. So one day I astonished the family by breaking into verse. It was the occasion of my sixth birthday and the supper table was spread like a feast. The centrepiece was a cold boiled ham, a poem in coral and ivory. Flanking it in seductive variety were cookies, scones and cakes. For a high tea it was a tribute even to a pampered brat like myself. As I looked at it in eager anticipation, an idea came into my head. Grandfather was sharpening the knife to cut the ham, when suddenly he remembered he had forgotten to say grace. It was then I broke in.

"Please, Grandpapa, can I say grace this time?"

All eyes turned to me, and I could see disapproval shaping in their faces. But I did not give them a chance to check me. Bowing my head reverently I began:

> "God bless the cakes and bless the jam;
> Bless the cheese and the cold boiled ham;

Bless the scones Aunt Jeannie makes,
And save us all from belly aches. Amen."

I remember their staring silence and my apprehension. I expected to be punished, but I need not have feared. There was a burst of appreciation that today seems to me incredibly naive. For years after they told the story of my grace till it ended by enraging me.

This was my first poetic flutter, and to my thinking it suggests tendencies in flights to come. First, it had to do with the table, and much of my work has been inspired by food and drink. Second, it was concrete in character, and I have always distrusted the abstract. Third, it had a tendency to be coarse, as witness the use of the word "belly" when I might just as well have said "stomach." But I have always favoured an Anglo-Saxon word to a Latin one, and in my earthiness I have followed my kinsman Burns. So, you see, even in that first bit of doggerel there were foreshadowed defects of my later verse.

FROM "BOOK FOUR: MANHOOD"

Chapter One

Steerage Emigrant

"Hurrah!" says I. "Launched on the great adventure at last." The day was charming and I was seated on the forward hatch of the tramp steamer. The sea was a shimmering, gold-spangled plain through which we ploughed. It welcomed us, laughing and leaping in little waves. The sky was without a cloud. Never before had I seen a cloudless sky, never before set foot on a ship. I looked around with happy eyes. On the tarred cover of the hatch two men had chalked a checker board and were playing with potato chips. They had sallow faces and wore cloth caps. A slender boy with a sensitive face was cuddling a fiddle.

"I'm a pitman," he told me. "There's a lot of us going to the coal mines." I was surprised. In the Long Grey Town colliers had been looked on as the scum of the country, but these men were gentle and intelligent. They had a pride in their calling. They told me they would rather work underground than above. They were well paid and doing work of high social value. Pitmen, I found, were a proud folk, self-respecting and independent. The world should be grateful to them.

Watching the game was a grey-haired man. "I am a hatter," he told me. "My son has taken up a homestead on the prairie and is farming it. I'm going to join him. My! but I'm looking forward to the land after a lifetime spent in a city street. I'm going to tend the garden, chop wood and draw water. It's like being born again. I've sent my wife ahead. She's waiting for me. I'm sure we're going to be awful happy." ... Near him was a fine, upstanding young man. "I played football for Renton," he told us. "I hope there's a team in Medicine Hat. In Scotland I was a wee frog in a big puddle; now it may be different. Football's a grand game. It's all I care for."

Farm hands were returning for the spring work after spending the winter in the old country. They were glad to be going back to what they now regarded as their home. All had taken up land and looked forward to a bright future. Quite another crowd were the drovers who had come over with shipments of cattle. They were wild fellows, who drank and swore and scoffed at the idea of settling down.

But all told me I could get work easily, and this thought added to my exhilaration. The air was so tonic; the sea rippled in rosy waves; everyone seemed full of hope and happiness. They were going to a land where there was work and welcome for all. How quickly the time passed! I was so interested in the fresh types and the new expressions. With the cruel egoism of youth, I seldom thought of the life I had left behind. I rarely remembered my family and my friends, and they grew vaguer as time went on. The past was memory, the future dream. To live was to squeeze the essence of the moment.

That is what I tried to do. I welcomed the hardship with spirit. I did not mind poor food and hard berths. I was part of the game. A vagabond life, I thought, may be more constructive than a sedentary one. I would give myself three years of roaming, then settle down. I had a pocket edition of *An Amateur Emigrant,* and I compared my experience with Stevenson's, wishing I could write half as well as he.

There was one drawback, however. I had put the wrong label on my Gladstone bag and it was stowed away in the hold. All my toilet articles and changes of clothes were in it, so that I had nothing but those in which I stood. Every day my collar grew grimier and my chin shaggier. I shunned observation. Shabby, unshorn, I shrank into my shell. There were some bonnie lassies on board but I became invisible to them. I took comfort in the thought that I was actually roughing it from the start, and wondered how the philosophy of Stevenson would have stood the strain.

As our voyage neared its end, expectation mounted to excitement. There was fog … icebergs … the bleak shores of Newfoundland. Quebec … toy-like houses … villages with church spires … a man driving a buggy. All evening I gazed shoreward, seeing moving lights and speculating on the mystery of the dim land. I looked forward to my first sight of a native Canadian with as much curiosity as if he had been a Patagonian.

I helped to make the usual collection for the steward, giving a half-crown, which I could ill afford. One old fellow gave a penny. When I suggested that it was insufficient he said with an air of generosity: "Well, I'll make it tippence."

Of course my eagerness was out of proportion to the event. I might have been Columbus discovering the New World, so excited was I. But my arrival in Canada was one of the great moments in my life and my emotions were correspondingly dynamic. We reached Quebec in the early hours where a solitary watchman greeted us from the wharf. He was a tallow-faced man with a goatee. He shouted in some strange lingo, then welcomed us with grand gestures.

With a rare eagerness I watched the unloading of the cargo. My eyes were riveted on the scene and no detail escaped me. I heard the longshoremen jabbering in that strange tongue. I breathed deeply the vitalizing air, I simmered with rapture. "Here I am," I said, "a traveller — I who was destined to be a stay-at-home. By my own will I have achieved this. I am where my boyhood friends will never be. I am superior to those who looked down on me. Now I can patronize the best of them; for does not travel bestow on one the garland of the experience?"

Vain thoughts, but they inflated me. It is not what we are but what we *think* we are that matters. At that moment I felt distinguished to a degree I have rarely felt since. And exultantly I reflected: "It is only the beginning. From now on, every day will be full of changing scenes and teeming with new characters. No more rubber-stamp living." So though no one envied me because I was poor and friendless, I envied no one because I was young and in love with life....

I saw nothing of Montreal. The train was waiting near the landing wharf and I had only time to buy a few provisions. We were going on an emigrant wagon. There were large racks on which we piled our baggage, and benches of varnished pine. There was no bedding of any kind and this pleased me. I welcomed hardship, I gloated in discomfort. That night I slept on the luggage rack, with my coat for a blanket and my Gladstone bag for a pillow. However, I was first up in the morning and held the toilet against a host of besiegers. There I arrayed myself in a Buffalo Bill costume Papa had bought for me in an auction room, for he too had a romantic conception of me. It consisted of a pair of high circus boots and a sombrero. Thus attired I felt equal to any occasion.

To my eyes, so anointed with wonder, the wilds of Ontario were fascinating. True I saw little but fire-scorched woods, and the occasional surprise of a lake. It was a blue eye staring up from the forest-grey, but it gave me a thrill. How happy I could be on its shores with a rod, a gun and a canoe! The wildness of the country charmed me. It was gloriously empty. A fellow had Room. Thoreau and Borrow fought in me, the one to make me live by a lake, the other to urge me to ramble on. If at that moment Sir Wilfred Laurier had offered to make me his secretary I would have politely refused. "No, sir," I would have said, "I want to wander and work with my hands."

To see the ordinary with eyes of marvel may be a gift; or it may be there is no ordinary and wonder is true vision. In any case it keeps one spiritually intact; and it must be a rare quality, for none of my fellow travellers had it. Most of them grumbled at the casual progress of our train, which dawdled to such an extent that I was tempted to jump off and run alongside. Good job I didn't, for that speed was deceptive and I should probably have been left behind.

In the coach ahead were a party of Armenians, accompanied by an interpreter. They were dressed like peasants. They made soup that was water with grease swimming in it. This, with bread, comprised a meal. I remarked to the interpreter on their poverty. He said:

"Don't you believe it. Every man of them has at least a hundred dollars tucked away in his jeans. Have you that much?" I hadn't. At that moment my entire capital was a dollar ninety-five cents.

The prairie delighted me by its very monotony. Indeed I did not find it dull. I saw cattle eating from straw stacks and ploughing with oxen. I said: "Here is my future home. I will settle on a section like this and dwell in one of these doll-like houses that look doubly diminutive in the vast emptiness."

We stopped at small villages whose names delighted me. One was called Moose Jaw. It consisted of a muddy street lined with shacks. In a small store I bought some provisions, spending the last of my money on hard tack, sardines and jam. I was beginning to worry about money. From now on the going would be hard.

In a saloon I saw some of the younger lads from the ship drinking and laughing. Among them was the football player. They were hilariously happy when suddenly came a warning whistle from the train. I jumped on as it was moving. Looking back I saw the party from the saloon running to catch it. Behind me was the Negro porter seeming anxious. "Dey cain't make it," he muttered. "Dey's gonna be left in dat dere burg." There were three of them. The first two managed to jump on; the third stumbled and slid under the train. The Negro made a grimace.

"He's killed for sure. Ain't dat no luck? Jes' when folks is goin' in for lunch! Dey ain't goin' to have no appetite."

The train stopped. Some distance away I saw a small crowd gathered round a figure on the ground. I ran back. On my way I passed a red boot and a sock and the protruding splinter of a shin bone; but I did not pick them up. Lying in the midst of the group was the footballer. His face was chalky white and he was moaning: "Mither! I want ma mither." Then a man came along holding a boot and a jagged section of bone and flesh. "Every wheel went over him," he said; "every bloody wheel."

As we approached Winnipeg, the hatter became very excited. He combed out his beard. His eyes shone with happiness.

"My wife's meeting me at the station. We'll all take the stage out to the homestead. Tomorrow I'll be raising vegetables in my own garden. I'll be chopping the firewood and bringing water from the well. Won't I be the happy man!" It was the moment he had dreamed of, and he kept dwelling on it. He would wear overalls and a broad-brimmed straw hat. No more felts for him. No more grubby streets. He was realizing the dream of a lifetime.

As we drew into the station a large, comely woman was awaiting him. Beside her was a young one, even more pleasing. Nimbly hopping from the train he embraced them.

"Where's my son?" he asked anxiously.

"Out at the farm. He was too busy to come in."

"Then we maun be gettin' out there. I'm jist dyin' to see the place. Let's get along."

But they hung back. "We're not going," they said excitedly. "We can't live on the prairie. We've taken rooms here in town and here we mean to stay."

The old chap stared in dismay. "But the garden and the chickens and all that?"

"If you want to you can go alone, but we're not going," said his wife.

Then the younger one broke in. "It's dreadful on the prairie. It's all right for European peasants, but for a civilized woman it's appalling. I'll never rejoin my husband there. I want him to sell the farm and come back to town." The elder took it up. "You're not going out there, John. You're just going to stay here with us two. We like Winnipeg, but the prairie — oh, it's simply terrible. You can get a job here. We've already got one promised for you. They want good hatters ..."

I left them arguing, and by the way they led him off I don't think he had any chance against them. I expect he spent the rest of his life cleaning and blocking hats.

This gave me my first inkling that life on the prairie was not all I had imagined. It rather depressed me, but I reflected: "Well, it doesn't matter. I have a ticket for British Columbia. I can keep going till I bump into the Pacific Ocean. After all, maybe the prairie is only fit for Swedes and Slovacs. Growing grain is not my idea of romance." Besides, the prairie was so devastatingly flat. I was afraid it might bore me. It did not seem a fit frame for a dashing young man who wore Napoleonic boots and a Spanish hat and who looked like the ringmaster in a circus. Yet I must admit my outfit caused little excitement. There were so many outlandish costumes around me, Hungarian, Italian, Roumanian, that mine seemed quite commonplace.

Arrived in Alberta I felt the same reluctance to grapple with grim reality. There the prairie was rolling, but it could not roll too much for me. I was beginning to feel a rolling stone anyhow. It was not that I lacked vitality. Indeed I was keyed up and effervescent with enthusiasm. However, all that did not incline me favourably to the job of making a hard living by the sweat of my brow. On the contrary, the more I voyaged, even though the going was tough, the more I wanted to keep going. Such was my westward impetus that only the barrier of the salt sea could arrest it. And I wondered if that could.

My big worry was financial. I had landed in Canada with five dollars in my pocket. Luckily I sold my Gladstone bag to a fellow passenger for ten dollars and bought for three a canvas contraption that better suited my circumstances. Then on the train I exchanged for six dollars a Harris tweed suit. At Winnipeg I got rid of my gun for a "ten spot." At Calgary I let my camera go for fifteen. My westward trail was studded with items of my outfit as I realized them in terms of cash. I felt some compunction when I thought of how poor Papa had combed auction rooms for these articles and presented them to me with such pride. Yet he got so much joy in doing it that the thought consoled me. My outfit served me well, though not in the way it was intended.

As I look back, I see myself a feckless young fool without any apprehension for the future. I had never worked hard, and already

I felt an aversion for strenuous forms of toil. Perhaps this was why I dallied, putting off the evil day when I would have to come to grips with reality. So in a spirit of irresponsibility I crossed the Rockies, revelling in the sheer glory of peak and glacier. Here was something greater than my imagination had ever conceived. As I looked awestruck at rivers roaring through canyon walls, I thought that these moments alone justified my joust at jeopardy. It was so gorgeous I grudged every minute I could not devour the scenery with my eyes, and got up in the first dawn light so that I should miss nothing. But I was alone. None of my companions shared my ecstasies.

Then we seemed to have left all that behind. I awoke one morning to find we were speeding through a land of forest to the sounding sea. My Nemesis of toil was nearing. I began to be afraid.

Chapter Two

Mud Pupil

I was standing in the green wonder of the primeval forest, who only two months before had been drooping in the grey drizzle of a Scotch city. Lover of contrasts, here was one that overwhelmed me. Where I had been pushing a pen, behold me now swinging an axe. Instead of grimy walls were pillared aisles of trees unbelievably tall. Pines made a cathedral hush around me. The silence was supreme, the aloneness absolute. I could have hugged myself for joy. Here was justification for slipping away from greasy commerce. Again I thought: Let my folly never give me anything more than this moment, I will have no regret.

But I looked without enthusiasm at the axe in my hand. Each stroke jarred me, and the thought that I was destroying life chilled me. I was a tree killer — I, who loved them and looked on them as friends. I would have enjoyed being a tree, but I would not have liked a clumsy young vandal to hack me down with a blunt blade. Let the wind lay me low when time rotted my heart; but to be prematurely slaughtered by my only enemy Man, and a poor city specimen at that — what a sorry fate!

Now *sawing* — that was another matter. I was operating on something already dead, to bring it to life again in heat and flame. As I worked the saw back and forth it seemed to sing a song of its usefulness. I liked the graceful body-swing, as it snored in the cut. I liked the sudden freedom as the block dropped away. I loved the sight and smell of the sawdust and the odour of the sticky gum. Above all, I was happy because I could dream. For the work was functional. It left my mind free to rove from the past to the future. And again, working with my body was good. I was making something useful, even if it were only firewood. I could not believe that writing figures in a book was either useful or constructive. And here I was, no longer a parasite but a fundamental worker.

Yes, I was richly happy as I swung to my cross-cut saw. What matter though I had not a cent in the world. Joy sang in me, for I had not a care. I had reduced life to simple elements. I wore the rough overalls of the toiler, the denim shirt and heavy boots; but I was prouder of them than I would have been of a suit from Savile Row. Lucky me, I thought, with so much of life before me and such a heart for enjoying it. For Youth itself was a source of exultation. So much happy living lay in front, I was sorry for folks even ten years my senior. I had still to spend the time they had used up. And I had no fear of the future. Bronzed by the sun, my muscles hardened by toil, I was in a new world, a pioneer, a trail-breaker.

Such my dreams as I sawed my way through a four-foot log and swung to the song of the saw. I did not realize that I was playing a part. Then as I paused to preen myself in my role of a "man in a world of men" I saw a movement in the bushes. A big, black head rose out of the brush. By gosh! a *bear....* It was standing on its hind legs eating berries. It would take a bunch of bushes in its arms, gather them together and pick off the fruit. It was leisurely and appreciative, but too near for my taste, so I gave a startled shout. Then the head vanished and I heard a crashing through the brush. Here, I thought, was something to write home about.

I was working for the MacTartans, a Shetland family who some ten years before had rounded Cape Horn to found a new home. The result of their adventure was a farm carved from the forest. The sons, Jock and Bung, who ran the ranch, were six-foot stalwarts with a genial tolerance and a gift for ragging their very green mud pupil. Pitted against them, I discovered that my gymnasium muscles were sadly wanting. True, my biceps compared imposingly with their stringy arms, yet when it came to the strain of a day's work I could not hold my own. I was ashamed of the way I played out so quickly when it came to packing hay in a hot mow, but my humiliation spurred me to grim effort and gradually my muscles took on the tough fibre of the labourer.

I soon found that there were some jobs I preferred to others. I liked work that left my mind free, that was not too hard, and that made no demands on either skill or resource. For instance, I hated handling horses. One had to give one's whole attention to them. Also I disliked competitive work, in which one had to keep up with the other fellow. I liked to toil alone, and I did not mind how monotonous the job as long as it was mechanical.

My first task was picking up stones from a field. It was of about an acre, yet I aimed to have it clear of stones in a day or two. So I collected them cordially, and carried them in a sack to the side of the field. But the more I picked the more there seemed to be. They were laughing at me, I thought — multiplying before my eyes. I grew discouraged. What price the fat little bank clerk who thought he was going to be a dashing cowboy! It seemed I was on the wrong side of the Rockies for a would-be bronco-buster.... My next job was even less to my taste. It was to weed a field of turnips. I had to crawl up the rows, tearing away the weeds, and eliminating most of the baby turnips. A cruel business. Surely weeds had a right to live. It was only because they were unwanted they were called weeds. The unwanted people of this world were weeds and should be destroyed. Poor weeds! Maybe I was one myself.... And the young turnips so ruthlessly sacrificed that their fortunate brothers should thrive and grow strong. Sad superfluous turnip plants! They made me think of the underdogs of the world.

With such musings I tried to lighten my labour, but my hands were worn raw and my back ached abominably. The heat was terrific. I wore a big-brimmed straw hat and my shirt hung outside my trousers. I was baked brown and stained with soil. To cheer me I looked at the blue purity of the sky, the mountains that rose to meet it, the unexplored bush that came right down to the clearing.... Here was a dream world worthy of a dreamer. I was quite alone. The silence was one of murmurous sound, of the droning of innumerable insects. The heat radiated like wavering sheets of cellophane. I hated the grovelling toil. I despised myself for doing it; but — well, if it was the price I had to pay for all this beauty, then I was glad to pay it. So with a sense of fulfilment I turned again to my turnip rows.

But soon haying began and I liked that better. The heat increased. Toward four in the afternoon it was a comfort to pitch in the shady side of the wagon. We brought buckets of water into which we dropped handfuls of oatmeal and drank as if we never could have enough. We fanned our torsos with our flapping shirts. We panted and sweated. It was a relief to unload the last wagon and go off to milk.

I never became a good milker. At first I was given the poorest cows so that I could not spoil them, but I fear they were none the better for my manipulation. A cow must be milked fast or she will hold up her milk. My cows all held up. Still, it was restful with my head butted into the cow's flank and my right leg between her two hind ones, so that she could not kick me over. She could switch her tail, though, giving me hard flicks of mingled hair and manure till I tied it to her leg.

The wife of the Jap farm hand used to help me with the milking. As she cowered under the cow she had a tiny baby strapped to her back. It was just like a doll but it was shamefully neglected. All day it lay in their wretched shack and never cried. It did not seem to know how. Flies crawled over its face, even walking into its wide black eyes, but it did not blink. It seemed to have lost all sensitiveness to discomfort and pain. It was inevitable that in the cold and damp of the winter it should perish. It did, and was buried, I was told, in a soapbox behind the cow barn.

In one of my first letters home I enclosed a mosquito that had bitten me. At first, despite my fatigue, they kept me awake at night, but I became inured to them. Soon they did not bother me, and their stings caused neither inflammation nor itching. Often after lunch, sitting in the sun with the boys, I would let a mosquito settle on an arm, dig down and swell with blood. The idea was to squash it just as it was full to capacity. Sometimes one waited a second too long and saw it take off, gorged to the gills. Then profanity was in order. Otherwise a broad red smudge testified to one's timing. The game was to see who could show the biggest blood splotch.

Apart from mosquitoes, sandflies were a pest in the early evening. They irritated, but did not bite hard. Worst of all was the black fly. It had a way of getting under one's collar. Its bite was poisonous and the swelling often lasted for days.

When I first visited London, after fifteen years spent in the wilds, I went into a shop in the Burlington Arcade. It was devoted entirely to ties and the display was a very gaudy one. I said: "I want a tie." The shopman said: "What school, sir?" I was taken aback. At first I wanted to say "Borstal," but thought better of it. Instead I said carelessly: "Oh, I don't care. Any old school will do as long as it's not too prismatic. I don't want it for a minstrel show." The shopmen nearly fell to the floor with horror. Disgustedly they sold me a contraption in orange and chocolate.

I wore it that night on the boat to France. I felt rather ashamed of it, thinking it in bad taste. However, I was roaming the deck when I saw a man wearing a similar one. He hailed me. "Good evening. I see we come from the same school." He pointed to my tie and I said: "Ha! Ha! Good old school."

"By Jove, yes. Good old Hangover. We did have some great rags there. You must have been long before my time, though."

"Oh, yes, about twenty years before, I suppose."

"How ripping! And still you think of the old school."

"By Jove! yes. Jolly old Hangover! How could I ever forget it!"

"No, indeed. Who was Head when you were there?"

"Head? ... by gad! it's so long ago and I've quite lost my memory for names. I remember we used to call him "Tuppence."

"It wasn't by chance Harvey?"

"That's it. Tuppence Harvey. Good old boy. Whacked me proper because I sauced the French Master. Frogs, we called him. Then there was the German Master. We called him Sausage. And the Chemistry Master was known as Stinks."

"Oh! I am surprised. So they taught chemistry then?"

"Yes, sort of experiment. Don't think they kept it up. Too modern.... Bad form and all that. Well, it was a great school and if you'll excuse me, I'm not feeling any too well. Rotten sailor, you know. So glad to have met you. Good old Hangover." So I beat a retreat and spent the rest of the voyage dodging him.

I relate this because I now found myself in a settlement glorified by the Old School Tie. I do not suppose that in all the Empire there was a community so dominated by the public school mentality. Here were people of the *pukka* type the snob novelists take for granted. Once I said to an Englishman: "The trouble with us is we think we are the finest people in all the world." He answered in amazement: "Well, we jolly well are, aren't we?"

In our colony the men were all Old School Tie boys. The older ones were often retired military or naval officers. They prided themselves that the settlement was a "little bit of old England, by Gad!" They dressed like squires and expected the hired man to touch his hat. They would tell you that they were not Canadians, they were British Columbians. Our community was also the haven for the Younger Sons. They were remittance men, sent out by their families who were glad to be rid of them. They kept ponies and played polo. They dressed in yellow leggings, knee breeches and Norfolk jackets. Many of these young bloods came to the house in the evening and the conversation consisted entirely of horses and dogs, guns and fishing. One would have thought that art and literature did not exist. Indeed, to have mentioned such subjects would have tabbed one a bit of a bounder. As I sat tongue-tied in their company, no doubt they regarded me with suspicion. How often I wished I could steal away and read a book, any kind of book.

Such was the unique colony in which I now found myself. The men I met were sublimely sure of themselves. They took it for granted that their race was the salt of the earth and their class the flower of that race. Can it be wondered that my inferiority complex flourished in their midst and that I felt a grubby vulgarian. They regarded me with such patronizing sufferance I felt it was a privilege to endure them.

★

And our settlement was as poor as it was proud. It is interesting to note how a community can get along without money. With us currency was so scarce it was almost non-existent. A silver dollar was almost something to put in a glass case. Business was done by barter. The farmers traded their grain, milk, butter, eggs and fruit for flour, tea, tobacco and sugar. Yet ours was a society in which there was no want. All were poor; few had any real money, and no one seemed to need it.

What I will call the Snob crowd came for the most part from impoverished county families who jealously preserved the customs of their class. While sons and husbands worked in the fields, the womenfolk, dolled up in old-fashioned finery, drove in rickety buggies with superannuated farm horses, to leave cards on their friends. They lived in a mid-Victorian atmosphere of tea, tattle and tennis. Sunday church was the great gathering place. It was Anglican of course, as the native Canadian usually went to Chapel.

I do not know what the future has to offer us in the way of a classless society, but when I think of the deep cleavage that divided our community I feel as if I had lived in a past century. The English emigrants regarded the Canadian pioneers with disdain and called them mossbacks. On the other hand, the Canadian frontiersmen who had carved homes from the wilderness spoke of "damn fool Englishmen" and felt for them contempt and dislike.

But one thing they had in common — a determination to work hard. With his gospel of stern toil the Canadian had converted the Englishman. It was either that or go under. And the Englishman, snob though he might be, was a sport and a fighter. He would not let the native beat him in the field. The patrician must prove himself the equal of the roughneck; so he pitched in for all he was worth, and in time he too came to accept the gospel of toil. Thus the standard of merit with us was a man's fitness to do hard physical work. If you could sweat all down your back you were a worthy member of society. If you could not, you were a loafer and beyond the pale. Laziness was the worst reproach that could be levelled against one, and few dared invite it.

I realized this quite early. At first it was pride made me hold up my end; then it was a decision that if I had to do a thing I might as well do it well. For instance, I was told to clean out a pigsty. The manure was packed so tight it was like cement. I could have dawdled all day at the job. I might have dreamed the hours away, for one can dream even in a pigsty. But I plied my four-pronged fork with a will and had the job finished by noon. It was some satisfaction that when I sat down to lunch the stink of me was so strong the female members of the family had to leave the table.

The harvest days were over and I had been initiated into most forms of farm work. Some of them I liked; some I hated. It made me feel cheap to rise at five-thirty in the morning and fetch the cows from the wet bush. The field work was not so bad. Pitching hay or grain was enjoyable, for my muscles responded to the task. Getting in the potatoes and the roots was not unpleasant, for it involved no hard labour. Gathering the apples in the orchard was like a charming game, with all around the changing foliage and the bracing air of Indian summer. Best of all was the threshing. We joined in to form a bee. We had a fine lunch and found the day almost a holiday. We joked and laughed, making a play out of toil. I volunteered for the tail of the carrier, which was a dusty job, but not physically exhausting. I always preferred dirty work to strenuous effort.

So passed my apprenticeship to farm labour. I acquitted myself well, because there was nothing else I could do. I worked harder than ever in my life; or rather I worked hard for the first time in my life. And from the first I realized that I hated hard work. Yes, with a feeling of horror I now knew that I had made a hideous mistake. For from now on, nothing but hard work lay before me. I had sold myself to serfdom. I had freedom only to starve. I had relinquished my heritage of easy living for the grimmest life I could have chosen. True, farm work was not so gruelling as other forms of labour, but there was no end to it. I had plunged myself into a morass from which I saw no way out.

On the other hand, I was never so strong and healthy. Yet that would get me nowhere. As a farm labourer I was not as good as the Jap who worked alongside me, and I felt he despised me. Yes, I had brought myself down to a low level. But I consoled myself that if my work was not so constructive outwardly, it might be inwardly. All experience may be good, even the bad. And I still had my cowboy complex, though it had suffered severe discouragement. The first time I mounted a horse was when Jock MacTartan told me to get on the bare back of a bronco, then gave it a whack on the rump. It made off at a mad gallop, while I held on by its mane. For about a mile I slithered around, finally locking my arms about its neck. Fortunately I managed to stick on.

Then one day Bung took me for a ride to visit some people and have tea. I wore my circus boots and white flannel trousers. I rather fancied myself as a dashing cavalier, but when I tried to descend from the saddle I found I was glued to it. At the tea party was a fat girl who made a poem on my plight. Afterward she became famous as a writer. Most people know her name so I will not give it; but if she reads this she may remember that her virgin muse was first inspired by the gory seat of my pants. After that, I felt less cowboy-minded. It was nice to have experience, but I felt I was going to pay bitterly for mine.

Chapter Three

Backwoods Ranch

The frame shack cowered in the shadow of the pines. Ramshackle, rain-sodden and innocent of paint, it made a disreputable blot in the clearing. Knee-high grass grew up to its walls and a rickety scaffolding caged it in. Thirty years before, young Hank had rigged up that scaffolding, intending to add another story to his home. He had answered an ad in which an attractive widow wanted a loving mate. She was to come out and join him and they would be married in the new house. But something slipped and the lady backed out. Young Hank had not the heart to take down the scaffolding, so there it remained, a witness of frustrated hopes and dreams.... And now old Hank was the same slow-moving mossback he had been thirty years ago. Rather a lovable man, gentle, patient and slovenly, he was lonely. He wanted someone to keep him company during the winter, and I had taken on the job.

So behold me installed in my new home at the end of everything. For it was the most outlying house in the settlement, and beyond it was a land that had never been crossed by human foot. The shack stood in a clearing, engulfed by Douglas pines three hundred feet high. Enough had been felled to give it breathing space, and to ensure that none were near enough to crash on it in a day of storm. The fallen trees lay criss-cross where they had been chopped down, and made a barrier around us. Fireweed grew up to the very door.

A narrow trail led to a small prairie where coarse grass grew, which Hank cut for hay. He had about twenty head of cattle that roamed the mountain all summer and came home in winter. I was really living on a cattle ranch, a cowboy without a horse. Hank had a lazy man's ideal of farming, the less labour the better. It was also mine.

The shack consisted of two sections, the living room and a bedroom. There was also a cubbyhole under the roof where Hank slept. He mounted to it by a ladder, drawing it after him at night. He was believed to have a sum of money hidden there and to be afraid of robbers. He ceased doing this when I came, but I never saw his den. I believe the reason he discouraged visits was that it was very filthy. Every morning he descended carrying a "jerry" which he told me had once belonged to the Premier of the Province. He was very proud of it, and it was precious, as he suffered from prostatitis.

I had the bedroom to sleep in, but it had no bed. Indeed, it had no furniture at all. I couched on the floor, lying on a buffalo robe and wrapped in a mackinaw blanket. And from the moment I went there, for all of seven years, I never slept between the sheets.

Primed with my newly discovered hate of hard labour, I energetically cultivated laziness. I had little to do but light the morning fire, sweep out the living room, bake the bread and help Hank to feed his stock. I also used to saw wood and pile it for the fire. Outside of that I was my own master.

Oh, the joy of liberty after six months of slavery! In that time I had done enough to hold me for a year. Again I declare — I like farming. It is the healthfulest of lives and the most useful. It is full of interest and excitement; but there is a lot of drudgery and its chores are endless. When another man's toil is done he can forget it, but a farmer's is never done.

Even today I could enjoy having a small farm if I could hire another man to do the work. I would pay him and pity him, but I would not want to help him. He could milk and clean the barn and feed the pigs. I would give him my moral support, but I would not lift a finger to aid him. For seven years I lived *on* a farm and my interest never flagged. Theoretically I was an authority on agriculture. I read many books and could talk convincingly from pigs to poultry. Thus by avoiding contact with the soil I kept my enthusiasm for it.

Yes, I was happy because I belonged to myself again. Freedom was the finest thing in the world. Later I came to think health more important; but in youth liberty is more to be prized. I was as careless as a breeze. I gave the future no thought. When the evil day came I would meet it; in the meantime let me live lyrically. But I would control my destiny. I would never allow myself to be shaped by circumstances.

Perhaps I might become a writer. The thought was always at the back of my mind. I might commit all kinds of folly but my pen would save me in the end. It may have been that instinctive confidence that made me so jaunty in assurance and challenge-ful of fate. All this, I thought, was but a preparation. Someday I would get my chance and I would take it. Yet how many like me have dreamed and dawdled on the dreary road to failure! I did not realize how I had been mentally starved during the past six months till I found in the shack a pile of *Harper's* magazines. It seemed like a treasure to me. I devoured them, and never did I get such delight from the printed page. Avidly I read, finding each word vital, each phrase pregnant.

We get from a writer what we bring to him, and sometimes we get more than he intended. Our intelligence fuses with his, and his words go deeper than ever he purposed. We may read a passage a dozen times and it leaves us unmoved; then there comes a special mood when it burns like a living flame. We must be hungry to appreciate literary fare. In my case I was famished. I read those magazines from end to end. Nothing in them bored me, much enraptured me. Every page had the pulse of life in it, and many passages had the preciousness of words engraved on brass. But most luminous of all were some articles on Southern California. They dealt with the fruitlands, and had wonderful photographs of groves and orchards. These articles were like a beacon light to me. They gave me a new incentive, a fresh inspiration.

As I dreamed over them I vowed I would visit that earthly paradise. I would pick oranges and grapefruit, olives, figs, walnuts, in that wonderful sunshine. I would work in drying sheds and canning factories. Serenely I announced my intention: "I'm going to Riverside to be a fruit-grower." It was so easy to make my dreams come true. More prosperous people were tied down; I was free to voyage where I willed. The price might be poverty, even material failure.... Well, I was willing to pay for it. As I looked at the clod-minded youths around me I felt that they were in a rut. My plans might be excitingly uncertain, but I was on the trail of adventure.

To reach our shack one had to tramp three miles through the woods. We had no near neighbours, the closest being a half-hour hike through the brush. This was a dwarf who lived with his mother in a cabin halfway to the settlement.

The old lady was tall and straight, with silvery hair and handsome features. She had a number of sons and daughters equally handsome, but she cared more for her misshapen offspring than for all the others. It was as if she were trying to make up to him for the horror of his birth. At first sight he affected me painfully. Later I got used to him and came rather to like him, or at least to feel pity for him. I would help him to get his sheep into the fold, or do other chores around the house. For he had little arms like flippers and tiny twisted legs that allowed him to squat on the ground with imperceptible effort. He could neither run on his stubby feet nor do much with his pudgy hands. But he had the torso of a normal man and a head twice as big.

He did not appreciate the solicitude of his mother; in fact, I sometimes thought he hated her for having brought him into the world. He snarled at her and looked with rancour at his stalwart brothers. He said to me once: "Why couldn't she have made such a good job of *me*? Or why didn't she smother me in my cradle?"

He was the cruellest man I have ever known. He seemed to get real pleasure from the infliction of pain on animals, and his chief victim was his old grey mare. She was skin and bone but he drove her mercilessly. On her back she had a big open sore that was full of maggots. To the lash of his whip he had attached a wire nail, and with this he used to flick the mare on the raw place. It made her jump and pull like mad.

One day, trudging the snowy trail, I heard the jingle of sleigh bells and there was the dwarf, with his old grey mare. He ordered me to get on the sleigh, for he had a peremptory way that brooked no denial. After we had driven a little distance he handed me the reins, and diving in the straw of the sleigh box he brought out a bottle of whiskey; then producing a knife with a corkscrew, he told me to open it. He had a fierce manner and I was a little afraid, so I complied. It was something he could not do himself, yet in helping him I had a feeling of guilt. Brute though he was, there was something manly about him. I realized that here was a being who did not know the meaning of fear. Now he showed it, for tilting the raw liquor to his lips he drank long and deep. When he put down the bottle it was almost half empty. Then after asking me to take a drink, he made me cork the bottle and hide it under the straw. He took the reins again, but after a few yards he fell senseless.

As I drove him home the mare kept looking back as if she knew what had happened. Perhaps she was unused to such gentle handling, but she became a little unruly, often swerving dangerously close to the ditch. There was one place at the bend of the road where she came so near to upsetting us I was scared. And as she looked back it seemed as if she was laughing.

The old lady received me in a pained way as I packed the dwarf on my back and dumped him down on his bed. "I don't know where he got the liquor," I said; "I just helped drive him home."

"I know," she said wearily. "It's the God-damned saloon-keepers. They let him have it, though they have been told by the police not to. Anything to make a dirty dollar. Oh, he's broken my heart long ago!"

I got the bottle and gave it to her. She poured the liquor into the dirt. At that time I was not hostile to hooch and it hurt to see good whisky wasted. However, it happened to be rye. If it had been Scotch I could not have avoided a restraining hand. So feeling that I had done a good deed, I turned out the mare and went home.

Next day the dwarf appeared at the shack. "The bottle," he said eagerly. He was trembling and if ever a man needed a drink he did. When I told him what had happened he burst into a torrent of abuse. Then he turned his wrath on the old lady and his face was murderous. His hands clutched as if her would like to have her by the throat. I was afraid and had a sense of tragedy. For the next few days as I passed their cabin after dark I would watch for a light in the window. I reflected, however, that with his tiny arms and childish hands he could scarcely do her harm. Still I had a feeling of foreboding and I said to myself: "This is going to end badly." It did, but not in the way I feared. It was old Hank who told me the sequel.

"I was talkin' to the old lady, who was skeered about him, when we spied the mare trottin' up the trail. She turned in at the gate. Then I saw that there was no one in the wagon. Wonder she didn't knock down that gatepost. Well, I drove her back over the road, and where it makes a bend, I found him in the ditch.

The marks of the wheels were halfway down the bank. He was dead all right. He'd been drunk and gone to sleep in the drivin' seat. Curious thing, there was a dent in his skull like the blow of a shod hoof. And as I lifted him the horse put up her head and whinnied like she was laughin'. Sounded like she was downright glad. Well, she had reason to be. And say, it may be a notion on my part, but I reckon that old mare jest took her revenge."

Old Hank was mighty decent to me. He taught me how to make bread and I became the family baker. Good bread needs good kneading. We used yeast cakes to make it rise, and it was always an anxious moment watching the oven. Sometimes it rose too much and threatened to invade the floor. Sometimes it was sadly flat, but we would eat it all the same. I also learned to build a fire, using a silver of pitch, whittlings and strips of pine. In a minute I would have a hearty blaze, and in ten more a flaming backlog. A fire was a grand comfort, as it was often bitterly cold. In my bedroom I might as well have been in the open air for my breath froze on the blanket.

I kept thinking of the Sun-land. It was a new dream for me, and I lived for the day when I could make a stake to take me there. In the meantime I got Hank to tell me about California, where he had lived many years. He was garrulous and I was a good listener. Bent and bearded, his pipe was rarely absent from his mouth, and he was constantly relighting it with coals from the fire. He had four brothers who looked like apostles. Hank was the black sheep. He had been a bit of a Casanova, and still nosed round certain bitches of the settlement.

When not reading I roamed the woods with my rifle, bringing home grouse and pheasants. One had to shoot them on the head, so I often missed; but I bagged enough to keep the pot boiling. Once in a while I would get a deer. However, they were so graceful and innocent I felt guilty every time I killed one. Often, too, I had to pack the meat for miles; yet it was such delicious eating I counted the toil well spent.

One day I followed the trail till I came to a little lake. A trout stream flowed into it. I had a dream of making my home there. I would have a canoe and a log cabin. I would fish, hunt, raise a few potatoes, and maybe keep a few sheep. There, far from the fever and fret of life, I would live like Thoreau, a backwoods philosopher.

I will always remember the long evenings by the big open fireplace in the red glow of the backlog. On one side would lie the old dog, on the other the old cat, both the picture of peace. I would try to read, but presently would listen to Hank yarning of his love life. He had a cask of sweet cider and during the evening he would treat me to a glass.

Then one evening Bung MacTartan came in, and the cider flowed freely. After the fifth glass I gave up, but the other two kept right on. Finally the old man drew a full bucket and vowed they would drink it before morning. I went to bed, but though I slept soundly I could hear at intervals Hank singing *Britannia, the Pride of the Ocean*. They finished the bucket and he slept on the kitchen floor.

Happy days! I exuded health and energy. I used to visit the neighbours, for though I loved my loneliness I had reactions when I craved society. And here I established a contrast between my present and my previous life.

Then I had belonged to the snob side of the settlement; now I found myself a member of the mossback section. No longer did the men with the knee breeches and the stock ties accept me. I had become almost a pariah. For I found I much preferred the class with which I now mixed. Small farmers for the most part, they had built their log barns and carved their stump-garnished fields from the virgin forest. They were a simple, hearty people. To me they were friendly, though with a certain distrust that I tried to break down. It was the struggle between Canadian democracy and English conservatism, disdain on one side and dislike on the other.

No doubt I antagonized my former friends by my democratic brashness. I wore a black shirt, a white tie and a black stetson. I was playing the part of a roughneck. I dropped my English accent and tried to adopt the vernacular. I even expressed some socialistic ideas, but found about me an absolute ignorance on the subject. The community was individualistic to the backbone, and I realized that any preachments for the betterment of the underdog comes ill from one who is himself an underdog.

I think that even the mossbacks looked down on me as a specimen of the "damphool English." It was only by my entertainment value that I finally was accepted as one of them. Old Hank happened to have a battered banjo and I soon made myself master of it. That is to say, I learned the three principal keys and was able to chord while I sang well-known songs.

And here let me say a word as to my musical obsession. Ever since I can remember I have played some instrument. I began as a small boy with the penny whistle. I played *God Save the Queen*, then went on to *Auld Lang Syne*. I found I could play any tune I could hold in my head, so I ranged over the songs of Scotland till I became fairly good at them. When other boys were romping I would stay indoors and tootle on my whistle. I could hear their glad shouts, but as I trilled and warbled I was happier than they. From the whistle I went to a flute, then to a piccolo. From the piccolo I switched to the concertina which I played for years. With the concertina I discovered harmony as well as melody. This gave me infinite pleasure because I was finding it out for myself. It was crude and elementary harmony, but I felt like a real music-maker.

My musical education was arrested early in life, and — of all things — by a *kiss*. When I was nine I took piano lessons and had for a teacher a spinster who seemed to fancy me. She tried to sit on the stool, and frequently embarrassed me by putting her arm around me. Then one day she actually kissed me. I went away, scrubbing vigorously at my cheek. I vowed I would never go back. I was getting on nicely. I could play *Nellie Bly* with variations, but I dropped the piano from that moment. I sometimes think, but for that osculatory indiscretion, I might have been a real musician.

It was this ability to entertain a crowd that now won me popularity. I was asked to surprise parties and to social evenings. I strummed the banjo and improvised ditties. I sang old songs with familiar choruses. I soon had the company joining in. Community singing is primitive, but among these simple folks, in a log schoolhouse on the fringe of the virgin forest, it sounded cheerful and friendly. Often I would return from these gatherings after midnight. I would set out over a six-mile trail in the pitchy dark. Usually I told my way by looking up at the stars, for the treetops made distinctive patterns against the sky. Once, however, I stepped forward and felt nothing under me. I had a moment of fear, wondering how far I was going to fall. I was relieved when I hit bottom about six feet down, for a little further along it was thirty. Arrived home I would throw myself on the floor, roll in my blanket and sleep like a dog.

The winter was hard. There was snow everywhere, yet under the trees it was light and patchy. From the settlement came the music of sleigh bells, but in the forest the only sound was the rustling of my feet as I crushed through the low brush and withered fern. The air was as bracing as wine, and after three or four hours of tramping I would return home ravenous as a wolf. Most of all, I loved to tramp the forest in the moonlight. The moon has never failed to make me feel fantastical. I had been a moon-child and now I was a moon-man, answering its call, and worshipping it in the deep glades of the woodland. At those moments I had a feeling of pure spirit, as if I were alone on the planet, alone with the moon. I believe I have spent more time staring into the face of the moon than any other fool mortal.

Often in the evening after old Hank had gone to bed, taking the only lamp, I would sit in the fire-light, seeing pictures in the flame. It was then I had an itch to write something, and a sense of frustration overwhelmed me. I could not express all the emotion I felt. I would sit brooding till the fire died down, then creep, still musing, to my blanket. I had a feeling of secret excitement. I did not know where I was going, nor what would become of me, but I had faith that my good angel would save me in the end.

Well, spring was nigh and my happy winter must soon close. Once again I must sell myself. However, it would mean earning money that would allow me to travel. For my mind was made up. I would work hard all summer and in the fall I would go South. I would winter in California. That was my dream, and how it inspired me! I had no fear of the future, only an intense awareness of the present and anxiety to create experience, so that one day I might be able to write about it. As Morley Roberts got his material for *A Western Avernus*, so I would get mine by self-sought adventure. Oh, it was good to be free to shape one's own destiny, and perhaps through one's very failures to forge success!

FROM "BOOK SEVEN: WHITE HORSE"

Chapter One

White Horse Arrival

"It's a tough country," said the Captain as we sailed up the Inland Passage. "Nothing but the God-damned pines. One gets sick of the sight of them."

I could not share his lack of enthusiasm. To me the journey north was one of wonder and joy. I wondered at the blue blaze of the glaciers. I wondered at the mountains glooming and gleaming in savage splendour. But most of all I wondered at myself — enjoying so much wonder without it costing me a single cent. It was the first time I had ever made a voyage at the expense of someone else; and, believe me, it tripled the enjoyment. And to think that I was being paid for having a marvellous time! Not only my pleasure was being given me free, but I was being handed two dollars a day for accepting it. To my Scotch mind it just didn't make sense.

So I got to thinking.... How gorgeous it would be to live all my life at the expense of others! And so easy, too. I had only to acquire a certain amount of capital, and the interest on it would absolve me from further effort. No doubt it might seem immoral to sit on one's stern and let the worker contribute to one's ease. But so many sound citizens did, and no reproach to them. From the receiver of bank interest to the bloated coupon clipper, they were all in the parasite class. They consumed without producing. Like lice they lived on the back of the toiler. But it was the ambition of every toiler to become a parasite in his turn, so it was all right. Society was run that way.

Then an idea came to me. I, too, would become a capitalist and live on unearned increment. Oh, I would be modest in my demands. Did not Thoreau say that one is wealthy according to the number of things one can do without? Give me a dollar a day and I would defy the devil. Five thousand at five per cent would give me twenty dollars a month. I could get by on that, and maybe make more by my pen. There was my Escape Idea cropping up again. And at the back of my mind always the Author Complex. Perhaps I could dodge my destiny of being a pot-bellied banker, and even publish a little book. At my own expense, of course. I might become one of those amateur authors who are such a nuisance. It would salve my vanity. AN AUTHOR. A poor wretch with dreams, but somehow different from the crowd. All this I thought in the moonlight of mountain magnificence; inspired by sublime scenery to sordid schemes of self-enrichment, because in the end they meant escape to freedom.

Skagway was wreathed in rain when I took the train for White Horse. But immediately the snow began, and soon there were six feet of it on either side of the climbing track. Far below I could see the old trail of ninety-eight, but I did not dramatize it. It looked tough enough, though. I was glad of the comfort of this funny little train, perhaps the most expensive in the world. Had not my ticket, for about a hundred miles of transportation, cost me twenty-five dollars? There were few passengers, and the windows were opaque with ice. I could not see much of the scenery, but what I did glimpse was dreary and depressing. Stunted pines pricked through the snow, and cruel crags reared over black abysmal lakes. A tough country indeed. I was glad I had not been one of those grim stalwarts of the Great Stampede.

At the Yukon frontier I encountered my first Mountie. He failed to make a favourable impression, for he pounced on a package containing a pair of felt boots I had bought in Skagway. He demanded two dollars duty. As I paid I could have kicked myself with them. Two dollars shot to Hades! A nice beginning to my campaign of economic independence.

As I stepped onto the White Horse platform it seemed jammed with coonskin coats. But for the rosy faces of the men inside them, it might have been a coon carnival. Then one of them addressed me.

"Better put on your coat."

"I'm not cold. How cold is it?"

"About thirty below. You don't feel it because you're a cheechaco. Your blood's like soup. When you've been here a year you'll get cold conscious.... By the way, I'm your Manager. Come along to the house." As he took me to my new home he was no doubt thinking: Another of the duds Head Office dump on us. Well, we must make the best of it.

So there and then I began what was to be one of the happiest periods of my life. For I found a real home such as I had not enjoyed since I left my own. There were four of us, the Manager, his wife, the Teller, and myself, and we surely made things sparkle.

The Manager had the unique distinction of being the world's only sea captain to turn banker. Of an eminent clerical family, but of an adventurous mind, he had defied the family tradition by taking to the ocean. He might have been a parson; he preferred to be a tar. Then, after roving the Seven Seas, he decided that he and Neptune had just about enough. He would give the land a chance. So he did, but soon he realized that working on a farm was a mug's game. There were easier ways of winning one's meal ticket, and banking might be a good bet.

There are two types of managers, the bureaucratic and the popular. Our skipper was of the latter. He was perhaps the most popular man in town. He was a virtuoso in slang, and his conversation was rich with it. He was a good mixer, oozed geniality, and had great gifts of chaff and humour. His wife was little more than a girl, with a *chic* that was Parisian. Unusually pretty and dainty of figure, in the setting of that rough mining camp, she stood out like a jewel in a junk heap. Yet she looked after us with a maternal solicitude that won our gratitude. She called us her "boys" and we called her "Missis." Few real families of four were more united and happy.

My colleague, the Teller, was a brilliant boy, as surely destined to success as I was to failure. He might have been a millionaire if he had not preferred to nurse the millions of others. As it was, he did pretty well for himself. He was a mass of energy that nothing seemed to exhaust. He had an insatiable appetite for life and a great gift for popularity. He excelled in games, was a hunter, a fisherman, and as keen a swimmer as myself. In all gatherings he was a human dynamo. He neither drank nor smoked and claimed he had never tasted tea or coffee in his life. In fact he was so viceless that he was almost vicious. One day I said to him:

"It's unfair to be so virtuous. It gives you such an edge over the other fellow. A drinking man like myself can't compete with you. Every time I buy a whisky and soda, you're that much ahead of me financially. You are exploiting your continence. There is nothing so immoral as morality."

He said: "No doubt you are right. I am cashing in on my exemplary conduct, but I have a good reason. Every day of my life I write a letter to a girl. It is my object to marry that girl, and every dollar I save brings me nearer wedded bliss. To an outsider I may seem a hoarder, but I have a definite aim. I am like granite in my resolve to win to matrimony."

"You mean to win to loss of liberty. Well, I am just as keen to win to freedom. So I am going to match you as a miser. From now on I mean to save every cent I can. So enthusiastic am I in my conception of myself as a future capitalist, I am cutting out the hooch for good." From then on, I put fifty of my sixty dollars a month into a savings account and watched with joy my nest-egg grow. I stinted myself the smallest pleasures. I scrimped, I scraped. Thrift grows on one. The more I saved the more I wanted to save. And all because of my wish to win to liberty. The bonds of the bank were of velvet, but they chafed all the same. Let me be my own master and take orders from no man. By means of capital let me defy capital and its power to enslave me. And at the back of all this was my desire to achieve authorship.

The Teller was intensely popular, while I was never popular in all my existence. Maybe I shrank from it, maybe I disliked it. Due to my solitary spirit I always wanted to take a back seat. I was as morose as a malamute. But my reticence was partly due to shyness, partly to indifference. I had no disdain for those around me; on the contrary I admired them because they could do so many things I could not. So I enjoyed the popularity of my colleague and trotted meekly at his heels. After all, he was a man of action, I a feckless dreamer.

Yet we were a happy quartet, and I do not recall a sour note to mar our harmony. Meals were occasions of sheer merriment. The Missis would sit in Dresden china daintiness, with a lot of fluffy fal-lals in front, which had a way of getting involved with the sauce. Then the Skipper would shout: "Here, you should have a tin chute hung round your neck, sopping up all the gravy." Then he would make a racy remark, and she would say: "Hubs, if you don't stop your nonsense I'll leave the table." But she would laugh all the while at his drolleries, delivered with never the crack of a smile.

In the Yukon there are practically only two seasons. Spring is negligible; summer comes with a swoop — with midnight melody of birds and myriads of mosquitoes. It was thrilling to see the snow so suddenly vanish, and the brown earth bob up; to watch the ice crack, break and go out in rearing slabs; to behold the eager green springing to the caress of the lingering sun. It was a magic change that happened almost overnight, giving one a sense of unreality.

Then from Outside came the inflowing tide of workers resuming their jobs, and residents returning to their homes. All had enthusiastic tales of their travels, but declared they were glad to be back. The shipwrights returned, the pilots and crews of the boats reappeared; the scene suddenly became a bustling one as every train brought new crowds going into the Interior. Then navigation opened, and the season was in full swing.

During the next five months there was little time to spare from work. We were kept busy at the office, for our town was the gateway to the North. The stream of travel was in full spate, while the local mines were working night and day. In fact, there was little darkness, and we were able to play tennis at midnight. We also paid a daily visit to the swimming hole, a pool formed by the back-up of the river. On Sundays we never failed to attend church, because the Skipper was a strict sectarian and insisted we decorate the family pew. He was head deacon and used to pass the plate, saying: "Come on, you old stiff, loosen up," or some similar remark. It was of him I thought when in one of my ballads I used the lines:

> Me that's a pillar of the church an' takes the
> rake-off there,
> An' says: "God damn you, dig for the Lord," if
> the boys don't ante fair.

But the publishers deemed the couplet sacrilegious, and refused to include it in the ballad.

After a time the Skipper said to me: "You have a pious mug. I think you'd make a good deacon." So I became one, and passed the plate in my turn, adjuring the tightwads to come through. I enjoyed that dramatic moment when I held the collection before the Parson, and he gave it his blessing. He himself was a literary man, and when he was not writing sermons he was composing bestsellers. He published a score of novels, many of which were popular. So far as I knew he was the only one in that community who had a taste for letters.

The two handsomest men in the Yukon were friends of mine, and curiously enough, met tragic deaths. One was Superintendent Engineer of the fleet of river steamers — tall, dark and desperately good-looking. He was a bachelor, and many of the women, married and single, angled for him. He did not encourage them; but, like all sailors, he was fond of horses and would occasionally ask one of his female admirers, duly chaperoned, to go for a drive.

On one of those occasions I was walking in the woods, when I met his party returning. They were in great trouble. He had invited two ladies to come for a drive, but on a trail behind the town they had met a pack train. His horses bolted, and he was thrown out and dragged, his leg catching in the wheel. Somehow he had hung on to the lines, and finally pulled the team to a standstill. Now he was in great pain, but tried not to show it. The women were in tears, and I drove the sorry party back to town. He had been injured internally from his fall, and had to go Outside to have an operation. Everything was going on all right. It was a simple matter of straightening out some twisted bowels, and he was duly sewn up again. Then the nurse missed a pair of scissors. To the horror of everyone it was found that they had been left in the body. So they had to operate again, but it was too much. The poor chap died, a victim of someone's carelessness.

My second friend was the nephew of an earl and related to half the English nobility. He could have posed for a statue of Adonis, being six feet two of stalwart manhood, with a proud carriage that made women look at him in admiration. He might have been a cinema star or a lieutenant commander in the Royal Navy. But when I first knew him he was a deck hand on a river steamboat. Why, I don't know. He was as clean living as he was clean limbed, with a fresh, frank face, and polished manners. Yet there he was, in a blue jersey, working on the deck of a stern-wheeler on the Yukon. If it had been a windjammer on the high seas I could have understood it. There was romance and danger there. But here on the placid river — if he had wanted to shirk the perils of sailoring, he could not have found a more secure billet. Yet even the Yukon has its perils....

One peaceful evening the steamer was nosing its way slowly upstream, pushing in front a scow laden with hundreds of small tin barrels. My friend was smoking a cigarette on the forward deck, leaning on the rail and looking dreamily up the river. In the distance a solitary duck was flighting downstream, and soon it would arrive directly overhead. A young cabin boy, slim and blond, ran to get his gun. A well-directed shot would tumble the duck on deck. But in his haste, he tripped, and the guns went off, bang into those tin barrels of ... *gunpowder.*

There was no explosion, just a great gust of flame that enveloped the steamer. The boy was blown onto the upper deck, a blackened cinder all that was left of him. High in the pilot house the Captain ran the boat into the bank. The flame-swept decks below were strewn with charred bodies, among them my friend. He died a few hours later. He asked to see me, and his last words were: "God curse the man who invented gunpowder."

What an incomprehensible world it seemed! An insignificant shrimp like myself permitted to survive while so many fine fellows were stamped out. More and more I believed in my guardian angel, and the experience of a lifetime has strengthened that belief. I know it is absurd and irrational, but I have steered through so many troubled waters to a serene haven that I cannot help fancying a guiding hand on the rudder.

And what a crazy world! Here was I, a lifelong agnostic, carrying the plate in church. I reconciled it with my convictions, for though I may not believe in religion, I believe in churches. They give me a sense of social stability. And I respect the *spirit* of religion, that reverence for the finer things of life. Churches are a rallying point in the fight for a heaven on earth. Not everyone can stomach my scientific materialism, but I would willingly sacrifice my sense of reason for a return to the faith of my fathers.

So summer passed, the hectic summer of a community trying to cram into four months the work of an entire year. Then the crowds who had flowed in with the spring began to flow out again. It was a human tide whose final ebbing was one wild welter of escape. The last boats were jammed beyond capacity, and the work was a mad scurry to handle the final exodus. Then the river congealed. The boats docked for the winter; navigation closed. The great river froze solid overnight, the season was at an end, and the real life of the Yukon began.

Chapter Two

Conflagration

When the Great Cold came to the Yukon it clamped the land tight as a drum. The transients scurried out, and the residents squatted snugly in. They were the sourdoughs; the land belonged to them; the others were but parasites living on its bounty. This is what we felt as we settled down to the Long Night. It was a comfortable feeling to be shut off from the world with its woes and worries; for we had none of the first and few of the latter. In the High North, winter is long, lonely and cruelly cold, but to the sourdough it is the season best beloved. For then he makes for himself a world of his own, full of happy, helpful people. The Wild brings out virtues we do not find easily in cities — brotherhood, sympathy, high honesty. As if to combat the harshness of nature, human nature makes an effort to be at its best.

As it was my ambition to be a true sourdough, I welcomed the winter more than most. Its sunny cold exhilarated me. Its below-zero air was as bracing as champagne. Our work in the bank dropped to a quarter of its volume, so that I could take things easy. I joyed to think that for the coming six months I could loaf and dream. For now I realized my dreaming was creative, that from my reveries came thoughts and fancies I might one day put on paper. It was an incubation of all worthwhile in my life.

I have never been popular. To be popular is to win the applause of people whose esteem is often not worth the winning.

I was polite and pleasant, but leaned back socially. I became notorious as a solitary walker, going off by myself as soon as work was done, into the Great White Silence. My lonely walks were my real life; the sheer joy of them thrilled me. I exulted in my love of nature, and rarely have I been happier.

At four o'clock I would close my ledger for the day. I had a little cocker spaniel who would doze all afternoon by the stove, but from time to time would look inquiringly at the big clock. Then, as surely as four struck, he would run to the closet and fetch my arctics. On my way through town other dogs would join us, till sometimes I had five, leaping and barking joyously around me. Then I would climb the bench above the town and strike through the woods. There were trails everywhere, and slender pines on which chipmunks barked shrewishly. Sometimes I would shake a tree till I dislodged the little creature. The dogs would wait, full of excitement, and make a dash for it as it fell; but they would never catch it, for which I was devoutly thankful.... Oh, those tramps in that world of crystalline purity, when I shared the joy of my canine companions! And my return after three hours of march, so keen set for supper, with glowing cheeks and sparkling eyes! Never was life more wonderful.

Then on Sundays, with lunch in my pocket, I would go for the entire day on snowshoes, striking across the river and exploring the snowy waste beyond. I would break trail under the pines, feeling supremely alone in the dazzling solitude, and filled with a rapture I have rarely known. It was then I realized the poetry of my surroundings, but did not yet dream of trying to put it into words. I just felt it with that inarticulate sense people feel in the presence of serene beauty. But I most loved the woods in the silver trance of the moon. Then I would steal away like a wild thing, feeling something akin to ecstasy in that fantasy of light and shade. The moon seemed my friend, calling on me to express the rapture that flooded me.

Of course we had other occupations in the evening, for in winter we sourdoughs organized our lives in friendliness and cheer. In our community rarely a night passed when there was not some social distraction. The skating rink was a scene of gaiety and glamour. We met our girls, and to the music of the orchestra we waltzed on the ice. Or there would be the toboggan slide on the hill. A few swift flights, and the world seemed so bright we wanted to shout and sing. There was something intoxicating in that wonderful air. It made the flame of life burn fiercely and impelled one to creative effort....

But specially in the realm of entertainment did we excel. We had whist drives, which I hated, and dances which I loved. Also, in the club, we had a handball court, and a big hall we used for indoor baseball. The latter we played with a soft ball that bounced from the walls. It was exciting. We had evening matches which aroused with enthusiasm. I do not believe as small a community ever packed so much pleasure into its leisure.

Our dances were very proper — not like those of the Settlement, where many of the boys carried hip flasks. There was enough inebriation in the air without the added stimulus of alcohol. In my three years in White Horse, I don't think I ever tasted a drop of hooch. Drinking means more drinking, and the expense of it just didn't fit in with my economy plan. Then again, the girls at the dances looked so bright one did not need to be lit up to appreciate them. They danced divinely, for all Yukoners excelled at that art. The men learnt in the dance halls, while the women were naturally on their toes.

Fire was the great fear. We had a well-organized fire brigade. We were drilled and instructed, and when an alarm sounded we were expected to be at our posts. Our equipment consisted of rolls of hose mounted on runners, and a pumping station, where in the winter the water was kept hot to prevent it freezing in the pipes. We had over a thousand yards of hose, so that if a fire was anywhere close, we could play two jets on the flames. Turning out at night at fifty degrees below zero was a ghastly business. Often the water froze in the pipes, and they had to be uncoupled. If we got wet we were immediately sheathed in ice, while to touch a bit of metal was agony. Many a frostbite resulted from a careless handling of the hose, yet in our furs and heavy mittens it was difficult to work efficiently. Altogether, getting up at night to a fire was the worst kind of a nightmare; but the occasion was so desperate no one dared to shirk.

One morning in early spring we were aroused by the fire siren. It was around three o'clock, and we cursed as we rushed to the scene. It was grey dawn, evil and askew. Others passed us pulling on their clothes as they ran. I heard them cry: "It's the White Pass Hotel." Already a crowd was gathered near the hotel and, in half-dressed excitement, the guests were gaining the street. Smoke was pouring from the building, but as yet there was no sign of fire.

"Hurry up there with the water," I heard a shout. Then another. "We can't get into the pump house." We had the hose laid, the nozzles pointed, and we waited for the water that would speedily lay the smoke. An easy job.... Buy why did the water not come? Again a shout of fury: "The pump house door is locked. The engineer is not at his post."

"Where the hell is the bastard?"

"Look in Lousetown," said one.

"Or in the poker game at Pete's," said another.

"Maybe the son-of-a-bitch is soused," suggested a third.

All scattered to find him, as in the meantime the smoke increased in volume. Presently I saw a crowd returning with a stupefied little man in their midst. He fumbled with the key of the engine room, badly rattled and afraid of the furious men who looked as if they wanted to lynch him.

Now all would soon be well. The hotel was only a hundred yards away from the pump house. We could get two streams on the fire and quickly master it. Everything was in place awaiting the water.... How long it seemed to be in coming! But the engine had to be started, and the engineer had lost his head. Others were helping him, probably hindering him. Every second counted as the smoke grew thicker, blacker, deeper. A breathless excitement gripped us. Would the water never come? Hose in hands, with nozzles pointing, we waited, prayed, cursed....

Thank God! At last the pipes swelled and the strong jets shot out. We were saved. We would soon get the fire under control. We inundated the centre of the building where the smoke was thickest. It faltered, almost died away. Soon we would have conquered that interior flame.... Now all was over. The smoke had ceased. All we had to do was to ply the hose till the drenched woodwork ceased to smoulder. We prepared to return to our beds....

Suddenly, to our horror, the saving stream ceased. Not a drop of water came forth. At the same time the fire, as if mocking our dismay, burst out again. There was another blanket of black smoke.... "Quick! See what's wrong!" shouted the crowd, and a rush was made to the pump room. Men were yelling frantically for water. Then I could see them dragging out the wretched engineer, who seemed to be in a state of collapse. I heard a shout of panic: "There's no more water in the tanks. He's let them run dry. We're lost. We can't fight the fire."

Despair fell on the milling crowd. Some were cursing, some weeping, some praying. And there they stood staring at those limp hose pipes from which no water came. We were helpless and, even as we looked, the fire, as if in triumph, shot out a great blaze of flame that dominated the smoke. The holocaust was under way.

It was useless to try to save the hotel. We must rescue all else we could. On the street, right and left, frantic storekeepers were carrying their goods onto the road. On the other side of the street from the hotel was a fine grocery store. The grey-haired proprietor was on the roof, swishing over it buckets of water that were being handed up to him. The street was wide. Surely there was no danger.... But even then the water on the roof began to steam, and quite suddenly a tongue of flame licked it hungrily. Scorched horribly, the old man on the roof rolled down and fell into the street. In another moment the structure was ablaze.

The two buildings were now like braziers, and at the station opposite, the employees of the White Pass Railway were trying to save their records. The distance was so great that surely no fire could jump it. Then the station started to blaze; then the freight shed. Then the fire, rejoicing in its strength, leapt across the track and attacked the storehouses. It seemed now as if the whole town was doomed. The buildings next the hotel and grocery were blazing fiercely, and the storekeepers, having carried out all they could, were crying as they watched the rest burn. Further down the street other storekeepers were still trying to salvage their stock. They begged us to help them, till at last the heat beat them back, and they, too, joined the hopeless, staring line in the middle of the road. I ran along till I came to a grocery store kept by a friend of mine. His daughter, a fragile girl, was shouldering sacks of potatoes and dumping them into the street. Excitement gave her extraordinary strength.

I espied some cans of gasoline in the back of the shop and told her to never mind the potatoes. As the heat grew fiercer we packed out the gasoline. It seemed as if nothing had any weight to me. My strength was tripled and hers doubled at the least. Other merchants were carrying out all they could grab up, using little discrimination. Many seemed to have lost their heads. I saw a dry goods man lugging bolts of cotton, while rolls of silk lay on his shelves. It was one blind frenzy to save all one could in the path of the advancing flame.

Suddenly I heard the Manager calling me: "Come on. The bank's in danger." Even though it was isolated, the fire had raced to the block opposite us. Panting, we arrived on the scene.

Fortunately there were four big barrels of rain water in the yard, and with buckets we drenched the wooden sides of the building. We worked feverishly, but as we swished the water upward, the wood began to smoke. The building across the street burst into flame. Fortunately, it was only a small one, or we would have been lost. For a panic-stricken moment I thought we were doomed. I knew we would have to save the records and let our own property perish. It was touch and go.... Then the Skipper, with the agility of an old salt, climbed to a perilous position on the balcony and kept a constant deluge playing on the steaming walls. There were three of us forming a chain to pass buckets up to him. With every ounce of strength we possessed we kept the stream of water going. Even the Missis, still looking decorative, lugged huge buckets on the scene.

At last the building opposite burnt out and we knew we were safe. What a relief! We were exhausted, grimy, parched, but, oh, so happy! Yet our joy seemed unworthy of us, when we looked around and saw bare space and smouldering ruin. Almost the entire town had been wiped out. Ironically enough, the buildings that had been saved were the Customs, the Court House, the Post Office. To these add the bank, and you can understand the bitterness of the townspeople when they commented that those who were spared were those who had least need to be. Well, it was over. What had been a thriving and happy community, a few hours before, was now a charred and smoking eyesore.

The summer that followed was the most hectic I have ever known. We crammed the work of a year into four months. First, an army of carpenters arrived to rebuild the town, and before its cinders had ceased to smoulder, merchants were again doing business. They put up tents and began selling off their salvaged goods. They must have done pretty well out of the insurance, for their new stores were finer than the old, and their stock richer. Before the spring was well advanced the town was rebuilt better than ever.

Then the stream of travel began. Swiftly it thickened like a flood — first the migrants returning from a winter in the South, then the seasonal workers, then a host of tourists. Soon we were in the spate up to our necks. The office was full nearly all the time, and often we had to work late. Again I managed to play a little tennis along about midnight, and cursed the everlasting song of the birds and the eternal whine of the mosquitoes. Then, with the usual mad rush of escape, the season closed, the snow fell, and the Great Peace began.

It was like gaining the calm of a cove after a stormy sea. Now our Yukon was restored to us. The strangers had departed, and we who remained were like a big family. With a sigh of contented lethargy I settled down to do as little as possible. But there came a change in our merry quartet. The Teller was transferred to Dawson and I took his place. Before he left he and I compared bank accounts. To my great joy I had attained the thousand dollar mark. Of course he had much more, but we congratulated one another. He was nearer his marriage, I my freedom.

Optimistically I reckoned: "It's the first thousand that counts," and I determined to save harder than ever. But, oh, what a long way to go before I could buy my independence! And it was only here in the Yukon I could hope to do so. If I had been Outside it would have taken me five years to save a thousand dollars.

I was succeeded on the ledger by a champion tennis player, a handsome fellow, with a quick Irish wit and a fine singing voice. His gift for popularity made up for my lack. We had a common taste for entertainment, and got up theatricals. I put on *The Area Belle*, with the female parts taken by members of the Mounted Police. And in the months that followed I cultivated my capacity for idleness. I took enough exercise to keep fit, picked melodies on a borrowed banjo, read light fiction. But as I lived a life of complacent happiness I little dreamed that the most wonderful an exciting event of my life was awaiting me just around the corner.

Chapter Three

First Book

I reckon that about my only claim to social consideration at this time was an entertainer, and a pretty punk one at that. I could sing a song and vamp an accompaniment, but mainly I was a prize specimen of that ingenuous ass, the amateur reciter. The chief items on my repertoire were: *Casey at the Bat*, *Gunga Din*, and the *Face on the Barroom Floor.* They were effective enough, but the moment came when they were staled by repetition, and at that time I was asked to take part in a church concert. What to do?

I was pondering over the problem when I ran into Stroller White, the editor of the *White Horse Star*. The Stroller was a remarkable man, a noted humourist of the North. Occasionally I had sent him bits of verse which he had accepted cordially. Now he addressed me: "I hear you're going to do a piece at the church concert. Why don't you write a poem for it? Give us something about our own bit of earth. We sure would appreciate it. There's a rich pay streak waiting for someone to work. Why don't you go in and stake it?"

I thanked him and said I would think it over. I went for a long walk, and did think, considerably. The idea intrigued me, but I hadn't the foggiest notion how I was going to proceed. All I knew was that I wanted to write a dramatic ballad suitable for recitation. I questioned very much if I would be able, for I started from nothing. I doubt if ever another successful ballad has been produced out of such unbelievable blankness. I said to myself:

"First, you have to have a theme. What about revenge? ... Then you have to have a story to embody your theme. What about the old triangle, the faithless wife, the betrayed husband? Sure fire stuff.... Give it a setting in a Yukon saloon and make the two guys shoot it out.... No, that would be too banal. Give a new twist to it. What about introducing music? Tell the story by musical suggestion. That would be different, maybe interesting...."

All of which shows my synthetic approach to the job. Yet as I returned from my walk I had nothing doped out. It was a Saturday night, and from the various bars I heard sounds of revelry. The line popped into my mind: "A bunch of the boys were whooping it up," and it stuck there. Good enough for a start.

Arrived home I did not want to disturb the sleeping house; but I was on fire to get started, so I crawled softly down to the dark office. I would work in my teller's cage. But I had not reckoned with the ledger-keeper in the guard room. He woke from a dream in which he had been playing single-handed against two tennis champions, and licking them. Suddenly he heard a noise near the safe. Burglars! Looking through the trap door he saw a furtive shadow. He gripped his revolver, and closing his eyes, he pointed it at the skulking shade.... Fortunately he was a poor shot or the *Shooting of Dan McGrew* might never have been written. No doubt some people will say: "Unfortunately," and I sympathize with them. Anyhow, with the sensation of a bullet whizzing past my head, and a detonation ringing in my ears, the ballad was achieved.

For it came so easily to me in my excited state that I was amazed at my facility. It was as if someone was whispering in my ear. As I wrote stanza after stanza, the story seemed to evolve of itself. It was a marvellous experience. Where I had difficulty in finding a rhyme, I bypassed it, and sometimes when I had my rhyme pat I left the filling out of the line for future consideration. In any case, before I crawled to bed at five in the morning, my ballad was in the bag.

So that's the story behind "McGrew." The speaker, through his own emotions, tells the story of the Stranger whose matrimonial experience presumably resembled his own. It suggests the power of music to stir the subconscious and awaken dormant passions; but at the time I wrote it I don't think any such idea was in my mind. All I thought of was to make a dramatic monologue, which, owing to the cuss words, I could not recite at the church concert after all.

I put the Lady Lou away in a drawer and forgot about her. Having cost me so little effort, I did not think the work could have any value. How my old professor of literature would have snorted with disgust over it! Probably it handicaps a writer to be a scholar and a gentleman. I could crook my little finger over a tea cup, and prattle about Pater, but what did it avail me? Better the college of crude reality and the culture of the common lot.

I did not write anything more for a month, and my second ballad was the result of an accident. One evening I was at a loose end, so thought I would call on a girlfriend. When I arrived at the house I found a party in progress. I would have backed out, but was pressed to join the festive band. As an uninvited guest I consented to nibble a nut. Peeved at my position, I was staring gloomily at a fat fellow across the table. He was a big mining man from Dawson, and he scarcely acknowledged his introduction to a little bank clerk. Portly and important, he was smoking a big cigar with a gilt band. Suddenly he said: "I'll tell you a story Jack London never got." Then he spun a yarn of a man who cremated his pal. It had a surprise climax which occasioned much laughter. I did not join, for I had a feeling that here was a decisive moment of destiny. I still remember how a great excitement usurped me. Here was a perfect ballad subject. The fat man who ignored me went his way to bankruptcy, but he had pointed me the road to fortune.

A prey to feverish impatience, I excused myself and took my leave. It was one of those nights of brilliant moonlight that almost goad me to madness. I took the woodland trail, my mind seething with excitement and a strange ecstasy. As I started in: *There are strange things done in the midnight sun*, verse after verse developed with scarce a check. As I clinched my rhymes I tucked the finished stanza away in my head and tackled the next. For six hours I tramped those silver glades, and when I rolled happily into bed, my ballad was cinched. Next day, with scarcely any effort of memory I put it on paper. Word and rhyme came eagerly to heel. My moonlight improvisation was secure and, though I did not know it, "McGee" was to be the keystone of my success.

I carelessly put my second ballad with my first and went my unsuspecting way. I did my duties cheerfully, thankful for my well-being and glorying in the open air. On my long tramps in the woods I carried a book of poetry, usually Kipling, and would rant poetic stanzas to chipmunks and porcupines.

One early spring I stood on the heights of Miles Canyon, with all about me a magnificent panorama. I breathed deeply, taking the beauty of it right into me. Then suddenly the line popped into my head: *I have gazed on naked grandeur where there's nothing else to gaze on.* My mentor seemed to be at my ear again, prompting, whispering, and I went right on. Maybe the two-syllabled rhyme helped me, for rhyme has always been a lure and a challenge. So again I hammered out a complete poem in the course of my walk. I entitled it *The Call of the Wild.* Its inspiration was the spring in my blood, and the wild scenery above the White Horse Rapids.

But my spate of inspiration was just beginning. In the two months that followed, I wrote something every day, and always on my lonely walks on the trails. I looked forward to them because

I knew the Voice would whisper in my ear, and that I would just as surely express my feelings. It was the outlet of the exultant joy that glowed in me. I was so brilliantly happy. Sometimes I thought I would burst with sheer delight. Words and rhymes came to me without any effort. I bubbled verse like an artesian well. I wrote the *Spell of the Yukon*, *The Law of the Yukon* and many others, a solitary pedestrian pounding out his rhymes from the intense gusto of living.

And as I finished each poem I filed it away with the others and forgot it. It never occurred to me to set any value on my work. It was just a diversion, maybe a foolish one. The impulse to express my rapture in a world of beauty and grandeur was stronger than myself, and I did it with no thought of publication.

But nature was not enough. I wrote of human nature, of the life of a mining camp, of the rough miners and the dance-hall girls. Vice seemed to me a more vital subject for poetry than virtue, more colourful, more dramatic, so I specialized in the Red Light atmosphere. And every day my pile of manuscripts grew higher, and I piled my shirts on them and forgot them. Then, as suddenly as it had begun, the flow of inspiration ceased. My bits of verse lay where I left them, neglected and forgotten for more than a year.

It was ever thus with me — bursts of creative energy, then lapses into lethargy. Apathy gripped me, so that I loathed the work I had done. A new enthusiasm would seize me and I would drive in another direction. I was temperamental, unpredictable. It might be months before I put pen to paper again; and in the meantime, in a slovenly roll held by an elastic band, my sheaf of verse lay at the bottom of a bureau drawer....

One day I was cleaning out my bureau when I came on that miserable manuscript. I looked at it bitterly. How much time had I wasted in idle scribbling! What folly and frustration! Then a fantastic, an incredible idea came to me. Reading it over I thought some of the stuff wasn't half bad. So I gave it to the Missis to glance at — very humbly and apologetically.

"Some of it's not so dusty," she opined. "Why not make a little book out of it, and give it to your friends for Christmas? It would be such a nice souvenir of the Yukon. Of course you would have to leave out such rough things as that McGrew poem. Also the McGee one, and a lot of things like *The Harpy* and *My Madonna.* They're a bit too frank."

I quite agreed, though at the last moment a sudden impulse made me shove them in with the others. Then Fate took a hand. I had just received a hundred dollar bonus for Christmas, so I decided that, instead of sending it to swell my savings, I would squander it in egregious authorship. I would herd my flock into a snug fold. I visioned a tiny volume of verse which I would present to pals, who would receive it with that embarrassment with which one accepts books from amateur authors. I would get a hundred copies printed, and maybe during my lifetime I could bestow them, with apologetic wistfulness, on my kindly acquaintances.

"Here is my final gesture of literary impotence," I said. "It is my farewell to literature, a monument on the grave of my misguided Muse. Now I am finished with poetic folly for good. I will study finance and become a stuffy little banker."

But before I staked my hundred dollars, my Scotch mind suggested that I might find some sucker to share my risk. So I went to the village Shylock, a fellow Scot, from whom I occasionally borrowed a ten spot at an interest rate of ten per cent a month.

"I've written a book," I said. "I'm having it published. Do you want to buy a half interest? It will cost you fifty dollars."

"Whit's yer book aboot?"

"Oh, just poetry."

"Poetry!" He almost leapt into the air. "D'ye take me for daft? Who buys poetry in this blasted burg? Not a damned soul. Look at all them padded poets I've had on my shelf for years. I never read a line of the stuff myself, but I'm well stuck with them padded poets. Now if it was stories like that Rex Beach writes, well, I might consider it. But poetry, laddie, oh, no. Ye can jist stick yer poetry up yer bonnie wee behind."

He was so rude I went away like a whipped dog. Yet years after, when he realized that his fifty dollars would have brought him in about fifty thousand, I think it broke his heart. I know it would have broken mine if I had been obliged to give him half the dough that book brought me in royalties.

Well, that was that. So I arranged my pieces, retyped them and sent them, care of Papa, to a firm of publishers who did amateur work. I remember so well the morning I posted that envelope. "Good riddance of bad rubbish," I thought, as I dropped it in the letter box, and instantly regretted my act. I did not register the envelope, I felt so careless and indifferent, and told myself: "Silly ass! Why didn't you burn the stuff?" I ordered a hundred copies, or as many as my cheque would cover. How people would laugh when the book came out! It would be the joke of the town. I would be regarded as one of those half-baked drivellers who dream instead of doing honest-to-God work.

Well, let them jeer. I would slink away and lick my wounds in secret. With my sensitive, self-torturing nature, I would mock my own misery. I would laugh with them at my cheap vanity. Never again would I make that kind of a fool of myself ... never again.

Chapter Four

Success

One day I had a letter from the publisher. It was quite a long letter, and it returned my cheque.

"There," I thought. "They don't want to publish my book. Too coarse, no doubt. They are sending me back my money." I was busy on the cash at the moment, and had no time to read the letter, but my feelings were of relief tinctured with chagrin. I had been about to make a fool of myself. Well, I would burn the darned stuff. So much the better.

When I was free I took up the letter. What was this? With a growing sense of stupefaction, I read. With a sense of unbelief, I reread. The words danced before my eyes. But it was a dance of joy. And at the same moment my whole being seemed lit up with rapture. For the letter told quite a story. It seemed that when they sent the manuscript to their composing room, the foreman noticed how quickly the typesetting had been completed. "The fastest job ever done in the office," he said. He smelled a rat, as it were. Taking the galley proofs to the office, he had shown them around. One of the travellers had scanned them carelessly, then become suddenly enthusiastic. He was an amateur reciter, and it was the McGee ballad that attracted him. He said: "Here, let me see.... This looks like the real thing." He had declaimed it to the staff with great effect. Then he cried: "Say, just lemme have those proofs. Maybe I can *sell* this stuff."

He did. He went around the trade reciting McGee, and booking orders so fast it made his head swim. He dropped everything else to push the book.... This was the story the publishers told me at some length in their letter. They told it with jubilation in the telling. Then they added that they had sold seventeen hundred copies from the galley proofs alone, and only in their city. Would I allow them to be my publishers, and they would pay me a ten per cent royalty on a dollar book?

Would I? WOULD I? I telegraphed acceptance so quick I did not give them a chance to change their minds. Then I went for a long walk, reading over and over my wonderful letter. My dreams were coming true. I would be an author, and not an amateur one. Already I had made a hundred and seventy dollars. A gold mine! But I did not think of the money. It was the glory of achieving something, I, who thought I was a dud. I was living in an enchanted world. It seemed as if the woods, the birds, the sky shared my joy. I sang and leaped like a wild thing....

Then, having exhausted my energy, I sobered down and began to take a calmer view of the situation. I mustn't indulge in foolish hopes. No, I would have a modest success, a bit of money, a little publicity. Well, better that than the kicks in the rear that had hitherto been my portion. But let me quote, as nearly as I can remember, the words of a well-known broadcaster.

> "In the composing room the men who set up the words got so enthusiastic they went about reciting them like crazy schoolboys. They took the sheets home, spouted them to their spouses, and shouted them to their neighbours over the garden fence. On trains going west salesmen read them from the galley proofs to receptive roughnecks; while in the bars of the prairie towns drummers declaimed them to the boys in the back room. Rarely has there been such a riot over the printing of a book. And to the amazement of the publishers, before it came out many thousands of copies were sold."

All this I did not even suspect. I went about my work, strummed my banjo, walked the woods and carried on in my humble way. But in the back of my mind was the sweetness of achievement.

I told no one but the Missis of what I had done, till suddenly the first spring mail brought me a package containing copies of my brain baby. I gave them away apologetically, and they were received with embarrassment. People in that town hardly ever read verse, and now I was putting them in a spot. They would be forced to scan my book, to pay me the compliments of politeness demanded. That was taking a mean advantage of friendship. I almost felt like begging their pardon for bothering them with my egregious effort.

Yet strange to say, even the least literary of my friends seemed to find something extenuating in it, while a few were quite enthusiastic. People whom I had never suspected of poetic leanings impulsively shook my hand. A lawyer we called the Judge, who up to now had never noticed me, said with feeling: "My boy, I've read your book. It's out of sight. I mean it — out of sight." Coming from an old whisky soak I appreciated the compliment.

My own feelings, when I caressed this bratling of my muse, were, I suppose, like the rapture of a mother over her firstborn. I gazed with awe and emotion at a slim, drab, insignificant volume. Yet it was a part of me, compounded of my ecstasy and anguish. I would rot in my shroud, but it would remain a testimony to my brief breath of being. Already it was being sold in the shops of the town. My Shylock had taken twenty copies on the understanding that I would take them off his hands if he got stuck with them. But soon he came to me, looking bewildered.

"Say, laddie, I've sold out of all them books I ordered. Could ye jist let me have a dizzen of yours at the trade price?" So I let him have them out of the two dozen I had ordered for myself, and he went off happy. But in three days he was back again to say he was sold out and had telegraphed to the publisher for half a hundred by the first mail.

It indeed surprised me that people were actually *buying* my book, and I felt a little guilty about it. It did not seem to me worth a dollar. It was a shame to take the money. At the foot of each title page was printed: AUTHOR'S EDITION. I realized these must have belonged to the original hundred I had ordered at my own expense. I believe that today there are only two copies of this edition in existence, and recently one was sold to a California collector for a hundred dollars.

It is interesting to record the reaction of the citizens to my book. Many thought me a presumptuous young pup, trying to exploit the town to my profit. To some I was a freak, to others a fourflusher. A few liked it and complimented me mildly, half afraid to show too much appreciation. No one saw in it a record-breaking success.

My chief antagonism came from the church. The first to express disapproval was the chief deacon. One morning he came to the bank where I was counting cash. His voice was dry, his manner sour. He said: "My wife's been reading your book, and she and the ladies of the sewing circle think that it is a pity you should have written so much about the bad women of the town and said nothing about the good ones."

"Well," I said, scratching my head, "we take the good ones for granted. But you see, it's story stuff I'm after, and vice has more colour than virtue. I write to please the public, and, though I have nothing against virtue, I've frequently remarked that a lot of people look on it as rather a bore."

He gaped with horror and answered me eloquently with silence. There, I thought, is another enemy. I imagine he wanted me to resign from the church, but I clung to my collection plate like a drowning sailor to a life buoy. It seemed my sole hold on respectability.

Then, with the opening of the season, public opinion began to change. Citizens returned from the Outside with the news that my book was a good seller. It was in all the bookstores and people were talking about it. It was said I was making real money, yes, hundreds of dollars, out of it. And to most, money was the standard of success. If a book sold well, why, it must be good. If a man made money, well, he must be smart.

So they began to look at me with consideration. And when the tourists came in, their respect increased. For every tourist had a copy of the book and quoted it with enthusiasm. They crowded to the bank, pushing through my wicket with requests for autographs. The other members of the staff sicked them onto me, deriving a sardonic glee from my embarrassment.

Pretty soon it seemed as if I was one of the attractions of the town, perhaps the main one. Blushingly I sought to evade the demonstrations of spectacled female admirers, and fled to the forest glades. But in my teller's cage I was a mark for them, and they spouted my stuff to me *ad nauseum*. Some of them even suggested I was a celebrity, and I had only to go outside to realize my vogue.

So ended another season. It had been very exhilarating. Then the snows came, sparkling zero weather and the Yukon we all loved. But I was not to enjoy another winter there. I was told I was due for three months' leave, and was forced to take a long holiday *with* pay. I bade goodbye to the White Horse with great regret. It was a brave little burg, birthplace of my prosperity. I had been brilliantly happy there. Every day had been enjoyable. Today they tell me it's populously important and flourishing. I have never revisited it, but I cherish the three years I spent there as one of my fondest memories.

FROM "BOOK EIGHT: THE GOLD-BORN CITY"

Chapter One

Dawson Arrival

I was not feeling very gay about my coming holiday. I did not want to leave the Yukon. Fancy being peeved because one had to take a three months' vacation with full pay! But it was like that. My savings account had been fattening for three years, and now I could no longer feed it. I would have to buy my own meal ticket and spend my salary in holiday expenses. Perhaps more than my salary, Well, I had that royalty money to help me out.

I landed from the steamer in fog and rain, a sample of the weather most of my stay on the Coast. I lived in a boarding house with twenty boarders and one bath. Contrary to my expectation I found my book was little known, and I was a small frog in a big puddle. I walked around the park in cheerless drizzles and revisited the scenes of my former hardships. I tried to imagine I was again broke and friendless, hugging myself when I realized I was neither. In the raw, damp weather I caught colds, from which in the Yukon I was immune. The climate here was indeed detestable, and I hated my enforced holiday. Then there was the chance I might not be sent back to the North. That would be a catastrophe. I realized how much I loved the Yukon, and how something in my nature linked me to it. I would be heartbroken if I could not return. Besides, I wanted to write more about it, to interpret it. I felt I had another book in me, and would be desperate if I did not get a chance to do it.

So my hapless holiday passed, and the day came when I must report to the Inspector. He was the same gruff character. He made no reference to my literary effort, but then none of the bank officials did. I think they resented my trespass into the Land of Letters, for they ignored my book. If they had known it would ultimately sell a million copies, maybe they would have been more cordial. I don't know, though. Officials must be stand-offish with their underlings. I have always hated authority and loathed discipline, so the pomposity of the man behind the desk arouses my spleen.

But I do not like to think this of the Inspector who played such a vital role in my life. I like to think that he had read my book, and that he wanted to give me a chance to write another. Perhaps under his frosty exterior beat a sympathetic heart that was willing to give a puling poet a break. Yes, I believe that; for with a twinkle in his eye he said: "Well, you'll be sorry to year you're going back to the North. I have decided to send you to Dawson as teller."

At these words joy possessed me. I think he saw it, for he thawed a bit and wished me quite a genial goodbye. No shaking hands, of course. No personal feeling could enter into his relation with those under him. He was making moves on a giant chessboard, in which human interest was barred.... How it must be fun to play God!

I never saw him again; but I will always consider him the benevolent arbitrar of my destiny, even if unwittingly so. For there is no doubt it was that last move on the board that assured my fortune. So, as he lies in an honoured grave, let a humble pawn lay a wreath of gratitude in his memory.

As I went north again my mood was of serene happiness and of faith in the future. After its first spurt my book was not so hot. But I believed it would be a steady seller. Well, I felt sure there was a lot of copy up there waiting for me to grab it. I was keen to get on the job. I wanted to write the story of the Yukon from the inside, and the essential story of the Yukon was that of the Klondike. In prose or in verse no one had done it. Perhaps I would be the one to work out that vein of rich ore. Maybe I would be the Bret Harte of the Northland.

So, nursing my conceit, I journeyed north again. Oh, but it was good to get away from the muggy coast, and to greet the great silence of the snows! Even the loneliness was friendly, for it was in harmony with my spirit. Here was my land, the grandest on earth, and it was welcoming me home. I would be its interpreter because I was one with it. And this feeling has never left me. The Yukon was the source of my first real inspiration. Of all my life, the eight years I spent there are the ones I would most like to live over.

From White Horse to Dawson was six days by open sleigh. It was then I realized the vastness of the land and its unconquerable reservation. The temperature was about thirty below zero. With bells jingling, we swept through a fairy land of crystalline loveliness, each pine bough freighted with lace and gems, and a stillness that made silence seem like sound. Day after day, serene and sunny solitude, as we hunched in our coon coats, half doped by the monotony of bitter brightness.

Our breath froze on our fur collars; our lashes and eyebrows were hoar; our cheeks pinky bright, as we took shallow breaths of the Arctic air. Every now and then the driver would have to break icicles out of the nostrils of the horses. Sometimes the sleigh would upset, and often we would have to get out and push through waist-high snow drifts. Twice a day we stopped at roadhouses to change horses. There we would find a meal prepared and be obliged to eat. As we had no exercise, we suffered from surfeited stomachs and had to take laxatives. Meals and beds cost two dollars each. When we woke up in the morning we would say: "Six o'clock, six dollars."

It was dark when we got to Dawson. A gloomy lad, who looked like Abe Lincoln, met me at the stage. "I am a reception committee of one," he said gravely, "come to direct you to the bank mess, and also to warn you."

"About what?" I said alarmed.

"Well, your reputation has gone ahead for bawdiness and booze. Mind you, for myself I kinda sympathize with you, but the other boys are on the pious side. You must never let them hear bad language such as you use in your book. And they would be so horrified if you referred to the Tenderloin. We have meetings and sing hymns every evening. No doubt you will join us in prayer."

"It's O.K. with me," I said, willing to be agreeable. "But say, how long have *you* been here?"

"Since ninety-nine. I came the hard way. Started from Edmonton. It took me two years." I marvelled. I had come the easy way — by Pullman. It had taken me two weeks. Incidentally, today it can be done in two days. However, I looked at him with reverence. Two years on the trail! …

"I'm gold-buyer at the bank," he went on. "You can't fool me on dust and nuggets. Gold Run, Sulphur, Hunker, Dominion — I can tell them at a glance. I do nothing all day but buy gold dust."

My reverence swelled to the point of worship. Here was a real old-timer, a sourdough of sourdoughs. I walked with him along a street that bordered the frozen Yukon. Lights were dim in cabins, and shadows shuffled past. My felt shoes squeaked in the dry snow. Like a frozen prairie lay the river, menacingly mysterious. We walked the dim street till we came to a low dark building.

"The bank mess. It used to be the bank. First a tent, then this. Ah, if these log walls could talk! You know, there's enough gold dust under the floor boards to make a fortune. They used to sling it around pretty reckless in the old days."

From the interior came sounds of rejoicing, and as he pushed open the double door there was a blaze of light and a burst of cheers. In a long, low room a dozen fellows were variously engaged. Some were standing up to a small bar, some playing cards. One was strumming on a piano. Then there was a shout: "Hail to the lousy Bard." "The Bard of Bawdyville," announced the pianist, "come to poison our innocent minds with his vicious verse.

> Hail poet, known as Ruddy Kip,
> Who paints for us the Yukon chip:
> Underneath a lamp of red
> Sighing softly: 'Come to bed.'"

"You've got me wrong, fellows," I protested. But I was shouted down, and a glass of whisky was pressed into my hand. Feeling like a lamb in a den of wolves, I drank the fiery stuff. The room reeled round and, exhausted, I sank into a big armchair. A Jap cook, entering from the kitchen to announce dinner, saved me from utter collapse.

The meal that followed was well cooked and copious. At the head of the table sat the Accountant, a youth with a high-pitched voice and spectacles. Supposed to be responsible for the decorum of the board, he took a book from his pocket and read with concentration all through the meal. I was just able to see that it was *Moby Dick*, for I was getting into a state where seeing is in duplicate. Before each of us was a bottle of beer. Next me was a lad with a cherubic face; he was so blond his head looked like a peeled turnip.

"Drink your beer," he told me. "We're supposed to finish our bottles. You see, we have the brewery account, and have to live up to it. It's good beer, though. No hardship to get it down."

We had soup, roast beef, apple dumpling, and the tone of the table was ribald. In fact its revelry was Rabelaisian; but in its midst, the spectacled youth read on imperturbably.

"You must excuse him," said my neighbour. "He's absent-minded. You see, he was born at sea, and he's been at sea ever since."

As we reached the dessert, men in uniform dropped in. "From the Mounted Police," said the baby-faced youth. "The barracks are next door."

Each visitor was hailed with yells of welcome and often a burst of song. Here was one greeting sung to the tune of *John Brown's Body*. Suppose the entrant was Mayor Jenkins, they sang:

> Poor old Jenkins has a boil upon his … um;
> Poor old Jenkins has a boil upon his … um;
> Poor old Jenkins has a boil upon his … um;
> And it hurts like heck when he sits.

It was not sung exactly like that. Certain words were vulgarized in a way the censor will not allow me to print; but the newcomers laughed, took out their pipes, and helped themselves to a drink at the bar. In the meantime the boys at the table finished their beer, and the hilarity rose to a climax. And in the midst of this maelstrom of mirth, an old man entered.

"Hooray! Here's Sandy with the mail," they shouted. Then up rose the chant: "Poor old Sandy" … etc. Sandy was the bank messenger, very Scotch and morally austere. His weakness was for whisky, and once in a while he would go on a bat that lasted for days. But he was so sober between whiles the bank winked at his lapses from grace. He had saved tenaciously, till now he was reputed almost wealthy.

He handed to each member of the staff the mail that had come in by stage; but at the last he held a letter in his hand, peering at it through his spectacles. "I'm thinkin' it's for the new clerrk," he said, handing it to me.

"From my publisher," I guessed, for an alcoholic blur was over my vision. Then a cheque fluttered down. Taking it up I saw a number one and some zeros. "Looks like ten dollars," I said, and I asked my neighbour to confirm my guess. But his eyes were even more muzzy than my own.

"Looks like a hundred to me," he hazarded. "Here, Sandy, you're the only sober man in the crowd — what's this cheque the bloody poet's been getting?"

Sandy peered at it. His face assumed a look of awe. "My gosh, mon," he said, "yon cheque's for a *thousand dollars*." It was, too. And the letter read: Account of Royalties. I was too dazed to realize it, as the cheque was passed from hand to hand. Some suggested it was a fake and advised me to use it for toilet paper; but old Sandy put out a restraining hand, and reverently returned it to me. "Pit it safely in yer pooch, laddie. It'll come handy one o' thae days." Respect was written on his face. If the others were impressed they concealed it carefully. "Here's a guy just made a grand," one shouted. "The occasion calls for a bottle of hooch — nay, two bottles. Hey, brother, what about it?"

"Three bottles," I said.

"That'll set you back ten bucks, sweetheart."

"Okay," I said; so they produced three bottles of Black and White, and glasses were filled. Then more of the Mounted Police boys, scenting booze from afar, trickled in, and soon there was quite a crowd. In its midst I sat bemused and a little incoherent, when the Accountant grabbed me by the arm.

"Come and I'll show you your quarters," he said; and steered me upstairs to a warm, friendly room, with a bed I loved at first sight. "A bunch of the boys are whooping it up all right," he laughed. "I thought I'd better rescue you before things got too hot. They're good chaps but a bit boisterous. And you must be all in after your day on the trail. Better get some sleep. By the way, I've a lot of books I can lend you any time you feel like it. I'm the only one here that reads to any extent. No one else reads poetry. I think Kipling's great, but I've just got a book called *A Shropshire Lad* that's the goods. I'll pass it on to you.... Well, good night.

Better lock your door." Later I was sorry I had not taken his advice, for I was aroused from a sound sleep by someone shaking me. Four dim figures were in my room, and from below came sounds of revelry.

"Two ladies wanna meet poet. Lovely ladies. Come on, pal. Mustn't disappoint nice girls."

I protested drowsily. "Let me get some clothes on and I'll be right down."

"No, no. Clothes not necessary. Come on down as you are."

I was horror-stricken, when suddenly I felt myself seized and pinioned. Then I realized how helpless a man is with four others hanging onto his limbs. Though I fought frantically I might have been a baby in their hands. Shrieking with laughter they carried me down to the crowded mess room. The whisky was still holding out. A poker party was in progress, and two girls sat at the piano.

And right in the middle of the floor I was dumped down. Fortunately I had on my pyjamas, but unluckily they were a pair I had worn on my trip. They were badly creased and not too clean. As I rose from the floor I felt a sorry sight. Standing there I tried to smooth down my garments, hoping there were no gaping apertures, as I was introduced to the girls. Then I grabbed a sofa blanket and draped myself in it. After which I was given a whisky and it began over again. In the end I was induced to sit at the piano and sing some of my songs, and not the most respectable at that. It was in the wee small hours when I was able to sneak off to bed, yet still the boys were whooping it up.

Chapter Two

Second Book

Next morning I was aroused by the Accountant. Grinning cheerfully he asked me how I was feeling.

"Pretty rotten. I've a helluva hangover."

"Some strong coffee will buck you up. Remember you have to interview the Manager."

The latter was in his office reading his morning mail. In a crisp voice he bade me be seated. I was feeling a bit disgruntled; but I had in my pocket a cheque for a thousand dollars, so I lacked some of my usual humility. I thought: It's the old trick, keeping me waiting to impress me with his importance. He's saying to himself: "Here's a guy that's published a book and thinks he's Somebody. But we'll soon show him that, as far as the bank goes, he's just piddling little nobody."

I quite appreciated his attitude. He was about my own age, but he had more banking in his little finger than I had in my whole carcass. As usual I was in a false position. I had been in one all my life, and I was getting a bit sick of it. But I had to take things as they were. Only I was minded to have done with false positions. Up to now I had been an escapist; now I realized I was a rebel as well. And then I knew the reason — that thousand-dollar cheque.

And here let me interpolate a note of petulance. I have always resented stuffed-shirtism. Why should a man who drinks with you at a bar assume an attitude of dignity behind his roll-top desk? Dignity is the camouflage of charlatans. What man is dignified with his pants down, or in the act of perpetuating his species? Dignified men are hypocrites and frauds. No man who has the honesty to see himself as he really is can be anything but humble. Only fools can take themselves seriously.... With these thoughts passing through my mind I sat waiting to be addressed. I was a poor little piker who must be kept in his place. Well, it would be all right. I would be humble yet awhile, but the time would come when I would reverse all that. The Manager addressed me sharply by my surname, and I sirred him respectfully, and he gave me my orders. And all the time I was saying: "Oh, hell! How long, how long?"

But that day as I was balancing my cash he came to me examining my cheque, and scratching his head. "All this money," he said. "What does it represent?"

"Verse," I said. "Just verse."

He looked bewildered. "It's a strange world." He sighed and scratched his head; and I agreed it was indeed a strange world.

The more easy money one gets the more one wants — up to a certain point. With me it was the five-thousand-dollar mark. To attain that I was willing to deny myself the pleasures others enjoyed. I cultivated thrift to the point of frugality. I gloated over my growing bank balance; but it was not love of money that made me save so eagerly; it was the hope of freedom. If I achieved the reputation of a tightwad, it was put down to my Scotch nationality. To some extent maybe it was. Yet a Scot is always ready to buy a drink, and I shunned even that. On Sunday I allowed myself a cigar after dinner, and lit it on the way to church. But when I arrived at the door, it would be only half smoked, so I would stick it in the snow and retrieve it when I came out. The others chaffed me about this, but at the time it seemed to me a natural thing to do.

One day the Manager came to me with my laundry bill. He said: "You know, I suppose, that the bank pays for your laundry. If your bill was too high we might complain, but yours is surprisingly low. I have here accounts for other members of the staff amounting to six and seven dollars each. Yours amounts to a dollar thirty-five cents. Do you realize that your washing is not costing you anything?"

Grinning, I answered in my broadest Scotch: "Ay, sir; I ken the laundering's free, but *the rubbing's awful harrd on the shirts*." And being quite a charming chap he went away laughing.

I imagine economy is a virtue only when it is a necessity. I practised penury so many years that it almost became a habit. When prosperity came it was hard to break myself of cheese-paring. The carefulness imposed on me by years of grinding poverty had entered into my system, and I was incapable of lavishness. Even today I am happier in modest comfort than in the lap of luxury, and the bravery of extravagance gives me a feeling of guilt.

But my lucre-grubbing period, however unworthy, was limited to the time it took me to gain the sum that was to assure me social security. After that I lost all interest in money, and cultivated a comfortable ignorance of my financial standing. All I knew was that it was improving all the time; but never again did I watch the mounting total in my bank book and gloat over it, as I did in those days of struggle to escape the curse of poverty.

My success in saving was stimulated by the ease of my efforts. Royalties were now coming in from the States, and for some time I had been getting cheques of twenty-five dollars a month. Suddenly they jumped to fifty, then a hundred, then a hundred and fifty. There they seemed to be stabilized. From all sources it looked as if I were making four thousand a year from my literary work, while the bank was paying me nine hundred. I gave myself furiously to thinking....

As a teller I was not a success and far from happy. I, who hated responsibility, was accountable for big sums of money every day. I worried over all that currency in my care. My fear of making a mistake made me over cautious, so that I was slow in paying out. At the close of the day my nervousness in balancing my cash amounted to fear. I seldom got a first-shot balance and generally had to hunt for shortage. This meant a feverish moment of anxiety till I found my error, and left me with a headache that lasted till dinner time. In my painstaking way I was a poor man to be on the cash.

Another reason was that I failed to ingratiate myself with the customers. A teller's greatest asset is his affability. A customer likes to be greeted with a gay word, a humorous sally. I never had the gift of facile chaff. In my strict attention to business I was grim and monosyllabic. Still, in my four years as a teller I handled millions of dollars, and I never lost a cent. In fact with my small "overs" I kept myself in tobacco money.

To succeed in a bank one must have its interest at heart. As time went on I found that my chief aim was to draw my salary and to do as little as possible for it. And this growing dislike for my job increased my determination to be done with it for good. If I could only be sure that my present income from writing would keep up?

... Then it was borne on me that I must follow up my success with a second book. There was no opportunity to write during the rush and scurry of the summer. After a hard day on the cash I was too tired in the evening to do anything but rest. However, I could at least assemble the material against the time when I would have the vitality to use it. And this I proceeded to do.

After my years in White Horse it was not hard for me to adjust myself to the new setting. Dawson was five times bigger, but its character of a small town was the same. From a one-time population of forty thousand, it had dropped to four, and was on the way to become a ghost. Buildings were being deserted and left to ruin. Less than a third of the dwellings were occupied.

Of course, the old landmarks remained, and even a dance hall was running when I first arrived. But this was speedily closed down. For the community was now influenced by the churches and the lodges. The townsfolk were great joiners, and nearly every one belonged to secret societies. I was a Wow-Wow and an Arctic Brother, though I never went very far with either. Brotherhood was not much in my line. I suspected that many members joined out of self-interest; but I have never been a climber and I disapprove of social discrimination.

Among my Arctic Brothers, however, I met many who had come in over the trail of ninety-eight. I wormed their stories out of them and tucked away many a colourful yarn. They were glad to find an eager listener, so I goaded their memories till they felt they were collaborating with me. I was like a reporter, ferreting out details of a story that would be a scoop. My only wonder was that no other writer had grabbed the rich stuff waiting to be won.

At midnight I wandered the streets of the abandoned town, with the light still strong enough to read by. I tried to summon up the ghosts of the Argonauts. The log cabins, in their desolation, were pathetic reminders of a populous past. I loved the midnight melancholy of the haunted streets, with the misguided birds singing, and the neglected flowers springing. As I pensively roamed these empty ways, a solitary and dreamful mourner, ghosts were all about me, whispering and pleading in the mystic twilight. Thus I absorbed an atmosphere that eluded all others; thus I garnered material for another book. Oh, my Dawson of those days was a rich soil from which I reaped a plentiful harvest!

The writing of my second book might be considered a *tour de force*. I had my material in the bag, and I did the book in four months, working from midnight till three in the morning. Any other hours were impossible because of the rumpus about me. The boys were forever whooping it up, and the only quiet I could get was in the small hours. So I would go to bed at nine and sleep till twelve. Then I would make myself a pot of black tea and begin to write. When I went to bed for good I would be so imaginatively excited I could not sleep, and would rise for breakfast feeling as if I were suffering from a hangover. It was tough going, but I kept doggedly at it.

In writing this book I had to *think* more than I usually do. I don't like to have to think as I write. I prefer to sit down, and hope for the stuff to come, and if I wish hard enough it generally does come. If it doesn't, I say: "Oh, to hell with it," and wait for the proper mood. But this time I really had to get down and dig. Instead of my usual joyous exuberance, I blasted out my rhymes with grim determination. When I finished the last line my relief was enormous.

By all precedents this volume should have been a failure. It was forced. It was a product of the midnight oil. It was that luckless effort, a second book, written to follow up the success of the first. A first book is rarely written. It just happens. It is usually a compilation of happy efforts, composed with no thought of a book. A second book is deliberately intended, sometimes even written to order. It is self-conscious, premeditated. There is a difference in collecting scattered verse for a volume, and constructively making one. My second book should have been a dud.... Well, it wasn't.

It succeeded because it was sheerly of the North. It was steeped in the spirit of the Klondike. It was written on the spot and reeking with reality. All of it dealt with the subarctic scene. There was little lyric verse, and most of the descriptive ballads were over long, but it expressed the spirit of the Yukon more than anything I have done. Technically it was an improvement on my first work, and as usual I revelled in rhyme. Altogether I thought I had made a neat job; so, with every confidence I sent it to the publishers.

What was my dismay when I received a letter telling me they were loath to publish it. Anger succeeded amazement, and I immediately telegraphed them to hand the manuscript to a rival firm. I received a wire by return: *Reconsidering decision. Await letter.* This made me madder than ever. I wired back: *Reconsideration superfluous. Have advised other firm to take over.* Then I received a telegram from the other firm: *Will be glad to publish anything you write.* So, sitting pretty, I awaited the arrival of the next mail.

There were two letters, one from the rival firm, offering to take the book on my own conditions. The second was from my publishers. In their first letter they had complained of the coarseness of my language and of my lack of morality. As a highly respectable firm with church connections they thought its publication would reflect discredit on their reputation. Also on my own. They suggested I scrap the book and write another of purer tone. Now, however, with my threat of publishing elsewhere, they entirely changed their position. They begged me to make certain minor changes, and to leave out one particular ballad dealing with the Tenderloin.

I thought it great fun pitting one publisher against another. Cynically I sat back and enjoyed myself. I wrote, pointing out that I had no reputation to consider, and that morality had nothing to do with literature. However, I wanted all my work to appear under the one imprint, so I said I would remove the offending ballad, but it would cost them five per cent more royalty. It did....

Thus ended my first fight for freedom of expression. The book was a success, and soon after I had a cheque for three thousand dollars.

Chapter Three

Dawson Dreamer

Having completed my five-thousand-dollar plan I at once entered into a second one. Ten thousand would put me in a spot where I could thumb my nose at the world. And it looked as if that delightful gesture might not be far off. My American royalties, coming in an ever-increasing flow, were augmented from England, so that I likened my bank account to a pool being constantly fed by small streams. It was a pleasant thought that the work was done, and I had just to await the awards. That is the most charming thing about authorship — having written two books I could now sit down and do nothing for the rest of my life.

As it was, I did nothing for two years. After making a book by furiously working for four months, I let my pen lie idle for the other twenty-four. I loathed the thought of writing and wondered if the desire to express myself in authorship would ever return. And in all my life thereafter my work average has been about four months in two years. Between whiles I let my mind lie fallow, dreamed and loafed. It's fine to do nothing at all, and for two years I did it exultantly. That is, as far as the bank would let me. I was drawing my salary and had to earn it. But with the slipping of the town my duties became so light they ceased to weigh on me.

Clear of my work by four o'clock, I would go for a two-hour tramp up the snowy trail along the Klondike. At night, if there was a moon, I might climb to the Midnight Dome. The evenings gave a choice of diversion. There was always the skating rink with bands twice a week, and although the town was on the skids there were still numbers of pretty girls. But on the rink all girls looked charming. Their eyes sparkled, their cheeks glowed and they chattered like magpies.

There were also snowshoe parties when we climbed the spruce-clad hills to the glow of torches. Or straw rides on sleighs, singing to the jingle of bells as we returned to the mess for supper. Bobsleighing was less to my liking. We had a bob that held eight and used to coast from the hill to the river bank. We had spills and bruises and, as we crossed the town, my heart was often in my mouth. If ever we encountered traffic I shuddered to think of the consequences. And one night we did....

Our steersman was a corporal of the Mounties with the reputation of a daredevil. He took us down the hill like a flash and we streaked for the level of the water front. Before us was the main street and the snow bank of the river. At that late hour there should have been no traffic, but suddenly a team emerged from the night. It was pulling a big sleigh loaded with goods for the creeks, and it was right in our path. I tucked my head and closed my eyes. We all did. We were packed so tight it was impossible to extricate ourselves. I thought: Curse bobsleighing. Now what's going to happen?

Nothing did. We heard the shrill whinny of horses and the shouts of the driver. Then we were a hundred yards away, safe on the Yukon, while the freighter was driving on. We stared at each other then looked at our captain. He grinned: "That was a close call. I couldn't take you past the heads of the team so I took you under their bellies. Anyone kicked?" We answered cheerfully in the negative, but agreed to call it a night.

As regards indoor recreation, there was an embarrassment of choice. We had two dances a week and frequent balls. There were also card parties and dinners. At dinners, even in the best-heated circles, one's feet were freezing under the table. Silk socks and patent leather shoes were poor protection against the Arctic cold. Better be snug in bed with a Whodunit yarn.

Yes, it was a glorious time — not much work, lots of fun, money flowing in. I was in the pink of health and incredibly happy. I recited at concerts and helped with dramatic shows. I danced into the small hours. I did everything but curl, drink whisky and play poker. I looked on curling as an old man's game, while hooch and cards meant spending money, and I was determined to save mine. For my precious capital was mounting month by month and freedom glowed before me like a star.

But with summer all that changed. The rush of work absorbed our vitality again and social pleasure almost ceased. Once more I was kept busy in the bank and the best I could do was to take a fishing trip on Sunday. I usually went up the Klondike, and it was on these excursions the idea came to me: "Why don't you write a novel of the gold rush? You have the field to yourself. The most colourful episode in Northern History is there to be put in fiction form. No other writer knows the Yukon as you do. There's your chance. It's really up to you."

I let the idea incubate I my mind, and soon it imposed on me as something I *must* do. It seemed a duty. My book must be an authentic record of the Great Stampede and of the gold delirium on a big canvas. The characters must be types, the treatment a blend of realism and romance. It must be....

Anyway that's how I visioned it as I whipped two-pound greyling from the pools of the Klondike not far from the scene of Carmack's discovery. No doubt it was bumptious of me to conceive myself as a novelist, but I had two successes to my credit and my confidence was unbounded. Although in other fields I was diffident, when it came to roping up a bunch of words and licking them into shape I felt I could hold my own with most. Maybe I couldn't, but I believed I could; and if one thinks one can do a thing, and tries hard enough, one generally can.

So there I was, happy again in the coils of creation and with my Klondike novel crystallizing in my mind. It seemed already as if I had the whole proposition clinched. My book would be the only fictional record of the gold rush. I would document myself like a Zola. I would work on old sourdoughs and get their stories. I would brood over the scenes they described till they were more real in my mind than in theirs. It would be I who suffered their hardships and exulted in their triumphs. Vicariously I would be one of the vintage of ninety-eight. I would re-create a past that otherwise would be lost forever.

Grandiose dreams! Glorious conceit! It's great to believe in oneself. It's half the battle. I leapt to high heaven and came down clutching handfuls of stars. I envied no one on earth. I felt I would shirk no hard work, no sacrifice to attain my end. I, personally, did not matter, only my job. In those days I would have cheerfully given my life to write one immortal book.

So wrapped in delicious dreams the summer passed and once more winter locked us in. Now was the time to tackle the field of fiction. But to my disgust I found I could not settle down to write. I had my stuff in the bag yet I could do nothing with it. My words came with difficulty, my imagination lagged. Something was wrong.

Then I realized that I needed seclusion to brood in. Contact with others threw me off my literary stride. I craved isolation to write easily, and if I could not write easily I could not do so at all.

One day I was brooding over this when the Manager called me to his private room. "What have I done now?" I thought, and felt I did not care very much. But instead of keeping me on the carpet he told me to take the chair.

"I have here," he said impressively, "a telegram from the Inspector. You are appointed relieving Manager at White Horse and are to report immediately. That means you'll have to leave by the first stage. Short notice, but it's promotion and I congratulate you."

My first feeling was pride that I was considered fit to fill a manager's post; my second, dismay that I was unfit. A manager's job! Why, it would worry me to death. I am a meek soul. I cannot give orders to others, though I find it hard to take them. I am incapable of authority. I could not refuse a customer a loan, though I would be afraid to grant him one. I would lie awake nights worrying over my securities. I who dreaded responsibility would have all the care of the branch on my shoulders. It would be perfect hell.... And then again, I did not want to return to White Horse. I always hated an anticlimax. Besides there was my novel. I was all set up to do it and I could only do it right here. It was the thought of my coming book that most weighed with me. Oh, no, it was quite out of the question that I should leave Dawson. Doubtless the Manager thought I was overwhelmed by the prospect. As I sat there speechless, he was giving me time to grasp my good luck.

"Of course," he said deprecatingly, "the appointment may only be temporary, really a sort of Vice Manager." At last I found my tongue. I said slowly: "The 'vice' part would be all right; I don't know about the other."

He stared. "Why don't you appreciate your promotion? I think you are most fortunate."

I said: "Maybe. I know I should jump at the job. There's only one obstacle in the way."

"Obstacle! Why, what could that be?" I thought again of my novel. That seemed to outweigh everything, but I could not tell him so. Then suddenly I heard my voice speaking. I listened to it and to my amazement I heard it saying: "It's just that I'm ... resigning. I'm giving three months' notice that I'm leaving the bank."

There! The monumental decision was taken. I breathed freely again. I went on: "You see, sir, my literary work is having considerable vogue at present. I want to follow it up by writing more books when the going's good."

He gave me a long look. "If it's a fair question, how much are you making?"

"Oh, about five thousand a year from my books and a thousand from the bank. Six in all."

He sort of gasped. "Why, it's more than I'm making myself." Then like magic his manner changed. He dropped the manager stuff and met me as man to man. He was friendly and affable as he went on. "You're probably right. Nothing like striking while the iron's hot. Grasp your opportunities. The trouble is we bankers don't get any. If I were in your place I would certainly take a chance. So instead of congratulating you on your appointment I congratulate you on your judgment in refusing it. Well, I will write the Inspector you have resigned and you can hand me your formal letter to that effect."

So I went back to my cage, but I was a little ashamed. I was not so sure of myself. I composed my letter with a feeling that perhaps I had been premature in my bid for liberty. I am timid and I fear the irrevocable. Perhaps my impulse had been foolish. Well, I was on my own now, pitted against the world. I had burnt my ships and I wondered if I had been wise.... But the next mail reassured me. In it was my bank book and I saw with a heart-bound that my balance ran to five figures. Not very far, but just over the ten thousand mark. Almost unbelievingly I looked at the total. And to think that only a few years ago I had been gnawing a banana peel and trying to kid myself it was a beefsteak. Now I had a stake for life. The interest on this would keep the wolf permanently from the door. And I vowed nothing would pry me loose from my nest-egg.

From that moment I lost interest in money. I told the publishers to place all the royalties to my account, and I never knew to a few thousands what I possessed. Three rivulets were feeding the reservoir of my fortune, but I ignored them. I became as indifferent to filthy lucre as I had formerly been keen. It seemed just a series of bookkeeping entries. It was hard to realize I could turn those symbols into material possessions. Anyway I didn't want material possessions. I wanted freedom — two square meals a day, some rags and a roof.

And that reminded me — I had to seek another home. I found one in a cabin high on the hillside. Behind it was the mountain; below, the valley of the Yukon. The view was inspiring, the isolation all I could have wished. But what attracted me was a pair of moose horns that branched above the door. They seemed a symbol of success, like the Winged Victory.

The cabin was of logs with a porch on which I slung a hammock. There was a sitting room and bedroom, both furnished with monastic simplicity. The sitting room had a small table, two chairs and a stove. I had a drum fitted into the stovepipe, so that the heat was conserved and I could dry clothes inside. The draught in the stove was so good I could light a fire in two minutes, and in ten the sides would be glowing red; then I could choke it off so that it would burn for ten hours. In the bedroom I had only a bed, a double one with good springs. I heated water on the stove for tea, but I took my meals out. I ordered a load of wood, bought an axe and chopped enough for months to come. I hung my photos on the wall, bought blankets, flannelette sheets and some cushions. I had the sitting room painted a pale blue and a double door put on. Everything was snug and shipshape in what was to be my home for two years.

Came the day when I was due to leave the bank. I am afraid I rather sentimentalized the scene. I made my usual entries in the books, told myself I was doing them for the last time. I put away the friendly tools of my trade and looked round the office where I had passed so many peaceful hours. I kept saying: "It is the last time I will ever do this … and this. Goodbye forever." It was characteristic of me that I should try to feel sad and exploit such an occasion. Of course, much of my emotion was phony.

Yet I will always be grateful to the financial institution that took me under its wing and sheltered me so many years. The work had been pleasant, precise and profitable. I had been comfortably looked after and treated with more consideration than ever I had known before. I will always have a kindly feeling toward the bank, and if I had to start over again I might begin in a worse way. If a man has no particular talent, likes an uneventful life, and has domestic ambitions he should appreciate the paternal care of a Temple of Mammon.

I passed my last evening in the mess with the same regret. It had been the scene of many a wild night of souse and song. We were a Rabelaisian gang but we were in tune with the rugged North. The mess was like a club where good fellows got together and the hooch-bird sang. The latch-string was outside the door, the glad glass waiting. Despite the racket I had consummated a book there. Well, I no longer belonged to it and as I left, it was as if a door had closed irrevocably on my past.

FROM "BOOK TEN: THE SPELL OF THE YUKON"

Chapter One

The Athabasca

I took the stage coach from Edmonton to Athabasca Landing. It was a two-day trip, and we stopped overnight at a roadhouse. There was a shiny automobile which claimed to go there and back in the same day. "'Tain't possible," said the driver of the stage, contemptuously squirting a stream of tobacco juice in its direction. "It's all of a hundred miles and that young jerk thinks he can make it was his benzene buggy in four hours. I'd hate to take a chance on it. Machines ain't never agoin' to take the place o'hosses."

I agreed with him. It would have been nice to arrive in Athabasca Landing for lunch instead of two days later, but, "It can't be done," I told the driver.

"Never will be done," he said, cracking his whip. "Oh, I grant you there's some good in machines — sewing machines and harvesters, and the like, but it don't do to expect too much. Horseless carriages ain't practical. Why, someday some crazy mutt will be claiming that they can make us fly in the air like birds. It don't make sense." I agreed it didn't. And later on, I more than agreed; for the car that passed us so proudly was stuck in a mudhole. The chauffeur hailed us and we pulled it out. The springs were broken, so we left it stalled by the side of the road.

There were four other passengers. One was a drummer for drugstore supplies. He was making a first trip to the Landing and figured he was a pioneer. Later, he told me his orders had far exceeded his hopes. He was very friendly, but knocked two of the others. "English snobs," he said. "They think themselves better than everybody else."

"You have to understand them," I said. Could one never get away from these race enmities? Being Scotch I got along with everyone. But the two alleged Englishmen ignored the drugstore man while I tried to be neutral.

The fact that they were going into the North with me made it natural that I should be friendly with them. They were brothers, one a mining engineer, the other a naval officer. They were going into the Coppermine country to prospect, and had an outfit for two years. The Engineer was tall and wiry, serenely confident, resourceful and without fear. He was a leader of men and would have made a splendid soldier. The brother was trim and well set, with a naval appreciation of discipline. A third was travelling with them, a Swedish doctor who was inclined to be melancholy.

★

Athabasca Landing was then a huddle of shacks; but it was booming, and that night at the hotel it was difficult to get a seat for dinner. My neighbour was a grizzled old-timer. When I offered him a cigarette he said: "I ain't got no use for them pimp-sticks." He told me of how he had discovered an old Indian woman on an island in the river, where she had been left to die according to the custom of the tribe. He said: "I made a raft, dumped her on it and started her downstream. I figgered that drownin' was better than starvin' to death."

We could not get beds at the hotel, so a Chinaman who ran a hash joint let us sleep in his back room. It was bare but clean. I spread my blanket on the floor and rolled in it. I cannot say I slept like a top, for the floor was no softer than any other, but I gloried in its very hardness. I was roughing it again, and I felt the exultation that comes from doing things the hard way. I did not even envy my companions snoring in their cosy sleeping bags.

The next day was spent in preparations for our departure. The Landing was abustle with spring activity and the Company was the centre of all movement. I went into the office where two men were standing over a blueprint. It was a plan of the newly conceived townsite.

"There you are," said one, "a chance to make your fortune. There's a corner lot you can have for three hundred dollars. In time it will be worth three thousand." If he had said "thirty thousand" he might have been nearer the mark. At that time I think I had enough money to buy the whole townsite; but I am glad I did not, for then I might have become a multimillionaire, and such a fate I would not wish on any one.

I was introduced to the second of the two, and right there I met the great man of the Mackenzie. Just as Joe Boyle was the King of the Yukon, so Jim Cornwall was Lord of the Athabasca. They were of similar type, stalwart and handsome. With their strong frames and bold features they might have been Roman emperors. They typified all that the word Man implies. Both were pioneers, fearless, confident, dominating. And here I wish to pay tribute to two of the great men of the High North — Klondike Joe and Peace River Jim.

At an early hour the following day we started out. We had two canoes, in one of which were the Brothers, and in the other the Swedish doctor, an Indian guide and myself. Henry the guide was young and husky but inclined to be sullen. He sat in the stern while I sat in the bow and the doctor amidships. We all paddled vigorously; that is, the doctor and I did. Henry seemed to think that his duty lay in steering, though the river was smooth and offered no obstacles. So he sat wafting his paddle wisely in the water, while we dug in like niggers. In paddling there is always a tendency to think the other fellow is not putting as much guts into it as you are. It's so easy to let the blade slip through the water. I've even done it myself.

But sitting in the bow of a canoe slipping down a strange stream is a joy hard to match. Especially if the river has a good current, is narrow and deep, and turns corners every few hundred yards. One looks ahead with expectation, if not with excitement. There was a mother duck with a swarm of ducklings that kept in front of us for miles, squattering and protesting. She had not the sense to draw into the side, but sought safely round the first bend. So presently, when we rounded the corner, there she was protesting our passage as if she owned the river. Only the coming of night relieved the situation.

In a gap in the brushwood we landed for lunch and lit a fire. We had bread, butter, canned salmon and tinned pineapple, copiously washed down with tea. Around three o'clock the Engineer, who had constituted himself leader, gave us each a slab of chocolate. So for ten minutes we drifted, blissfully chewing. I have always been an ardent chocolate eater, but never did I appreciate it as I did then. As reluctantly I resumed my paddle I was muttering: "You damn fool, why are you doing this? You don't have to. You might be lounging in a lobby of a hotel with a cigar and a cocktail, or toying with a tea cup and chattering to an incendiary blonde. These others are going in on business. They hope to make a fortune. But why are *you* doing it? Just because you have a silly notion in your head that you want to do something with a tang of adventure. Bah! you fake pathfinder, you phony explorer, turn back while there is yet time."

But I knew that nothing would have made me turn back, and I was happy in the thought. I was going to accomplish something worthwhile. I was even prepared to risk my life. I was young, strong, active, and I had not enough sense to be scared. A fifty-fifty chance of survival was good enough for me.

We made camp just before nightfall. I put up my little mosquito tent, cut some brush, spread my slicker over it and used my kit bag for a pillow. We had supper of tinned soup, bacon, jam and tea. In the morning we had bacon, tea and marmalade. As these are typical meals I will not repeat our menu.

The night was cold and damp. I shivered under my big blanket and envied the others their sleeping bags. I rose to a misty, miserable morning and took with much distaste to a river steaming in the rising sun. These heavy, overshadowing trees and mud banks were depressing.

At dinner I learned the reason of the lack of geniality on the part of Henry. The scows bearing supplies for the Company's posts had gone downstream a few days before. He should have made one of a hilarious party, but he had been told to wait behind and take me in a canoe. He missed his merry comrades and resented me. I reciprocated his resentment. Through long unuse my canoe muscles were flabby, and putting them to work for nine hours aroused them to painful protest. They were reluctant to resume, but there was no respite for them. The Britannic Brothers surged ahead, and for the honour of Scotland and Sweden we had to keep up.

So I turned my crankiness on Henry who lolled so loftily in the stern. I could understand that a canoe with two paddles a side would need a steersman, but I failed to see how the feeble efforts of a Scotsman and a Swede called for one. Of course he was supposed to be a white-water man, though no boulders mushroomed up to meet us and the only rapids were ripples. I could have taken his job but I had not the nerve to demand it. To my mind he looked on me as a sucker and he was playing me for all he was worth. So I gloomily humped tons of water past me, and cursed myself for letting my poor biceps in for this galley-slave stuff.

Fortunately the river widened and became more interesting. We were in an oil region. The banks showed signs of it. In spots they looked like asphalt. There was a strong odour of oil in the air; it floated like a scum on the water and when we flung down lighted matches the nearby river was covered with a blue flame.

Toward evening we heard a roaring in the distance. It grew louder and soon we came on the cause of it. Rising about twenty feet into the air was a flaming jet of natural gas. It had been vigorous and vocal for twenty-five years, and I am told it is roaring and blazing to this day.

I was mighty glad that evening when our leader decided to make camp. It was fairly late and our crew was disgruntled. The doctor was paddle-peevish, Henry vicious. He expressed his irritation by suddenly starting to paddle. And how! Our puny efforts were put to shame. With every stroke he seemed to lift the canoe out of the water. His paddle bent almost to breaking and the river surged and swirled around it. His example gave us guts, so that we swept ahead of the other canoe with shouts of derision. The Brothers rallied to the challenge but it was of no avail. They could not catch up, and soon we heard them shouting to call it a day.

It was with joy I rigged up my one-man tent. I must have done this a hundred times during the trip and I never failed to get a kick out of it. It was so quickly and easily done. The tent consisted of an oblong sheet of canvas with a rope dividing it, and cords at each corner. You attached one end of the rope to a tree and the other end to another tree and pulled it tight. You attached the cords to shrubs or roots, also, pulling them tight. Your canvas made a roof, sloping on each side of the central rope, and from the interior dropped mosquito netting forming a space about seven feet by four. It could be set up in a minute; then rains might drum and mosquitoes hum, but you were dry and immune.

Sometimes I would cut boughs and spread my waterproof dunnage bag and my slicker over them. Then wrapped in my seven-point blanket, with my shirts for a pillow, I was so happy I did not envy the others their snug sleeping bags.

On the afternoon of the third day we caught up with the fleet of the Company. A dozen barges were strung along the bank as if supper was in preparation. We were allotted one of them and the canoes were lifted on board. As I joyfully relinquished my paddle, I marked for the first time a grin on the face of Henry. He said: "You heap good canoe man. You work very good. Next time I let you take him steer." We parted friends, but as I ruefully massaged my aching muscles, I resolved there would be no next time.

A dozen passengers were distributed over the barges and they received us with that patronizing friendliness old voyagers reserve for new. We installed ourselves in the hold of our vessel that was loaded with flour, then going ashore we erected our tents. The captain of the flotilla, a chunky Dane, had selected a camp site on a grassy bank and the scene was cheerful. A cook was preparing mulligan stew, tables and benches had been set up, and the various passengers were whiling away the time until the bell rang for supper.

I made myself acquainted. There was an Indian Agent and his assistant, the first Canadian, the other English. Already their two wives were at loggerheads, yet they were going to pass three years together. I foresaw heaps of trouble.

It was jolly, however, to sit down to a decent meal again. We had soup, fried hash, beans, hot biscuits, pie and coffee. The rest of the evening was passed in lively conversation, but quite early the camp was asleep. The Indians curled in the holds of the barges, while I was happy and snug in my tiny tent.

I felt still happier next morning when we embarked after a ham and egg breakfast. I had nothing to do now but make myself comfy and behold the banks go by. Also, I was able to enjoy my laziness the more by watching the work of others. For the barge was propelled by Indians with huge oars. There were four on each side and the scullers had arranged little runways of flour sacks up which they ran then fell back letting their weight be the power behind the stroke. Like machines they worked together, with grunts when it came to the pull-back. They saved themselves all possible strain; but for eight hours a day they kept it up, three steps forward, three back.

I watched the banks of the widening river. I read, I dozed. It was pleasant but boring. I looked forward to meals and felt I was putting on flesh. I enjoyed the picturesque scene, the string of barges, the timing oars, the steersman in the stern with his long sweep. The Indians depended on this trip. They made enough out of it to keep them in grub for the rest of the year. Though they worked hard they seemed to enjoy it, and their camps at night were songful. The sailing of the Hudson's Bay fleet was a gala occasion from which they took some sobering up.

There was nothing to mar the pleasant monotony, except when it rained and we had to cower under tarpaulins. We crawled ashore for a meal below a stretched awning, then slunk back to our shelter in the hold of our barge. It was hot under cover and the mosquitoes were pestiferous. I regretted my little tent.

The only exciting spot on the trip was the descent of a series of rapids. The Engineer suggested we get out a canoe and run them. It was a needless bit of bravado, but I felt I must take part. So I sat in the bow as we tackled the tossing river. I loosened the laces of my high boots and when we reached the danger point I prudently slipped them off. The Engineer gave me a contemptuous look, but he happened to be wearing moccasins. I saw he had no confidence in me. He warned me to sit still and leave everything to him; but when a big boulder suddenly shot up I poked it out of the way. We slewed sideways, half turned over, and it looked nasty. However, a canoe takes a lot of upsetting, and before I had time to be scared we were in smooth water. Behind us was a swirling, tossing welter of white foam and brown boulders. But if we got through triumphantly others were not so fortunate. One of the barges ran on a rock and had to be hauled off. The steersman said he was so distracted by our adventure he could not concentrate on his own job. The accident was blamed on our canoe and from then on we were forbidden to do these silly stunts.

Fort MacMurray was a bustle of spring activity. We were welcomed with enthusiasm, bringing news and booze. The little settlement was hectic, and the whisky-starved population was making up for lost time. The scene was like a fiesta, for it was the end of months of cold and deprivation and the opening of a season of sunshine and plenty. It was hard to realize what our arrival meant to those few whites, half-breeds and Indians; that it was their only contact during a whole year with the outside world.

Canoe, scow, steamer — that is a pretty progression toward comfort, and I was able to appreciate my stateroom in the boat that was to take me on the next stage of my journey. I lost no time in installing myself. True, the cabin was misty with mosquitoes but my curtains were snug, and from behind them I watched the angry swarm that craved my blood. I enjoyed their efforts to get at me, while their ferocious hum was music in my ears.

I donned moccasins and slacks and prepared for a spell of delicious laziness. In the week that followed I lolled the deck, watching the Indians unload the scows. I enjoyed seeing them work because my own efforts were confined to filling and smoking my pipe. Spitting in the river I laughed to think that I had done with the battle of life. I had gone so low there was no lower, and I had fought my way up. Still in my youth I need never do another tap of work. I need never think of money, because for every dollar I spent I made two. It seemed fantastic — rags to riches. A knack of romping rhyme had brought me fortune.

So smoking my pipe I watched the Indians load the boat. They were carrying sacks of flour aboard. They had slings and headbands. Four sacks was the accepted load, but as I watched, one of them told the chargers to put on an extra sack. Then waving to me he climbed from the hold of the barge to the deck of the ship. He was a small man and no doubt was packing twice his own weight. But these fellows were woodmen. They had not the puny legs of the canoe Indians.

At last we were loaded and ready to start. As we edged into the stream I was not sorry. I looked forward to my coming adventure. I found that my design to go to Dawson gave me a certain glamour; but the Indian Agent, an ex-parson, took a gloomy view. He said: "You're not going alone?"

"I hope so," I said airily. "I'll need guides to cross the divide, but once I get to the Yukon watershed it should be plain sailing."

He shook his head solemnly. "Young man, you're going to your *doom*."

It wasn't very tactful of him, was it?

Chapter Two

The Mackenzie River

It took us a week to switch cargo and start on our trip down river. Before we left I saw the Indians begin their long track back to the Landing. They took the barges in stages upstream, one at a time with about a hundred men on the hauling line. Attached to the big rope were looped tump-lines, and each man threw himself eagerly into his harness. As they strained and tugged they shouted and cheered. It was a Volga boatman scene, only these fellows seemed to enjoy their effort. They were barefooted, the banks were steep and wooded, the going hard; but they had been doing it for years and at the end was home and rest until another spring.

Our way down river was so leisurely it seemed casual. We stopped at small trading posts and were welcomed with pathetic joy as we left supplies for another year. The white men were like children, innocent of the outer world and unused to company. Many had a strained, furtive look. Their avidity to greet us and their sadness to see us go told of lonely lives in a hostile setting. When the steamer returned it would pick up their season's pack, leaving them prisoned again for many midnight months. Such a life would have driven me mad. Perhaps it did them, a little.

Always amphibian I never could see water but what I wanted to wrap a packet of it around me. So the swift swirling river tempted me till someone said: "Don't. Only last month a priest was caught in the undertow and never seen again." Being pig-headed I laughed and dived boldly. At once I was gripped by an angry current and swept downstream. I struggled frantically, feeling childishly helpless. I thought I was done for, but by a desperate effort I edged inshore about a mile further down.

Hanging onto a sweeper that whipped the water I was so happy I recked little of my plight. Yet it was a sorry one, naked in that mosquito-misty bush. All the way back to camp they attacked me in swarms and I beat them off with branches. As I arrived exhausted I wondered: "Inscrutable Providence! Why should a poor priest perish and a sinner like myself be saved?"

It was nice to be on the boat churning down the muddy current. It was restful and easygoing. More or less the passengers were interesting. Indeed most people are if you probe them a little. I tried a bit of Somerset Maugham technique on them, turning them into stories I was too lazy to write.

For instance, the Government had an idea the Indians might be made to farm, and to teach them were sending in two agents and an ox. The head agent had been a preacher; his assistant was a war veteran. Already the two disliked each other, while their respective wives were spitting fire. Behold a setting for a tragic story of Arctic antagonisms.

Also antagonistic were the Churchmen. We had on board two priests and two Episcopalian missionaries. Each couple regarded the other with studied politeness and on Sunday held separate services at opposite ends of the boat. When I told these people the intention of my journey they seemed rather appalled. One of the priests, an ideal shepherd of the Wild with a long silvery beard, warned me almost with emotion: "Whatever you do, don't go alone. To travel by oneself in the Arctic is to court death. I know, because I've lived here all my life. A single slip and you are lost." I took his words jauntily. Up to now my plans had been vague. I had thought to get guides for the worst of the way, but to drift down rivers by myself. There was no credit in doing the trip with a party, and to be alone was fascinatingly foolhardy. I was airily confident, eager enough to be a fool.

★

At Smith's Landing our boat trip came to an end. A series of rapids made the river impossible to navigate, so the cargo had to be carried over a twenty-mile portage to Fort Smith, where we took another steamer. These Hudson's Bay posts are pretty much alike, built of logs on a high bluff overlooking the river. They form three sides of a square, with small and frequent windows so that they can be defended from Indian attack. Not that there was much risk, as the natives in these part are hardly of the fighting kind. However, when we reached Fort Simpson we found it in a ferment of excitement.

On the way up we had been hearing rumours of hostility and possible insurrection. It was really rather absurd, but the wives of the two agents took it seriously. In fact, they talked of returning in the boat. I don't think they were scared of the red men; it was probably funk in the face of a winter of exile. And the reason for all the trouble was that placid and comfortable beast, our ox OSCAR.

Now Oscar and I were particular pals, and with my preferences for animals over humans I would often ride in his barge and keep him company. He seemed to appreciate my society, gazing at me with his big, calm eyes. I caressed, groomed and fed him, loving his bovine odour. So when we beached at Fort Simpson and Oscar was landed, it was I who led him ashore. Then I had a bright idea — let me mount on his back and ride him into the village in triumph. What a sight for the poor Indians! Almost like a circus. They should receive me with acclamation.

But I was sadly deceived. Instead of with rejoicing I was met by sour silence. In grim groups the Indians gathered, gazing at me with frowning faces. In nasty knots they scowled and gloomed. Their hostility was so marked I abandoned Oscar, but even then I could see I was regarded with rancour. As I approached one of the groups and hailed them in Chinook every man turned his back on me.

"Perhaps it's the way I'm dressed," I muttered; for I was wearing high boots, a khaki costume and a cowboy hat. "Maybe they take me for one of the Mounted Police. Evidently they have bad consciences and don't care for the Mounties...." But, no, they seemed friendly enough with a trooper who accosted them, though it might have been the spell of his scarlet tunic. Me they regarded as an enemy.... Why?

Then I found out. It seemed they considered me a minion of the Government that was going to make them slaves of the soil. Oscar was a symbol of agricultural serfdom. True, he might be brother to the wood bison that roamed their solitudes, but they, like the bison, were wild and free. And they were going to remain that way. The white man wanted to seize their lands and make farmers of them. He would trap them like wood bison and turn them into Oscars.... No, they did not want to be civilized. They were warriors, slayers of the bear and the wolf. No truck gardens and Oscars for them.

And the traders supported them, maybe egged them on. They did not want the Indians other than procurers of fur. They wanted to buy skins from them, not grain. It was their game to keep the native wild and free. This Government bug that the North might be made to yield harvests and the red man harnessed to the plough was all hooey. The North was a wilderness, hopeless, barren. It would never be any good except to shelter the savage and the brute. And behold, I was the fall guy who bore the brunt of Indian animosity. They identified *me* with the attempt to enslave them. It was all so silly; yet they were like children, and all the time I was at Simpson I gave them a wide berth. Even as I roamed the woods I had a feeling of being stalked. It got so that I finally gave up the land and took to the water.

This was partly because I became the possessor of the finest birch-bark canoe in the North. I bought it at Great Slave Lake from an old Indian who was considered the best canoe-maker of his tribe. He judged it his masterpiece and truly it was like a flame upon the water. A gaudy patchwork of purple, scarlet, primrose and silver, it danced on the ripple as lightly as a leaf. The old man sighed as he parted with it. He had gone far to select the bark. He had sewn it with wood fibre and lashed it with willow wands. There was not a nut nor a nail anywhere. It had taken him a year to fashion, and now he looked at it with the sadness of an artist who sees his finest work being sold. With reluctance he took the twenty-five dollars I offered him.

So now, far from the sullen Indians who wanted to pot me in the back, I darted up and down the river in my fairy canoe. It was as nervous as a thoroughbred, but I soon mastered it, swaying to its rhythm and feeling as if it were part of me. I was confident that nothing could upset me, and nothing ever did. Even in the most riotous rapids it rode exultantly. I christened it *Coquette*, and to the admiration of at least myself I demonstrated its qualities.

There was another, however, who shared my enthusiasm. He was an amateur explorer who aimed to become a real one. He had made some minor expeditions, but now he proposed to cross from the Mackenzie to Hudson Bay. He had only a vague idea of the route and was depending on the Eskimos to help him. He would winter in the interior, taking two years to cross the continent. I do not think his purpose was scientific. Rather, he was pushed by the idea of exalting himself in his own eyes, if not in those of the public. He was young, rich, handsome, eager to make a bid for fame. He had a big canoe with supplies for a year, and a guide who was both water-wise and wood-wise. He was sure of success as he told me his plans, but somehow I felt he was not the man for the part.

One day he invited me to lunch in his cabin, and we were smoking afterward when a silky field mouse ran across the floor. "Let's play football with it," he cried, and with his moccasined feet began to kick it around the room. "Let the poor thing go," I said; at which he was surprised, for I think he was insensitive to animal suffering. I had also been told he was inconsiderate to the natives and had accepted presents from the Eskimos without giving anything in return.

I remember the morning he started out. The day was sunny and serene, and the canoe was deep in the water. The explorer looked glum and subdued. I think he was scared at the thought of the job he had undertaken. I accompanied them a little way in *Coquette*, and as I waved a final farewell I felt a sudden sympathy for him. Sadly I watched his canoe dwindle to a speck in the distance. There! he was off on a two-thousand-mile trip into the unknown. For two years that was the last I heard of him. Then news filtered out that two white men had been murdered by natives. It was said the explorer had kicked an Eskimo who had promptly spitted him with a spear. I remembered the mouse and was not surprised. There was something arrogant and tactless in him. It was a pity, though; for the tribe also slew his companion who was one of the best guides in the North.

At last we left Fort Simpson and embarked on the mighty Mackenzie. I am not going into details of our trip, but I enjoyed every moment of it. Nothing is more delightful than a river voyage, for it is easy, intimate, varied and safe. We visited a score of Forts and met many Factors who hailed from the Hebrides. Highlandmen make the best officers of the Company, because they are hardy, used to loneliness and good traders. It is a saturnine life that takes men of determined sanity to endure it. These Hudson's Bay posts were of a mine for the storyteller, but the grim men who manned them had no sense of the romance of destiny.

Fascinating books have been written on this trip. I made copious notes intending to add another volume to the list, but other events crowded on me and I never got round to it.

Imaginative work ousted mere reportage of the Wild. However, isolated incidents stand out. I remember landing in the grey dawn, where three men were huddled over a tiny fire, eating breakfast of fried bacon. One was an old Scotch guide who was reckoned tough even in a land where most are inured to hardship. The second was a tall Englishman with a monocle. Straight and slim he stood, sipping his coffee that steamed in the eager air. He spoke with a soft voice and a nonchalant drawl. "Just come out of the Barren Lands," he said casually. "Went in after musk ox.... No, didn't bag a single head. The other chaps had all the luck.... But I'm going in again and hope to do better."

I marvelled a little. Here was a man of high society, son of an earl, who preferred to rough it in the wilds. He was blue-eyed and blond, with the look of a viking. He said he liked the life and had no desire to return to England. I had suspected the explorer of swank but this man was innocent of it. No fear of him boring you at the club or writing a book about his exploits.

The third party was a thin little man with a wiry beard. He was called Hornby and was a relative of the famous Lancashire cricketer. He had spent many winters in the shadow of the Pole and was an authority on the Coppermine country. Several years later he went in with two lads and all three perished in the wilderness. One of the boys left a diary which is a most poignant human document. It is published in the Penguin Library under the title of *Unflinching*.

One day an Indian came to the Post to tell us that a cabin belonging to two trappers had been closed for a month or more. The men had not been seen, but an evil odour was coming from it. An investigation seemed advisable, so we set out in two canoes. There was a captain of the Mounties, a sergeant, two troopers and several others. We saw the cabin from far off, situated on a high bluff. In its very stillness there was something sinister. As we approached we were met by an appalling stench. It seemed to grip us by the throat. I gagged and shuddered, for the odour was of decaying human flesh.

The door was bolted, but the sergeant and a trooper picked up a log and charged it. At the third assault it caved in. Immediately a black cloud like smoke poured forth. But it was a seething cloud composed of thousands of big blue-bottled flies. There in the gaudy sunshine they trumpeted their freedom. There was something obscene about them, they were so bloated and greasy. We watched them pour forth and spread into the clean, sweet air. Only when the cloud thinned did we advance. Then half-suffocated by the stench I peeped into the cabin.

Everything was tidy, even clean, but in the gloom at the rear I saw a sight that made my flesh creep. On two bunks, one over the other, two men were lying. Yet it was hard to tell they were human beings, for heaping over them were hills of greasy husks that had once been the homes of maggots. All that was visible of them were their hands and faces. They had skeleton hands, dimly seen through parchment-like skin. Their faces were skulls covered with the same oily integument. Beneath the caved-in mask that had been their faces countless maggots could be seen crawling and feeding.

In the case of one man the skull had been smashed in, and jagged bone showed brain cavities cleaned by the crawling worm. The grinning skulls were pillowed in cushions of rank hair of a foul ashen colour. The hair had continued to grow after their death till it was now a foot long. Their beards, too, had grown till, like some vile fungus, their chests were matted with horrible hair. Then looking closer I saw that this hair was in constant movement, agitated like the long grass of a prairie. I could not understand this undulation till I saw it was caused by legions of lice moving in endless activity round the hair roots. There in that jungle of rancid hair, armies of lice were fighting, feasting, breeding in an obscene world of their own.

On the floor lay a rifle and in it one discharged shell. An empty vial of carbolic acid lay near. Evidently the top man had been killed by the cartridge, his skull having been shattered at close range. The lower man clutched his guts as if in agony. Near the bunk was a small notebook with a glazed cover. It was partly an account book, partly an irregular diary. There were entries regarding pelts and their prices, also stores and their costs. But its main interest was the human one. There was evidence of early dissension between the writer and his partner, developing into hate and finally into murderous resolution. Here to the best of my memory is the gist of the diary:

> Spud gets more peevish every day. Seems I've picked a punk for a partner. We're just beginning the winter. If I could quit I would.

Again:

> We are snapping at one another like crazy curs. Nothing seems to please Spud. He's trying to pick a row with me but I won't give him a chance. Wish this winter was over.

Later:

> Spud gets more and more cranky. I believe he hates me. I think he would like to kill me. I must watch out for him.

A week later:

We are no more on speaking terms. Today he walked round the table rather than ask me to pass the sugar. He makes me afraid, staring at me with his big, glassy eyes.

Again:

I'm afraid Spud is going mad. I'm feared for my life. I can't sleep nights thinking he'll knife me in the dark. We each cook our own meals now.

Then an entry in a nervous, shaky hand:

We had a bloody fight. He got hold of this diary and tried to read it. We wrestled for it. I got it back but we had a hellish scrap. Now he wants a chance to kill me. Well, I must get him first.

Then:

Have decided to kill Spud. Will blow out his brains with my rifle.

At last entry, almost indecipherable:

Have killed poor Spud. He was sleeping and would never know. Now I must kill myself. Curse this cruel land! It drives us crazy. God forgive me. Goodbye, folks....

"It's the old story," said the sergeant. "One of them guys goes nuts, croaks his partner then does himself in. It's tough on us, though. We've got to bury the bastards."

We were nearing the mouth of the muddy Mackenzie. I was not sorry. The river had grown so wide that from one bank the other was dim on the horizon. The shores were clay, rising to levels of tundra with low hills in the far distance. A ghastly, God-forsaken land. Our company had grown small and we were inclined to bore one another. Nevertheless the trip had been enjoyable and comes back to me in vivid memories. For instance:

The Grand Falls of the Athabasca when I caught a queer fish in the pool below the cascade, I don't know what it was but "it didn't taste so good." Also as I fished I saw a scow coming over the falls. It tilted so I thought it was going to somersault. I sure hand it out to that pilot....

The long wait at Fort Smith, where, regardless of superstition, the Engineer shot a pelican. He also painted his canoe scarlet. It was so pretty in its gingerbread gloss, but he had to have it a tomato colour.

Posts where we lingered for days in leisured unloading, after a preliminary night of poker and booze. We were so welcome it was hard to refuse to celebrate. Many of the Factors were a little queer, for it was not easy to live that life and remain normal. Only a routine of order and discipline saved them. Once they lost their grip they were done....

The feeling of the vast valley of the Mackenzie and of the few men who roamed and ruled it. There was only a score of them yet they were as well-known as if they lived in a village. Stefansson was the uncrowned king of the Arctic, but the others were fearless, hardy, tried and true. Nearly all met tragic deaths.

The Mackenzie was more murderous than the Yukon. Its law was harder, its tribute higher. It killed most of those I knew.

Fort Macpherson stood on a high bluff overlooking the junction of the Mackenzie and the Peel. It was just like other Posts, only more important. The Factor was an old man called John North who had spent his life in the service of the Company. He was a rare character with a pretty perception of writing. I say this because he had read some of my books.... Egregious vanity of an author! In any case his patriarchal white beard suggested sagacity, and, judging by the manly half-breeds in sight, fecundity. He sold me sacks of flour and sides of bacon and gave me good advice. It was mostly: "Don't. Don't go on. Go back the way you came, like a good little boy."

Another pessimist was the officer of the Mounties. "Don't you do it," he said. "Just think of the Lost Patrol." I did think of it and was impressed. Every winter a police force of three made the cross-country trip to the Yukon and back. It was a notable achievement, calling for skill and stamina. But the last party had failed to reach Dawson and an expedition had been sent in search of them.

"A chain is only as strong as its weakest link," said the sergeant, leaving me to infer that one of the party had fallen sick and let the others down. I think he expected me to reconstruct the tragedy in verse; but I never like to write about realities, so the Ballad of the Lost Patrol was left unperpetrated.

On the flat near the river a tribe of Eskimos were camped, and I set up my tent among them. They were semi-civilized, for they had gramophones that played hymns and they punished their children. I saw one urchin being chastised. The mother held his hand as with a strip of whalebone she pounded his palm. It reminded me of my own boyhood, but I never howled so lustily as that kid.

Despite the heat the tribe wore their costumes of caribou skin and their odour was penetrating. As a Swede trapper put it: "I don't like the huskies. The men get mad at you if you won't sleep with their wives, and the damn women stink so there's no fun in it. A man doesn't mind lending you his wife so long as it's casual. Only when it gets sentimental he sharpens his spear. After all, what does a little copulation more or less matter?"

I became friendly with the Chief, who was an artist, and squatted in his tent where we looked at one another, trying not to feel fools. If he had been educated we could have sat on the terrace of the Café du Dôme and talked art. Humorously we sketched each other. Then he gave me a fish hook of walrus ivory, and I gave him my safety razor. I reckoned if I was going to blaze a trail to the Yukon I would be more in character with a beard.

As time went on I worried more and more about my coming trip. In a few days the steamer would start south, severing my last link with civilization. It would be so easy to step on board again and take the easy way out. Every one urged me to, but I thought: If you do it you'll never respect yourself again. As a trailblazer you'll be a chunk of cheese. So with a sense of destiny I watched the boat pull out. I bade farewell to friends who looked at me with mournful eyes, as if they never expected to see me again. Well, that was that. I was doomed to get out the hard way or spend the winter in the Arctic.

In these disconsolate days my canoe was small comfort to me. There it lay on the mud, a streak of primrose and crimson. Beside it lay a kayak of one-man size. It belonged to the son of the chief and he sadly wanted to swap it for *Coquette*. We would dart about on the river, he in the canoe, I in the kayak. I was tempted to take his offer, for it would have been unique to cross the Rockies with such a craft. But it was tippy and could not have held enough grub for the trip.

So there I was, stranded on the beach with no hope of getting away. My first idea had been to get Indians to go with me as far as the Divide and from there shove off on my own. It would be all downstream, on rivers easy to navigate. That I would be alone pleased me mightily. That there was considerable possibility of me perishing did not occur to me. But I found the Indians would not carry my canoe to headwaters. The distance was over a hundred miles and the trail almost impassable. It was doubtful if the frail craft could stand the trip. Though I offered to pay them their winter's rations they steadfastly refused. Thus I learned that in the North money could not buy everything.

What to do? Everyone discouraged me, and it seemed I was up a blind alley. I was planning to spend the next nine months in the Arctic when an unbelievable bit of luck happened to me.

Chapter Three

The Rat River

One day while loafing on the beach with my friends the Eskimos I saw a scow come up the river. Two men were sculling while a woman squatted in the stern. As they drew near I went to meet them. One man was big, with a fiery beard and a bold belly. The other was small, with a grey bristle. A poke bonnet and Mother Hubbard could not conceal the woman's comeliness.

"I'm Captain McTosh," said the big man, "of the gallant craft *Ophelia*, en route for Dawson."

"Not in that thing," I gasped.

"Don't disparage *Ophelia*. She's going to be the first scow to cross the Rockies. How would you like to sign on as her crew?"

"Okay with me," I said; so there and then it was arranged I was to share the effort and the expense. Hurrah! I thought; soon

I will be back in my little cabin, my troubles over. Little did I dream they were about to begin.

I quickly got to know them. The mate of the *Ophelia* was the rat-grey little man. His name was Jake Skilly. "I'm a trapper," he told me. "Mac's a lousy trader. You can tell it by his guts."

"Now, Jake," said the Lady who was Mrs. McTosh, "don't be mean. Ever since we left you've done nothing but grizzle."

"I'm not sayin' a word agin you, ma'am. You're the finest little woman in the Arctic."

"Considering I'm the only one. You know, I came north on our honeymoon," she told me. "I thought it would be romantic, but I don't know.... McTosh, being Scotch, took a honeymoon trip by himself before he married me. He went right round the world, gave himself a grand time. But wait till I get Outside. Won't I make things sparkle."

I guessed she would, too. She was a lively one, as pretty as was peppy. With resignation and a copy of Shakespeare she had followed her red-haired Romeo into the wilderness. "I can quote the bard by the yard," she said. "We read him through the Long Night. We decided to take one book and concentrate on it. Well, I'm going out to make up for a lot of loneliness."

She certainly deserved a good time. I could see them cooped in their cabin through the weary winter, reading William by the light of a seal-oil lamp. A tough part for a woman to play, but she was made of rare stuff.

"McTosh is a free trader," she said, "and hates the Company. He won't visit the Post on the hill, and nothing would make him set foot on their steamer. Hence *Ophelia*."

Jake was a wiry, wizened man with a perpetual grouch. He, too, hated the Company, and for no price would he sell them a pelt. He was one of half a dozen white men who thought nothing of going off alone into the winter wild, of building an ice house in the blizzard, of living on raw fish so rotten he poked a hole in the skin and sucked out the substance. He boasted that he and Stefansson were the only two who could live off the land. He had traplines on the Mackenzie Delta and his pack of white fox ran into hundreds of skins.

These were to be my companions for many days, and as I set out with them my heart was gay. The Eskimos crowded down to see us off. I had Jake with me in the canoe, while in the scow were the trader and his wife, with the two Indians to help. At last I was on my way, and this time it was going to be the real thing.

Paddling up the Peel River was serenely monotonous. Mud banks mounted to stark grey tundra as the stream wound wearily through desolation. Yet toward evening we came on a glittering pool. I got out my line and the spoon had hardly touched the water when it was seized by a huge fish. In a few minutes the canoe was alive with scaly monsters. Pulling them in became so tedious we went ashore and made a meal. They had little flavour; their flesh was soft and I left most of my catch on the bank. They were what were known as "coneys." That is the only place I ever saw them.

Toward evening we came to the mouth of the Rat River and there made camp. As it was one of many similar camps I had better describe it. While we put up the tents the Lady prepared supper. Jake built the fire, whittling a bit of dry driftwood then nursing the tiny flame into a blaze by adding chips of increasing size. After which he would fetch the water and set the kettle to boil. Meantime the Lady had opened the flour sack and poured into it a small pan of water in which some yeast cakes had been dissolved. She let the water be absorbed by the flour, mixing it into a paste which she moulded into bannocks. These she fried in bacon fat, at the same time cooking two strips of bacon for each of us. Then she brewed the tea and told us supper was served.

This was our usual meal, sometimes augmented by blueberries which she stewed slightly and sprinkled sparingly with sugar. We had neither beans, rice nor canned food of any kind. So for over six weeks I lived on bannocks, bacon, blueberries and *bohea* and never worked harder nor felt better.

I always loved to put up my tiny tent. At Fort Resolution I had swapped my big blanket for a rabbit's foot robe. This was made of skin taken from the legs of rabbits and woven into a loose texture. It was thick, fluffy and very light, an ideal covering for the country. Many a night I blessed it. Snuggled in it, with beneath me my slicker and waterproof dunnage bag I was so cosy I laughed for sheer joy.

After breakfast, a repetition of supper, we started up the Rat River. At the mouth it was hardly fifty feet wide. Willows overhung the water and the air was heavy. Mists of mosquitoes rose to meet us but we were prepared. Over our hats we wore nets that fell to the shoulder, while our gloves were of the gauntlet type. Thus equipped, though they buzzed round us in clouds, we could laugh at them. The mosquito is the scourge of the region. Even when eating it was necessary to wear a net. At Fort Norman I once walked in the woods with the Engineer. He was a few paces in front when I said: "I didn't notice you wearing a grey jumper." "It's bright blue," he laughed. And in truth he was so sheathed with a film of mosquitoes you would have sworn his back was grey. But here on the Rat River they attained their greatest density. To show a bit of bare flesh was to be set on ferociously. No citronella lotions deterred them. We drank our tea under our veils and the dregs in our cups often consisted of drowned insects.

The lower reaches of the Rat were a series of deep pools and long stretches of still water. All of the first day the canoe leapt eagerly forward , but toward evening there were signs of change. As the river rose to hilly land the water became sprightly. It danced and sparkled, it was merry and mocking. By these tokens we knew our days of placid paddling were over. And sure enough next morning we ran into rough stuff. After buffeting it a bit we were obliged to give up and load *Coquette* on the scow. From then on we had to fight every inch of the way.

And now a word as to my canoe comrade. He was a cigarette fiend of the most desperate brand. He smoked all through meals, and if I awoke at night I would see a tiny glow coming from his tent, so that I imagined he smoked in his sleep. As we paddled upstream he would ask me to hang onto a branch while he rolled a fresh cigarette. This happened very fifteen minutes. He made his cigarette from plug tobacco, cut with his jackknife, rolling it in a half-page of an old magazine. With avidity he inhaled the strong smoke deep into his lungs. If he went ten minutes without a "coffin nail" a wild look came into his eyes and he trembled violently. It was as if his nervous system depended on tobacco.

He had a cadaverous face that made me think of a wolf. But he was a fine type of the Arctic adventurer. What stories he could tell! … Of winters when he relied for food on fish caught through a hole in the ice; of months of darkness and silence when he was forced to eat his dog; of days spent in an ice house in the heart of a blizzard.… What yarns the man could spin of starvation, cold, loneliness. He told them simply, casually and without self-pity.

The only time he showed bitterness was when he spoke of his father. The old man had been a disciplinarian, and when Jake told of his juvenile pants being warmed his face was convulsed with wrath. All the hardships of his life left him unmoved, but these boyish beltings were something he could never forget. Now his dad had died leaving him two thousand dollars, and he was going out to claim it; but what he would have liked more would have been to lambast the old man's hide for the drubbings he had received.

There were six of us on the scow and the water was mean. It showed white teeth, resenting our invasion. *Ophelia* weighed half a ton, so it was going to be a tough job to take her up in this angry flood. At first we poled hopefully, making good progress. Then the bushy banks gave way to gravel bars and the water grew shallow. Even with four poles we found it difficult to advance. Ruefully it was decided to begin what must be our chief means of navigation — tracking.

Then it was I began to realize what I had let myself in for. We were to haul this hulk up to the Divide and over to the other side. It was grotesque, incredible. I had imagined I would use my canoe for most of the trip, and here I was roped in to do a job that would have made a Volga boatman look like a slacker. But it was too late to draw back, so I thought of my old maxim: "If you have to do a thing you hate like hell to do, do it for all you're damn well worth."

With apprehension I watched McTosh uncoil a hundred feet of rope from *Ophelia's* hold and line it along the bank. With distaste I saw him attach smaller ropes with rolled sacks to fit one's shoulders. With dismay I saw him indicate a particular harness and ask me if it were to my liking. If you had demanded of a galley slave if his oar was to his fancy he would have replied with more enthusiasm.

And henceforth my role was to be that of a yoke-ox and a beaver, with the working capacity of both. Why did I not take that boat out? For in all my life I never worked so hard as I did in the next few weeks. As I tugged, strained, plunged knee-deep in water, panted and lunged forward in my sling of sacking, I muttered: "What a bloody fool you are! Why do you do those things? And you are *paying* for the privilege." Well, I suppose it was for the good of my soul, and if I had not done it I would not have been able to write about it today.

Fortunately the water was tepid, and as long as the stream was not waist-high it was a pleasure to wade. I cut off my trousers at the knee and slit my boots at the ankle, so that the water could gush in and out. I tried wearing moccasins, but they slipped on the smooth boulders and were worn out in two days. My high boots with nailed soles were just the thing. They gripped the rock so that I was able to put my guts into the pull. And I did. I determined that none of the others would put it over on me. In my effort to play the game maybe I exaggerated, but I do not think I ever let myself down.

It was a great life, twelve hours a day on a tow line and most of the time in the water. For one thing it cured me of corns that had bothered me for years. One day I took off my boots and stared at feet so immaculate I was lost in admiration. And since then they have remained so innocent of bunions and other blemishes. If only the rest of my carcass was as worthy of approbation as my feet I might hope to be a movie star.

Twelve hours a day on the track line! … True, we had spells off every three hours, when we would throw ourselves exhausted on a gravel bar, make a fire and have some grub. We needed it. While the Lady fried her bannock, the water drooled from our mouths. As I watched her cook I kept swallowing my saliva and wishing there was twice as much grub. But in that case I could not have thrown myself into the water and heaved like a Volga boatman. These Russians must have been foxing, I thought. At least they could sing. For us there was no thought of vocalism. We hoarded our breath for angry water.

★

I don't like the phrase "borrowed time." Do we not all live on it, more or less? Who has not had half a dozen close calls? We brush shoulders with death every day and do not know it. It takes a narrow shave to make us realize how precarious is existence. On the Rat River I had one of these. We had sculled up a deep pool between two canyon walls, with a rock jutting at its upper end. Beyond was a run of white water. It was waist-deep and the bottom was paved with round boulders. Jake was poling *Ophelia*, keeping her head to the current. Four of us were on the track line, bent low, our chests breasting the current. It was the toughest pull we had ever had. With muscles taut we inched the scow upstream, fighting every step. Often we would be motionless, just holding our own.

I was bent almost double in the foam, when suddenly I was jerked off my feet. Between me and the sky was a wall of water. I was being dragged downstream, my back bumping over the boulders. I was utterly helpless, with over me a slab of seething foam like a coffin lid. Goodbye, world, I thought.... Would the bumping never cease? ... Then suddenly it did, and McTosh was fishing me out more dead than alive. I was hauled to the gravel bar where they worked over me. My back felt broken, my bones too, but a slug of brandy brought me round. Said McTosh: "What a grand headline in the papers you've gone and spoiled. *Yukon Bard Meets Watery Doom*." I thought his levity was ill-timed. I appreciated more the ministrations of his Lady who made a fuss over me with sympathy and hot tea.

What had happened was that Jake's pole had slipped, letting the scow slew sideways to the current. As *Ophelia* swung downstream he lost control of her. Being at the end of the track line I was thrown more violently than the others, and dragged under. I completely disappeared, so that they could only stare with horror at my watery grave. But they had not reckoned with that rock so providentially placed at the mouth of the canyon. The scow struck it and stuck there long enough for Jake to get control. Undoubtedly that snag of stone saved my life. Otherwise I would have been dragged into deep water and drowned in a few moments. We did not go any further that day. I was weak and wild-headed; but after a night of rest I took my place once more on the track line.

And indeed I was needed. In the struggle before us every one was called on to give of his best. Even the Lady lashed herself to the straining rope, pulling like a little man. We were launched on a bold adventure and the river was doing its best to balk us. The idea, it seemed to say, of trying to take a scow over the Rockies! It had never been done, never would be done.

As we plunged and panted, our eyes were fixed on the muddle of mountains ahead. They seemed impossible to pass; yet as we strained upward a path opened for us. It's like Life, I thought banally. Difficulties daunt us, but if we tackle them with a high heart barriers break down and the way is clear.

Let me describe a typical scene.... We have come to where the valley opens out, and the river forks in a dozen channels. We select the likeliest stream and explore it. It is only a few inches deep and studded with boulders. How I curse that unwieldy scow! How I hate these fur men and their stubbornness! Why couldn't they have a stout canoe for the job? Blast and damn *Ophelia*! Well, we will have to get the old bitch over somehow. So first we unload her and portage the stuff half-a-mile. It takes several hours packing everything through the thick brush. Then we proceed to boost her over the boulders, scraping her bottom all the way. At one place we deepen the channel, at another build a wing dam. Often we have to get under the scow and heft her on.

Though there are five of us it is a heartbreaking job to hoist her foot by foot over that rocky bed. Heartbreaking, too, to see mile after mile of the same gravel ahead of us. But, oh, what joy when we come on a channel deep enough to float us a little! And again, what despair when we see another devastating reach of rock and rubble!

There were days when we made only half-a-mile after weary efforts through a dozen hours. But luckily the weather was lovely and the water warm. One did not mind being in it for ten hours a day. In other circumstances I might have worried about catching a chill, but I never felt better. I gave no further thought to bewailing my lot; my only idea was to extricate myself. So I laboured to the limit and kept grinning even when things were grim. A dauntless smile, I thought, is worth a million dollars. I put up a big bluff as if I were playing a lusty game and enjoying it.

I did enjoy some of it too — squatting on a sand bar and swallowing my spittle as I watched the bannock bake; smoking my after-supper pipe and retiring to my tent, where I would dig a hole to set my hip bone and sleep like a hound after a hunt. As I dozed off, I would see the glow of Jake's cigarette in his tent and hear the McToshes love-making in theirs. Lucky devil, McTosh, I thought; and I knew Jake thought so too.

As we climbed higher, the mountains closed around us and the river narrowed to a single channel. But it forked at one point, so that we were in doubt which was the main stream. Though we took the branch that carried the biggest bulk of water we were uneasy. It should lead us to a little lake at the height of the Divide. To miss that lake would be disaster.

It took so little to cheer me in those direful days. As we toiled upward we saw a high hill with a face of black soil. The stream ran bang into this and was diverted by it. But what gave me a pleasure as intense as it was simple was that the water which up to now had been obscure suddenly became crystal clear. It seemed to make such a difference to one's morale ploughing up a current that was pure and sparkling after weeks of wading in a murky stream.

One day the Indians announced that they were quitting. It was a bitter blow but there was nothing to do about it. The leader said he had to get home to the christening of his baby boy, while the other professed to be the godfather. Of course I knew they were sick of the grilling toil, and grimly I suspected that as guides they had lost their way. They wanted to leave us before we found them out. So we let them go, and with evident joy they departed. For Indians they had worked hard, but they had never seemed contented. The job had been harder than they had bargained for. As I watched them moving swiftly downstream, taking shortcuts and soon disappearing in the distance, I figured it would take them three days to travel the distance it had taken us three weeks to cover.

Their desertion made our travail ever so much harder, and to make matters worse we were losing heart. Day after day it became more difficult to keep the grin on my face as the fear grew on me that we were not on the right stream. But so far no one dared echo my doubt. Then one afternoon, after an unusually discouraging day, we flung ourselves on a sandspit for a cup of tea. As we gazed upward the stream narrowed and the valley looked as if it led to nowhere. McTosh was grim.

"Looks like we're lost. Well, if we come to a blind alley we can only go back till we find the right fork and try again."

The others glumly agreed, but I felt less stout-hearted. My spirit rebelled. If nothing would make him abandon his damned scow I was determined I would not help him to lug it over any more mountains. I would desert them. Alone I would make my way back to Macpherson. In *Coquette* I could make a good time.

We were too down-hearted to go any further that day and decided to make camp. Our supper was passed in silence; but after we had finished our bannocks and tea, to get away from the others I went for a stroll upstream. I thought I would climb a tree, after the manner of the Indians, and try to see ahead. I selected a promising pine on a grassy bank and was preparing to scale it when I observed that the bark had been blazed by an axe. To my amazement I saw that on the white surface was faintly pencilled a name. I made it out — BUFFALO JONES. So that well-known character had passed here on his way to the Klondike, behold his endorsement on the tree trunk.

Of course I had to announce my good news is the most casual way, as if it were scarcely worth mentioning. But the other rose to instant excitement and made me take them to the tree. I was mighty glad I had not suggested leaving them, and that night I slept better than I had done since the Indians deserted us. Indeed, so elated was I by my discovery that for the next week my exertions were herculean. No one hefted *Ophelia* more enthusiastically than I, and as I helped to heave her upstream I almost liked her. For I had a vision of myself in my Dawson cabin, swinging in my hammock, with the river gleaming blue and the birds singing. Oh, how I would rest and read and sleep! No more wandering for little Willie. But to the others I posed as their saviour.

"You were about to turn back," I gibed. "I was prepared to go on despite all hell. But for my exploring spirit you would have rotted away the winter with the snot-nosed Eskimos."

With these words I put my entire guts into the job and let no one beat me to it. And there was need, for the way was the worst yet. The stream narrowed to a brook, then a ditch overgrown with willows. Suddenly we realized we were on the height of land forming the Divide. We were no longer climbing. We were pushing on the level. We were pulling over a small prairie....

And Glory be! there in the near distance was a small lake, shining like a jewel under the cold blue sky.

Chapter Four

The Bell River

That was a great moment. I felt as if it almost repaid me for the privation I had undergone. There was the lake about a mile away, and beyond it the Pass, wild and savage, the stark mountains looking as if they were cast of iron. Yet how to reach the lake was a problem. Luckily half the distance was dry tundra and fairly level, so once more we unloaded the cargo and emptied the scow. Then, using the four poles and the mast for rails and skids, we pushed it forward. In places we were able to use the poles as rollers, so that foot by foot we worked *Ophelia* nearer the glacial waters.

When we reached the true tundra progress was easier. There was water and squashy mud through which we were able to slither our old ark, but half the time we would be waist deep in icy slime. Niggerheads promised a footing then wobbled under our weight. However, they aided us, till at last the ground grew so swampy we were able to go on board and pole the rest of the way. So after ten weary hours of labour our craft splashed into a sudden depth of clear, cold water.

But we still had to return for our cargo. Although it was late it was broad daylight, and we decided to finish the job that night. I made three trips carrying my flour and bacon, trying to make stepping-stones of the niggerheads and failing because they wiggled under my weight. A hundred times I sank to my waist in the intervening mud and struggled up again. This was doubly hard with a sixty-pound sack of flour on my back. Sometimes I thought my heart would burst with the effort, and despite the chill air I was soaked with sweat.

But the fourth trip was the worst, for this time I had to pack my canoe. True, it did not weigh any more than a sack of flour, but it was so much harder to balance. I carried it in the Indian way, with the paddles crossed as a back brace and a sling from the thwarts to make a band round my head. Thus fixed it was easy packing on the level, but in the muskeg it was hell. Time after time I had to throw it down and rest till my strength came back. Well, after an hour of that, I reached the water's edge, and wasn't I glad to launch it on the smooth surface?

The little lake was clear and still. It reflected the sky coldly. Looking down I saw strange Arctic weeds, and half expected to see some primeval monster rise up and grab for me. These secret waters made me shudder; but it was so good to be in the canoe again that, despite my exhaustion, I began to sing. Now, I thought, it will be easy going; and I blessed this gem of a lake that fathered streams flowing into the valley of the Mackenzie and the watershed of the Yukon.

It was a weird camp at the height of the Divide, with the midnight sun shining like a great red ball. There were sudden squalls of pelting rain, and the loneliness had a sinister quality that struck fear in me. The little lake shuddered as it shone. One had an "end of the world" feeling, as if this was the final word in desolation. As I looked at these iron mountains towering above the Pass I felt crushed with awe.

Having need of tent posts, I went to cut some saplings, but all I could find was a tiny tree about four feet high. As thick as my thigh at the butt, it tapered to a tip when it reached my chest. It was gnarled and grizzled, with sparse, tough leafage. I swung my axe vigorously, but the blade bounded back. It was as if I had struck a chunk of rubber with a croquet mallet. Again and again I swung, but the axe refused to make the faintest indentation in that horny trunk. A keen blade when I started, its edge now turned in disgust. That tiny tree seemed just the toughest thing on earth. Then I realized that it was very, very old, maybe a hundred years. It was a triumph of life over extinction. This pygmy pine was a symbol of the cruelty and frustration of the Arctic. It should have been three hundred feet high — a glorious, a majestic tree. I bowed before its brave defiance and craved its pardon for having planned an assault on its life.

So weary were we, we remained at that camp a whole day. During the night, hail hammered on our tents and mine collapsed under the onslaught. But there were no mosquitoes, so I used it as a covering. What a wretched night of cold and bitter wind, a weird red sun looking down on us with a bleary, dissipated eye!

I could not sleep, mainly because I worried about the stream that was to take us down to the Yukon. I could see no sign of it and the thought that we had been deceived made me sick. However, scouting round in the early morning, I saw a fringe of willows at the far end of the little plateau, and found it concealed a deep gully at the bottom of which brawled a lusty torrent.

"What a bonnie wee burn," said McTosh, all eagerness to launch *Ophelia*. So for the last time I got under her bottom and hefted for all I was worth. We tried to let her down by a rope; but I must admit I did not hang on very hard, and it was with a vicious joy I saw her break away and crash through embattled willows to the foaming water.

I followed with my canoe and a happy heart. As I embarked on that babbling brook I was singing a song about Maggie and when she and I were young. And for the next three hours I kept singing over and over that refrain, but alas! mechanically, and no longer with joy. For the trip down that "bonnie wee burn" was a bit of hell. The waters that came down at Lodore were a ripple to it.

Fortunately my canoe was well balanced and ballasted. My two sacks of flour and my dunnage bag were stowed amidships and everything was snug. Nevertheless, at moments I thought I would be upset. The water seemed to seize *Coquette* with a giant hand and shake her as a terrier does a rat. It descended in a series of rapids varied by small cascades, so that often, waist deep in foam, I was forced to get out and line the canoe. Once I was dragged after it into a deep pool and had to swim. At other times I thought my frail craft would be smashed like an eggshell. Sometimes it would be gripped by fang-like boulders and held clear out of the water. Often it tilted till the water came over the thwarts, but always it righted itself. I fought desperately to steer and clear it, for I was alone now and realized what it would mean if I upset and lost my grub. And all the time, through seething cauldrons and whirling pools, with clenched teeth I never ceased to sing of Maggie and the old mill stream.

Well, it was over at last. Just as I was beginning to despair, I saw a stretch of smooth water and knew I had reached the river that was to carry me the next stage of my journey. And on a grassy bank I found *Ophelia*. The party were exhausted, having had even a worse time than I. The men were grim, surly and sopping wet. I think they resented the absence of my help. They listened without sympathy as I related my woes on that rampageous river. It was then I took a definite dislike to them.

When things were bad I had been humble, but now the way seemed clear I felt independent. McTosh had left his belly on the Rat River and was inclined to be chesty about it. He and Jake were at loggerheads — the cause, the Lady. To this day I have never decided whether Mrs. McTosh was beautiful or not. I never saw her without her poke bonnet and Mother Hubbard, but I prefer to conserve the illusion that she was as lovely as she was charming. Anyway Jake thought so, and was forever fussing around her in a way that would have made any husband an understudy for Othello.

Another reason for their bickering was that Jake, with the money coming to him by his father's death, wanted to set up a trading post. True, it would be a few hundred miles from their territory, but even at that distance it would hurt their trade. Also, with the idea of bucking the Company, he talked of cutting prices. The others protested, but with bitter rancour he vowed he would get even with a certain Factor who, he declared, had refused to sell him flour when he was starving.

However, the chief reason why Jake was so cantankerous was that he had been obliged to cut down his smoking. He had only three magazines left and he looked at them anxiously. Paper was precious to him. It meant cigarettes, the chief need of his existence....

This was the state of affairs when I hauled *Coquette* on the bank and emptied a few gallons of water out of her. None of my food was spoiled; the flour had caked on the outside of the sacks, keeping it dry: while my dunnage bag was so well waterproofed my clothes were not even damp. But the canoe had been badly strained and was leaking at many of the seams. I spent two hours doctoring it. This was done with resin chewed in the mouth and applied to the leak. I went over every seam, inch by inch, sucking vigorously. If I drew in any air I plastered gum over the place till suction was no longer possible. The gum soon hardened and the mend was made. I liked this job so much that I often wished my canoe would leak so that I could show my skill in repairing it.

The others, however, had fared worse than I. The scow had been strained in the torrent and the boards had sprung so that it was half full of water. Their precious bales of fur were wet and were now drying on the bank. So they decided to draw *Ophelia* out of the river, upend her and caulk the seams of her bottom. I felt no desire to give them a hand. McTosh loved her like a father, but I hated her with the venom of the bitter days I had spent heaving her over the Summit.

To a lesser degree Jake shared my dislike. He looked longingly at my canoe. He was an expert paddle man and he loved its lightness and grace. He envied me when I announced my intention of shoving off on my own. For I had now decided to carry out my first plan and travel alone for the rest of the trip. Otherwise there would be no sport in it. Of course I knew I was taking a risk. A sprained ankle would mean helplessness. Loss of grub would be starvation. A dozen accidents could happen, and if one was alone the results might be fatal. I do not wish to exaggerate the risks I was taking, but they were obvious even to my jaunty spirit.

Behold me then light-heartedly launched on the bosom of the Bell River. I wanted to call it *la belle rivière*, for of all I have known it was the most beautiful. Perhaps I thought this because of its contrast with the vicious little stream from which I had just escaped. From turbulence I swept to tranquility. Imagine a river about seventy yards in width, with a surface as smooth as a mirror, and a gentle, placid current confined in banks of verdant green. It was nowhere deeper than six feet, and so crystal clear I could distinguish every pebble on the bottom. An idyllic stream, worthy of Arcadia.

And along its banks were fur and feather of Arcadian innocence. All the ptarmigan of the region must have come here to nest. Every few yards sat a mother with her chicks. They were brown, not like the snow-white birds I had hitherto seen. And beyond them in the low bush were myriads of rabbits. They, too, were russet brown, but with the coming of the snow they would turn white and I would know them as the Arctic hare. Thus Nature took care of her children. And as if I were a bear and not interested in them they were unafraid of me. I could have knocked them over with my paddle, for they scarce troubled to get out of my way. But I had neither time nor taste for killing. Anyway, I thought that at that season they must be pretty tough.

And fish! I never saw so many fish. If I peered into that pellucid water I could see them nose to the current weaving and wavering in shoals. Indeed, in some places, against a bed of silver gravel, they made a mosaic of light and shade. But I did not try to catch them. It was too easy. A flick of my rod and I had one. Five minutes and I had a fry fit for a family. However, they were soft of flesh and flat of flavour. I preferred my rusty bacon; for I had such a craving for fat I could have eaten tallow.

So day after day I drifted dreamily, under a cloudless sky in an air that was gentle and warm as a caress. Sometimes I wished for a book of poems, and often I would lie at full length in the canoe and let the current bear me along. The banks were rounded with sward and I knew there were no rapids. My mind was at peace because I had no thought of danger. What could harm me here in this sylvan solitude? I had lots of grub — bannocks, bacon, blueberries. I made my pots of tea on the bank whenever I felt bored, and at night I chose a grove for my tent. The ground would be dry and fragrant with crushed pine cones. Sometimes before supper I would have a swim. It was glorious to be alone like that.

And I was really, truly alone. I felt that if I had drawn a hundred-mile circle around me there would not have been a human soul in its compass. As I hugged my fire of an evening I gloated over my solitude. As I dawdled downstream I felt so free and careless I was in no hurry for company. After two hundred miles of the Bell I would come on the Porcupine, but I was in no rush to reach it. I wanted this beautiful stream to unwind forever.

Once as I went to fill my billy from a pool I got a glimpse of stranger in its clear mirror. I saw a brown, bearded creature in an old khaki shirt cut off at the shoulders and hanging in rags. His pants had been hacked off at the knees and were also in shreds. His legs and arms were brown and bare. What a savage! Then I laughed with delight, for the stranger was myself. I was lean as a rake, with a waist that caved in so that I could almost span it with my hands. I christened that country the Land of Lean Bellies, for a paunch there was unthinkable. Not even a modest melon.

I rarely used my paddle and one evening I was drifting lazily when in the far distance I thought I saw something moving up the bank. I was always on the lookout for bear so I put some shells in my Remington and set it in readiness. But as I drew near I discerned two objects moving dark against the shingle. To my great excitement I made out they were men. Who could they be? Rarely did human beings come to this wild place. This river was but a frail scratch on the map. Then I saw they were poling a canoe upstream.

Our surprise was mutual and they greeted me with joy. They were tall men, bronzed, bearded and tough as whalebone. They had been prospecting all summer and were going up the Bell to trap through the winter. Having been away from civilization for two years, they wanted the news. But the first thing they asked was: "What was the result of the Corbett-Fitzsimmons prize fight?" Of all world events, that was to them the most vital. So late by the campfire we smoked and yarned, and early next morning they left me.

In placid peace for days and days I drifted down my river of dreams. Most of my dreams were of Dawson, my cabin and the work I planned to do. On the Mackenzie I had gathered a lot of material that was different. As I paddled I mulled over this and saw ballads in the making. How I longed to get at them!

Then the river changed. It spraddled out with many a sand bar where I had to step into the suave stream and ease off the canoe. I went bare-legged, for mosquitoes were no longer in evidence. And I watched eagerly for my first sight of the Porcupine. It must be near now. The banks were a tangle of driftwood, blanched and weathered, so that making a fire was the work of a moment. Ever so often I would run *Coquette* on a sandspit and boil a billy of tea. Strong, sweet, stimulating, it never seemed so good.

Then one day I saw ahead the broad flow of the river that was to carry me on the next stage of my journey. Instead of green the water was olive brown. I was greatly elated and dug my paddle into it, singing joyously as I went. The current was stronger, and when the wind rose there were little waves. In paces the river was several hundred yards wide, so that when the breeze blew upstream it kept me humping.

Then the weather worsened and there were cloud bursts, when I would make a dash for the nearest bank and get my tent up. It only took two minutes to make the canvas taut, but by that time the torrent would be drumming down. However, inside I would be dry and warm, and I would immediately go to sleep. There were two days of rain during which I kept to the tent, sleeping most of the time. I blessed the cosy comfort of my rabbits' foot robe and wondered how the crew of the *Ophelia* were getting along.

One day passing the mouth of a small stream I was attracted by a domelike hill of many colours. It was a little way inland and I was curious to have a closer look, so I beached *Coquette* and strode up the creek. I had not gone far when I saw a mother goose with six young ones. They were almost full grown, but lacked their pin feathers and could not rise from the ground. They made a frantic effort to reach the water but I barred the way with my paddle and laid four of them low. They must have been very fragile, for light blows killed them instantly. Then the mother and two of her brood reached the water where they found safety in swimming.

Rather ruefully I laid my four geese on the bank. I had killed them in the excitement of the moment and now I regretted it. I could eat one, or maybe two, but four was beyond me. So as I went to climb that prismatic hill I was feeling rather glum. How could I cook my goose? To fry it in the pan would be difficult. Could I not roast it or bake it in ashes?

I reached the foot of the hill that looked dovelike in the evening light. It made me think of a sacred mount in its sweet serenity. Its surface was composed of spongy moss of many colours, rose, orange, lemon, pomegranate. I gained the top and in a hollow in that fungus-like growth, I lay down and went to sleep. I had no fear of night falling, for there was no night. No one would steal *Coquette*. There on the beach she lay, friendly, willing, patient. And alongside her lay my four geese....

I woke with a start. I must have slept for hours. For a moment I wondered where I was, then I looked down and saw my canoe. But a man was standing beside it, and with a feeling of alarm I went plunging downhill, going up to my knees with every leap in the spongy moss.

Chapter Five

The Porcupine

As I drew nearer, to my great relief I saw that it was Jake. He was sitting on *Coquette*, gazing grimly at my geese. A little way down the bank was *Ophelia*, hitched to a trunk. McTosh was making camp, while the Lady was preparing tea. I was mighty glad to see them again. I was fed up with loneliness, and my conscience had troubled me for my desertion of them. Now we would have a happy reunion. I would welcome them with my geese. Four people, four geese. The Lady would cook them in her big pot, and we would each eat one.

Our greetings were cordial yet casual. It might have been yesterday we parted instead of two weeks before. I found them the worse for wear and sensed things were not going well. It was the Lady who enlightened me. "It's Jake. He's just the crankiest thing, worrying about his cigarette paper. He's only got one *Argosy* left, and when that's done he says he'll go nuts. I'm glad we caught up with you. Maybe it'll change his ideas some."

We all fell to plucking the geese and boiled them in the big enamelled pail. They were cased in fat and so tender the flesh seemed to melt in the mouth. As I wolfed down delicious morsels I had less regret for slaughtering them.

We were gorged and gladsome when a sudden squall came up and we had to rush to the tents to avoid getting drenched. All day we were prisoned on that beach by heavy rain. Jake and McTosh had a furious row. The Captain wanted to go on but Jake refused. He was very surly and looked livid and fleshless. His jaw muscles jerked nervously; his fingers twitched in the gesture of rolling a cigarette. He had cut himself down to one an hour now and was taking it hard. You could see he lived for the moment he could twist his magazine paper round his shredded tobacco and light up. Then his whole being would light up too, and he would be almost genial again. Otherwise he and McTosh were snarling at each other like two malamutes over a mildewed bone.

Next day Jake took me aside. "Let me go with you," he begged. "I can't stand that carroty son-of-a-bitch a day longer. If it wasn't for the little woman I'd have slugged him before now. If I go with him I may do it yet. Curse him. I hate his guts!" This could be taken literally, for the Trader had got back his belly again, yet lost none of the arrogance its absence had evoked. However, nothing could have justified Jake's bitterness as he launched into a stream of profanity that made me wonder if he was sane. I did not like his suggestion to take him with me, but I said I would consider it. The question was whether the McTosh couple could handle the scow alone. Jake insisted:

"They'll be all right. From now on the river's easy. They can go to sleep and the current will take them right down to Fort

Yukon." I demurred, but next day the Lady came to me rather pleadingly. "I wish you'd let Jake go with you. I'm afraid of him and McTosh coming to blows. It's all I can do to keep them from mixing it. Besides, he had only enough paper for three days and you can make better time in the canoe. You can wait for us at Rampart.... Why can't he smoke a pipe like all decent men? I can't understand it. His God-damn cigarette is the only way he can get satisfaction. Believe me, that guy's nuts."

This seemed a cheerful reason for wishing him on me, but she was so worried I finally agreed. Immediately an atmosphere of relief settled down on the party. We picked the bones of the goslings and parted on the best of terms. As Jake took his place in the stern of *Coquette* he looked almost amiable. Beside him lay the solitary *Argosy* that represented the last of his paper. I looked at it anxiously as page by page it went up in smoke. Well, in three days we should be at Rampart, the trading post on the Porcupine, and there he would get all the paper he wanted.

We took the river at a swift lick and I cursed my partner who kept me humping to keep up with him. After so much dawdling it seemed tough to be obliged to sweat again. With vicious rage I dug into the water and the banks slipped by as never before. What with the current and our spirited paddling it seemed to me we must be making ten miles an hour. I would have rebelled but my eyes kept roving to that solitary magazine.

"How many pages left, Jake?" I asked.

"About thirty," he told me gloomily.

I made a rapid calculation. Allowing twenty-four smokes a day, that gave us only two and a half days. Hum! I put more guts into my stroke. As I sat crisped in the bow I could hear his grating voice: "I think I oughta warn you, partner, if this paper pans out I'm liable to go bughouse."

"Nice cheerful prospect," I said. "And then what?"

"Well, ye mind that yarn ye told me of them two stiffs ye found in a cabin wi' their heads ablowed off? … I've jest been athinkin' that's what might happen to you an' me — if this here paper gives out." I laughed as at a merry jest, but as time went on I did not think it so funny. A homicidal maniac in the making is not the most pleasant for companions. I got to watching him more and more and my nervousness increased. And that night he told me: "Ye know, I always figgered if I run outa paper for cigarettes I'd be a fit candidate for the loony ward. Well, I'll tell ye what happened to me the winter I ate my dog.… A wolverine got into the cabin and chewed all my paper to pulp. I was just about to go daffy when I found the Bible my old mother gave me. I hated my dad but I sure did like Ma. I carried that there Bible everywhere. I never read it, but jest liked to have it by me, thinkin' it might come in useful. Well, it did — mighty useful. For I smoked it through from Genesis to Revelation. Damn poor smokin' at that, but it saved my life. Yes, sir, that Bible saved me from a bullet in my bean."

As I listened I was sorry I had no Bible to offer him. With growing alarm I watched that paper diminish. If only we would confine his smoking to the day; but at night when I woke up I could see the glow of his cigarette. In despair I paddled harder than ever. Thank Heaven! the Post by my reckoning was only a day away. I counted every hour. Then on the third morning I saw he was down to his last sheets.

Anxiously I looked ahead as I rounded each bend of the river. My arms and back were aching, but I had no thought of letting up. I felt we must make Rampart that day or there would be hell to pay. I begged Jake to go easy on his smokes, and he seemed to realize the crisis. He tried to get a grip on himself. But, oh, how he made that water churn! Then suddenly I felt like shouting with joy. We had not stopped for chow and it must have been late in the afternoon when we swung round a bend and there, a mile ahead, I saw the high bluffs of Rampart.

★

But what was the matter? An Indian woman stood on the landing beach and she was wildly waving us off. As we drew near she cried: "You no stop. All Injun heap sick. You catchum too. You go away much quick."

"But what the hell?" began Jake, when we saw two men coming down the path at a run. They also waved us to keep out. Both were white men, and one was big and burly.

"Don't come ashore," he cried. "We have smallpox at the Post. Yes, *smallpox*. Got it bad. All the Indians down with it. I'm the Doctor. Wait … I'll write you a note to say you haven't landed." He scribbled on a piece of paper and gave it to me. "There! That'll show you didn't go ashore. Otherwise you would be put in quarantine. You'd better get on your way and be careful to avoid any Indians you meet on the banks. Now I must hurry back. Have a hundred patients to look after."

He was going, when he turned again. "There's a launch on the way up with supplies. We've run out of vaccine. You might tell them to hurry.… Oh, and by the way, you wouldn't care to stay and give us a hand, would you?" To my eternal shame I excused myself. The thought of all that putridity revolted me. Yet here was a chance of making a real hero of myself. To volunteer to nurse in a smallpox camp — what a fine gesture! Well, I just hadn't the gizzard for it.

So I said I guessed I'd go on and wished him good luck. Then I started paddling downstream when I was aware of an uncomfortable silence behind me. Jake was not paddling. Instead he was looking at me with a glare of murderous hate.

"What's biting you?" I asked.

"The cigarette paper," he snarled. "Look! That's all I've got — two sheets. I wish I'd gone ashore with them guys."

"And maybe meet your death from smallpox."

"It's not smallpox I'm scared of. It's myself. When this paper is done I'll go screwy."

"It's not too late. I'll put you ashore. But you'll have to spend a month in quarantine."

"No, go on," he said sullenly. "There's that launch coming up. I'll take a chance on that. But look out for yourself. I'm not responsible anymore." So we paddled more furiously than ever: but we did not speak and I felt the tension between us was near to breaking point. Jake reduced his cigarettes to a minimum and used his paper parsimoniously. Yet even at that I saw that the end was approaching. I dreaded the crazy man behind me so much that I kept my loaded rifle in front of me. Then I heard him sneer: "Seems to me you're all fixed up to fire that there gun of yours."

"Might see a bear on the bank," I answered with affected carelessness.

He laughed harshly. "I've got an axe here might be useful if we saw … a bear. I'm a good man at throwin' an axe." No doubt he could get me with the axe before I could swing round with the rifle. Nice messy end to a misspent existence! As I bent to the paddle I felt my spine creep. The man was unbalanced, but whether to the point of insanity or not I could not determine. It is true he was a nicotine fiend and his nerves were sustained by tobacco. And only strong cigarettes could satisfy his craving. He loathed a pipe. Once when I handed him mine he returned it with repugnance.

And incidentally, lest it be thought that I exaggerate in my fear that my partner was going crazy, let me say that that was what ultimately happened. A few years later, in his lonely cabin on the Arctic Ocean, Jake went mad and shot off the top of his head.

*

That night after supper he suddenly demanded: "Gimme that bit o' paper the Doc gave you."

"What do you want to do with it?"

"Make a cigarette. Maybe two."

"No. It's going to save us a heap of trouble when we get to civilization. I won't give it up." I thought he was going to spring at me and prepared to yield the paper rather than fight for it. But he contented himself by cursing me and my ancestors, and over the campfire kept baiting me with the foulest abuse. In the end, however, he retired to his tent, taking the axe with him.

All that night I lay awake with my rifle ready to my hand. If he made any move to attack I was prepared to shoot. I would aim for his legs, I thought. But the night passed and he made no move. There was not even the usual cigarette glow from his tent. I was afraid now he might draw his throat across the axe blade. I felt anxious. So I rose early and called him, but he would not answer. I made breakfast with bacon and hot tea and called him again. This time he got up. I felt sorry for him, he looked so shrunken and abject. He refused to eat or drink.

"Look here, Jake," I said; "let's go on for another half day. We ought to meet that launch. If we don't I'll give you the Doc's paper and we can go back to the smallpox camp." His face brightened. He seemed a new man. He gulped down some strong tea and even tried my pipe. "Till noon," he stipulated.

It was about eleven when the canoe sprung a leak and I had to beach it. I was stooping over it on a gravel bar, sucking the seams, when I looked up and saw a tiny launch swinging round the bend. Was I glad? Oh, boy! I hailed it but Jake was before me. With a bound he was on board and a moment later he was drawing on a cigarette as if it had saved his life. From then on he was a changed man. He could not do enough for me. He insisted on performing all the chores of the camp, and in the evening, with his jackknife, he carved me a tiny model of a rabbit snare. It was his way making friends again. We talked as if nothing had marred our harmony, and everything went as merry as a church chime.

It never rains but it pours; for next morning we were gaily paddling around a bend when we almost butted into a small stern-wheel steamer. As we materialized from out of the blue a score of eyes were on us. At the sight of *Coquette*, dancing daintily on the wave, there were shouts of admiration. She was as gay and colourful as when I first bought her. Now she shot forward with an air of saucy triumph. So far as I was concerned it was her last dashing gesture and I tried to make it as dramatic as possible....

A dozen people were regarding the shapely craft as its owner, a bronzed and bearded individual, leapt lightly ashore. He looked like a scarecrow spewed out of the wild, with tattered pants hacked off at the knee and a khaki shirt cut clean at the shoulders. Lean as a greyhound, sinewy as a panther he ...

So I pictured myself, and truly I enjoyed the thrill of that moment — those wondering eyes on me, my sheer primitiveness as in my proud rags I strode up the gangplank. I felt nonchalant, yet arrogant. The Captain, very trim in white duck, met me halfway.

"I'm Captain Brown from Fairbanks."

"I'm from Edmonton," I said. There was a gasp from the crowd. "My partner's from Baffin Land," I added. Another gasp, then the Captain said: "You don't mean to say you've brought that canoe all the way?"

"Pretty near. But I'm figgering on going much further with it. I'm fixing on taking a passage with you." He looked doubtfully at me, so I went on rapidly: "I'll give you a cheque on Dawson for the passage of myself and my friend."

"It's not that," he said. "We hear there's smallpox at Rampart. You've not stopped there by any chance?"

I handed him the paper from the Doctor. He read it very carefully. "All right," he said at last. "But if you hadn't had this clearance I wouldn't have taken you. I admit we were scared. I was going to Rampart when I heard of the epidemic, so I turned back. Unfortunately I stuck a snag in the river and knocked a hole in the boat. We're trying to patch it up now by wedging sacks of flour in it."

"Lucky for me you struck that snag," I said, "for I've had enough of paddling for the rest of my life."

It was a long, sleepy trip up the Yukon and I spent it mainly in eating. At first the food made me sick but I soon got over that. From the table I went to my sunny stateroom and stretched on my berth, thinking with a sigh of ecstasy that my wanderings were over for a month of moons. I gained six pounds on the trip but was still lance-lean. I shaved off my beard and grinned at the hollow mug that confronted me. I borrowed a guitar from the steward and composed a song that the deck hands learned and sang for years after. It was called: *When the Ice-worms Nest Again.*

Jake made one sheepish and awkward appearance in the cabin then vanished into the steerage which seemed more to his taste. Once or twice I got a glimpse of him yarning with the deck hands, and I knew he spent hours playing cards with the stewards. Then just before we reached Dawson he came to me looking very humble.

"I want the loan of a hundred dollars," he said. "I lost five hundred in blackjack down below and pledged my furs in payment. I'll need some money when I get to town — enough to last me till I draw the dough the old man left me. I sure have made a bloody fool of myself."

Next time I saw him he repaid me my money and told me he had a job as a bartender. He had received his heritage and was very chesty about it. I told him to keep out of card games but I guess my advice fell on deaf ears. He was a born gambler and a reckless one.

Six months later I met him and he was very abject. He had gambled away all his capital and was heading for the Arctic again. I offered him another loan but he refused, saying he could not repay me. So he went away to trap and starve and suffer, and in the end to blow out his foolish brains.

Chapter Six

Home, Sweet Home

We reached Dawson at eleven in the evening and I immediately went ashore. What joy to see again that little sleeping town! With a sort of ecstasy I walked the old familiar streets. Ramshackle and unsightly they might be, but to me they were beautiful. I loved them for I had known so much happiness there. Down Front Street and up Main I wandered in the midnight daylight, meeting not a soul and wondering at my infatuation for this old burg. It felt like home to me and I was glad to be back.

I went into a pub and saw three men I knew. After the clean hardness of the men of the Wild they seemed greasy and grubby. They gazed at me strangely and with some suspicion. I looked like a tough character, one who might hold them up. I had to tell them who I was, and even then they hesitated to believe me. With the stamp of the Wild on me I felt a contempt for these men of the town. After a drink or two I went back to the boat. Next morning I had a gorgeous time introducing myself to so many old friends. "You're so thin," they remarked.

"So would you be," I answered, "if you had to live for three months on blueberries and pea-vine roots."

"Where did you come from?" they would ask. And I would reply with elaborate casualness: "Oh, I just dropped in from Edmonton." Then I would brag of the greatness of the Mackenzie Valley as compared to the Yukon. They were impressed. Here standards of the North prevailed, and the man from the Arctic strutted it over the man from the subarctic. So I swaggered round feeling pleased with myself; but as, after a week, no one took any more notice of me, I settled down to be an everyday Dawsonite. At first I was inclined to regret the sacrifice of my beard, but it made me look like a Rabbi. And besides, there were girls in the offing.

The first morning I went ashore and climbed the hill to my cabin. It had such a pathetic, deserted look, as if it had missed me. Now it seemed to welcome me again, and its moose horns over the porch were like arms stretched out to me. As I unlocked the door I thought I saw my own ghost on the threshold. I caressed the rude walls and the rough furniture and loved them. I made the bed with two thick blankets and my rabbits' foot robe. Here, said I, is my haven and here I rest till the spirit moves me to mush on.

It seems queer to me now.... I was able to live in a fine room in a *de luxe* hotel in any city in the world, and yet I just wanted my bare cabin in this near-ghost town. I wanted the winter to clamp down on me and shut me off from the world outside. Again I would be a hermit, living my own life in my own way. Oh, I know I was looked on as a strange individual, morose and unsocial; but to be solitary was not uncommon in the North. And I was of the North, its lover, its living voice. Dawson was my home; I had no thought of ever deserting it.

Such was my attitude as with exultant happiness I settled down to months of simple living. Once more I would supremely belong to myself. So I had the cabin re-papered and the stove revised. It was very bright and warm *chez moi*. I got books from the library, a good guitar and a bath tub. Twice a day I would take a cold bath and so harden myself. All my life, even in the Arctic, I have never worn underclothes. The prickly sensation of my childish woollens is with me still.

So I resumed the old beloved habits, my rising around noon, my lunch of ham and eggs, raspberry pie and coffee. In the bakery of the old Swede I relaxed, and generally had a gang of sourdoughs round my table. Truly life was very agreeable, just as I wanted it to be. I kept at the peak of physical fitness and beat out my snowshoe trails in the woods and on the hills. It was on these solitary tramps I began to work again, spinning my fancies as I walked, and in the silence of my cabin converting them into words. Just as my first inspiration had been Kipling and my second the Ancient Mariner, now I was influenced by Bret Harte and Eugene Field. My material was uniquely my own, so that I might be forgiven for modelling myself on others. I had definitely abandoned the Yukon and my new work concerned the Mackenzie basin and the Arctic.

I used to write on the coarse rolls of paper used by paper-hangers, pinning them on the wall and printing my verses in big charcoal letters. Then I would pace back and forth before them, studying them, repeating them, trying to make them perfect. I wanted them to appeal to the eye as well as to the ear. I tried to avoid any literary quality. Verse, not poetry, is what I was after — something the man in the street would take notice of and the sweet old lady would paste in her album; something the schoolboy would spout and the fellow in a pub would quote. Yet I never wrote to please any one but myself; it just happened I belonged to the simple folks whom I liked to please.

So all that winter I worked at my book of verse; not too hard nor too anxiously, for I had lots of time and knew it would come out all right. My first book had been written with no thought of publication; my second was a *tour de force* produced in the small hours of the morning; but this one was a leisured and pleasant job spread over most of a year. For I was enjoying my winter too much to make it a strenuous one of work. Even in the coldest days I climbed to the summit of the Dome and returned to have my bath in freezing water. Sometimes, indeed, it consisted of me rubbing myself with chunks of ice. I practised physical culture till my muscles rippled, and often I would go off for days on a tramp up the creeks. And it was one of those trips I met with an adventure that inclined me to believe in a Special Providence.

Chapter Seven

Lost in the Wild

One morning, feeling a restless foot, I started out for Gold Run. The distance was nigh on fifty miles, but with bright weather and a crisp trail I thought nothing of that. I had an Indian lope I could keep up for hours. I ran in-toes and bent forward, with a swing movement of the arms. It was as if one was tumbling and checking oneself.

I reached the roadhouse that night, not too tired to visit some friends. On the following morning I decided to walk back, but thought I would take another trail. In a parka and moccasins I was in fine fettle. Soon I came to where the trail forked, and I took what seemed to be the likeliest branch. But I made a bad guess, for it got smaller as it went through the woods and finally petered out.

I had gone a mile out of my way; yet little troubled I turned and regained the right trail. It was in the open. The sun was brilliant, the cold about thirty below, the air like champagne. I was plumbful of pep, so I ran till I came to another fork in the trail. I took the left-hand branch as it seemed to head more directly for town. I had not loped along very far when I found the path led up to the mountains. I could see it streaking miles ahead to where stood a big roadhouse. I made for this, thinking to get my directions and maybe have lunch; but when I reached it I found it had long since been abandoned. I swithered whether to turn or go a little further. To beat back on my tracks would have meant another night in Gold Run. The trail was so good I thought I would venture on. Maybe I would strike a lone cabin in the waste.

Yet the trail kept ever climbing and I saw no sign of life. I was abysmally alone in a dazzling white wilderness. Even then I could have turned back, but I had that obstinacy that makes one loath to admit one is beaten. Besides, a Northman hates to give up a trail. I was feeling gloriously well, for I had climbed higher than I had imagined, and below me lay a white immensity of awe-inspiring desolation. So I turned again to the upward trail, convinced that I was foolish, but saying: "I'll go just a little further. Maybe beyond the next ridge I'll come on life." That was the temptation, ridge succeeding ridge and the hope that the next might reveal human habitation. Indeed, I might still have retraced my steps when some miles further on I saw in the diamond clarity a tiny cabin. It was remoter than I thought, and when I gained it to my dismay it was empty.

I was now committed to this trail. There was no returning. I must go wherever it led. I kept climbing higher and higher, into the hills which now closed behind me shutting out the valley. I had a trapped feeling but hurried on. What worried me was that the path dwindled so rapidly. It became a toe-track that switched from ridge to ridge but ever mounting. Little by little it grew fainter, till at last it failed. In front of me was virgin snow, and I found I was breaking trail. Then at last I realized I was lost.

★

In tense moments I always sing, and now I found myself crooning *The Bonnie Banks of Loch Lomond.* As I did so I thought of that long past day when I had walked the length of Loch Lomond in the rain. Since then I had followed so many strange trails and this might be the last. Night was coming on. If it caught me before I found shelter it would be hard to survive till dawn. So I ploughed ahead; for, though the snow had effaced it, there were still signs of the trail below. Sometimes the drift was knee-high, and then again it had been blown away revealing the hard track. All I could do was to follow it blindly. "By yon bonnie banks and by yon bonnie braes," I chanted as I stumbled on. Often the snow was up to my knees and I had to lift my legs high or flounder in the drift. Once I did, falling forward on my face, and strange to say I did not want to rise. I said: "It's lovely to rest a little in this white shroud," but the last word made me jerk upright. Not for a moment must I linger. To do so would be drowsiness, sleep, death. Already I could feel an almost invincible desire to close my eyes.... Just a short doze.... Fiercely I struggled against it then goaded myself on again.

I sang no longer. It was a fight with the Wild, a fight to the death. A nice end to a promising career. Frozen in the snow. Might be weeks before they found me up here in this huddle of peaks. Pity about that book. I might never see it published. On, on again. Never give up.... I saw the sun set like an angry boil, when suddenly I heard a scuffling in the snow, and up the steep bank sprang a bull moose. For a moment it stood huge and majestic against the setting sun. Then it vanished, leaving me wondering if I had dreamed.

Again I staggered on, fighting fatigue and refusing to quench my thirst with snow. That would have been fatal. I had not eaten since early morn but I did not think of hunger now. Indeed I did not think at all. I was on the verge of collapse and all I felt was the physical desire to lie down and rest and rest.... Then suddenly as I was about to give up, my second strength came to me. In a state almost resembling delirium I pressed desperately on.

I saw night fall, shadows obscure the trail; but I realized they were the shadows of pines. I had descended to the timber belt and the woods were all about me. In a kind of stupor I went on and on. Thank heaven, the snow was lighter under the trees; not much longer could I have kept up that plunging through the deep drifts. In a dull daze I saw that the moon was in the sky, shining down with a merciless clarity. The cold had grown intense; it must be forty-five below. Then in a flash of vision I knew it would be fatal to stumble on. I must find a tree and walk round and round it till morning; otherwise I would stagger in a snow bank and be lost for good. So I selected a big pine and began to beat down the snow at its base. Round this I must turn and turn all night, and the night was eighteen hours long. My chances of survival were pretty slim, but still I must fight on.

How long I turned around that tree I cannot tell. Perhaps thousands of times. At first I tried to count, then gave up. My feet rose and fell, my eyes closed, but I plodded my circle on that now hard-beaten snow. Strange thoughts came to me … "By yon bonnie banks and by yon bonnie braes" … I suppose I'll never see old Scotland again.… Darned shame to finish like this. I might have done such good work.… I think I'll just rest my back against the tree.… No, no, struggle on, you fool! Fight to the last.…

The moon seemed unnaturally bright. It was shining down on me in pity. Damn you, Moon! I don't want your pity. I've always been your lover and now you'll gleam over my snow-cold corpse. I, dreamer, joyous liver of life, so grateful for all good things, will lie white under the silver of your spell.… My legs were giving under me. Through the frosted collar of my parka I could see the diamond glitter of the moon.

There comes a time when the spirit can no longer conquer the flesh, when despite the gallant heart the foot fails. This came to me now. My muscles refused to function, my legs crumpled beneath me now. I sank on my knees, rose and sank again. And as

I kneeled there in the attitude of prayer my Special Providence came to my aid. Or was it the moon that saved me? For it seemed to burn brighter, brighter. It seemed to cry to me: "Look! Look!" And in the answer to the pleading of the moon I looked, and there in the shadow of the woods across a brief gully I saw ... A CABIN.

I wondered — could it be? Or was it only a mirage, a ghost cabin born of wistful thinking? I peered harder. No, it was beginning to take definite shape in that weird glamour. I never saw the moon make such an effort of brightness, and it now revealed the cabin clear as day in the silver glade. It was like a glimpse of heaven, and again I feared a cruel illusion. But it persisted, and at last I was convinced it was a reality. The cabin was there, had been there all the time. For hours and hours I had been tramping miles and miles around this pine with safety only a hundred yards away....

Now I must be careful. If I fell into a drift I was so weak I could never struggle out. So almost on hands and knees I worked my way to the cabin. There was a clearing in front. I rose and stumbled on. Of course the cabin would be empty, but it would shelter me. I would build a fire, get warm, sleep. I was saved. Yet I had a frantic fear that the door might be locked.... But no — bless that old Yukon law, the latchstring was outside. I pulled it and tripping over the threshold I fell on the floor.

Thank God, the cabin was not deserted. Someone lived there, but no one rose to welcome me. Still, there was the stove, and (Oh, blessed Yukon law) a heap of kindlings. Trembling with joy I filled the stove and lit them into flame. I piled in small wood, then bigger, and soon the stovepipe was glowing cherry red. What music as the flames roared up! How heavenly the heat! Cowering on the floor I let it soak into my hide.

Food! I must find something for I was ravenous. There was flour. No good. A can of beans! I hacked it open with my jackknife and heated it on the stove. As soon as it was warm I wolfed them from the can. I wanted to make tea but I was too tired. There were two bunks at one end of the cabin and some tumbled blankets in the lower. So after fixing the stove that it would burn for hours, I crawled into the bunk, curled up in the heavy blankets and lost consciousness.

I was awakened by the smell of frying bacon. What a heavenly odour! I sniffed back to awareness and opened my eyes. A huge man was standing by the stove. He had a shock of snow-white hair and a long grey beard. He looked like a reprobate Apostle Peter. He was bleary-eyed, dirty, dishevelled, like a man who was at the tail end of a fierce jag.

"Hullo!" I said.

"Hullo, young feller; I thought you was never agone to rouse. Been sleepin' yer haid off. It's high noon. Musta been petered out when ye got here. Lucky ye found the cabin. Reckon ye was losted."

"Yes, I was just about all in."

"Musta taken the old trail over the mountain. Hain't been used for years. Pretty tough goin'. Well, now yer here I hope yer fixin' to stay a bit. I got lots o' grub. Just come from town where a feller staked me. I'm puttin' down a shaft in the side of the mountain an' could do with a bit of help, so what?"

"I'm sorry. I'm going back to town. I work there."

"What might ye be workin' at?"

"I tap a typewriter."

"Sounds easy. One of them clurrks, I guess. Well, it takes all kinds of folks to make a world. I'm a hard-rock miner, name of Joe Rich. Helluva name to give a man that's been poor all his life. But I'll strike it yet. I'll die a millionaire. Have ye heard of me back in the old burg?" I seemed to have a vague remembrance of a man of his name. I could not recall its nature, but there was something sinister in it.

"I'm not sure," I said. "Are you well-known there?"

"Well-known ... why, say! there ain't a girl in Lousetown don't know old Joe. I kin make things sparkle some. I'm seventy-three an' feel like a four-year-old. Say, I brought a box of eggs from town. What about hittin' you with a slab of hen-fruit?"

I was agreeable and we wolfed bacon and eggs. There was bread too. His hands were filthy yet I did not seem to mind. I ate heartily, but best of all was the boiling tea. I felt grateful; however when he suggested I remain with him a few days I demurred. There was egg on his beard and his cabin was dirty. Weakly I told him I would remain there that night, yet even as I did so I had strange misgivings. Again that suggestion of something sinister came back to me.

After eating he suggested we visit his mine. It consisted of a hole in the ground ten feet across and six deep. I knew nothing about mineral rock so I listened as he talked of stringers and veins and the mother lode. He had it here, he said, if he could only go deep enough. "There's a fortune in that there hole. You can see it stickin' out — gold-bearin' quartz. I've just been to town havin' some of it analyzed an' it's rich. If I had only capital an' lots of help, I'd be a muckin' millionaire.

He had a profound voice and he roared in his enthusiasm. Then with a flying leap he landed in the middle of the hole. I marvelled at his agility when suddenly I saw his face turn to me with a look of alarm. He gave one gasp and staggered to the brim of the pit. He was hanging on to the edge and about to collapse when I grabbed his arms. With all my strength I tried to hoist him up. He was a heavy man but he managed to help me so that he was not all dead weight. Desperately he fought, gasping and gazing at me with frightened eyes. Finally, with an effort that strained my muscles to the limit, I got him on the level ground, and there he lay like one in a swoon. At last he roused. "That there mine near proved my grave. I shoulda thought before I jumped. Before I went to town I made a big fire to thaw out the ground. That hole's full of gas. Mighta been aspzyated. Reckon, buddy, you saved my life."

"Well, you saved mine, so we can shake on it."

"Better still, we'll go back to the cabin an' bloody well celebrate."

He produced a bottle of Scotch and we began to drink. We stoked up the stove, made ourselves comfortable and finished the bottle. He drank about four-fifths, I the remainder. Then he opened a second bottle. I retired, however, but he seemed to be keeping it up. I was roused by him gripping me by the shoulder and shaking me roughly. "Come on an' join me, partner. You're a hell of a sport to let a man drink alone." Reluctantly I rose and accepted a glass. He was pretty well tanked up by this time and he grew worse as the night went on. He yarned of his travels in Australia, South Africa, Bolivia. He had followed the gold lure all his life. I began to be interested, for the whisky was stimulating my mind. But there was one country of which he did not talk, the High North. He had tales about every other but this in which he lived. Again I racked my brain to discover what it was holding back about this unkempt old man.

Tired at last and only half sober I threw myself on my bunk. Alone, he fell into a brooding silence broken by mutterings and lurid oaths. He was like an evil being, haunted by memories of past misdeeds. Suddenly I was aware of him shaking me more violently than before. "Get up, you damned little shrimp," he roared. "I want to talk to you." In a half daze I felt myself being hauled from the blankets and hurled into the only chair. There I slumped, wide-eyed and wondering. Was this man a maniac? If so I was out of luck. I seemed to have a specialty of encountering crazy characters, first that mannikin Jake, then this Colossus. He poised before me, his eyes burning, his face inflamed and distorted.

"I've a feelin' I wanna tell you sompthin'. I've jes' gotto. I've never told it to a human soul so it's between us two. But if you ever blab, by the horns of Moses, I'll let the daylight through your hide." Menacingly he took a shotgun from the wall. "Yes, I'll puncture your gizzard wi' buckshot till it looks like colander."

"Please don't tell me," I faltered. "I don't want to know your secret."

"You've got to," he shouted, flourishing the gun. "I'm tired of bein' the only one to carry it round. If I tell it to you it'll help me, an' you look a nice guy."

"Well, go on," I said with resignation. "Spill it."

At that he threw down the gun and burst into a roar of laughter. "Kindo skeered ye, didn't I? Why, lad, I wouldn't harm a rabbit. And that's what you look like, a skeered rabbit. 'Fraid I'll hurt ye. You think I'm a killer? Why, I never killed a man in my life an' never will. But you know what they call me in the North? … *Cannibal Joe.*"

Then I remembered. It was the story of two prospectors in the Barren Lands. After a year one returned alone with a tale of hardship and starvation. They had been lost for months in the Winter Wild. They had used up their grub and been forced to live on the country. His partner had succumbed but this man had struggled on and made his way to safety. It was a great story of an epic battle that should have left him an emaciated wreck. But curiously enough he looked well fed. Also the dog he brought back was well conditioned. It was strange. Then some Indians came in with story of the corpse of a white man with the flesh cut away. All evidence pointed to it being the dead partner. Suspicions were roused. It was even hinted that the survivor had killed his mate and lived on him. It had happened before, and would happen again in that insensate North that turns men into brutes and lunatics. Well, here was the survivor himself, ready to tell his story … and I did not want to listen.

As I stared at him he had a fit of fury. He grabbed up the gun again. "You don't believe I ate Bob?" he raved. "You don't think I'm a cannibal? Say you don't or I'll riddle your guts."

"I certainly don't," I said. "I'm sure you would never do such a thing. The idea!"

He subsided. "No, I wouldn't. I'd perish first. Bob was the best pal I ever had. We'd a died for one another. When he passed on it was a knock out for me, but his last words showed he thought as much of me for he whispers: 'Joe, if my dead corpse is any good to you, use it. You know what I mean. Don't hesitate; maybe I can be the means of savin' your life. So long, pard.' Them was his last words, so help me God. Well, I did use him…." He paused, fixing me with his burning eyes. Suddenly he became like a crazy man. "Not that," he shrieked. "Not what you think. I never et Bob. I never et a single slice of him. No, that's not what I want to tell you … What did I do? Listen — God curse me! I never et Bob, but *I fed him to the dogs and I et the bloody dogs*." With that he collapsed on the floor and lay like a dead man.

When I woke in the morning there was my host standing by the fire frying eggs and bacon. He showed no sign of a hangover. With his white beard and snowy hair he was mild, almost gentle. He made me think of Walt Whitman.

After we had eaten he sped me on my way. He seemed glad to be rid of me now, and as we parted he remarked almost casually:

"Say, friend, if ye had a bad dream last night ye jest wanto ferget it. Y'understand?" I understood. And that is why I have forgotten … till now.

Chapter Eight

And Last

I finished my book in the late spring but still I lingered. Dawson had meant much to me and I had been happy there. I was loath to go, for I felt I would be leaving behind me part of myself. So I remained until the last boat. As I wrote some verses bidding goodbye to my cabin I knew they meant farewell to so much that was familiar and dear.

My plan was to go to the South Seas. I imagined I had the gift of golden indolence and suspected that as an adventurer I was a bit of baloney. I dreamed of palms, starry-eyed sirens, strumming ukuleles on coral strands. I could realize all that. I was young, free and I had no more need to work. I had done my share of roving. Let me rest in colourful security.

So I thought, but at the same moment an editor was saying: "Here's a guy that loves excitement and action. He is dedicated to adventure and doesn't mind taking any old chance. Now he's at a loose end. Let's send this bold boy to the blood bath of the Balkans. Give him a chance to show his guts." Thus I got a letter proposing to make a war correspondent out of me, and with curses in my heart I cabled acceptance. Then with my book of verse in my valise, superb as to health but uncouth through long living near to Nature, I departed for sophisticated Europe.

As the steamer passed the mouth of the Klondike I was as blue as burning brimstone. There was the grey face of the Slide, the green summit of the Dome, the brown town clinging to the river bank. It was not beautiful but it was very dear to me. I knew every nook and corner, so that it seemed to be a Self I was leaving behind. Poor old Town, so wistful, so weary. "You're leaving me too," it seemed to say. "Like so many, you are abandoning me. I have sheltered you, nourished you, brought you cheer, and now you disregard me and turn to others more fair." And I answered: "I swear, I will come back. I will live with you again and renew the joy and comfort I have known. You have been more to me than any other of my resting places. I am grateful and will never forget. Yes, I will come back."

But I never did. Only yesterday an airline offered to fly me up there in two days, and I refused. It would have saddened me to see dust and rust where once hummed a rousing town; hundreds where were thousands; tumbledown cabins, mouldering warehouses....

And as I looked my last, my eyes rested on my cabin high on the hill. The door seemed to open and I saw a solitary figure waving his pipe in farewell — the ghost of my dead youth. No, I do not want to meet that reproachful wraith again. He might say: "You promised to do so much; you have done so little."

And I had a further thought that saddened me even more. I felt I was not only quitting Dawson but the North itself. Nine years of my life I had given it and it was in my blood. It had inspired and sustained me, brought me fortune and a meed of fame. I thought I knew it better than most men and could express its secret spirit. Maybe I should have remained there and devoted my life to singing and writing of it.... "I will come back," I said again. "I will be true to the North." But over thirty years have passed and I have not returned. Now I know I never will....

FROM

Harper of Heaven

Chapter Five

The Latin Quarter

I will never forget my first forenoon in Paris. As I stepped forth the morn looked like a newly minted coin — ringing with rapture. Rills of clear water glittered in the gutters and the trees flirted their first April finery. Curdles of cloud accentuated the ingenuous blue of the sky. "Notre Dame," I called to a cabman. Cheerily he grinned and with a flourish of his whip we were off. He wore a glazed tile hat, a black cape and was as rubicund as the *cocher* of my dreams. Indeed, as we ambled along, so many things made me think of dreams coming true. My reading of Paris had been ravenous; from every corner remembered names leapt at me. I was living again in the pages of Hugo, Daudet, Zola. In that adorable Spring morn each twist and turn gave me a new thrill. I felt as if I were coming home and my heart sang. Here, I thought, is where I fit in. I will remain at least a couple of months ... I remained for fifteen years.

Poignant moment! Notre Dame at last. I had studied a model in the Metropolitan Museum so that the original looked like an old friend. It was even more beautiful than I had hoped, and sitting in the serene square I regarded it with beatitude. Bless the Gods who have given me the gift of rapture, for that marvellous morning I knew ecstasy as I have never known it since. Yes, all that immemorial day one radiant moment crowded on another, till I felt like shouting from sheer joy that surged within me.

After a blissful spell of contemplation I started out on the grandest walk in the world. Skirting the Seine, past hundreds of book-bins, till I came to the Institut de France, I crossed the Pont des Arts to the Louvre. Then I kept on up the Tuileries to the Place de la Concorde. From there I mounted the Champs Elysees to the Arc de Triomphe. On that brilliant day everything was at its best and I had no words to fashion my delight. So from one seductive street to another I marched on till I came to the Madeleine and from there to the Opera.

After a leisurely lunch on the terrace of the Café de la Paix I resumed my enthusiastic exploration. The Eiffel Tower, the Invalides, the Boul' Miche' and the Luxembourg — I visited them that afternoon and though I was footsore, in the evening I climbed to the Sacré Coeur and Montmartre. But my joy was sustained to the last, till with prayer of thanksgiving I crowned the most delectable day of my life. To be young, free, primed with romance and with a full purse — what could be nearer to Paradise than Paris in the spring?

Soon I left my seven-franc room near the station and took a four-franc mansard in an old hotel on the Quai Voltaire. From there I could watch the Seine, its toy-like steamers, its strings of barges, its torpid fishermen. The shining river, the trim quays, the gay green of the poplars and the book-bins beneath all gave me an exquisite pleasure, so that I dreamed for hours by my mansard window. From it I could see the spires of the Sainte Chapelle and the towers of Notre Dame, while down river were the gay gardens of the Tuileries, with the lacework of bridges culminating in the Pont Alexandre. That panorama never failed to enchant me, so that from dawn to dark I could sit there entranced.

Absorbed in my city I was some time in making human contacts. The first was the Paris correspondent of a New York daily who interviewed me at my hotel after ordering a golden omelette. As he gobbled and gabbled I listened with admiration. An Englishman with a rich voice he knew every capital in Europe. "Come with me to breakfast at Ciro's tomorrow at noon," he said. By that he meant lunch but I took him literally, and he was a little chagrined when I asked for ham and eggs and tea. Even the great Ciro shrugged his shoulders.

"I'm cross with our New York office," my host told me. "I sent them a story of a Prince sailing from India with a cargo of monies and they printed it 'a cargo of monkeys.' All the time they try to make a monkey out of me. I think I'll resign.... Have you any girl friends? I can introduce you to some of the little dancers of the Opera, but I warn you presents of hats are very expensive, and the simpler they are the more they cost." This discouraged me so that I declined his kind offices. How one vice will cancel out another! My Scotch parsimony has always prevented me making a fool of myself where women are concerned. To my mind not the most beautiful woman in Paris was worth a thousand francs for an evening of distraction.

I would never be a dashing blade like my newspaper friend. He had a personality I lacked and he made me look a poor dub, even though I *had* written bestsellers. I visioned success for him and I was not wrong. In the World War he became a Colonel, wrote a book, made a handsome marriage and clinched his career with a knighthood.

My best friends were a Canadian couple, and they too symbolised the romance of destiny. Sweethearts in the same prairie village, linked by a love of art, they had studied in city schools and finally gravitated to Paris. From there they roamed with brush and sketchbook through Europe, returning with joy to their studio in Montparnasse. Theirs was an ideal marriage for not only were they devoted in their ordinary lives, but their art was a spiritual passion binding them. So in their painting and etching they shared each other's pains and triumphs. In their perfect partnership they inspired me, and for years I enjoyed their gentle friendship, until like so many they passed on....

Through them I met other painters till gradually my life took an artistic trend, and I conceived myself in the role of a *rapin*. At school I had been tops in design and had a knack of sketching from life. When other boys were playing I spent happy hours copying pictures from *Punch*. In those days I dreamed of being a real artist, and here I was playing at being on; for I bought a sketchbook and took lessons in the studio of Colorossa in the Rue de la Grande Chaumiére.

For one franc we were admitted to the life class where with some trepidation I watched the girl model undress. As it was the first time I had seen a naked female I fear my conscientious nudes were affected by my modesty. However, with sepia pencils sharpened to a long point I succeeded in getting good effects of light and shade. I learned a lot of painter lingo and looked wise when I stood before a picture, I went to *salons* dressed in a broad-rimmed hat with a butterfly tie and velveteen jacket. I dramatized myself in my new *role*, for, like an actor, I was never happy unless I was playing a part. Most people play one character in their lives; I have enacted a dozen, and always with my whole heart.

This *Vie de Bohème* must have lasted a year, during which I learned to loaf on the terrace of the Dôme Café, waggle a smudgy thumb as I talked of modelling, make surreptitious sketches of my fellow wine-bibbers and pile up my own stack of saucers. Drinking so continuously I stuck to small *bocks* which did me little harm and I reverted to my pipe. I also visited the picture galleries, of which the Luxembourg was most to my taste — the Louvre lulling me to somnolence. On the other hand excessive modernism irritated me, and when a Russian woman showed me a cubistic nude in which even the sex organ was rectangular I gazed without conviction....

I got to know many of the long-haired freaks who spent their time between the Dôme and the Rotonde, crossing from the one to the other their only exercise. Poles and Swedes were peculiar enough but the Muscovites were the maddest of all. There were middle-west Americans, too, who absorbed the colour of the Quarter to the point of eccentricity. One of the charms of living in Europe is its leisurely appeal. There is not the goad to achievement of the New World and life often becomes a protracted holiday in which one dreams of doing things instead of getting them done.

On the other hand, however, were American artists who worked with passion, grudging every moment they could not be at their easels. They would be off in the early morning to the country, painting with eager intensity, and when the light failed returning tired but tranquil to their studios. Often I would accompany them on their daily excursions to the banks of the Marne, sketching amateurishly while they plied the professional brush. Yet I had a feeling they were exploiting beauty while I was worshipping it.

For outside of their own job I found them singularly uninteresting. Their beloved work done, all they wanted was to play snooker or go to a silly cinema. As a rule they cared neither for music nor for literature. Outside of painting nothing much mattered. But what a blithe brotherhood! Their technical absorption saved them from that introspection that is the curse of the author. Yet writers are more broadminded. The whole world is their *atelier* and their lives are richer. So, though I would have loved to be either an artist or a musician I think that I would still prefer to be a modest inkslinger.

But soon I began to weary of my assumed role of a camp follower of art. This came to a head when a man invited me to a tea one Sunday. He was a designer of book plates, balanced between literature and art. In his studio were two men — the first small and thin, with a pear-shaped head, a Swinburnian brow, dark eloquent eyes and crinkly black hair. The other was also short, but sturdy, with a round face, sharp eyes peering through glasses, and a virile manner. I was introduced to them: "James Stephens, the Irish poet, and Gellett Burgess, the American humourist."

I was thrilled — two men I had always admired yet never hoped to meet. Long before I had dreamed of writing I had read Burgess, when to quote his book on Bromides was a *cachet* of cleverness. Stephens I knew through his *Crock of Gold*, and though I never dared to emulate his poetry I feel that he inspired me. And now to have both launched at me casually over the tea cups! …

In my velveteen coat and *Lavallière* tie I felt something of a *poseur*, but when Burgess asked me why I was not whooping it up in the Yukon I answered with dignity that I was an art student, experimenting in the life of the Quarter.

Soon the talk turned to poetry. Stephens asked me what I thought was finest in Tennyson and I answered: *"Ulysses."* When the others seemed to agree I felt rather bucked. Then both men recited some of their poems and I was asked to give one of mine. This I did with diffidence, for I felt that a chap who recites his own stuff is a bit of an ass. However, I tried my best and Stephens said loftily: "Very good *newspaper* verse." I was so humble at the time I felt flattered at the compliment.

Burgess was the finest swimmer of any writer I have ever known. I am myself a waterdog and like de Maupassant love to float far from shore, enjoying between sea and sky an ineffable remoteness from the world. But Burgess with powerful strokes would cleave the waves till finally he vanished from sight. I would watch anxiously for a long spell, fearing he might have taken cramp. Then, suddenly, with that same swishing stroke, he would disengage himself from the horizon and soon his short, sturdy form would emerge from the foam.

In contrast Stephens looked pale and frail, a man of delicate health, due no doubt to the privations of youth inured to poverty.

I saw something of him as at one time we rented his Paris apartment. It was a loft over a machine shop converted into living quarters, and when the various machines got going the place vibrated with a demoniac intensity. In an ear-shattering din we jiggled and joggled. Afflicted as with Saint Vitus' dance I could not steady my hand to shave, and when I went down to the *bistro* for a *bock* I jerked most of my beer on to the table. How could my landlord have written his radiant poetry in such a racket?

But I think most of it was achieved as he strode the streets or in the midst of a crowded café, for he had a most enviable gift of detachment. In the hubbub of some busy *bistro* he could write of linnets and lonely gods. As I saw him stride the grey streets he made me think of a faun and I half expected him to break into a dance to the playing of inaudible pipes of Pan. Or as he huddled in some sordid pub I fancied him squatting with nimble goats on a thymy hill.

Sitting under the leafy foam of the *Closerie des Lilas* he would read me his latest poem written on the back of an old envelope. He sang rather than recited, weaving to and fro in lyric ecstasy and chanting the lovely words with a thick brogue. Like many poets he was an egoist and surveyed the writing fraternity from a Hill of Derision. "There are only two great living authors," he would tell me, "and the other is meself." He would not say who the first was. He spoke rather patronisingly of a new book called *Ulysses* written by one James Joyce. I listened to him reverently. I suspected he scorned me, but I admired his work so much I yielded him homage.

Once he asked me if I had any offspring, and I answered: "No, I'm afraid I have not the paternal temperament." He said: "Neither have I but begorra! I have the childer." He wore an eye-glass, though his collar was attached in some weird way to his singlet, and once when I remarked on the disparity between his attire and his monocle he snapped: "Ye can look at me clothes and ye can look at me eye-glass and ye can strike an average." …

His wife was the most charming of women, pretty as a picture. She once said: "The Services are the best tenants I ever had and the only ones who left the apartment as clean as they found it."

These literary lights of my salad days looked, I fear, with a justifiable disdain on the brash boy from the Yukon, but one who put me severely in my place was the great Edmund Gosse. I was asked to meet him by a friend who was a collector of celebrities and bought an evening-dress suit for the occasion. Gosse was handsome, distinguished, a famous talker. On this occasion he held us enthralled with his stories of Browning, Rosetti, Swinburne. As he did so he gestured with a nice edition of my latest book of verse, but never had the grace to open it. "Rather of pretty binding," he remarked grudgingly, but the author he ignored. He did not address a word to me during the entire evening. I was rather relieved because, if he had never read a line of my work neither had I of his, and between writers that creates an awkward situation. Nevertheless, his supercilious attitude galled me and as the party broke up I observed to Edmund: "We have at least one thing in common — our names are French." As *gosse* is a slang term for "kid" my remark was received in freezing silence.

In those days I took contumely meekly. I regarded myself as a cross between Kipling and G.R. Sims. I was inclined to agree with the dispraise of the mandarins of letters. If people did not buy my books they might purchase others more worthy. I was sorry I was an obstructionist in the fair path of poesy but I did not see what I could do about it. Alas, I write as I feel! I fear I can never do otherwise.

I am shortish by New World standards but average by European ones. However, most of the *literati* I met at this time were "sawn-offs." I have mentioned Burgess and Stephens. Another was blond James Hopper, writer of short stories. He was half French and perhaps that was why he loved to live in France. Like myself he was reticent and self-effacing, so that when we sat together on the terrace of a café conversation languished. No doubt he was hypnotized by the passing throng, or maybe dreaming one of his distinguished stories.

Another short man, a contrast to the brooding Hopper, was dark, loquacious Jeffrey Farnol. He gobbled life with avidity. We had the same publishers and when he offered them *The Broad Highway* they objected that it was too lengthy. Savagely he tore out a chunk from the middle, saying: "That will make it short enough." Even then it was overlong but they accepted it and it was an instantaneous success. In Paris society he wore a huge pair of knee-high boots, but despite them he was gay and ebullient as if he had on dancing pumps.

By way of a change I met a Big Man in Brentano's. He had a distinguished look and the salesman whispered: "Richard Harding Davis." My old hero! I watched him with admiring respect. He was well groomed and handsome, but he did not look a hale man. As I saw myself the picture of health I did not wish to be in his shoes. I was wise, for shortly after I read of his death.

Meeting those masters of my craft was to turn my mind to writing again. For long the very thought of it had irked me; till I wondered if I would pen another line. Then suddenly the old urge came back. For months it had not mattered; now it seemed to be all that mattered. My fallow period was over; I was desperate to ride myself of the thoughts that seethed in my brain. But what really started me was a chance meeting with a man who was to become my dearest friend.

Chapter Six

Bohemian Days

I was sitting lonely on the terrace of the Dôme when an oldish man approached me. He made me think of a Skye terrier, for he had a shaggy moustache and friendly blue eyes under a thatch of eyebrow. He addressed me with a Scotch accent that immediately appealed to me.

"Peter McQuattie's my name. I'm a journalist of sorts and I would like to write an article on you for the *Morning Post*."

"Let's have a drink," said I. I called the waiter and though it was early in the day he ordered a *Pernod*. Then, chain-smoking, he told me of himself.

"I was a school teacher in a wee Scotch toon but I always longed for a larger life. Paris particularly allured me, so when a millionaire offered me a post to tutor his son with a year's stay in France I accepted it as Fate. For some time we lived in Tours where one of my friends was Hugh Walpole, then a young student with no thought of writing. Hugh wanted to make a pact of life friendship with me, but somehow he wasn't my sort — didn't have enough of the devil in him. I liked to smoke and drink and tell salty yarns and I'm not very strong on skirt resistance. Hugh was too respectable for me. I like freedom and variety — so I've never married. Are you single?"

"For the moment: but I'd like a wife and a home. Everyone comes to it in the end."

"I never will. I'm a born bachelor. I've a little apartment underneath the tiles and I'm happy as the day is long. I meet my pals, do a bit of writing, make just enough to jog along. I'd rather be like that than be Head in a Scotch school. I came to France for a year and now I've been over twenty. At times it's been hard but I've scraped by. Always enough for a crust and a wee dram.

And how I've loved poetry! I can quote it by the yard."

"For God's sake don't quote mine."

"I might if I get drunk enough. But, come on, man — ye'll no refuse to help a fellow Scot. Tell me something about yersel' for my article."

The result was a column in the *Morning Post*, for which he was paid ten guineas and went on a big binge. But such successes were not frequent. As Paris correspondent for a Sunday paper he made three pounds a week. Once in a while he sold a short story to a cheap weekly and the quid or two it brought him was reason for a celebration. After a fling he was often hard up but only once did he ask me to help him. When he repaid me I tactlessly remarked: "You're the first of my friends who ever returned to me the money they borrowed." He bristled and said: "D'ye think I'd have asked for a loan if I wasn't sure I could pay ye back?" And never again would he accept a penny of aid from me.

But he was incorrigibly lazy. Day after day he would sit on the terrace of the Dôme greeting his friends. I think his failure as a writer was because he was a great talker. He was the garrulous Scot with a talent for detail, that made his conversation realistic and riveting. I loved to get him gabbing and could have listened to him all night. Even stories he had told me before seemed more interesting in the re-telling. But his conversational gift was really his curse for it made him too convivial.

However, the dream of his life was to write a book about Paris. It was to be called *Youth and a City*, and was to recapture his first rapture on arriving. He had conceived it twenty years before and each year he had decided to make a beginning. But perhaps laziness intervened; or it may have been that he was dismayed at the job and had secret doubts if he could fulfil it. So always he put it off for another year. Then one day I said to him: "I think I'll write a novel on Paris and the Latin Quarter and youth and rapture," but he gave me what I called his "school master look."

"You haven't been here long enough," he said. "You don't know the City." So I told him: "You've been here too long. You know it over well. You'll never write your book."

I hoped that would goad him; but no, he hesitated to make a start. So I went off to the country and wrote and wrote. I said nothing to him about it, then months later I went to him. "Here's your book," I said, "Only *I* wrote it. I did it in six months, but I kept my nose to the grindstone. It's the only way." He agreed, yet I could see something shrank affrighted in him. I am sure he realised then he would never write his book, and though he spoke of it hopefully to his dying day he never got beyond the title.

One day Peter sought me eagerly. His eyes bulged with joy as he said: "Who d'ye think's coming to see me, all the way from Clydeside? — my old pal Neil Munro." I, too, was excited, for Neil was at that time our leading Scotch novelist. I had never read any of his books which were what I called "tushery." They were historical and though he had a pretty style modelled on Stevenson, I was too much a lover of the present to be interested in the past. Yet, to meet a man who writes books, even though one doesn't care to read them, is thrilling enough, and I was happy indeed when that evening in the Napolitan I was introduced to the only Scots author with more than a local reputation.

The "Nap" was the café where the journalists foregathered, and I found them toasting our celebrity. Neil was a slim, fair man, not outwardly striking, yet giving an impression of being fey. He asked me about my work and I assured him I was doing nothing with great enthusiasm. He shook his head sadly: "I'd give a lot to be independent and write only books. But there's the grey grind of a newspaper office, and by the time I get home my imagination just won't work. Yet my heart's in the Highlands, in the good old days when clansmen clashed and claymores flashed. I was born a hundred years too late." "Damned if I feel that way," I told him. "I'd rather be here drinking a bonny dram with you than stinking in the coffin of the great Sir Walter. But I get your point, and here's to Romance."

I liked Neil a lot. We got on fine. Besides being a good writer he was a good fellow, enjoying his liquor and not above listening to a racy yarn. He was my kind, human all through. And that evening we had a great feed in Larue's. There were present Adam of *The Times*, Jerrold and Grey of *The Telegraph*, MacAlpine of the *Daily Mail*, Hill of the *Montreal Star*, Donahoe the Australian journalist, Peter, Neil Munro and myself. What a glorious, uproarious evening! Grand lads they were, with a great thirst and a rollicking wit. How the table rang with their sallies! ... Yet today, of all that gleeful gang, only I am left alive.

Another celebrity I met at that time was Ibáñez, the Spanish novelist. Fisher Unwin was our mutual publisher, and I acted as interpreter between them. Blasco was as romantic looking as Neil was prosaic. He was brimming over with a vitality that would not let him rest a moment. A big, handsome, dynamic man.... Yet, when I met him years later he was walking across the courtyard of the Louvre with a worn and weary air. Gone was his exuberant zest. He was flabby and stooped with dull eyes and a pasty face. He told me he was having trouble with the Spanish Government who had denounced him as a traitor, while even the French authorities regarded him invidiously. Rich, world famous but broken-hearted, soon after he passed on. I believe his last regret was that he could not die fighting for his country.

These literary contacts kindled in me the spark of inspiration and soon it burst into a blaze. In the meantime I wrote a series of articles on Paris. Into them I put all my enthusiasm and zest for living. From every facet I flashed joy as I wrote of my beloved city. It was easy to write those articles for I was so supremely happy. Again and again I thanked the Gods for their gift of ecstasy. Little things that others took for granted — my morning *croissant* and coffee on the terrace of a tavern, my reflective pipe, my lonely walk along the Seine, evenings under the trees in the purple twilight — all of these were to me sources of divine content. I was amazed at my former idleness and rattled on my typewriter with exuberant ease. Again I discovered the rich satisfaction of creative effort. How I radiated joy! It did not seem right to be so lyric with gladness. I was so happy it almost hurt.

Now I had resumed work I wanted to do nothing else, and I neglected Peter. I had no time to waste in café loafing. I despised the four-flushers and failures who crowded the Dôme. "A bunch of boozing wasters," I told him. "Don't let yourself be one of them." But after twenty years of it he was too much of a *flâneur* to reform. Shaking his head sadly he ordered another Pernod, while indignantly I strode away.... Always a tremendous walker I indulged in it more violently than ever. No man had ever stauncher legs and they carried me all over Paris till I came to know it like my pocket. And the better I knew it the more I loved it. At one moment I do not believe there was another writer of English who knew the City as well as I.

More and more I came to despise the sodden sybarites of the Quarter; then, as the demand came for more articles I realised I must broaden my field, so I went to Barbizon. I was enchanted with the woodland. Dithyrambic with delight I wondered how I could bear to live anywhere else. And truly after sun-baked streets those cool, leafy aisles seemed heavenly. So I walked the forest far and wide, thinking it a fairy land. I embraced trees and caressed boulders for the joy they gave me. Sometimes in the solitude of a green glade I laughed like a lunatic from sheer ecstasy.

But in the evenings I was often intoxicated by more than sun and sky. There were many artists in the forest and after their day of work they were inclined to make merry. The vine bequeathed to us the jewelled joy of its mellowing so that we drank till the night ended in a rich, confused rapture. And it was on one of those occasions I had a curious adventure.

*

Oh yes, I was a little drunk as I walked from the tavern to my hotel in Barbizon. The distance was some three kilometres and the way lay through the forest; but I knew the trail and the moon was bright. The walk would serve to sober me. So after a final glass I set out. I sang as I marched, with a step that did not wobble too much. When one is lit up distances don't seem to matter. The miles pass like magic and soon one tumbles into bed. So I went singing along, ever so pleased with myself and all the rest of the world when — suddenly I saw it — a LION.

Incredulously I rubbed my eyes. It was in a forest glade and the moon was like silver. At first I thought it was a fantastic boulder, then I took it for a forgotten bit of sculpture, for it was as still as stone, staring at me. Sombrely I reflected: "I'm pickled and I'm just seeing things. Must cut down on the booze.... Pythons or pink elephants I could understand. But *lions* — no Sir!" So, bravely I went up to the brute. I would dispel this apparition of my drink-distorted brain. I would ... When suddenly that lion *snarled*. How it happened I don't know but in two shakes of that big cat's tail I was six feet up the nearest birch and still climbing. But when I looked down again from what I judged was a height discouraging to lions there was nothing there.

"Let this be a lesson to me," I thought gloomily. "From now on the water-wagon has a new passenger. No more fruity old vintage for me." But prudently I stayed up that tree for a full hour and when I descended it was with a precipitation much greater than I intended. Bruised and shaken I returned to my inn and went to bed without saying a word to anyone. I was not going to expose myself to derision and disbelief.

And next morning, with a bit of a hangover, I was dully drinking my morning coffee when Gerrard, the sheep painter, said to me abruptly. "Well, they shot the lion." "Lion!" I exclaimed. "Yes. Is it possible you didn't hear? There was a lion loose in the woods last night. The Pathé people were making a picture over Melun way. It was one of those jungle stories and they built a compound and hired a live lion from the Zoo to give the scene atmosphere. But the palisade wasn't high enough and the brute leapt it and got away. Rather nasty if anyone had encountered it. But an expert rifleman got it in the early dawn. Lucky shot, for it was a big brute and considered dangerous.... You were out late. You didn't happen to trip over a stray lion by any chance?" I shook my head sourly, knowing that if I had said "yes" I would have been the butt of all that ribald gang. Still, I thought — what I vowed about the water-wagon goes — with latitude.

There are at least five inducements to live in a foreign land — freedom, strangeness, irresponsibility, romance and adventure. It was the hope of a little of this last that finally started me roving again. For the moment I was fed up with Paris, so I brought a push-bike and started off with no definite goal. The first day I did fifty miles with enthusiasm, the second, ten with a sore fanny. From then on I averaged twenty, depending on the distance between pubs. When I found one that was sympathetic I stayed and wrote an article. In that way I pedalled up and down Normandy, then went on to Brittany.

The Breton country charmed me, and I lingered lazily in that Land of Wooden Shoes. I wrote of the fisher-folk of Finisterre, and its cider-swigging sons of the soil. I did some swigging myself, in oak-panelled taverns or sunny seashore *buvettes*, and the more I saw of Brittany the more it grew on me. From the sky-blue sardine nets of Douarnanez to the grim cairns of Carnac; from the quaint *coiffes* of Concarneau to the brilliant brocades of Landerneau; from the fantastic offshore rocks to the grey stone cottages with their oak-fringed farms — How I loved it! I called it the Land of Little Fields and wrote articles about it.

Then one day I happened on a village that seemed lovelier than all. In a sea coast famed for its charm its beauty took my breath away. Tiny bays of golden sand were caught between rugged arms of rock with beyond a blaze of gorse and broom. Off shore were fairy isles, then a large one shutting in the bay from the outer ocean. It was an island of fantastic battlements and cliffs of grotesque device, and when the tide went out one could walk to it across miles of green-pooled sand. Clad only in trunks I would go daily to the tidal flats, coming back with lobsters, conger eels and jumbo shrimps. My body became Indian brown and all alone on that waste of reed-strewn pool I felt a nearness to nature I had long missed. As I stalked the sands with spear and shrimping net I was like a primitive savage. When the tide came up I would swim a mile or so, returning lazily to my cove. There I would linger, dreaming on a heather-clad headland and longing to express lyrically my feeling for the loveliness about me.

But somehow my eyes always went to a little red-roofed house that stood on a sea-jutting rock. It was far apart from any other and seemed so lonely. It was flanked by coves of golden sand and backed by a yellow blaze of gorse. Somehow, wherever I gazed, my eyes returned to that little house till at last it seemed to call to me saying: "I am empty and sad. I want to be lived in. Please take pity on me. Buy me. You will love me. You will never, never be sorry...."

So I asked the landlord of my hotel: "What about the little red-roofed house on the point? Is it really for sale?" He answered: "Everything is for sale, Monsieur, if you are willing to pay the price. But this one will be high. It belongs to the *Maire* and is the apple of his eye. He built it himself and really it is a jewel. But he is a hard man and wants too much — twenty-five thousand francs — completely furnished, of course."

"It seems exorbitant," I said. "Would he not come down a bit?" But the landlord said: "Not if you begged him with your *derrière* sticking out of your pants. He is hard as nails. He will never take a franc less."

However, my host had given me an idea and next day I interviewed the *Maire* at his home. He was indeed a gnarled and withered man who looked as hard as hickory, and behind him was a moustached wife who seemed equally difficult to deal with. I had made myself as miserable as possible, though I had drawn the line at exposing my *derrière*. But I wore stained pants, a ragged shirt, a broken straw hat and disreputable sandals. Even the natives appeared more respectable. "I want to buy your house," I said, "and I offer you seventeen thousand francs."

He looked me up and down. "My poor Monsieur, you mock me," he began. But I checked him. "Wait a moment. I do not know if I will be able to pay you even that sum. All I possess is seven thousand francs. I will have to beg, borrow or steal the other ten. I do not know if I can do so, but I will pay you seven thousand now and try to pay you the balance by noon on Saturday. If I cannot I will forfeit the seven thousand."

With that I took from my ragged shirt seven lovely *milles* and spread them before him. Dubiously he looked at them. Then I overheard his wife whisper: "He's a poor devil. He will never raise the balance. You take a chance, my brave Gustave."

Her eyes were fixed greedily on the notes, so reluctantly he took them. Then he made out a document in duplicate in which he agreed to sell me the entire property in the state it stood for seventeen thousand francs, seven thousand down to be forfeited if three days later the balance of ten thousand was not paid. Then we all signed and I went away.

That night I took the Paris train, withdrew ten thousand francs from the bank and the following day I was back. With the local lawyer I arrived at eleven on the fateful Saturday. On the way we had to ferry over on a small boat and I was worried we might not be able to get there in time. "If this boat upsets I'll swim," I vowed, "but I'll be right there with that dough." However, we reached the *Maire*'s house a few minutes before the time had expired and I'll never forget the look of disgust on his face as he saw me. For now I was togged up in flannels made by a Paris tailor and I overheard Madame whisper, "My poor Gustave you should never have trusted him. I told you he was a Monsieur." However, they put the best face on it, the papers were signed, the payment made, the place was mine.

It was difficult for the *Maire* to conceal his chagrin. Yet he proved a good sport. "Would you not like to make an inventory?" he asked "You know the house is furnished, even to silver and bed linen. Everything complete."

"Not quite," I grumbled. "You've forgotten a car for the garage. But I know you're honest people and I trust you to leave everything as it is. I do not want to see the interior of the house. I fell in love with the outside and I want the inside to be a pleasure in store."

I returned to Paris that day after a final float over my house. DREAM HAVEN I called it, and I wanted to keep it a dream, something insubstantial and only half conceived. I had a whimsical feeling I did not want to realise it too quickly. So I went back to Peter and the Dôme and Montparnasse. "I have a home, old man," I said. "And now what I want is a *wife*. I am ready for the greatest of all life's adventures — Marriage."

Chapter Nine

Ambulance Driver

Although I was over military age when war broke out I felt keen to join up. I fancied the Seaforth Highlanders, so I went to the recruiting office and offered myself. To my surprise a varicose vein in my leg disqualified me. "You can't wear puttees with that thing," snapped a medical officer. As I had understated my age and darkened my hair I went wearily away. When he yelled after me: "Shut the door!" I did so with a bang. But it was just as well, for that battalion of the Seaforths was practically wiped out in the Somme. Had it not been for an innocent bulge in my left calf I would probably now be lying near my brother in a grave in Flanders Field. Sometimes a blemish is a blessing.

Then I took counsel of my good friend John Buchan, a man whose brilliance dazzled me. Had he not gone to my old University, gained a scholarship for Balliol, written a dozen books, become a Member of Parliament? He was also partner in a big publishing firm and head of a famous news agency. So young, with so many irons in the fire. Yet I do not think he dreamed of the high honours that would ultimately be his. At that moment he was a ranking Colonel and writing a history of the War.

I met him in the lounge of the Hotel Scribe. He had a slim figure and a sensitive face under a bulging brow. When I told him I wanted to join the ranks he shook his head. "Join the Officers' Training Corps and get a commission. We want men like you." I disagreed, for I knew myself better than that. Though I can obey ardently I cannot command. Always that inferiority complex. I am incapable of handling men, while responsibility unnerves me. All of which I tried to explain to John but left him unconvinced.

So we went to a Burns Banquet where he made the speech of the evening. As I sat by his side he told me his health was so delicate at times he had to go to bed for a month. On these occasions he would write a book. He had just finished *Greenmantle*, which had sold twenty thousand copies in advance. I marvelled at his facility and his success. He commented on the absence of a haggis, saying: "A Burns Banquet without the haggis is like *Hamlet* without the Prince." For so fine a scholar he had a rich sense of humour, and it was a grievous pity a man of such grace and distinction should meet with an untimely death.

Having been thwarted in my effort to get into the War on the ground floor, I thought of my Balkan experienced and wondered if I could not be a correspondent. Accordingly I offered myself to my old syndicate and was accredited on the same conditions. So I went round hospitals and training centres, doing my best to grab colourful stuff. One of my articles described the arrival of a train of wounded at Rennes; but it was hard getting such gory material, so I went to Calais.

In those days war correspondents were anathema to the High Command, and to be caught near the firing line was a dire offense. The best one could do was to snoop as closely as possible. At the Station Hotel of Calais were a brilliant band of journalists, but they depended on leave men and Blighty victims for their stories. I was not very successful. The regular newspaper men got tips that left me an outsider. I did not get much help from them; but one and all said: "If you value your skin don't go near Dunkirk."

I reflected: "If I'm the man for my job I *must* get to Dunkirk...." But how? The train was running, yet I should be arrested at the station. Well, why go to the station? There was a village a few miles out of town where the train stopped. I would get off and walk the rest of the way. So I slipped on to the train which was full of soldiers and country people. I thought they looked at me queerly, but suspected no evil.

Hopping off at the little station I made my way to a café where the *patron* hailed me with some surprise. He spoke to me in a lingo I first thought was German so I hastened to disavow any knowledge of that language. He explained, however, that it was Flemish, and served me with beer. As I drank I was conscious of that atmosphere of suspicion. The other drinkers hushed their talk and eyed me distrustfully, till feeling a little uncomfortable I rose and went my way. As I did so I saw the landlord rush to the telephone.

I did not take the direct road to Dunkirk. If I did so I might be stopped, as I would have been at the station. So I found a byway and entered the town by the suburbs. Soon I was in its centre, where in a big café I ordered tea, bread and butter. As I sat there I felt serenely happy. I had been smart. I had evaded the authorities. I was on the track of something that might be worthwhile.

And indeed the town was full of interest for a news-starved scribe. I saw numbers of Indian troops looking strangely out of place in the mud and rain. I spoke to weary *poilus* fresh from the Front. I could hear the cannonading and it gave me a thrill of delight. I beheld my first string of German prisoners in grey-green coats, marching methodically. Troops were being landed in the Port and supply columns congested the narrow streets. All day I dodged from one vantage point to another, seeing a hundred things I was not supposed to see. And I was innocently happy thinking how I was getting ahead of the boys back in Calais.

That evening I was arrested. I was watching ambulances load the wounded on a train when suddenly a *gendarme* pounced on me. He was dark and truculent. His bushy eyebrows met over his hawk-like nose and his eyes were angry. He demanded my papers; then instead of telling me they were in order he curtly ordered me to follow him. He took me to an office where sat a Major with a good humoured face that grew stern as soon as a he looked at my passport. I could not blame him. That passport was a record of my travels over much of Europe. It had all kinds of outlandish visas, including German ones. It was really a sinister document. After examining it he turned me over to the *gendarme* whom he called Gaspard. The eyes of Gaspard gleamed with triumph. It was he who had made this arrest. As he told me gloatingly, the whole police force had been combing the town for me since morning. Only he with his superior acumen had calculated that sooner or later I would seek the station, and for hours he had lain in wait.

Now he had nabbed a dangerous spy — for it seemed that was how I was regarded. My surreptitious entry into the town, my innocent evasion of the police, my equivocal passport, all went to convince Gaspart that I was an *espion de premier ordre*. This he told me, fiercely, pointing a big revolver with my navel for its bull's eye. As he accused me a crowd collected — menacing, murmuring, glaring, so that now Gaspard became my bulwark barring me from their wrath. For at that moment Dunkirk was having a wave of spy fever, and they were shooting suspects at sight. I wondered if I, too, might not be a victim; though I did not take the matter too seriously. Yet I was marched through the streets with a big pistol jabbing at my spine, for Gaspard was taking no chances. He dared me to make a break for liberty, when he would have shot me like a dog.

Then followed what I will always consider to be a doleful experience. First I was interviewed by a General. He was severe, but when he looked over my passport he became grim. He kept all my papers, congratulated Gaspard, then had me conducted to a guard room where I was locked in. It had whitewashed walls, a small barred window and was unfurnished but for two chairs. I sat on one of these and, putting my feet on the other, I tried to make myself comfortable. But I did not like the look of things. I had a feeling they might shoot first and inquire after.

That was a nasty night, I did not sleep for worrying over what the dawn would bring forth. It brought forth Gaspard. He grinned ruefully and told me he had instructions to take me before the English Captain of the Port. My hopes rose. Now I would have a chance to square myself. So again I was marched through streets and streets accompanied by a vindictive mob who hissed *"Espion!"* I was painfully glad when I was shown into the presence of the Port Captain. He sat behind a big desk while in a far corner, behind a small desk, sat a naval cadet. Gaspard handed him my various credentials which he examined grimly, giving me a piercing look from time to time. Finally he turned to Gaspard. "These papers seem to be in order. Why have you arrested this man?"

I heard Gaspard explain that I had entered Dunkirk by a back way and all day had evaded arrest. As he did so I saw the cadet start and gaze at me as if petrified. More than anything else that made me grasp the gravity of my situation. I was in serious danger. Then for the first time in my life I realised *I had a heart*. I was conscious of a steady pounding going on inside my chest. "You're in a tough spot, laddie," I thought.

That Captain, too, seemed amazed at my audacity. "What have you to say yourself?" he snapped. "It's quite correct," I said. "I did come into Dunkirk by the back door; but in Calais the boys told me it was the only way to make it, so I took a chance. Risk is my job. I had to get a story for my paper and I did not think I was doing anything really wrong. Some of the other chaps did it."

He grinned wryly. "But you are aware you have no right to be here, and the faster you get out the better. As for this spy business, let me tell you you've had a narrow escape. There's a big scare on and they seem to have lost their heads. Only this morning they shot half a dozen poor devils off hand. I am sure some of them were innocent. If I had not been here to intervene you might have been one of them. Now take your papers and GET OUT!"

Then rising, he shook his hands with me, saying to the flabbergasted Gaspard: "This man is innocent. You may release him." I thanked the Captain fervently. As I went into the street Gaspard was there. He said: "In spite of it all, I believe you are a spy." I wanted to thumb my nose at him but I only gave him a look of contempt. So with a sense of escape I strode to the station where I took the train for Calais. When I got to the hotel I told the boys of my adventure and they roared with laughter. To be shot as a spy seemed a "helluva joke."

This escapade disgusted me with the correspondent game. "If I could only get a break," I reflected, "I could put it over these newspaper guys. The only one doing decent stuff is an amateur called Philip Gibbs and the others call his work 'sob stories.' What they do is just common reporting, without distinction or imagination...." Yet despite my defeat I felt I must make another try to get a ringside seat at the Big Show.

Back in Paris I got two good stories. One evening in the Place Clichy I saw a crowd milling around a drunk Tommy. He was an elderly man, small and wiry, covered with mud and wearing a woollen nightcap. I rescued him from a mob of women who were affectionately mauling him, and bought him a bottle of wine. "We got it pretty 'ot, Sir," he told me. "I'm the only one left of our lot. Them Youlans would have speared me like a hog if I 'adn't shammed dead, lying under a gun carriage.... But oh, the time we 'ad on the way to Mons! The men cheered us, the women kissed us and they gave us so much wine we was urinating red. But the coming back was bloody. How I felt ashamed to face them same people! But they gave me this tam o' shanter because I lost me 'elmet."

He hung on to his rifle, however, and still was full of fight. "I want to go back to Mons," he kept saying, "and 'ave another go at 'em." But the Army thought otherwise. They gave the old chap a Victoria Cross and kept him at home as a training sergeant.

Then one night I saw crowds lining one of the Montmartre streets. They were mostly women, some of whom would break away to kiss one of the soldiers who were passing in a column. Many of these soldiers were black. Their teeth flashed ferociously as they grinned at us. All were in full fighting kit yet their spirits seemed high, for they were going forward to the Battle of the Marne. I stood there all night long and in the dim light I saw the Foreign Legion file past. Then regiment after regiment of colonial troops. Then what seemed to be every taxi in Paris crammed with cheering *poilus*. It was an inspiring sight and only in the dim dawn did I go home too tired to write my story.

The next few days were heavy with anxiety. I knew nothing, heard nothing as we gazed anxiously in the direction where one of the greatest battles of history was being fought. But we thought that Paris was doomed, and the following week would see the *Boche* marching under the *Arc de Triomphe*. Though most of my friends scrammed, I decided I would stick it. The weather had been brooding and sinister, but the Sunday dawned bright and clear and somehow we all sensed that a miracle had happened. Apprehensively we had been waiting to hear the guns of the enemy; now all was silent. Only later did we know that one of the most glorious pages in history had just been written.

I was eating my heart out to think I could not get into the thick of things, when I saw in the paper that an American Ambulance Unit was being formed and that drivers were needed. I applied for further information and received a letter from one of the leaders asking me to meet him at the Hotel Meurice. "It's like this," he told me, "a bunch of the boys were whooping it up in the Ritz Bar when someone suggested that we form an Ambulance Corps. We all had cars and were willing to turn them into ambulances and drive them ourselves, so we decided to offer our services to the French Government. They accepted. Now we are attached to the army of Foch. But we need young men who are not afraid to rough it and have a taste for adventure. If you join us we will send you to the Front, only you must promise not to write a word on anything you see."

Of course I promised, though that was the very thing I meant to do. But that was for the future to realise. In the meantime I went to London, bought a uniform and felt rather a fool in it. Being what they called a "gentleman driver" I had an officer's standing. This embarrassed me. I was not a fighting man, yet *pukka* soldiers were saluting me. I got so that when I saw a Tommy coming I would dodge round a block. I did not wear my Red Cross arm band, for I was ashamed I was not a combatant. Though I did not want to kill I was willing to take a chance of being killed. If only I could get some *gore* on my uniform I might feel better. Anyway, I was no longer a nosy newspaper slacker. . . .

A week later I was driving an ambulance under fire. It was on a long stretch of Flanders road, and I had five wounded in my car. This road was raked by German battery as I hurried over it. Suddenly I heard a shell burst. I saw a cloud of black smoke, while gravel and stones spattered the car. I hesitated to dash on or to stop; but my orders had been to do the latter, so I put on the brakes. A good job too, for ahead there was another explosion with a mushroom of evil black smoke. I had three walking wounded and two stretcher cases, so with the air of the first, I got the stretchers into the ditch and there we waited till dusk. I had felt no fear, only a thrill that had something of pleasure in it. I had been under fire. I could go back to Chelsea now and take a salute.

Our headquarters were in a *château* where we slept on the floor and had food provided by the French army. But we all contributed for extras so that our fare compared favourably with the best officers' mess. Dinner every evening was a scene of hilarity.

Wine flowed freely and everyone was in high spirits. Perhaps there was something feverish in our gaiety, for we were keyed up by the events of the day. We joked, laughed, sang, told stories, anything to make us forget the roar of the cannon that sometimes seemed to rock the ground about us. It may seem a dreadful thing to say, but we were actually *enjoying* the war.

Taxi jobs took up our days and by work well done we earned our evening gaiety. When not on duty I would go for long walks through fields where crops were rich with promise. It was a peaceful scene, though in the distance I could hear the guns, like the flapping of a gigantic blanket, and sometimes clouds of smoke would stain the horizon. Often I gained a knoll from which I could see spires of villages that were in enemy hands, and I would wonder wistfully what was happening there. Overhead at all times were Hun places, dodging between silver puffs of shell-burst. I watched them, hoping to see one brought down, but they seemed to enjoy a miraculous safety. In these fields of Picardy the contrast between peace and war was brought home to me, with the peasants ploughing peacefully under the very guns. I was happy, for I was in uniform and proving myself worthy to wear it. Somehow I did not think of writing any more. All I wanted was to be a good soldier, even if I were a phony one.

Despite the usefulness of my work I began to long for something more exciting, so volunteered for outpost duty. We had several posts close to the First Aid Stations, and kept cars there day and night. There were two of us to a car and we were relieved every ten days. The life was rough, for we had to sleep in our clothes on the floor of a ruined cottage, or in a tent or dugout. We were exposed to shell-fire, at least to a direct hit, so that as we slept we felt we were in the hands of Providence. Usually we resigned ourselves on a bad night of bombing, thinking that if a shell did get us we would never be any the wiser. Soon the cannonading ceased to keep us awake; it was the rats that really annoyed us. A rat running across one's chest can feel as heavy as a sheep, and one of my best laughs was to see a big grey one chewing the beard of an old *poilu* by my side.

The night driving was the worst. We could not show the faintest light and the roads were pitted with shell holes. It was nerve-racking, crawling on low speed, with a badly wounded man along those coal-black devastated roads. Once I had a soldier die in my car — but I prefer to forget that. There is so much I want to forget. Those who went through the horror of war never want to talk about it. But if there was a slaughter, there was also laughter. We would laugh a lot, mostly about nothing, and we became very callous, grumbling if brains or guts soiled the car. We were sorry for the poor devils but saw so many they were like shadows.

I always begged to go forward with the stretcher men to fetch the wounded from the front line. There were two men to a stretcher and they were glad of a third to spell them off. I loved those trips to the firing trench, or even into No Man's Land. We made them during the day when we had cover, but when we were exposed we took the wounded after dark. The danger enhanced the heartening feeling of saving life. All of us were keen on those hazards for they gave us a pride in our job. We felt a certain shame that we were not fighting men. However, most of us were middle age, while the younger ones were American citizens and that country had not yet come in. Grand fellows all — I never expected to work with finer.

In the early stages of the war I felt no fear. I used to prowl close to the front line, and once or twice got myself into trouble. In some cases the German trenches were only a few yards away, so I got a thrill out of the nearness. To think that I was exposed to fire bolstered my self-respect, and sometimes I would leap out of a trench in full sight of the enemy lines. I was a show-off and a fool. That I did not get a bullet in my hide was no fault of mine, for I loved the twang of them. But towards the end I got jumpy, hating the nearby crash of a shell and its concussion. War does not improve on acquaintance. It resolves itself into filth, confusion, boredom. Though I tried to avoid the latter by courting danger in the end I came to realise I had a yellow streak a yard wide.

After a month or so at the various advance posts it was grand to get back to the peace of the *château*. I had a wonderful feeling of relaxation and a sense of duty done. Oh, the goodness of the golden garden! — loafing, dreaming, forgetting that so few miles away men were murdering each other. How beautiful this world could be! Yet we must make it hell. Strolling in the radiant sweetness of those sunny alleys I thought: Why cannot it always be like this? … And once again it seemed to me I heard my *Harps of Heaven*.

Of course it was not always so serene. We had time of battle, big and small, which were strenuous enough. Often for nights there would be no sleep as the stream of wounded kept us on the run. As a rule the bigger the battle the smaller the danger; for then things were organized so that we took up our loads less close to the fighting zone. But there was always the same long, straight road lined with walking wounded who threw away their rifle cartridges as they trudged to the rear; always the same metallic atmosphere, the din, the concussion, the apathy of the soldiers, the excitability of the officers; then to the rear the sweating surgeons, their bare arms gay with gore; the hospitals where one helped to carry severed limbs, unexpectedly heavy, and dump them in a ditch.

Night brought no respite. With star shells brilliant about us we scurried back and forth, clearing hundreds of cases between dark and dawn. The difficulty was to keep awake. Often we dozed over the wheel till a jolt would tell us we were running into a ditch. To fall asleep was deadly, and only when we were empty did we flirt with death. But the weariness was overwhelming and there was no rest. I remember one night in a furious electric storm; it was far from the Front but it seemed as if the thunder and lightning were trying to mimic it. How I laughed at that paltry imitation. The thunder might crash, the lightning flash, it was as nothing compared to the roar of the guns and the blast of the shells. I who had always hated thunderstorms now jeered at the puny efforts of the heavens. Man could so easily out-horror nature I would never be afraid of storms again.

But so grateful was the lull after battle we would soon forget it in happy comradeship. We would utterly ignore the War, being more interested in eating and drinking. In fact liquid refreshment played a big part in our lives. I was very proud of the Corps in these days, and felt privileged to be a member. It really did a memorable job both in the Champagne and the Verdun show. Later I was asked to be its historian and write a book about it. However, I had not the time at the moment for my real war book was in the matrix.

I was happy with the Ambulance Corps. With our gallant lads and ramshackle cars we did worthy work. We had many distinguished visitors, among them Granville Barker. I offered to take him to a danger point, but he said he would only accompany me if I would write his obituary. In our mess we did not talk shop and I never heard a word of smut. The standard of duty and devotion was high, while above all our Chief commanded our affection. Oh, it was a grand life! I would have gone on with it until the end had not a queer sickness befallen me.

Chapter Twenty-Six

Leningrad

My first impression of Leningrad station was of shabby meanness. It was old and grimy, not at all like the swank border terminus. From the packed platform peasants gazed at us unbelievingly. Who were these plump and dapper strangers? By the way they stared we might have been from another planet. They looked at our clothes with envious wonder. Well they might, for they had been told that in foreign countries there was nothing but misery. Only in happy Russia were people well clad, well fed. We must be pillars of capitalism.

They did not resent us because, at heart, they too were capitalist. Aren't we all? We love to live on unearned increment, and clip our coupons, wishing we had more. I like Russians but I dislike Communists, and it is pleasant to think that in Russia only ten per cent of the population are Marx-minded. And it is only on the faces of the latter one sees our envy of the well-dressed stranger. The others, no doubt, are envious, but there is no hate in their hearts.

A girl with a patched skirt took charge of us and we were caught up in the machinery of Intourist. Tattered porters grabbed our baggage. They looked so hungry one wanted to tip them but we were told tips were taboo. However, it was pleasant to be herded like sheep with nothing to worry about. Cars were awaiting us. Everything was arranged.

"Hotel Astoria," said the girl guide. "The best in Leningrad," said the Drummer.

I have nothing but good to say about Intourist. They treated us well, and though I travelled second class I had the best hotels and bedrooms with baths. The organization was good. If the employees were sometimes indifferent is it not the same with Government servants everywhere? But why, I wonder, *is* Intourist? In all countries they have fine offices which, I am sure, do not pay expenses. It is not the money brought into the country, for this is small. And it is not to welcome sympathizers, for most tourists are hostile. I think it is to prove that Russia is making progress. One is shown all that is worth seeing and steered away from the unsightly. They are naively proud of the advance they have made. Before the war they were a hundred years behind civilized Europe. Now they are about thirty, and in that time they may overtake us. But will they keep it up? I question it. I do not believe Russia will ever attain the culture of France. Just as Japan has remained Asiatic, so will the land of the Soviets.

I will never forget my first impression of Leningrad. There was an open vastness about it, a lavish spaciousness. No pedestrian proposition this. At the thought of perambulative sight-seeing my legs ached. Is there any other city that offers such wide vistas, and stretches with such assured majesty? True, one noted the streets needed repair, the paving was broken, the asphalt caved in. The buildings were unpainted and crumbling in decay. And the further one went the more one was conscious of poverty and neglect. Even as we thrilled at the magnificent prospect we were bumped by the roughness of the road. Even as we were roused to admiration by the monuments and mansions we were conscious of corruption and decline.

The Hotel Astoria is historic. It stands in the shadow of St. Isaac's Cathedral and in olden days was the scene of civic splendours. It also played a part in the Revolution. As we drew up a porter advanced who looked like an admiral. There were several of these door porters, old-style Russians with beards and shabby uniforms. The hall porters were of the Soviet type, lean-jawed, unshaven, in black shirts and sandals. The old men were sad and gentle; the young insolent and cynical.

We surrendered our passports and were given rooms. As I went up in a lift I could realize that this hotel had been palatial. There was a drawing room to each floor, furnished with faded splendour of the past; and in an alcove a chamber-maid in black, with cap and apron of lace. She seemed to fit the elegance of the alcove with its overhead lighting. As a rule she sat at a Louis Quinze table, looking like a French maid in a Parisian setting. The effect of these reception rooms from the passing elevator was theatrical.

By a long corridor I reached my chamber. A bristly valet in a dirty blouse showed me in. It was large and over full of furniture. There was a sofa, seven chairs, a round table. Everything was dingy, faded, none too clean. The closed window gave on a court, the air was warm and stale. The wash basin had no plug and had become detached from the wall, so that only the water pipe held it in place. I mention this to show how everything pertaining to the old *régime* is being allowed to go to ruin. As a relic of Czarism the Hotel Astoria seemed to be doomed.

It was two o'clock, so after a hasty wash I dashed down to lunch. But I need not have worried for it was just beginning. I found a place in the dining room that looked out on the Cathedral and hoped for the waiter. There were seven of them with soiled linen jackets over shabby street clothes. After ten minutes or so one of them approached me leisurely. "Ticket!" he snapped.

I gave him my Intourist coupon for a midday meal and he handed me a bill of fare in French. I decided to make my lunch as Russian as possible, so I chose caviar, bortsch, boiled sturgeon and ice cream. My experience is that from the time of ordering a meal and receiving it half an hour elapses. At first you are impatient but after a while you get used to it. There seemed to be no hurry and one ceased to hurry oneself. I would not have minded waiting if the man had brought me what I ordered; but he forgot the caviar, gave me cabbage soup which *repeated* all day, served me fried sturgeon instead of boiled, and ordinary ice cream instead of *Pêche Melba*. However, I accepted everything meekly, washing it down with the inevitable glass of tea.

Afterwards I learned to do better. I insisted on caviar with every meal, the black Beluga — not the red tinned stuff; I got the real bortsch, blood red and turning to pink as I added cream; I found sturgeon hard and gluey and came to prefer stergel. I stuck to ice cream, which is made in Government factories and of good quality. I drank Narzan or pink lemonade. Occasionally I had gobbits of lamb, impaled on a dagger. One got enormous helpings. If you ordered chicken half the bird was served. The food was rich and satisfying; but, after all, I was staying at the first hotel in Leningrad.

I succeeded, however, in accelerating the service, so that instead of waiting half an hour for food a quarter sufficed. This is how it happened ... There was a waiter of an aristocratic type who suggested the old regime. He was very melancholy, with a faraway look in his eyes. Perhaps he was dreaming of the gilded past in which he had been an honoured guest where he was now a shabby servitor. In his slow distracted way he waited on us, looking so sad I felt sorry for him. Then one day I suggested to the Drummer: "Suppose we try to tip him."

"Don't you do it," he warned. "It's against the rules of the Soviet Constitution. It's an insult not only to them, but to Stalin and all the Kremlin gang. He will resent it. There will be a scene. We'll have the whole bunch down on us."

"I don't care," I told him. "I'm sorry for the poor devil. I'll try to slip him a rouble." I was nervous about it but I plucked up my courage, thinking that at the worst I could only be conducted to the frontier. The dramatic moment arrived. The Prince, as we called him, was standing in a trance near the door, a dirty serviette over his arm. I tickled the palm of his hand with a bill and the effect was magical. Eagerly he grabbed it while his face lit up with a smile of joy. In a moment he was bowing us to the door, holding it open for us. I have never seen a tip so thankfully received. After that I did it all the time, and people wondered why I got served so quickly. Tipping may be forbidden in Russia, but because of that tips are doubly welcome. Never did I have one refused.

"I want a comb," I said to the Drummer. "Let's seek one on the Nevsky Prospect."

So we strolled forth and soon found ourselves in that famous thoroughfare. The packed pavements were streams of shabby humanity, jostling in the hot sunshine. Most of the men wore only short sleeved cotton shirts, shoddy trousers and sandals on bare feet. Of the women not one in a hundred had a hat, and only a few "perms." They walked with the loose freedom of the corsetless, their breasts proudly advanced, their hips unrestrained. Their bare feet squeezed into high-heeled shoes. They seemed sensual in a healthy way, while their broad faces had a contented look.

By comparison with the packed pavements the great boulevard looked like a desert. I supposed it must be the broadest street in the world, for the crowds on the opposite side seemed dim and distant, and the policeman stationed in the middle were like remote mannikins. They were alert, however, for when we decided to make a dash across, a shrill whistle arrested us. As we were already halfway over and the policeman was two hundred yards distant I suggested we keep a-going; but we saw a Red soldier turn in his tracks and go back, so we, too, obediently retraced our steps.

The Nevsky Prospect, avenue once so proud and opulent, had fallen on evil days. Again one noted that passion to blot out the past and to show, by degrading its monuments, how futile and abortive it had been. Says your Bolshevist: "Let us obliterate this accursed heritage and live only for the future. All that is beautiful we hate because it was conceived under Czarism, and we will do all we can to reduce its grace to misery and derision."

This was visible in the Nevsky Prospect, but most of all it showed in the shops, once so richly cosmopolitan. Mirrors were cracked, cabinets broken, silver brackets wrenched away. The inlaid woodwork was scarred and filthied, while the Red riffraff eddied about the products of the Soviet Union which boasts that only Russian goods are sold in Russia. There was no attempt at display. In most cases the shop windows were almost empty, which did not prevent them being besieged by a mob of buyers, eager to turn their roubles into something concrete. To them, deprived so long of the needs of life, even banality seemed beauty.

It was easier to print roubles than to produce goods and the first had outpaced the second. It was more important to make tractors than to make shoes, yet the man who makes tractors wants to spend his wages on clothes. As he finds few of these his roubles often remain unspent. For instance, in a furrier's shop was a consignment of squirrel coats. They were his whole stock and they would be sold that evening. A mob of women were pawing and grabbing at them, trying them on before cracked but bevelled mirrors. They were shapeless as a sack, though the fur seemed fair. And as I stood in that lamentable shop I saw a woman who had the look of a factory worker exchange a roll of paper money for a graceless fur mantle. In the days of the Czar she would have worked a lifetime to own such a coat. No wonder she looked radiant.

The next shop I did not enter, for a crowd of two hundred waited to go in. Some of them had been there for hours, green roubles clutched in sweat hands to be exchanged for a pair of shoes. For buying shoes is slower business than buying sugar. One has to have some sort of a fit, hence the long line that extended round the block. Yet many would go home shoeless, for before they could pass those portals the consignment would be gone.

The third shop filled me with a frantic desire to escape, for the air made me want to vomit. The counters were piled with pork products, chiefly various kinds of sausage. There were also canned goods and groceries. But the mob of buyers was assailing the stock with such avidity it looked as if it would soon be exhausted. To make a purchase one had first to buy a ticket for the exact sum. This was exchanged for the article desired. There was no quibbling. You took what was slung at you by a snappish shopman who did not conceal his contempt for the crowd. They were Government employees and their job was to serve the customer, not to please him. I was glad to get away from the mass of smelly humanity that stood three deep for a can of peaches or a pound of tea. Then I remembered I had come to buy a comb.

In a shop near the Black Cathedral of Kazan I thought I might find what I wanted. It was below the level of the street and jammed with women buyers. There were half a dozen shop girls in grey slip-overs, and seen in the dim light they were unusually discouraging. I tackled the nearest but she turned her back on me. To the next I seemed to be invisible. A third deigned to regard me with distinctive dislike, and to her I confided my need, by making the motion of combing my silvery locks. After gazing at me for a moment with proletarian disdain she brought me a card of *small tooth combs*. In my best Scotch accent I advised her to keep them for her own use and left the shop.

Outside I found the Drummer in conversation with a stranger. He introduced me. "A Jew boy who wants to speak English with us. He says he has only studied it a month and already he's a wonder." The young man was about twenty, tall, slim, handsome. He had silky black hair, velvet brown eyes, clear pale complexion and fine aquiline features. His clothing consisted of a cotton shirt, old cotton trousers and broken canvas shoes. In short, he suggested grievous poverty. Yet in his hand he held a fistful of roubles.

He spoke English, halting over each word and bringing it out with difficulty. I told him of my attempt to buy a comb, so he volunteered to help me. We re-entered the shop and the girl was impressed by his air of assurance. She brought us a card of celluloid combs, very thin and flimsy. I took one and the Jew boy said he would take one also. Then he said: "I'll pay for yours. I have lots of money — two thousand roubles." Of course I told him the thing was impossible even if he had two hundred thousand; but I would gladly pay for his, which I did.

Then we rejoined the Drummer and our new friend offered to accompany us on our promenade. At a lemonade kiosk he wanted to buy us a drink but we did not fancy the pinkish liquid. As we walked he told us he had just received a scholarship of two thousand roubles and was going to study electrical engineering. Meantime he played the accordion in a jazz band. I noted his long, delicate hands and asked if he played the piano. He said he played Chopin, Beethoven, Mozart. He would love to devote himself to music but there was no money in it. He could do better in electricity. He was handsome, vivacious, charming. Standing there in his rags with his pockets full of roubles he made a curious impression on me.

"It's funny he hangs on to us like this," I said to the Drummer. "He's delightful, but I imagine he's got some game on." "I think so too," said the Drummer. "He's too clever to be disinterested. We'll wait and see what happens."

We decided to visit the Black Cathedral which had been turned into an anti-religious museum. The Jew boy insisted on paying our entry fee so that we had some difficulty in refunding him his money. Always he kept harping on that two thousand roubles and displaying a big roll of bills.... The museum was instituted to show that Religion was founded on Fear and fostered by Ignorance. It tried to prove that belief and superstition were one and that the church down the ages had been the enemy of human enlightenment. Beginning with primitive man it claimed that religion had its birth in darkness and dreams, and that from the gods of the jungle grew the Deity idea through the centuries.

It showed the sinister side of worship, the blood rites, the massacres done in the name of the Church. In places it was a veritable Chamber of Horrors, Inquisition cells, witch doctors, bones of saints, and holy relics which the public were invited to regard with ridicule. To me it seemed grotesque. It slammed religion so savagely that in the end one sympathized with it. Soon it became a comic show; yet here were bands of school children conducted by their teachers and told how the Church and Capitalism were the twin oppressors of mankind.

But though this interested the Drummer I noticed that it bored our Jew friend. He admitted it was the first time he had been in the place and refused to answer our queries, saying he did not know. Then he began to ply us with questions about America, prices, social conditions and the chances of making money. From his eagerness it was apparent he regarded the States as an earthly paradise and would have given one of his eyes to go there. And he would have been a success, for he had charm, looks, intelligence. But there was no hope for him. He must make the best of this Russia where he was a prisoner for life.

All this he made plain to us and we felt rather sorry for him. Then at last he revealed his interest in us and why he cultivated us so assiduously. It was *Clothes*.... "Look at me," he said. "I am a begger, yet I have two thousand roubles. I want to be dressed like you. I want American clothes, English clothes. I want coat, suit, trousers, shirt, tie, shoes — yes, above all, shoes. Please, please sell me some clothes — any clothes. I give you all the money you want. I don't care for money. I want to dress like you. Please you sell me ... No?"

We tried to explain that we were only travelling with what we actually needed and that our shoes would not fit him. "That's all right," he told us. "Fit no matter. Leather good, cloth good. That good for me. Come, I give you all my money — two thousand roubles. You give me suit, shoes, shirt, tie, I dress like American...."

It struck us that if we accepted his offer we could be put in prison for illegal trading. Perhaps he was an *agent provocateur.* Again we assured him we had nothing to sell. Yet he pleaded desperately. He would meet us anytime, anywhere. He would come to our hotel that evening. He touched our suits wistfully. He begged for my old school tie and the Drummer's silk socks, but by this time we were so scared of him we were adamant. Then suddenly he saw it was no good. He was beaten, and all at once his manner changed. He became cool and contemptuous. Looking like a nobleman even in his rags he drew himself up and bowed icily. Then without a word of goodbye he turned on his heel and was lost in the crowd.

Chapter Twenty-Seven

Pushkin

A section of the fine but faded lobby of the Astoria was devoted to the office of Intourist. Here a pretty girl arranged the daily excursions. There are certain trips you are encouraged to take. Factories, hospitals and social centres are considered more worthy of your attention than art museums and historical monuments. Yet the latter are not entirely debarred and it was with considerable eagerness I elected to visit the Palace of Pushkin.

An ancient bus jolted us over a rough road, while from its floor came an evil odour. It was like stale vomit; indeed two of our party were sick owing to the bumpy motion. They were French school teachers and, of course, Communists. I noticed a large, peasant looking woman smiling at me and wondered if I was making a conquest, despite my silver locks. However, it turned out she was our guide.

Intourist guides sometimes complain that visitors try to seduce them, yet nearly all with whom I came in contact with were in no danger in that way. Rash would have been the Casanova who would have dared to lay siege to them; but one of them haughtily turned down the Drummer when he offered to buy her ice cream. I have no doubt she thought he had designs, though being rickety and otherwise ill favoured, she might have considered herself safe.

However, our present guide, though hardly worthy of seduction, was a personable female, fat and fortyish, with stockings and a turban of canary colour. She spoke English with little accent and told us she was preparing to take her final exam for a professorship in that language. Her husband was an engineer, so that between them they made a snug income and approximated to the bourgeois type. Yet she was a good Communist, defending the system with spirit. In answer to my polite curiosity she told me her first name was Tamara.

On our way to Pushkin we passed through a slummy district and saw before a shop a line of customers extending down the block. There was something desperate about that patient column, or would have been if they had been waiting for food. But Tamara told us it was for silk stockings. The guides did not like us to notice these long queues and tried to explain them by the temporary shortage of luxury goods.

In this section of the city much building was going on, and the expansion was encouraged by the Government, as it developed a Leningrad of Soviet origin. To house the workers in the nearby factories huge blocks of apartment buildings were going up. The apartments consisted of two rooms each, with a communal kitchen for every seven. They were box-like constructions of concrete, as if the architect had aimed at ugliness instead of beauty. There were more aesthetic houses of red brick, but these were designed for Government departments. Here I saw a groping for something essentially Soviet in architecture, but so far no clearly defined style has developed.

Emerging from this industrial zone we found ourselves in a farming region. In the distance were factory-like buildings, while the road was lined with log cabins of the old Russian type. There would be a slovenly garden, mud-plastered walls, a patched roof of rotting thatch. Half-naked children played without enthusiasm, while bare-footed women fetched water from the wells. The scene suggested a procrastinating people, who took life easily, preferring to suffer sordid conditions than to make any effort to rise above them. Here is the traditional Russian peasant and it will take a lot of communising to change him. Progress may go forward in a series of drives but, these exhausted, human nature will triumph in the end.

★

Entering Pushkin through an arched gateway we found ourselves in a broad avenue, flanked by houses that resembled small *châteaux*. Now they served as institutions for the people. But beauty and Communism do not click, so everything was allowed to run down — lawns strewn with refuse, crumbling stone and rotting woodwork. But please do not think I complain of this democratic decadence, for I have only to think of the old Czarist regime to feel as ruthless a Communist as the best.

And now as we drew up before the Palace of Pushkin I surveyed with amazement its vast proportions. In the olden days it must have rivalled Versailles in beauty and splendour. Its ornate façade stretched in a terraced vista, fronted by fountain, garden and grove down to a lovely lake. But it would take a dozen chapters to describe this palace which is so beautiful even the Bolsheviks held it inviolate. However, they preserve it not for its beauty but as an object lesson. The people are admitted free, then … well, listen to the guide:

"Look how good we are to you. In the olden days you could not have entered here even on your bended knees. Now you are welcome, for it belongs to You, the People. Look at this magnificence born of your sweat and toil. In hunger and poverty your fathers built up these palaces; in sickness and suffering they lived like beasts to bring this beauty into being. They were treated like dogs, unfit to breathe the air of the gilded domes their bleeding hands lifted to high heaven. But now *you* breathe it. You laugh and feel at home in these splendid halls, for they are yours. Their former masters died the death of dogs and it is your turn to triumph. You see how they lusted and orgied and mocked your misery. Now it is you who rejoice and give thanks to the glory of Communism, for it has delivered you from hell and given you a new heaven."

Pretty propaganda! No wonder these lovely floors are kept polished by human scarecrows, these exquisite walls preserved by emaciated artists, for they are damning proofs of a dark and iniquitous past. And so from all parts of the land the People are brought to see them, not to admire, but to condemn them as infamous and degrading exhibits of Imperial oppression. Tamara was something of an artist, yet after pointing out some rare bit of loveliness she conscientiously gave her approval a proletarian twist. But obviously she loved beauty for its own sake, for her propaganda lacked fervour. Then again her sense of humour balked her, for she was one of the few I met who seemed to have it. That's what is the matter with Marxism. It lacks a saving sense of humour, forgetting that only stupid people take themselves seriously. The peasants are more intelligent. They laugh, and most of all at themselves. But then no one likes the peasants — except the peasants.

But to return to Pushkin.... It struck me as a country edition of the Winter Palace. There were the same succession of marvellous halls crammed with richness. You passed rapidly from one vast room to another, and each seemed to surpass the former in beauty. All were so different as to make a bewildering contrast; yet their number was so great you had to go through them quickly, so that your final impression was one of despairing satiety. They merged into a picture of barbaric magnificence, of sybaritic splendour. There are over a thousand rooms in the Winter Palace, and I do not know how many in Pushkin, but Tamara almost sprinted to get them in. Continually she spurred us on, then she would remember her job, stop short, and shoot off a line of dope boosting the Soviets.

After a bit the Drummer and I got on to these interludes and as she yawned in the midst of a harangue we told her to cut the cackle and show us the sights. The pictures alone were a show in themselves. There were many paintings of Catherine the Great, though our guide reproved me when I called her "Great." She was, said Tamara, a horrid woman, given to eating and drinking and sleeping in turn with every soldier in her regiment. The last she did not express in my rude language, but hinted at it delicately.

As a matter of fact that was the feature of Catherine that interested the Drummer most, but Tamara would not him draw her on this subject, and was disgusted when he avowed his admiration for the Imperial nymphomaniac. On the other hand, she said Peter the Great really deserved his title. There was a Man. He would have made a good Communist. Communists like Peter because he once worked in a shipyard and was a ruthless character.

There was another band of sight-seers led by an earnest girl guide who was handing them propaganda by the yard. They were peasants and she addressed them like children. The women had bright blouses and bad teeth, the men were hulking oafs. But the moment they saw our little party the guide might have been talking to four walls. With eyes wide and gaping jaws they stared at us as if they had never seen a foreigner before — which probably they hadn't. And as they followed on our heels they continued to regard us as one of the wonders of the Palace, which otherwise seemed to bore them. As some of the girls nudged and tittered I accused the Drummer of making his usual killing, and perhaps I was not far out. No doubt some village damsel went home to dream not of the marvels of Pushkin but of the dashing stranger fresh from another world.

We were foot-sore and fed up with banqueting halls where dinners lasted all night, and boudoirs where the insatiable Catherine entertained her lovers. We were weary of halls of lapis lazuli and amber and porcelain. We wanted to see human stuff, and that was to be the climax of our visit, the intimate Palace of the Czar. Since the massacre in the vast square before the Winter Palace the Czar hated it. A kindly soul, he retired to Pushkin and lived a life almost bourgeois in its simplicity. That part of the Palace near the lake was occupied by the Royal family and is ideally beautiful. The swarded banks slope to the water, while noble trees preen themselves in its sky-blue mirror. With their ice cream kiosks and rowdy rowboats even the proletariat cannot mar its charm.

It is when one enters the series of rooms one realizes that kings and princes are no more than plain people and their pomp and pride a hollow sham. Perhaps it was for this reason the Government preserved those rooms exactly as the family of the Czar left them. But the feeling aroused in the intelligent observer is one of pity. However, such commiseration is foreign to Communist mentality and the hordes who pour through these rooms get the Soviet slant on the exhibition. For these intimate vestiges of Royal domesticity are shown to the vulgar public in a spirit of jeering bravado, even the bathrooms and water closets being exposed to the gloating gaze. Besides being sad there is something indecent about it, but there is little decency in the Communist character. Even Tamara looked on it with sheer contempt, as if the Royal family were vermin who deserved to be stamped out.

I don't think there is any remorse in Russia for that massacre, and perhaps they were right in what they did. The continued existence of the Czar and his son might have led to efforts to restore him to the throne. Better sacrifice a dozen lives than risk the slaughter of a million. There will never again be a Czar of the Russias and this is to the good, for hateful as is the new regime the old one was detestable. Deep as is my disgust for Bolshevism, at the thought of Czarism I become an ardent Communist.

Of the score or so of rooms that make up the Royal suite three remain vivid in my memory. This first is a Council Chamber panelled in exotic wood. There is a marble table that during the war used to be spread with maps, and round this the Czar and his generals would spend hours. Here, warmed by good wine and smoking their cigars, they decided the fate of millions. That amateur soldier, the Czar, had the last word ... No, I am wrong. The last word was still more amateur. It came from the Czarina. For overhanging the Council table was a gallery and here sat the Czarina with Rasputin. And it was she, prompted by Rasputin, who had the final say. Often a decision would be countermanded at the last moment by the brutish monk who was the real ruler of Russia. I sometimes wonder if other councils of war are not equally irresponsible.

The second room was the living room. It was of medium proportions, and had rather a low ceiling. Stairs led to a gallery behind, which in turn led to the sleeping quarters. To the right was the Czar's writing-table — small, leather-covered and of horse-shoe shape. On it were his pens and inkwell, just as when he wrote his last letter. There he used to sit smiling, dreaming and watching his family. On the opposite side of the room was a vast divan in brown velvet, and on this the children used to throw themselves, romping or sitting clustered over a book. To the rear, like a cushioned throne, was the chair of the Czarina. It needed little imagination to picture that scene of loving gaiety. Yet here was the girl guide of the peasant group telling them that the Czar was an ogre and his children a brood of vampires.

The third room was most pathetic of all. It was the nursery of the little Prince, spacious and overlooking the lake. In the sunshine it must have been bright and joyous. The feature of it was one of those toboggan slides so common to Russian nurseries. But this was a giant one. Mounted by a winding stair it was about twelve feet high, and its shining surface projected one far on to the polished parquet below. I confess I myself longed to have a shot at it. In the space under it, as in a garage, was a little electric automobile, along with tricycles and other toys, all exquisite and expensive. The guide pointed to these with malicious joy, asking her following to compare this opulence with the wretched homes of those who contributed to it. "These monsters got what they merited," said she, and her flock agreed.

On the walls were pictures of the Czar and Czarina. He looked a bearded manikin, but she … well, I stood gazing at her portrait for five minutes, she was so lovely. There was a haunting melancholy in her expression, no hint of haughtiness, just serene beauty. Was there ever a Queen who looked so well the part? On the wall opposite was a painting of Marie Antoinette who seemed dowdy in comparison. This portrait was given by Poincaré and at the time it was regarded as an evil omen. Now the two queens gaze mournfully at each other across the nursery of the little prince.

I came away from Pushkin feeling a sincere pity for the tragic Romanoffs. It left an impression on me which its big sister, the Winter Palace, did nothing to efface. The Winter Palace might be compared to the Louvre with its buildings straightened out and laid in a line. It is said to have a thousand and fifty separate halls. These give on a corridor so long that looking down it one cannot see the end. Tamara guided us with a hangover look. She said she had been studying for her examination but I suspected she had been making whoopee. She galloped us through the rooms at racing speed, so that we had only a vague idea of their incredible magnificence. It would take a week to see them thoroughly and a book to tell about them. Catherine was partial to change — both in men and meals, and there was a dining room for every day in the year. Dinners used to last seven or eight hours, accompanied by music and interspersed with amorous interludes. All of these high jinks were, of course, duly emphasized by Tamara as examples of Imperial depravity.

The pictures alone would take days of study and there were many examples of classic art. Tamara grew almost enthusiastic as she pointed out the beauties of Rubens, a Rembrandt or a Murillo. She had been trained as a professional pianist but had fallen while skating and broken her thumb. Her great hope was to visit the United States where her husband might be sent to get technical experience. But I am sure if she were allowed to accompany him the Soviets would see them no more. "If," I say, for the Government has a way of holding wives and children as hostages against return. She complained bitterly that the climate of Leningrad was vile, and she wanted to live in Moscow. But her dream was of Caucasus, and she exulted in the thought that in a month she was due for a holiday in Yalta, where she could bathe in the Black Sea.

Chapter Twenty-Eight

The Singing Soldiers

Tamara, our guide of the banana yellow turban, was of the communist *bourgeoisie*, or perhaps I should say she was a silk stocking socialist. She took me aback by asking me how much money I made. I told her I was lazy and only earned enough to keep me in luxury, but the bulk of my bloated income came from dividends. At this my popularity suffered an eclipse, but I pointed out that many communists were capitalists, that the State Bank paid them three per cent on their savings and that this interest came from the exploitation of labour. She said it came from Rent. Everyone paid rent to the State to the extent of six per cent of their income and each person was entitled to twelve cubic feet of space. She earned six hundred roubles a month, her engineer husband a thousand roubles. She was very proud because she had a small apartment of two rooms and kitchen.

She tried to convince me that conditions in Russia were better than in other countries, and anything I said to the contrary was put down to boastful lying. She challenged me about prices, from silk stockings to motor cars, but owing to the fictitious value of the rouble we got so tangled up I was glad to change the subject. We were driving in a car which ran sweetly enough and I asked her about the price of gas. She asked the chauffeur. He did not know. He was a Government servant and got his petrol with his car. As only Government officials were allowed to own cars, petrol was a ration and had no market value.

By putting idiotic constructions to all she said I tried to neutralize her propaganda. In the square behind the old British Embassy was a mound under which one-hundred-and-sixty-five martyrs of the Revolution were buried. I insisted that the bodies should have been planted deeper, as the odour was quite distinct.

Expressing my concern for the children playing round this charnel heap I suggested chloride of lime. As she recited Pushkin about them I metaphorically held my nose. Poor Tamara! I'm afraid we did not click.

Like other guides she discouraged slumming, and was blind when misery heaved up. Once a street arab passed, his rags tied with string. I asked Tamara the whyness of him, but she declared I must have been mistaken. Misery did not exist in the Soviet Union. If she had encountered such a boy she would have investigated his case. He might be one of those pariahs who have no homes and used to be a plague. But now they had been sent to institutions and such cases were rare. Rare they might be, I insisted, but I had seen some of them. Quoth Tamara: "A great city cannot be cleaned up in a day."

Of beggars, too, I saw a number. They were very discreet, demanding charity ever so craintively. In the olden days Russians were kind to beggars, but Communists treat them with the harshest cruelty. They are spoken of as "those who won't work," and looked on as a discredit to the State. Yet tradition dies hard and people still give. "Never tip and never aid beggars," Tamara told me, so joyfully I did both.

I admit the job of eliminating misery in Russia is a tough one and no doubt it is making progress. But through the Red Realm poverty is dominant. In the large sense people do not live; they exist, and existence is full of fear, suppression and hardship. I mean hardship according to our standards, not Russian ones. If you have been used to a hovel two rooms seem a palace. The past was so black, the present seems golden. Yet in the United States no workman would submit to the standard of living in the Soviet today. He would not wear their best clothes, even to work in, and he would feed to the pigs much of the food they eat. The English worker on the dole can exist better than the Russian on full pay; while to live as the French worker does he would have to work eighty hours a week instead of forty.

*

It is difficult to sidestep the tentacular solicitude of Intourist; but on one or two occasions I evaded their clutches and roamed the streets. I went cautiously at first, frequently taking my bearings. The spaciousness of Leningrad is rather stultifying and my legs are no longer those of youth. I stared at the yellow Ministry of Marine and the vast Winter Palace. I paraded the Square of the Revolution and gazed at the Fortress of Peter and Paul. I followed the Nevsky River watching boys bathing. I saw semi-naked children playing in the streets. I beheld men and women with torsos nude, leaning from their windows. For in Russia there is no false modesty. Women suckle their children with breasts proudly displayed and urination is a frank function.

The crowd took little notice of me. Perhaps they thought that to stare would be to flatter me, for their eyes were cold and hard. The Drummer attracted attention, for he was dressed in the height of Broadway fashion. His shoes drew the eyes like a magnet. Of patent leather and white kid such a pair did not exist in all Sovietdom. One day as we stood in front of St. Isaac's Cathedral some boys threw paper aeroplanes over our heads, shouting loudly. An Englishman who was with us asked us: "Do you know what they are saying? They are shouting: 'See the aeroplanes of the Soviets flying over the profiteers.'" In the eyes of the crowd we were grinding capitalists and they hated us.

The public squares sagged in spots; the streets were ruggedly in disrepair. The mansions were broken fronted, with disconnected drainpipes, chipped masonry and crumbling ornamentation. All that was bourgeois was doomed to be torn down and replaced by box-like buildings that embodied the Soviet ideal of utility. In the meantime many mansions were used as lodging houses, their entrances dark and dirty, their windows dingily blank. From splendour to sordidness these homes of wealth and rank had fallen; from patrician refinement to proletarian filth.

The shops seemed open at all hours. Even at two in the morning the grocers and bakers were crowded. In a window of the latter I counted ten kinds of loaves, but they need only one, their own black bread, the most nourishing in the world. With that and cabbage soup they can thrive. Yet while the grocers were well stocked the green-grocers were almost empty, for they depended on supplies fresh from the country. I saw two men with crates of tomatoes selling them to a line of over a hundred women. One took the money while the other handed a pound of tomatoes to each person. And they had to take what they got without any wrapping. In another case it was green melons. As each man went away with his melon he would cut a wedge from it and eat it on the road home.

I saw no cafés but lots of cellar drinking-dens, dim with smoke and jammed with unshaven men. I saw numbers of drunks yet people gave them no attention even when they slept in the gutter. In other countries they would have been locked up, but here they were treated like naughty children. The Russian is a philosophic drinker who looks on getting drunk as a diversion. Many of the men wore hair cropped close and I do not remember seeing a single hat. I don't believe you could find in all Russia a claw-hammer coat. The bigshots affect the blouse of the peasant.

The name of Stalin must be uttered with reverence. The Drummer and I referred to him as Mrs. S. and thus were able to make him the butt of our jibes. Not that we had anything against him, but having him always thrown at us as a god rather soured us. As for Trotsky — Oh no, we never mentioned him. That might mean trouble; in Russia it is advisable not to argue but to agree to everything.

The women looked happier than the men. Ninety per cent had the look of workers; for a man must earn big pay to be able to keep his woman at home. Many wore high-heeled shoes and their chubby legs looked incongruous by comparison. Very rarely I saw one with stockings or a hat. But a few had pretty print dresses with patterns of flowers. That sort of thing is contagious. I saw a girl stop another woman and touch the stuff of her gown eagerly. There is coquetry even in the Communist heart. Under their dresses many wore only a brassiere and knickers. They walked with the freedom that comes from few clothes. Their breasts protruded, their hips swung. From a health standard they were fine women. Also from a breeding one, judging by the many that were *enceinte*. There was no stigma on bastardy. A woman might have as many natural children as she wished and was honoured for it. Abortion had gone out of fashion but free love was freer than ever.

Everywhere one saw pictures of Lenin and Stalin, some gigantic. Producing them seemed to be one of the industries of the country. It is said there is a portrait of Lenin for every three citizens; I should think there must be three pictures for every citizen. One gets fed up with those two Muscovite mugs, including Kalinin, looking like an elderly goat. Molotov always managed to be impressive, but I never saw a portrait of Litvinov.

The tram cars were unbelievably crowded. In the interior one could see a solid compost of humanity, with growing from it a forest of arms. And however full, there always seemed place for more. The capacity for compression of the people was only equalled by their optimism. At every halt they stormed the door, clinging to the steps in clusters while the conductor tried to kick them off. I saw him tumble one woman on to her fanny on the street. She shrieked wrathfully after the retreating car, then subsided into laughter. They were good natured about it, but there was no sentiment of gallantry. Women were ruthlessly elbowed aside, and men sat where the softer sex stood patiently. Thus the Communist shibboleth of the equality of the sexes was proclaimed.

Night in Leningrad was weird, theatrical and a little sinister. Owing to the vague lighting it was like a medieval scene. As you approached the river the vast spaciousness engulfed you. It was so old and historic, the shadows so massive, the roadway so deserted. The starlit river with its fortresses and palaces seemed one with the brooding sky. And one night as I wandered dreaming of the past suddenly I heard singing. It approached, growing louder, louder, till I was aware of a strange rhythm. Somehow the sound filled me with joy. On it came with a steady beat, a regiment of singing soldiers.

There must have been a thousand of them, marching twenty abreast, stepping as one man and singing as with a single voice. And how they sang! It was worthwhile coming all that way to hear. They seemed oblivious to everything as they chanted their melodies so wild and strange. Up and down the streets they went, singing for hours, just for their own joy. Every evening I sought to hear them and never ceased to be profoundly moved. In Moscow I only heard the raucous row of the radio, but the Singing Soldiers of Leningrad will always haunt me, and it was with that lovely memory I took my leave of a fascinating city.

Chapter Fifty

Exile's Return

The gaunt grey troopship edged from the dock and into the teeth of the growing gale. There was no one on the quay to cheer her going; she slipped away as surreptitiously as we had crept on her in the grey dawn. Yet only three days before, she had landed fifteen hundred G.I.s. Now she was hastening back for more, with fifteen sickly civilians as her only passengers. As we huddled on the hatch under the middle deck, shivering with cold, I wondered what was in store.

Perhaps because we had come on board so early everything seemed unprepared for us. We were relegated to the hospital section and I selected a four-cabin room, only to find that it was the Isolation Ward. However, it had a certain privacy, so we decided to take a chance of foul germs. The other cabins had ten berths or more, and were less snugly situated. All had steel posts supporting wire mattresses. In fact, the boat was a huge cage of steel without a splinter of wood to be seen. It was grimly utilitarian, a carrier of troops and war supplies, not of woe-begone exiles.

We had no tickets or papers of any kind, and no one took any notice of us as we climbed the steep gangplank. It seemed irregular to me — no check-up of any kind. We had paid two hundred dollars a passage; but it was not a passenger boat, so perhaps our presence was unofficial. In any case I had a feeling of evasion, and breathed a sigh of relief when at length we cast off. That was at four in the afternoon, and we had been told to be on board at eight that morning. In the interim we shuddered in the icy cold, and dreaded what discomforts awaited us.

Like a stealthy wraith the ship slipped into the gathering gloom, but we had little heart to admire the grandiose heights of Manhattan nor the grey Statue of Liberty. As we realized the lift and pitch of the seas we shrank into the cold, steel hostility of our cabins and huddled there. Yet it was impossible to sleep, for they turned on the heat and, from ice boxes, our staterooms became ovens. We had to open the door wide so that we heard the racket of the engines, besides the shrieking of the tempest. Once we got into such a roll it was difficult not to be tipped out of our berths. I was alarmed, but the calm face of a black steward reassured me. The ship was like an empty shell, he told me. We were bound to get all the tossing there was.

He looked for a rough trip, and was busy lashing down everything moveable. Our cabin gave on a big space between the middle deck and the lower, where was a huge hatch over the hold. It was covered with black tarpaulin and was our *salon* for the voyage. He was now roping it off, so that we could hang on to our deck chairs which had tendency to pile up in one corner. Crawling from this place up a steep steel ladder, and over a steel bulwark, I peered out. The sky was black, the decks awash, the howl of the storm terrifying. Precariously I balanced myself and crawled back to my berth. The slightest slip on that structure of steel might have been fatal.

For two days most of the passengers were sick, then one by one they began to show up for meals. And what meals! True, they were served in the soldiers' quarters, but of the very best. For supper we had *filet mignon* we had not tasted for ages, and wonderful ice cream. We were told it was food reserved for officers only, and they surely did themselves well. In no first-class passenger liner would we have been better fed than we were on that Victory troopship.

Immured in our floating barracks we tried to get our bearings. It was a strange situation. The ship suggested mystery as well as adventure — sort of soldier and sailor too. We felt somehow as if we had no right to be there. Yet our presence was recognized in a casual way, as if we were superior to stowaways who had bribed a passage. For certainly the boat was never intended to carry the likes of us. Its sheer efficiency appalled me. It was purposive to the point of fear. All that grim, grey steel, so cold and comfortless! I shivered as I descended to its bowels, and shuddered as I saw six tiers of metallic beds on metallic braces. How could those on the top stay on in rolling weather when a fall to that steel deck would be fatal? Yet on the return trips every berth was filled, and even the corridors were paved with sleeping bags.

On those return trips there were five relays for meals, yet the food was first class — for those who could eat it. Ice cream was served every evening, with Danish pastry and coffee, followed by a flicker show. There was a library consisting of narrow, paperbound books printed specially for the army. There were also musical instruments. I borrowed a guitar and an accordion and played continually. Every evening we had a Cinema. On one occasion I was thrilled to see that production of *The Spoilers* in which I appeared with Marlene. I never thought to view myself in mid-ocean, acting in a picture, to the applause of G.I.s and coloured stewards. Because I was a musician of sorts the latter were friendly. There was a guitarist among them who made me ashamed of my strumming, but none of them could swing *Roll out the Barrel* on the accordion.

It will be seen from all this that our voyage had its bright spots, to which the officers contributed. The Captain was a stalwart who tried to make me play medicine ball on the forward hatch but I had enough trouble to keep my own balance. The Purser was one of my fans and the various army officers in charge of transport were sociable and attentive to the ladies. There were three prospective brides among us, and an American Consul who organized a mock trial. Altogether it was amazing how we extemporized certain gaiety on that hatch between decks, even though the rolling would sometimes ball us up together. For my part, however, I did not feel any too cheerful. In that Isolation Ward cabin I must have caught some foul microbe, for I started on a session of flu. Huddled in my grey army blanket I coughed all night long and worried about the landing. What would be our fate? I heard that Marseilles was full of thieves who would steal our baggage, and there was not a hotel room to be had.

Two features of our Victory vessel I should like to mention. One was the engine room which must have been a source of pride, it was so lofty, so spacious, so clean. It was like an engineer's palace, quite out of proportion in its airy amplitude to the rest of the ship. The other scene was the washroom with its circle of a hundred toilet seats, close, naked, unadorned, with only a metal rod between them. I viewed that gleaming circle of porcelain with misgiving. Though its cleanliness was spotless I had no urge to respond to those hundred invitations. Maybe I am squeamish, but community commodity did not inspire me.

My sickness being sore upon me I spent the last two days on shipboard lying low and conserving my forces for the ordeal of landing. Even at its best it would be trying; but I was old and easily upset. Besides, I coughed continually. My weakness worried me; however, I thought: "This is the end of the trail. One last effort and I will be home … *home*." So as we neared Marseilles I crawled on deck. It was a cold, grey morning, and the great port looked like a graveyard of dead ships. There they were, nigh two hundred of them, half-sunk, tilted crazily, up-ended and awash. We edged into a wharf far from town that looked oddly abandoned in the chill sunshine. Pretty soon people dribbled down to meet us. Then a team of coloured soldiers appeared and made us fast to the wharf.

Gradually the crowd increased, and I watched it with interest. Once more I was gazing on the soil of France and soon I would tread it. If only I had not been so wretched I would have thought it a great moment…. Then the officials came aboard to check our money and give us landing tickets. They looked thin and shabby but were quite charming in the best French manner, and when the purser told them: "Don't take too long with these poor people. We have a nice lunch awaiting you," they brightened up and governed themselves accordingly. The Customs' men reduced their formalities to a minimum, being also conveniently short-sighted in the examination of our trunks. It was all delightfully friendly and futile, and French, and my heart warmed to these easy-going people who refused to take life too seriously. So I bade farewell to the hard bitterness of the boat and, with a last look at its grey hull, I turned to the amenities of the land.

For the moment there were not many. There were baggage men and money changers, but no hotel touts. Rooms were unattainable. Under the eyes of the police a shabby Jew offered to pay me twice the official price for U.S. dollars. I have no doubt it would have been all right, but I have always had a horror of the black market and would not take a chance. Then to our great joy the Man From Cook's arrived on the scene, and took entire charge of our situation. He handled the baggage, promising to reserve us tickets on the midnight autorail for Nice. How we blessed him, feeling that no money we could give him could repay him for all he did for us!

From the wharf we took a taxi to the station. It was dirty and broken down but the owner asked five hundred francs for the trip. However, for good value he took us for a ride through all the bombed and blasted parts of the city, which did not cheer us any. Having duly impressed us with its devastation he dumped us in front of the station where we sat on our baggage, afraid to leave it for a moment. There we ate lunches from the boat and talked to our fellow passengers.

Soon darkness fell but, owing to the few city lights, the scene became strangely sinister. A grizzly fog crept up from the sea, attacking my lungs so that my cough racked me. On the chill, bare platform we exiles cowered and shivered, yet the worst was yet to come. On inquiring at the ticket office about the night train for Nice we were told that *all places were taken.* What a shock! The prospect of sitting all night on that station platform unnerved me. At the best it would have been rather terrible; in my present state I believed it would be the death of me. I also worried about my family. In fact, we were all sunk in woe when Cook's man again appeared on the scene. It was all right, he assured me; I need not "make the bile." He had an arrangement with the conductor and by paying him a hundred francs each certain seats would be kept off the reservation list. Good old corrupt France! We were saved.

Squatting on our trunks in the ghoulish gloom and peering at the bleary lights of the Cannebière, Marseilles looked to us like a corpse city. Wraiths detached themselves from the grey mist and passed us shudderingly. It was just before Christmas, the coldest day of the year at its coldest hour. I tried to keep warm, dreading pneumonia, coughing my lungs out. I tried to cheer myself by thoughts of comforts ahead — my grand bed in the

Yellow Room, the sun glinting on the palm leaves as I pulled up the shutters, a friendly warmth in the radiators and breakfast of tea, toast and marmalade. That would be for the morning; in the meantime were four weary hours of waiting for the train. I paid the porters with dollar bills, but found they were better pleased with a ten cent packet of cigarettes. Indeed, we soon learned not to give away cigarettes by the packet. One or two were enough, and often more appreciated than a dozen. Cigarettes were almost currency at that time.

How would we find the apartment? Had it been looted? Would any of our stuff be saved? This was the question that agitated us as we sat in that grizzly gloom. After years of occupation the proud station was a sordid shambles. I prowled around, seeking for warmth but found it not. Everywhere icy drafts and a waiting room like a frigidaire. We were afraid to leave our baggage for a moment in case it might vanish, for sinister shapes lurked all about us. That four hours' wait seemed interminable, and only our hope that our troubles would soon be over saved us from utter despair. After all, we were lucky to get a train, even at this time of night. Only recently had communication been established, and some of the repaired bridges were temporary. Anything might happen. I began to fear Cook's man would fail us, and as the hour approached for our departure my anxiety increased.

When at the last moment he appeared I could have fallen on his neck. He had everything nicely fixed up, so that we passed before everyone in the crowd that clamoured to board the train. As we started I felt *unreasonably* happy, for a draft from the broken windows chilled us and we were really most uncomfortable. But the humming wheels seemed to sing: *Home, home*, and the names of the stations were like sweet music. Cannes, Antibes, Juan-les-Pins — how they rang joyously in my ears! The long years rolled away till it seemed I had been here but yesterday. Then, though cheated by the darkness of its precious approach — NICE. I was so eager to get out of the train I stumbled and fell my full length on the platform, hurting my hip, which did not help any. But little I cared. I breathed with ecstasy that ice-cold air and proclaimed its purity. My beloved Nice!

We acquired a porter who loaded our stuff on a handbarrow, keeping a sharp lookout in case it got stolen. We followed him through the familiar streets of the musical quarter — the rues Mozart, Rossini, Verdi — to our house in the Place Franklin. There it stood in the frail moonlight, as solid and handsome as when I last looked on it. But what a job we had to arouse the concierge at that hour of the morning! She was still the same, though her husband had died in the interval. We called her *Casque d'Or* because she wore a golden wig, and now even the wig welcomed us. She could not believe her eyes — thought we had all perished ... Yes, the apartment was as we had left it. Nothing had been touched. It was marvellous. Houses on every side had been looted but ours had been spared. It was simply that they did not *know* about it. Both Italians and Germans had passed up that rich booty lying open to their hands. How unbelievably lucky we were! As we entered into that familiar scene it was almost uncanny to find everything just as we had left it, down to the smallest detail.

Chapter Fifty-One

Home, Sweet Home

Of course the apartment was cold and stale as a dungeon, but we were all so tired we grabbed blankets and curled up in beds that smelled of moth balls. All night, however, I struggled with a racking cough and woke weak and wretched. I had to beg some bread for breakfast which we prepared over a spirit lamp. The bleak morn was sunless and forlorn. The palms dripped and the rose bushes were bare. No comfort in the garden. We scouted around, discovering a little food we had left five years before — sugar, tea, coffee, also precious soap. This cheered us a bit, but I had to go out into the biting cold to arrange for the electricity and gas to be turned on. As I went to the various bureaux my head was like to split and I had to sit down on many a bench.

As I went through the markets I noted how the shelves were bare. The shops looked miserably poor, the people pinched and shabby. They did not seem to laugh anymore. The girls were wearing wooden-soled shoes and coats made out of army blankets. The men were hollow-cheeked and pale. I got a painful impression of issue out of misery. Going to the bank I drew what little money I had to cope with the astronomical prices, but I could not buy bread because the bakers were closed. I had to borrow it again, and it was so bad it made us all sick. After waiting in line at a market barrow for an hour I bought a cabbage.

It was all like that. Take what you can get and think you're damn' lucky. Line up two hours for a loaf of bread that seems to contain sawdust and fills you with gas. No potatoes, no meat, no fish. Butter and eggs a dream of the past. Did they ever exist? No paper to wrap things in. A market woman charged me a franc for a twist of newsprint to form a poke. Once after a long line-up I was lucky enough to get a small salted cod which I had to carry home by the tail. And the anxiety of the queue! Would the stuff last till my time came? And how often it did not! In these first days people were living on a grey species of macaroni and half-rotted cauliflowers. Any vegetables one could get, such as leeks or salad, would be too green and give one dysentery. People looked so pinched and sad — thin too. How could anyone do a day's work on such a diet? G.I.s called the French a lazy lot, but in their own well-fed smugness they were unfit to judge.

Many of the girls rode bicycles and their legs looked thin and hard. But with their cheeks hollowed a little they were prettier than ever. Their high-heeled wooden or straw shoes made them look tall, and they wore their G.I. blanket coats with a gallant swagger. Bicycles were the favourite mode of locomotion, while there were taxi-bicycles where the owner pedalled in front of a light car that held two. All motor cars were fitted with weird and cumbrous contraptions that burned charcoal, and the roofs were packed with sacks of the fuel. Despite December weather few women wore stockings, and then usually sockinettes made of white homespun wool.

Everyone thought in terms of food, looking with avid wistfulness at shop windows where all was camouflage — empty boxes and bottles, with behind a few tinned foods at fantastic prices. I paid two hundred francs for a can of condensed milk, while candies, if you had coupons to buy them, cost you ten francs each. Tea, coffee and chocolate were unobtainable, while sugar had to be bought on the black market at three hundred francs a pound. True, we had ration cards for everything imaginable but there were no rations available. The sheer emptiness of the shops was appalling. It was indeed a weird world into which we had precipitated ourselves so recklessly.

Our first months were spent in trying to adapt ourselves to these rigorous conditions, and often we regretted that we had left Hollywood in such haste. It seemed the cards were stacked against us, for we happened on a spell of the coldest weather for twenty years. An icy wind swept down from the Alps, seeming to cut through one. I ventured out before my flu was completely cured and had a relapse. My doctor said I had just shaved pneumonia. I coughed incessantly and could scarce crawl from one bench to another. How anxiously I watched the bare ground, looking for the first sign of growth, for it meant food, vegetables, salads. The Earth would save us, but it was so long in coming to our rescue. More months of misery before glad spring greenness. I counted the days until we would be able to eat our fill again.

In the meantime I had lost ten pounds in weight, and was amazed to find my clothes fitting me so loosely. My family, too, went down with *grippe*, and they also had a tough time. For

Christmas dinner we had each a sardine and a potato. That was the saddest Christmas I have ever spent, for then the pinch of misery seemed to reach its climax. Even the blackest of black markets failed us. But we had streaks of luck — a few eggs at twenty-five francs each, a bit of pork at six hundred francs a kilo, a small ration of dates. How such small things brightened existence!

But best of all were our Red Cross parcels. We learned of these through the British Consul and half believed they saved our lives. They had originally been designed for prisoners of war, but now the surplus was being distributed to indigent Britishers. We were each entitled to one every fortnight and it was a wonderful day when we collected them. They contained tea, sugar, Klim, corned beef, Kam, chocolate, raisins, sardines, prunes, salmon, pilot biscuits, and — just imagine! jam, butter, cheese. How three semi-starving people gloated over all that wealth of food!

And how wonderful everything tasted. My taste buds developed a new sensitivity, so that everything I ate seemed delicious. Hard tack with a little jam — what joy! Klim — what cream was sweeter? Kam — no fresh sausage could be more tasty! Butter and cheese — we had almost forgotten what they tasted like. Bless the Red Cross! How the French people looked at us with envy as proudly we carried our provisions home! Not ten thousand francs could have bought one of these parcels.

Yes, their coming seemed to usher in a brighter day. We felt we were saved for we had those little delicacies that make life tolerable. Then our own parcels, sent off before we left, began to arrive and this too was an occasion for celebration. Now we had tea and coffee in abundance. Fruit cake, too, and candy and marmalade. And at this point our friends in Canada and the States came to our aid. Parcels began to pour in. Soon we were on Easy Street: in fact, building up a reserve. My daughter, who was in charge of the commissariat, took pride in her well-stocked cupboard. And with the spring days the sun warmed the apartment, so that for a few hours every afternoon we were comfortable again. We had been obliged to break up old furniture to keep the furnace going; now, except in the evening, we could let it go out. Nature was showing us mercy.

We blessed the sunshine that glimmered on the palm fronds in the morning, and I began to notice green sprouting from the ground. It was a moment of joy when I saw my first buds on the trees. We had weathered the evil season. Hope gleamed bright again. I was able to buy some coal on the black market, and sugar and meat of good quality, for I had succeeded in getting funds from abroad. At first I had been limited to the few greenbacks I had brought over, changing them at the official price. Now I had ample money and could spend freely. Again I went my walks on the high hills, greeted the blue sky and sang with cheer. Again, in my joy, like a sweet echo, I heard the *Harps of Heaven*.

And so it went on, every day an improvement on the one before. People looked happier; the markets began to fill. Things were dear, but they were on sale. With tomatoes, celery and new potatoes colour came back on the shelves. The pastry cooks sold us cakes of improving quality, the bread was better, the macaroni whiter. There was no longer that spirit of resignation. We looked forward with courage and confidence. But we could not look back on our austerity period without a shudder. Yet at its blackest there had been gleams of brightness. Everything is relative, and how we had enjoyed a warm radiator, a cup of tea, a sweet biscuit! And what a delight to parsimoniously nibble a morsel of chocolate!

But with the month of May came magic change, for from the hillside a burst of bloom cascaded into town and the markets were a foam of flowers. Tulips, lilies, violets, anemones, they lit the streets with a spirit of invincible delight. They cheered and exalted. Or perhaps it was the spate of fresh vegetables that brought smiles back again. Peas, beans, artichokes, young carrots, new potatoes — one could be a vegetarian happily, especially as eggs were more easy to get. Rationed foods were still a mockery, and meat was rare, but the bread became really enjoyable. Colour took the streets, too, as the women put on gay gowns of flowered print that fluttered in the sunshine. How gallantly the girls carried themselves on their high-heeled shoes, and slung their shoulder bags with gay coquetry!

Quite suddenly one felt a vast change in morale, the spirit of liberation at last. The uplift was so great one wanted to dance in the streets, and at the May festival the bars were festooned, the accordions rejoiced and the people revelled as never before. It was good to be alive again. The roses in my garden bloomed exultantly. The pergola was ablaze with them, and every room spilled over with gorgeous colour. The big mimosa tree was a sheen of gold; the cherry trees were gemmed with blossom. The swallows returned and skimmed low over the streets, while starlings made music in the orange trees.

Yet in the midst of such a renaissance of joy there were mementos of the Terror. At street corners one came on marble slabs to tell you that the pavement below had been crimsoned with Resistance blood. Near the Place Massena were tablets where two young patriots had been hanged, and the people forced to pass before them for two days. On every hand one heard hideous talks of starvation, cold, moral dejection. Yes, the people deserved to rejoice for they had been through hell. Now their hearts were buoyant again and instead of wry grimaces they gave you radiant smiles.

It was the old France of laughter and gaiety, of peace and plenty, for with the beginning of the fruit season the cornucopia seemed to brim over. There were cherries and strawberries, peaches and apricots, plums, greengages, grapes, pears, apples, all succeeding one another and in such abundance we seemed to be living on fruit. During the winter our chief plaint had been that we had forgotten its taste, and now this plenitude. One felt one was blessed. To me the *Harps of Heaven* sang serenely.

The Italian occupation had been easy, but the German one unbelievably brutal. The Gestapo was everywhere. They had their quarters in the Hermitage and the cells underneath were scenes of torture. Most of the Jews had been deported to the death chambers of Dachau and Auschwitz, and many Communists had been liquidated. But it was along the sea front the sign of the Occupation was most glaring. By forced labour the Boches had built a magnificent bastion that stretched for miles, skirting the promenade. Some of it was unfinished but the stones were there, ready to be put in place.

Now it made a beautiful sea wall behind which were forts and gun stations. Also on the beach, which was a bristle of barbed wire, were guard houses of steel and concrete. Every means had been taken to repel invaders and now it was wasted labour. For they were heaping the barbed wire in rusting masses, and demolishing the guard towers with dynamite. The promenade had been turned into a defence zone, the villas had been evacuated. In one of those my bank was situated. The officials had received twenty-four hours' notice to clear out, and in that time they had forced the strong boxes, put the contents into sacks and packed them off to a safe French bank.

Yes, I was lucky; for in our strong box were many precious bric-a-brac, all our silver plate, and the manuscripts of three unpublished books. All were saved by the energy of the bank officials. On the other hand my strong box in Paris was opened by the Germans who must have been badly fooled, for it contained nothing but out-of-date publishers' contracts. In Dinard, too, my safety deposit box was forced by the Boche, but it only contained some Life Annuity contracts that could not interest them.

And Nice was lucky too, for the city had escaped bombardment. It would have been so easy to make rubble of those shell-like houses with their red tiled roofs. A little destruction would have gone such a long way. The damage done by five minutes of shelling would have taken years to repair. The city might never have recovered, yet here it was smiling again and using German prisoners to work on its roads and its gutters. One saw hundreds of them, looking not so badly off. Indeed, those employed by the Americans were chipper to the point of arrogance.

The Yanks on leave dominated the water front. Those G.I.s were having the time of their lives, pursued by the French *poules* and lodged in the best hotels. They bought cartons of cigarettes in the canteens and traded them off in the black market. At night the more obstreperous roamed the streets uproariously, leaving broken windows in their wake. Then quite suddenly they seemed to vanish. Hotel after hotel was closed, till only the Ruhl remained. Their girls were sent to the hospital for treatment, and they, too, vanished overnight. It had been rather hectic and I was glad to see those signs of military occupation disappear. Yet the townspeople missed the cash the big Yanks squandered so lavishly.

So at last we had our own Nice back again, the Nice of the Carnival, of the Battle of Flowers, of the swarms of tourists. I hoped I would never set eyes on a khaki uniform again. To hell with war and all its paraphernalia! One should have been grateful to the men in uniform, but all one felt was a desire not to see any more of them. And perhaps I *was* grateful. At least I was thankful as I looked round my lovely apartment and saw everything in its place. By a miracle those precious things we had collected over half a lifetime had been spared to us. Pictures, statuettes, carpets, curtains of lace and velvet — they were our treasures even though their value was negligible. That picture I bought for a hundred francs in an old junk shop gave me the same serene pleasure as the day I carried it home twenty-five years before. Yes, our possessions were priceless because they conserved the essence of our years of happy living. To have lost them would have been the worst heartbreak of all.

And last but not least my beloved books, over a thousand, some rare and many in rich bindings — how thankful I was to have them restored to me! I dipped into them with inexpressible joy. My accordion too — it was still in tune. And my three guitars — their tone was as sweet as ever. How the Boches would have grabbed them if they had known! But perhaps they did, for the apartment above me, owned by a wealthy Jew, was stripped completely. Perhaps because I was British they left my stuff alone … but I doubt it.

And while I was marvelling at my immunity I had another bit of good news. The garagist in my Brittany village wrote to say he had saved my car. Three times the Germans had come to take it, but each time he had stalled them off. He had risked imprisonment to preserve my lovely little *Lancia*, and he wrote that he was putting it in shape for me. That reminded me I had another home, the dearest of all. How had things fared at Dream Haven? How was Tasie and her family? Had my house been smashed or looted? Had my trees been spared? … It was calling me, the spot on earth I most loved, begging me to return.

Chapter Fifty-Two

Return to Dream Haven

Seven years after our flight I returned to Dream Haven.

I was dusk when I entered the village and a summer storm was brooding. By lightning flashes I followed the path till I neared my home, but all I could see was a black pyramid of pines. My trees! With my own hands I had planted them, digging the hole and setting up the tiny sapling. Now each was forty feet high, with the girth of a woman's waist. How often in my exile I had worried about them, hoping they would be spared. Behold them a tiny forest, hiding the house from view. I hungered to see it, but the thunder roared and the rain poured, so I returned to the village.

On my way I called on the garagist who had saved my car. I grimy man of seventy, he greeted me with roars of joy; offering me his oily wrist to shake. Four times the Boche had tried to take away my *Lancia*, but he had dismantled it and hid the tires. "I told them it was mine," he said; "but if they had discovered me in the lie they would have shot me. Ah, what brutes! Fancy — ten thousand of them quartered in the village. They had their petrol pump in my garage and a soldier to guard it. All day he sat there, but I did not speak to him. Then one morning the Commandant came on him with his belt unbuttoned. He made him stand to attention, put on a glove, and slugged him three times on the jaw. Each time he knocked him down and made him stand to attention again.

"Oh he was a swine, that Commandant. He terrorized the village. He swore he would shoot anyone who uttered the word *Boche*. He evacuated all the houses near the sea. Your neighbour, the English lady who was seventy, he sent to a concentration camp. Your other neighbour, the dentist, got eighteen months in prison for reproaching a collaborator. That's the bitter part of it. We who were honest have to go on living with those who worked for the enemy. It doesn't pay to be a patriot."

That night I slept in the house of Tasie. Her joy at seeing me knew no bounds. Time and again she clutched my hand and held it. A bunchy old woman, grey-haired and spectacled. With pride she showed me her home, once a barn and pigsty, now a rustic residence of charm and taste, with whitewashed walls, oak beams, window nooks and a winding stairway. She was the richest woman in the village, owning half a dozen houses and a score of fields. "And I owe it all to you, Monsieur," she told me with tears in her eyes. 'When you first engaged me I hadn't a *sou*, and the five francs a day you paid me seemed a fortune."

This, however, wasn't exactly true. She owed it to her industry and shrewdness. With her small savings she began by buying the earth-floored hovel in which she lives, and by sweat and saving she forged her way to fortune. Property was cheap. When she saw a bargain she would come to me timidly and ask for the loan of a few thousand francs. She became the village washer-woman and bell-ringer, working day and night to repay her debt. So bit by bit, over thirty years, she realized a proud independence. A woman of deep integrity whose motto was: Never put off till tomorrow what you can do the day before yesterday.

To a Britisher expressions of gratitude are a bore so I switched the subject to the Occupation. No sooner had we gone than the Germans surged on the scene. The road was stiff with their cars. "Where is the Englishman," they cried, "who writes bad things about our Fuhrer? Escaped! Well, we will make sure...." So they crashed in the door, searched the house, started the radio. When Tasie arrived they were already at home. "English *kaput*," they sneered. "This ours now, always ours." Then as she sought to save the family photographs they drove her off, threatening to shoot her if she touched anything.

Soon the Commandant appeared. A slim man about my height, he too, sported a monocle. "This place pleases me," he said; "I will make it my headquarters." Then he looked at my shelves of books, remarking: "If I were not a German soldier it would please me to be an English gentleman. But this author is an enemy of my country. In his books does he not call us *Huns!* Well, if ever we are obliged to quit this charming spot we will leave behind us only a shambles."

So saying he selected the best of my Savile Row suits, my pearl grey and chalk-lined blue flannels, and monocle in eye strutted through the village. Then began the joyous loot in which all of value we possessed vanished overnight. Our silver and napery, our linen, embroidery, pictures, our carpets, curtains, clothes and shoes — all disappeared in a twinkling. The search was ruthless. With what sadistic joy they discovered my accordion under the roof-beam where I had hidden it. My grand piano, a Steinway, was shipped to Hamburg; my guitars, my motor bicycle were grabbed with delight. Indeed, in a few days everything that was easily transportable had vanished.

Twenty-five soldiers occupied the house, and no one was allowed to go near. As its commanding site gave it strategic value it was made a defensive point. Yet when Rommel came on a tour of inspection he called it a "mouse trap" and ordered it to be converted into a citadel. They began by breaching the walls for machine gun posts. They built pill boxes in the garden; they tunnelled and trenched till they transformed my home into a fortress.

They were fairly correct in their behaviour, but if they did not pursue the fair sex some of the women ran after *them*. A buxom wench who had been regarded as the village harlot, was soon running a *bordel* with a dozen women and girls to assist her. By night they played my accordion and drank champagne from my cellar. After the liberation every one of them were publicly cropped and marched up and down the village; while one girl, who had a portrait of Hitler in her room, was made to kiss it, as she paraded to the jeers of the populace. The Resistants were bitter. Few who had been friendly to the Boche escaped their vengeance. Our village vamp got three years in gaol, while some of the male Hitlerites were sent to the chain gang.

There were others who willingly had business dealings with the Germans. Many of these are now rich, but they will never live down the reproach levelled at them. Collaborationists! one shrugs with a look of contempt. Fortunately they were in a minority. The others, the Incorruptibles, refused to speak to or even look at a Boche. Even in the darkest hours they never lost hope. They were, it is true, only passive Resisters, but they conserved their honour. Lastly came the militant men, the real Resisters. Marcel, son of Tasie, was one of those, and was imprisoned for hoisting the tricolour on the church steeple. But most people lived in fear, for they had been told that the least act of revolt would result in the total destruction of the village.

*

Next morning I set out for Dream Haven. After the storm the land was glittering — the fields bright with buttercups and rich with growing grain. I wanted to bless each ear of wheat for its promise of bread to come. But my way was slow. Red-faced men with bellowing voices wrung my hand, while women unknown to me hailed me joyfully. The heartiness of their welcome surprised me. To them I was an exile returning home. I belonged to this strong, ruddy race and they received me with open arms. So after many haltings and greetings I came in sight of the sea. I was picking my way through a clover meadow when a huge, hairy man greeted me.

"Ah Monsieur, you go to see your poor house. But it has not suffered so much. Mine they razed to the ground. The stone they used for their ramparts, the wood to line their trenches. Yours still stands, and that is something. You were lucky the Commandant liked it. He had orders to blow it sky high, but he did not have time. The Americans came too quick. Oh the grand boys! How they drove the Boche out of the house, chased them across the fields, killed them in the wood yonder. What joy to see them! And so by a miracle, Monsieur, the Americans saved your home."

As I drew near the coppice behind which it lay, I hoped and feared in turn. First, I saw that all the fences had been torn down and the gateway was gone. Through pine-gloom I passed over a carpet of crushed cones to come on a wasteland that had once been my rose garden. A lone rose greeted me, and gratefully I plucked it. High grass hid the main alley while debris blocked the other paths. The approach was difficult. I walked warily, fearing traps....

There! I saw it at last — the old house. Sadly it seemed to welcome me, seeming to say: "Here I am, Master, broken, battered, weak and worn, but faithful to you still. For thirty years I sheltered you. Now, do not abandon me in my age and sorrow. Once again rejoice me with your music and your laughter...." And I said: "Home of my Heart, do not fear. I will not desert you. I will return and live in you, and love you as long as life shall last."

And as I gazed in sentimental reverie there was a scream and a crash. I started — it was only a shutter swinging in the wind. Then I saw that all the windows were broken, and the wind swept through the house, so that it moaned like a lost soul. Slowly I stumbled my way to the side that faced the sea. The red roof tiles were rusty, plaster peeled from the walls, but staunchly the house stood. Rommel himself had ordered it torn down and a bastion built in its place. Already they had made a beginning by breaching the wall and installing cement platforms for machine gun emplacements.

Seated on one of these, where rocks went ruggedly down, far and wide I scanned the sea. On the iron shore it crashed yeastily, tossing in peacock shades of blue and green to the empty islands that barred the ocean. A caller wind whipped the blood to ecstasy. Here was a grandeur and beauty the Boche could not destroy. This, at least, they had left me, and with the sight to glory in it. Gratefully I gazed till, turning at last with a strange reluctance, I entered the house where I had passed the best years of my life.

Grudgingly the door yielded to my key and I found myself in the hallway. The wind soughed in the corridors, the floor was splintered underfoot. The wainscotting was shattered, the tapestry torn away, the walls lettered with Boche inscriptions. Luckily the doors were intact, and I opened that leading to the salon. The first thing I saw was a strange piano, battered, upright, anonymous. It was cracked and tinny but easy to play, for it was so out of tune that if you struck a false note it sounded like a true one. I thumped out the *Harp That Once Through Tara's Halls*, and the music I evoked echoed weirdly in that deserted house.

The place had been gutted with ferocious enthusiasm. What little remained would not have tempted a travelling tinker. The rich tapestry that covered the walls had been ripped away, revealing them in their stark crudity. The woodwork had been systematically smashed, and everything that could not be removed had been deliberately damaged. A beautiful home wrecked, and I was too old to restore it. That was the worst of it: I had not the guts to begin over again.

Finding little to comfort me, bleakly I went from room to room. The bedrooms were bare and bedless, the kitchen an empty shell with only a ruined stove to show what it had been. In some rooms the destruction was complete. My roll-top desk and cabinet had been smashed; every wardrobe was doorless. My pictures had vanished and my library.... But fearing the fate of my beloved books I had left that to the last. Well, seemingly about a third of them remained but in such grievous state I was sorry they, too, had not been destroyed. For the pages were pulp, the covers rain-rotted. To a bookman a sad sight. Had they been left to mock me? And the others — fuel no doubt for a Boche bonfire. Well, that was that. No use crying over burned books. I was inclined to bewail the manuscript of my novel, *"And His Seed Forever"* but probably it was no good anyway. Of more account, to my thinking were my hundred bound volumes of *Punch*, my *Encyclopedia Britannica*, my big *Webster's Dictionary*. What a bonny blaze to rejoice the hearts of Vandals. Sick of staring at empty shelves I sought the sunshine of the garden!

Sitting by the well under the fig tree (where, if the publisher cares to print it you may see a picture of me) soberly I took stock. After all, things might have been worse. At least the house stood. One day all the able-bodied men of the village had been summoned to demolish it. They had refused, so the elders had been arrested. Seeing their fathers threatened with a firing squad the young men had yielded. But before they could make a start the Commandant had changed his mind. For the moment my house was saved. Less fortunate my neighbour and friend, an English lady who owned a gem of a *chalet* perched on a point. They used it as a target to test their fire. Now its sightless skeleton echoed the wail of the winds.

Yes, I was lucky. After all I *was* alive, while so many I had known had come to a sorry end. Radiant living might still be mine. Even in my wild garden there was beauty — gay gowans and impudent poppies. I could fold my hands and invite Peace. Patience, resignation, charity were mine. Largely I had learned the lesson of life.... So sitting in the quiet sunniness I looked up at Dream Haven and thought of the happy part it had played in the harmony of my days. I would never let the old shack down. As long as health remained I would go back every summer and sing and play and loaf and laugh. I would light the hearth fire and rouse the walls with cheer. And perhaps as I sought my rest with soft stars burning, I would hear again my mystic melody, my *Harps of Heaven*.

Chapter Fifty-Three

The End of the Trail

I am writing this on the terrace of a big brown villa, perched amid proud palms. Below me is the sapphire sea, and afar the Isle of Corsica glows like a golden ember in the diamond dawn. Olive groves wimple to the beach, waves flash like silver seagulls on the shingle. Twice daily I go down to play with them; I roam for hours on the mountainside, I muse on banks of rosemary and thyme.... A place one dreams of — Journey's End for a lifelong dreamer.

The villa is spacious and gracious. It has floors of marble, arches and Corinthian columns. Indeed, it once played an important part in the life of the community, for it was the official *bordel de luxe*. There was a *bidet* in every room, including the drawing room. Even now I feel it is harlot haunted, and somehow it tickles me to think I am ending my days in a house of ill fame.

Ending my days — there is a finality in the phrase that affronts me. I look on life as an Experiment in Longevity. When I was young I had three ambitions: to make a million dollars, to write twenty books, to live a hundred years. The last I will never do. I will have to content myself with a modest ninety. "Today," I tell myself, "you are bright-eyed and alert. The years will pass and you will toddle round, a perky Old Codger with a cheery smile. If Bernard Shaw can do it so can you. True, you are not a vegetarian, and if steaks and ale do not harm you you will continue to enjoy them. So with your back to the fire and your belly to the table you will still get a lot of fun out of living. And that's the sum of human wisdom — enjoy your days on earth, for they are all you will have to enjoy."

I had a mind to end this book on a gleeful note but I find it hard to do so. I hate to be serious and I am afraid to be a bore. Yet I have a feeling that these may be my last words and I want them to be worthy. So forgive me if a solemn note creeps in. After writing many pages to clarify my final relations to living, I am tearing them up. I prefer to hark back to a dead book of mine, and from it quote words that to me ring as truly as when I wrote them twenty-five years ago.

I am a professional ink-slinger and most of my life I have made my bread and butter by my pen. I like my job, but I have no foolish illusions as to its importance. Nor have I any but the most pessimistic views as to the permanent value of literary effort. The good will go with the bad. We who are sprats and don't matter may console ourselves that even the whales don't matter. In the long run we are all headed for the scrapheap; the Pantheons of today will be the Parthenons of tomorrow.

> What's the use of fortune? What's the good of
> fame?
> Rank and riches, pomp and power, the end is
> just the same:

We're nothing but a pack of fools that play a
silly game.

The devil of it is: we've got to play it, and it's the way we play that counts. It's the spirit of striving that matters. In expressing the best that is in us we are keeping alive the genius of the race. And however futile we consider the fight we must carry on. We may realize that pride is a sham, property an illusion, wealth vain … yet we must work or we will die. In our fashion each of us must serve Nature's purpose as she moves in us and through us to her inscrutable ends.

Every man who reaches the sober seventies should be a philosopher of sorts. With the years he acquires patience, tolerance, stoicism. He revises his values and begins to see existence as a whole. He realizes his insignificance, his mortality. In the end he is enriched by resignation and a cheerful acceptance of destiny.… But before he comes to this he may have a moment of self-searching. He may want to conceive some idea of what he is, and why he is. He would like to know what the whole thing means. Or at least satisfy himself that he can never satisfy himself. He would fain reach a final position of which he can approve, and not leave this earthly scene baffled and discontented. All this I have gone through.

Unfortunately I have a scientific mind. I would like to account for life in terms of physics and biology. I would explain emotions by chemical action. I would prove that everything that exists can be expressed in terms of Matter. I would conceive the Universe as a mechanism in which Man plays an automatic part. I would regard him as no more responsible for his actions than he is for his existence. Indeed, he owes his being to an act of brutal passion in which he is ignored. He is not so much a product as a by-product.…

All of which may be true, but it does not help us to happiness, and that is the aim of everyone. Materialism, Determinism, Agnosticism — these are bleak beliefs that lead us up a blind alley. Science does not supply *The Answer*, and after much muddling I have abandoned it. I realize that I am a fool and that I know nothing, yet I do not see that others know a great deal more. Baffled by the mystery that surrounds me I cease to puzzle over it. Having satisfied my lust for reality I am willing to return to illusion. I am resigned to a destiny I cannot fathom. I make the best of things and develop my capacity for enjoyment. I cease trying to probe the depths and take my happiness as it comes.

No doubt happiness is something different for each of us. Even to ourselves its character is constantly changing. I think, however, that, generally speaking, we all get about an even ration. In the long run the poor are almost as happy as the rich. Nature adjusts us to our circumstances so that whether we are peers or peasants we get our share of the sun. When it comes to the question of tastebuds or testicles the pleasure of travelling tinker is equal to that of the movie magnate.

Having been pushed around in my early days I demand in my seventies the right to comfort. I assert my claim to avoid anything that threatens my peace. I put my interests and those of my household before everything. I admit this is selfish, but I am not responsible for the state of the world and I feel it is not my affair to reform it. I give to charity but take care that my own needs are satisfied. I would not sit out a sermon but cheerfully I pay for the family pew. I denounce the unearned increment but I clip my coupons carefully. And in reaping the benefits of capital I am not ashamed, for I believe that those who condemn it most would do as I do if fortune came their way.

But at least I can say that for all the good I enjoy I am deeply grateful. If it were a tenth of what it is I believe I would still be grateful. Give me Ruskin and a rusk and I will mock the pomp of princes. Only let me rise in the morning feeling that I am *free*, and that the day before me is all my own to do with as I will. Only let me potter round my garden, joyously do my physical jerks and fuss over my toilet. Only let me eat my simple lunch with the appetite I have studiously unsophisticated. Let me walk the windy heath, returning rosily to tea. Let me sit in dressing gown and slippers before an open fire, stroking a cat that purrs, chatting of idle things, dipping into a pleasant book. Let me pass the long evenings in cheerful repose, and when the house is hushed let me take a last look at the stars, saying: "What a good day it's been. Rich, full, sweet. For all its happiness I thank whatever Gods may be. . . ."

So in my seventies this is what life means to me. Of course, to you it means something quite different. But whatever it does mean it should hold out happiness to you with both hands. If not, something is terribly wrong and the sooner you right it the better.

Happiness, in whatever form it comes, is not to be questioned. It is to be hugged to the heart. Illusion is to be cherished. On the surface of things is enchantment enough. Do not let us seek to see too clearly. Let us like painters be satisfied with appearance. Let us like children be satisfied with little things. In the simple joy of the heart let us forget inalterable destinies. From the gladness of birds, the rich tenderness of the rose, the lusty joy of roaring tides, let us learn to live radiantly.

Yet it is good to have some conception of what we are, and of the part we play. It will make us humble and at the same time glorify us. A conception of world destiny is as necessary to us as is a conception of human destiny. We are part of the Oneness of things, and through each of us moves the Eternal Purpose. We are at the mercy of no blind forced, but part of a sublime scheme. Let us believe in the wisdom of the world plan, and the ultimate triumph through law and order of the unknown and almighty energy.

Surely a faith in our Universe and our human destiny should satisfy us. Let us then put all futile gropings for a meaning of life out of our minds and come down to the pure joy of living. Let us worship Nature as she reveals herself in all simplicity and beauty. And if we live in usefulness and sanity according to her laws, cultivating happiness and sharing it with those near and dear to us, we will do more than well. The measure of our sunshine is the brightness we can kindle in the eyes of others.

In some cloistered garden we may walk with peace, and in the joy of little things our vain efforts to comprehend the universe may be forgotten. In tangible beauty is charm and solace. In visible nature is comfort. Let us be eager to be pleased; grateful for every gleam of sunshine. Nature can comfort us and bring us joy. Are we not her children? Let us try, if it so pleases us, to understand her with the minds of sages, but let us enjoy her with the hearts of children.

So in the end let us seek a quiet home, and with earth radiant about us, face the setting sun. With thankful eyes and grateful hearts let us rejoice that it has been granted to us to live the length of our years in a world of beauty — to understand much, to divine much, and to come at last through pleasant paths to peace. Peace and understanding! So with our last gaze let us face the serene sunset, content to have played our parts and saying humbly:

> "Nature, from whose bosom I come, take me back tenderly, lovingly. Forgive my faults, my failures, and now that my usefulness to you is ended, grant me to rest eternally."

ALL IS WELL

FROM

Why Not Grow Young? or Living for Longevity

Chapter Two

Health Before Everything

In the following pages I propose to show you how to grow young.... But can one?

Now that I am presuming that you are a townsman who up to the present has been too busy to give his body the care it deserves. If you are a countryman, throw this book out of the window. If you are a sick man, let the doctors deal with you. If you are a very poor man, alas! the grindstone is too near your nose to let you make proper heed of your health.

But being what you are — a sound, successful city man, let me tell you that *you are prematurely old.* It is almost inevitable. You are anything from five to ten years older than your age. But don't let it worry you. You may yet stage a comeback, make the age of your body tally with your actual one. You may restore the balance, find your true self again. And this is what I mean by GROWING YOUNG.

Yes, you can do it. We all can. And it is to help you I am writing this. I am a mere adventurer on the highway of health. I have not any letters after my name to impress you; nor am I a massive-muscled professor of physical culture, nor a food reformer with a stack of statistics. I detest dogmatism and do not pretend to authority. I write in the spirit of mild suggestion, and if you don't *click* with me, I'm not too proud to strain the point. I just want to talk over the subject of health with you, hoping we will find so much in common that my experiences may be of some use to you. Regard my book, if you regard it at all, as one of *inspiration.* It is to induce you to take stock, get a fresh grip, and hoist yourself on to a higher plane of health and happiness.

Health and High Health

Health and happiness! To me they seem inseparable.

> "To make my body a temple pure
> Wherein I live serene...."

With me the welfare of the body is a religion. I am an acolyte in the Temple of Health.

But by health I do not mean the everyday variety that consists in not being sick. Ever many of fifty who takes reasonable care of himself may enjoy this bovine brand of wellbeing. I mean what I call the Higher Health, that sense of superlative wellness that makes a man slap himself on the chest and say with gusto: "By Godfrey! ain't I feeling fine today!"

In youth we don't notice such super-health because we are accustomed to it; but in middle age it is rare enough to be remarked. It is not negative, but positive; not drab and passive, but brilliant and active. It expresses itself in an abundant vitality, a vivid rapture in living. It is distinguished by a zest of life almost lyrical. It is this I am at and would have you too take as your mark.

We all agree that the chief end of life is happiness, yet it is difficult to advise anyone how to be happy. To each it means something different. Some are happy in industry, some in idleness, some in cleanliness, some in dirt, some in virtue, some in vice. One wants a château, another a cottage. Each to his taste and tolerance for all. For me, I am happy in the quiet of my library or on a country walk, and if I were a prince or a plutocrat I should be profoundly miserable. The only suggestion one might make for general happiness is to recognize within rational limits universal liberty of expression.

But there is one avenue to happiness which may be recommended with reasonable confidence, and that is the highway of health. For though without health there can be no consistent happiness, one can think of it as arising from health alone. The lusty tinker in the ditch is more in love with life than the dyspeptic millionaire. Animal health is a mighty factor in the happiness problem. Keep your body fit and you'll make your mind rejoice.

Body Before Mind

But though a happy body usually means a happy mind, it by no means follow that a happy mind will make a happy body. It would be glorious if the spirit could so triumph over the flesh; but alas! The body has infinitely more power over the mind than the mind has over the body. A man with a perfectly sound body will never be immediately miserable, while it is rare for a sick man to be conspicuously gay. When we come then to the problem of securing happiness through health, it is the physical machine with which we should concern ourselves. If we want to get the maximum of fun out of life, let us begin with this body of ours.

That is why I am first and foremost a physical culture enthusiast. For after fifty health is increasingly due on the care we give our bodies. Through the harmony of the flesh we achieve the exaltation of the spirit. Mental serenity is profoundly physical in its source, and by the purification of the living tissue we are helped to attain the higher life.

Let us then put the health of the body before everything, for on it everything depends. Yet most of us insist in putting other foolish things first — money, fame, position, work. In their order I should say the three most precious gifts of life were Health, Liberty and Intellect. You may differ as to the second and third, but you will agree as to the first. And be it understood I mean High Health. Aim at perfection, for though you will fall far below it, in the effort to attain it you will raise yourself above the ordinary standard. Try to enjoy not merely the health that is fitting to your age, but that of a decade earlier.

Know Your Physical Self

But first of all get to know the structure of your body and its functioning. Are you not shockingly ignorant of that which is most vital to you? Can you give a clear account of the working of either your digestive or your circulatory system? Would you hire a chauffeur to run your Rolls Royce who had not the smallest knowledge of mechanics?

Yet as far as concerns your more exquisite mechanism that's just what you're doing. For the better you look after your human machine, the longer and sweeter it will run. The pity is that you treated it so brutally when it was new. It seems inevitable that we should spend the latter part of our lives trying to repair the damage we have done in the former.

Yet it is never too late to be reasonable, and be getting to know your body better you can learn to handle yourself better in the endurance race which is Longevity. Remind yourself, however, that as well as a healthy interest in the body, there is a morbid concern for it. The first is an interest in wellness, the second in illness. The first is a clear comprehension of your capacity for health, the second a nervous preoccupation with your capacity for sickness. By all means keep yourself under intelligent control, but never let imagination ride you. If you have a sane and balanced mind an understanding of your physical processes will only fortify you in serenity; but if you are one of those who go to bed because a toenail aches, you'd better leave such knowledge alone and take to tabloids.

At the same time it is your growing privilege to be a bit fussy about yourself. Occasionally it is not a bad thing to make mountains out of molehills, as long as you remember they really are molehills, and that your making mountains of them is only a trick to render you more cautious. As far as others are concerned, too, it is good policy to exaggerate your petty ailments. It makes people take you more seriously; and especially after sixty a little coddling is always on the side of safety.

The Discovery of Health

Health has been defined as physical unconsciousness, and though all physical unconsciousness is not health, the greatest compliment you can pay an organ is to be unaware of its existence. Young people don't know there's such a thing as health because they have it in abundance. But with the years we incline to become more and more health-conscious. To be health-conscious is to be a little sick, and I may hazard the opinion that after fifty most of us really *are* a little sick. There would be no such thing as health if it were not for the lack of it, and we begin to discover its existence just when we need it most.

But while health-consciousness may be a sign of impaired vitality, let me suggest that this only applies to the common variety of health. The Higher Health is essentially conscious; or rather, it is conscious of its unconsciousness. It is health-pride, something to be realized and savoured. It is a manifestation of the will to live *long*. As such it may be encouraged and developed, but it must never be permitted to become an obsession. Never let your body be a house of fear.

But by all means make health your hobby, or rather one of your hobbies. And remember again, I speak of the Higher Health. HEALTH BEFORE EVERYTHING. Let that text be largely framed on the wall of your mind. Let health be a definite study with you, and do not be satisfied with anything but the best. Try to make every day one of brilliant well-being. Believe that the time you spend in exercise will be added on to the end of your life; that the money you spend in caring for yourself will be returned with compound interest. Time and money put into the Bank of Health is the finest investment in the world. And this is no egotism, for by conserving yourself you are adding to your efficiency and social usefulness.

Let it be my effort, then, to arouse you to health enthusiasm, to inspire you with a desire for health perfection. For in so doing

I hope to increase your sum of happiness, to help you to grow in youth instead of in age, and to attain that ripeness and maturity that Nature intended you to enjoy. Let me be a gospeller of health, even if I have to din it into deaf ears.

[1]Estimates were made using the Environmental Defense Paper Calculator.